Deus Ex Machina

"Julie Kenner's fresh and fun dialogue keeps the readers engaged and entertained . . . a fun, fast-paced tale."
—*San Francisco Book Review*

"The latest imaginative and witty entry in Kenner's lively Demon series creates a vivid and intriguing fantasy world."
—*Booklist*

"Although this is the fifth in the series, it can stand alone. And then you'd want to go back and read the previous four! These are books that consistently deliver and never disappoint."
—*CK2S Kwips and Kritiques*

"Julie Kenner does a great job."
—*Night Owl Romance*

"Fans will appreciate Julie Kenner's profound glimpse at the human side of demon slaying beyond a bad hair or broken cuticle day."
—*The Best Reviews*

"I can't praise this series enough. Kenner is a talented and proficient storyteller. Combining urban fantasy, zombie-like demons, real-life situations, and just enough humor, the Demon-Hunting Soccer Mom series is one of which I can't get enough. And I love each episode no less than the previous. The series is fun and addictive. Don't miss it."
—*SciFiChick.com*

"A good book to read when you want to get away from the dull, boring life for a few."
—*Manic Readers*

Deja Demon

"A delightfully different take on the paranormal romance theme that will leave fans thirsting for more."
—*Monsters and Critics*

continued . . .

"Kate is as kick-butt tough as ever . . . fans of Julie Kenner's suburban fantasy will appreciate *Deja Demon*."
—*Genre Go Round Reviews*

Demons Are Forever

"[A] wonderful author . . . a fun premise . . . excellent characterization, intriguing stories, and snappy dialogue."
—*Fresh Fiction*

"Fizzy . . . Kenner's trademark cliffhanger finale promises further demonic escapades to come." —*Publishers Weekly*

"This is the third in Kenner's splendidly creative series featuring Kate, whose wickedly amusing adventures in demon hunting are a pure paranormal delight." —*Booklist*

"This chapter in Kenner's first-person, kick-butt adventures takes a darker turn, and a more serious tone, as Demon Hunter Kate Connor faces long odds and emotional turmoil. The terrific Kenner grabs you and doesn't let go!"
—*Romantic Times*

California Demon

"Kenner continues to put her fun, fresh twist on mommy-lit with another devilishly clever book." —*Booklist*

"Sassy!" —*Richmond.com*

"Plenty of action and humor. Kenner is at her irreverent best . . . delightfully amusing." —*The Best Reviews*

"A fun paranormal adventure that definitely appeals to moms!" —*Scribes World*

"More witty, funny, and poignant adventures from the marvelous Kenner." —*Romantic Times*

Carpe Demon

"I LOVED *CARPE DEMON*! . . . It was great fun; wonderfully clever. Ninety-nine percent of the wives and moms in the country will identify with this heroine. I mean, like who *hasn't* had to battle demons between car pools and playdates?"

—Jayne Ann Krentz, *New York Times*
bestselling author of *Fired Up*

"I welcome the novels that decide to be utterly over-the-top and imagine paranormal and superhero lives for their chick-lit heroines. Take *Carpe Demon* . . ."   —*Detroit Free Press*

"This book, as crammed with events as any suburban mom's calendar, shows you what would happen if Buffy got married and kept her past a secret. It's a hoot."

—Charlaine Harris, #1 *New York Times*
bestselling author of the Sookie Stackhouse novels

"What would happen if Buffy the Vampire Slayer got married, moved to the suburbs, and became a stay-at-home mom? She'd be a lot like Kate Connor, once a demon/vampire/zombie killer and now 'a glorified chauffeur for drill-team practice and Gymboree playdates' in San Diablo, California, that's what. But in Kenner's sprightly, fast-paced ode to kick-ass housewives, Kate finds herself battling evil once again. Readers will find spunky Kate hard not to root for in spheres both domestic and demonic."   —*Publishers Weekly*

"A +! This is a serious keeper—I am very ready for the next segment in Kate Connor's life!"

—*The Romance Readers Connection*

"Smart, fast-paced, unique—a blend of sophistication and wit that has you laughing out loud."

—Christine Feehan, #1 *New York Times*
bestselling author of *Water Bound*

continued . . .

Titles by Julie Kenner

CARPE DEMON
CALIFORNIA DEMON
DEMONS ARE FOREVER
DEJA DEMON
DEMON EX MACHINA

THE GOOD GHOULS' GUIDE TO GETTING EVEN
GOOD GOULS DO

FIRST LOVE

TAINTED
TORN
TURNED

Anthologies

HELL WITH THE LADIES
(with Kathleen O'Reilly and Dee Davis)

HELL ON HEELS
(with Kathleen O'Reilly and Dee Davis)

FENDI, FERRAGAMO, AND FANGS
(with Johanna Edwards and Serena Robar)

Demon
Ex Machina

Tales of a
Demon-Hunting
Soccer Mom

julie kenner

BERKLEY BOOKS, NEW YORK

THE BERKLEY PUBLISHING GROUP
Published by the Penguin Group
Penguin Group (USA) Inc.
375 Hudson Street, New York, New York 10014, USA
Penguin Group (Canada), 90 Eglinton Avenue East, Suite 700, Toronto, Ontario M4P 2Y3, Canada
(a division of Pearson Penguin Canada Inc.)
Penguin Books Ltd., 80 Strand, London WC2R 0RL, England
Penguin Group Ireland, 25 St. Stephen's Green, Dublin 2, Ireland (a division of Penguin Books Ltd.)
Penguin Group (Australia), 250 Camberwell Road, Camberwell, Victoria 3124, Australia
(a division of Pearson Australia Group Pty. Ltd.)
Penguin Books India Pvt. Ltd., 11 Community Centre, Panchsheel Park, New Delhi—110 017, India
Penguin Group (NZ), 67 Apollo Drive, Rosedale, North Shore 0632, New Zealand
(a division of Pearson New Zealand Ltd.)
Penguin Books (South Africa) (Pty.) Ltd., 24 Sturdee Avenue, Rosebank, Johannesburg 2196,
South Africa

Penguin Books Ltd., Registered Offices: 80 Strand, London WC2R 0RL, England

This is a work of fiction. Names, characters, places, and incidents either are the product of the author's imagination or are used fictitiously, and any resemblance to actual persons, living or dead, business establishments, events, or locales is entirely coincidental. The publisher does not have any control over and does not assume any responsibility for author or third-party websites or their content.

DEMON EX MACHINA

A Berkley Book / published by arrangement with the author

PRINTING HISTORY
Berkley trade paperback edition / October 2009
Berkley mass-market edition / November 2010

Copyright © 2009 by Julie Kenner.
Cover illustration by Mark Fredrickson.

ISBN: 978-0-425-23776-2

BERKLEY®
Berkley Books are published by The Berkley Publishing Group,
a division of Penguin Group (USA) Inc.,
375 Hudson Street, New York, New York 10014.
BERKLEY® is a registered trademark of Penguin Group (USA) Inc.
The "B" design is a trademark of Penguin Group (USA) Inc.

PRINTED IN THE UNITED STATES OF AMERICA

10 9 8 7 6 5 4 3 2 1

One

"Stuart!" I shouted from my post beside the old Dakota tomb, as the black-clad figure sprinted toward my husband.

Stuart had been crouched near the ground, his forehead creased with concentration as he poked at loose dirt atop an ancient grave site. Now he lurched to his feet, turning as he reached for the dagger he wore sheathed at his hip. The kind of move you saw in martial arts films, where the hero thrusts out a leg and cuts down his opponent with one sweep, then springs on top of the bad guy and presses the tip of his blade to his neck.

My husband, unfortunately, is not an action movie star.

Neither is he a trained Demon Hunter.

And instead of catching his attacker on the approach, thrusting out and defending himself with his blade, my husband toppled backward onto his ass. A string of sailor-quality curses escaped his lips as he rolled sideways trying to avoid the wraith who now leaped through the air, landing with a thud on Stuart's torso, knees on either side of my husband's chest, and both hands tight around his neck.

"Kate!" Stuart yelled as I dashed forward. "This is *not* what we talked about!" He twisted under his attacker, his predicament illuminated by the single lamppost in this section of the cemetery. "Off!"

Blue eyes under a black ski mask turned to me, and I nodded. The figure rose, peeled off the mask, and flashed a grin so wide and self-satisfied that I couldn't help but laugh.

"I don't have any more control over the demons than I do over my daughter, Stuart," I said. "You're the one who wanted to train."

"Did I hurt you?" Allie asked, offering a black-clad arm and hand to her stepfather.

He took her hand and hauled himself to his feet. "If by *hurt* you mean that I got my ass kicked by a fifteen-year-old kid, then, yeah, I guess you hurt me."

"Sorry." Her lips twitched. "But I'm not fifteen until next week." She turned deliberately to me. "And I want a video iPod and my own dagger." She turned, indicating the ivory hilt of the blade sheathed at the small of her back. "Not another one of your old ones. *Mine*. Unless you'd rather get me a crossbow?" she added, hopefully.

"I'll get right on that." I turned my attention back to Stuart. "Don't blame Allie," I said. "I told her no-holds-barred."

"I could have stabbed her!"

"Your dagger's rubber."

"Something else we need to discuss," he said, irritably. "Allie's packing some serious steel."

I crossed my arms over my chest and cocked my head, my expression one I used on the kids at least daily. A little fact that, considering the way he was eyeing me, wasn't lost on Stuart. "She's logged over a hundred training hours with that thing," I said, compelled to soften the blow to his ego.

"I know," he said. "I do. But I'm in a cemetery in the middle of the night in a town that apparently breeds demons. I'd like to go out armed with something that packs a little more punch than one of Timmy's toys."

The dagger did, in fact, belong to our toddler. A souvenir from a recent trip to SeaWorld. Either that or Peter Pan paraphernalia from the Disney Store. Honestly, it's hard to keep track.

"We're training, sweetheart," I said. "Like you said. Nonlethal is a good thing."

He grimaced, undoubtedly embarrassed by the fact that he'd been taken down by a girl who, on some level, probably considered this whole gig fair payback for various groundings and television bans over the years. Even so, his inner politician shined through, and he flashed Allie a genuine smile, the kind that made his eyes twinkle with pride. "At any rate, it was a nice move, kid. Your mom teach you that?"

"Cutter," she said, referring to our martial arts instructor. "But Mom's definitely got the moves," she added loyally.

Stuart glanced my way, his eyes soft. "Yeah," he said. "She does at that." He held out a hand, then tugged me close, and I sank against him, this moment of spontaneous affection reminding me that Stuart still loved me despite the secrets I'd kept from him. Despite the fact that he'd never really known the woman he'd married.

My name is Kate Connor, and I'm a Level Five Demon Hunter with *Forza Scura*, a secret arm of the Vatican that, at least in my hometown of San Diablo, California, isn't quite as secret as it's supposed to be. It's a whole, big, complicated thing, but ultimately it boils down to my recent return to active duty after a fifteen-year retirement.

Not that I'd been looking to return to the workforce. I'd been perfectly happy living a quiet suburban life with my not-so-quiet teenager and my even less quiet toddler. But when a demon explodes through your kitchen window intent on killing you, it kind of changes a girl's perspective, you know?

So, yeah, I'd gotten back on the job, in secret at first, though my best friend and my daughter learned the truth soon enough.

With Stuart, though, I'd clung to anonymity long after it was prudent to do so. The secrets had started to strain our marriage, and when Stuart finally learned the truth, he'd reacted with anger and fear. My heart still pinched when I recalled how he'd taken our son, Timmy, and moved out of our house, claiming that remaining with me was far too dangerous for a toddler.

I'd been heartbroken and furious. But once I'd calmed down and been able to think rationally, I had to admit that Stuart's fears weren't irrational. No matter how you sliced it, my secret profession boasted a high mortality rate. And trust me when I say that demons aren't squeamish about using civilians to achieve their own ends.

Then Stuart had come back, wanting to strengthen our marriage. Wanting to make things work. I'd cried tears of relief even as I'd silently smothered the guilt brought on by my joy. Because no matter how I tried to spin the situation in my head, there was no escaping the fact that Stuart had brought my baby back into evil's crosshairs.

I'd fight it.

I'd do everything in my power to prevent it.

And I'd hunt down like a dog any person or creature who threatened my kid.

But none of that changed the basic paradigm that the world was a dangerous place. Mine, more than most. And every day I did my job—every time I eradicated another smidgeon of evil from the world—I was ramping up the forces of darkness against myself and my family.

They were keeping score, the bad guys.

And one day, I knew they'd come to settle.

I shivered, and Stuart's arm tightened around me, bringing me back to myself and making me focus on the issue at hand. In the demon-hunting business, distraction could get you killed. And though we might only be training, it was a lesson I'd be wise to take to heart.

"So what did you do wrong?" I asked, moving away from him as I slid into my instructor persona.

"Other than wandering around a pitch-black graveyard, you mean? I shifted my focus. The ground caught my attention. I started thinking back, remembering the zombies. And I let down my guard."

"Good analysis," I said, duly impressed. When Stuart had first insisted that he wanted to train, I'd said no. My husband's no wimp, but at forty-two, and with a gym regimen that consisted of sporadic racquetball games with his buddies from the office, I wasn't certain he was the best candidate.

More than that, notwithstanding the rather huge secret I'd kept from him, our marriage had always been one of equals. And I didn't relish the idea of being suddenly in that power position, correcting his technique with weapons, or forcing him to run another mile.

He'd insisted, though, and when he'd pointed out that Timmy was safer with two parents who knew how to kick butt, I'd had no choice but to cave. And the truth was, he was doing great. He asked the right questions and had enough innate skill that the fight techniques and weapons training came easily to him. Not that I was going to send him out to defend the house against a horde of demonic attackers, but he hadn't injured himself with a knife or crossbow. And I considered that a damn good sign.

In the end, my fear about the shifting balance of power in our marriage turned out to be unfounded. Sure, there were awkward moments, but now that the bubble around my secret life had burst, I was enjoying the new experience of not having to squeeze my husband in around the edges of my reality.

And, yes, getting all hot and sweaty training together does have certain side benefits. And under the right circumstances, even learning to throw a dagger can be a damn sensual experience.

I knew that better than anyone, didn't I?

I shivered, thoughts of my first husband, Eric, intruding where they really didn't belong. Not now. Not with Stuart right there, the wounds on our relationship still raw and tender.

"They won't be back, will they?" Stuart's question caught me off guard and I cocked my head, confused. "Zombies," he clarified. "You talked to Father Corletti, right? Worked out a way to keep the beasts out of here?"

"I did," Allie said, the pride in her voice unmistakable.

We'd recently had a bit of a zombie infestation in San Diablo, and since I was keen on eradicating the smelly little beasts for good, I'd promised Allie a birthday party at her choice of venue if she could come up with a solution in less than a week.

It had taken her three days. And I hadn't been sure if I should burst with pride at my daughter's resourcefulness and brilliance, or cower in terror from the possibility that she'd want to hold her party at home. We'd be forced to sell the house simply because of the destruction wrought by two or three dozen partying teenagers. Either that or bring in a hazmat team for a week's worth of cleanup.

As it turned out, she'd selected the old Palace Theater, a classy choice with a rental price that included a cleanup crew. Bonus all the way around.

"We did salt and holy water and then we scattered a powder made from the bones of saints," Allie was saying, her comments directed more to Stuart than to me.

"Powder?"

She shrugged. "I guess they have barrels full of the stuff in the Vatican."

"Probably an overstatement," I inserted.

"Dunno," she admitted to me, then turned back to Stuart. "But Father Corletti overnighted us a couple of pounds, and Daddy and I used your fertilizer spreader to—What?" She leaned in, peering at his face, which did look a little queasy. "It's just ground-up bones. It's not like they pulverized living—"

He held up his hand, and she had the grace to stop. "You're telling me that you and your father came out here to the cemetery with my lawn tools and spread salt and saint bones?"

Allie glanced at me, her brow furrowed in confusion. I stared back at her, equally confused. And Stuart looked between the two of us, then sighed. "I'm seriously considering scheduling time every day," he said. "A few moments, all by myself, where I do nothing but sit and ponder the ramifications of what you do and what goes on around here."

I tensed, listening for warning bells in his voice. Signs he was scared or fed up or otherwise ready to bolt on me again. But all I heard was quiet resignation. And, surprisingly, a hint of respect, too.

He met my eyes. "She took a fertilizer spreader," he said, as if I hadn't already picked up on that little fact. "And because of that, no zombie is rising out of this cemetery."

"Is that good or bad?" Allie asked, voicing my exact question.

"It's a hell of a lot more than I've managed with the thing. I can't even get the dandelions to stop sprouting. So no vampires rising either, right?"

"Right," I said. "But I already told you I haven't seen any vampires in San Diablo."

"Better safe than sorry," he said stiffly, and I again regretted the way I'd boasted one night, telling him about the time I'd fried a few vamps with a Bic lighter and a travel-sized can of Aqua Net. "Come on, guys," I said. "Timmy's going to a birthday party at ten tomorrow, and I'd like to get at least a few hours' sleep before I spend two hours with fifteen screaming kiddos."

"One more go," Stuart said, and I nodded in agreement.

"I want you focused," I said to him as Allie pulled the black hood back over her face. Serious eyes peered out from a sea of black, and I turned my attention to my daughter. "You're in the shadows. Use your discretion when to attack, but don't pounce again. I don't think Stuart's ribs can take it."

"Probably not manly of me to admit, but your mother's right. I'd consider it a personal favor if you didn't break any bones tonight."

"No prob, Stuart," she said, then melted into the dark.

"You're on your own," I said, then took a step toward the shadows. The sharp *clang* of metal against rock stopped me, and I froze, trying to discern the direction from which the sound had come. "Allie?" I whispered, then jumped as she materialized a few feet in front of me.

"Not me," she said, her voice so low I could barely hear it.

I gestured for her to come closer even as I approached Stuart, my muscles tense, my senses hyperalert.

What is it? Stuart mouthed. I shook my head and held up my hand, palm flat, hoping to silently indicate that not only did I not know, but he needed to stay put while I figured it out.

I signaled again to Allie, and she correctly interpreted my hand flapping as orders to get closer to Stuart. I wasn't sure how keen Stuart would be on the concept of a fourteen-year-old girl helping to protect him, but right then I wasn't inclined to tread daintily on his masculine ego. To Allie's credit, she got right next to him and took his hand, as if to suggest that he was the one protecting her.

As for me, I moved slowly and silently out of the circle of light. I considered moving them to the dark as well, but decided against it. I'd rather be able to see them and know they were safe. In the shadows, anything could happen. A fact of which I was only too aware as I moved through the dark. The night seemed to close in on me, and I shivered, unable to shake the feeling that something was out there. Something other than us. Something watching.

Something waiting.

But waiting for what, I didn't know.

A thick layer of clouds hid a crescent moon, reducing the ambient light to next to nothing. I could barely see my hand in front of my face, and if a demon were crouched in waiting, it was quite likely he'd see me before I'd see him.

And that realization was my cue to get my family the hell out of there.

I stepped around a tall monument, planning to call to Stuart and Allie. I never got the words out, though, because of the sharp crack of a twig somewhere from the dark in front of Stuart.

I saw him tense and reach out, his hand going for the knife at Allie's back even as the figure appeared in front of him, just outside the circumference of light.

Stuart snatched the knife, then hauled back, taking aim even as I raced forward, a sharp cry of "No!" bursting from my lungs as I recognized the apparition for what it really was.

But it was too late. And all I could do was stand there as the lethal blade flew straight for Eddie's heart.

Two

Allie's scream joined mine, and I heard Stuart's sharp intake of breath even as the knife whipped, blade over hilt, toward the retired Demon Hunter.

I watched, helpless, as Eddie thrust his arm up in an effort to deflect the impact. But while he still had it going on at eighty-something, those reflexes weren't what they used to be, and he missed the knife by a solid two inches, then stumbled back as it connected—hard—with his chest.

"*No!*" Allie shouted, racing toward him with me right behind her. Stuart stood frozen, his eyes wide, his hand held in front of him as if it were something contaminated that he'd never seen before.

"*Goddamn*, that smarts." The voice, slightly irritated, came from the prone figure of Eddie on the ground, and those curmudgeonly tones danced on my ears like bells tolling my relief.

Allie skidded to a stop at his side, then helped him up, his Oscar the Grouch face more grumpy than usual, though

I supposed that was to be expected. He grunted, coughed, and proceeded to rub his head with gusto while Allie made soft noises, as if she were trying to calm an angry dog.

Dressed in black jeans, a black turtleneck, and a black knit cap, Eddie was the very picture of an octogenarian grave robber, and despite the circumstances, I couldn't help my smile. He aimed a gimlet eye at Stuart. "You trying to get your guest room back by offing me, pansy boy?"

"I didn't mean—" Stuart began, the fact that he was over-looking the "pansy" part of the equation underscoring ex-actly how freaked out he was.

Eddie, however, only chuckled. "Guess I'll have to quit calling you that, huh?" He rubbed his chest. "Got some-thing of an arm on you there, slugger. Just gotta learn to hit 'em with the blade, not the hilt."

"It's from lifting all those pansy-ass legal tomes," Stuart said, and Eddie's mirth-filled chuckle filled the air. "Builds muscle tone."

"Little more practice, and you'll have the pointy end of those things sliding through demon flesh in no time."

"Just so long as I don't take down any raggedly old men."

"Heh. I may be old, but I'm still spry."

How nice. After months of tension-filled coexistence, the two adult men in my household had finally connected. And all it had taken was for one to almost kill the other. If I'd known that, I could have shoved them in the backyard with a handful of knives weeks ago.

"You sure you're okay, Gramps?" Allie asked, her forehead crinkled with concern. "That hit really hard. You coulda broken some ribs."

Eddie thumbed himself on his chest. "Rock solid," he said, then held out his hand for her. She took it, leaning in next to him as he swung his arm around her shoulder and allowed her to help haul him to his feet. Dressed as they both were in head-to-toe black, I had to laugh. They looked like an advertisement for multi-generational ninja training, an image with added irony when you considered that they weren't actually related, though neither Allie nor Stuart knew that.

And, the truth was, Eddie had truly become Gramps. No, he wasn't Eric's grandfather, like I'd told Stuart so many months ago before I'd settled the then-loopy and involuntarily medicated former Hunter in our guest room. But somewhere between then and now, the fiction had become our reality. Eddie was family. A fact evidenced most strongly by Stuart's recent agreement to have his room wired for cable.

"Don't take this the wrong way," I said, lifting my hand up and down as I gestured to Eddie's midnight black outfit. "But why are you here?"

I'd asked Eddie to join our little training mission, with both him and Allie playing the role of wandering demons to Stuart's Hunter-in-training. He'd declined. Or, more accurately, he'd turned me down flat with a snort and a chuckle and the uniquely unhelpful comment that training Stuart was too little, too late, and if I was going to let my husband go out into the field, then I damn well better be training him to heel.

The sad part? I actually feared Eddie was right.

"Eh, Tammy's cable's down," he said. "Decided to call it an early night and see how lawyer-boy's training was going. Figured if you wanted me and the kid playing demon, it was the least I could do."

"You left a date with your girlfriend because her cable was down?" I repeated.

"Hell, yeah," he said. "Her DVD collection is crap."

Stuart and I exchanged a glance, and I caught the ever-so subtle shake of his head. I exhaled, backing down from my instinctive response to challenge Eddie's less-than-romantic approach to dating.

"We appreciate the help," I said, "but I think we're calling it a night."

A snort of protest from Eddie underscored Allie's anguished cry of, "But!" Even Stuart muttered protests.

Although I was probably being paranoid, I didn't back down. I'd felt something out there that made the hair on the back of my neck prickle, something other than Eddie lumbering through the dark.

As Eric had recently reminded me before all hell broke loose, I'd developed a Hunter's instincts over the years. Which meant that my vague sense of paranoia could very well be the minions of hell lining us all up in their sights.

I bit back a sigh, battle weary and tired, but knowing better than to ignore the inevitable. Something was brewing in San Diablo.

So what else was new?

I cocked my head vaguely in the direction of the parking lot. "Come on, guys. I'm serious. We'll do this again next week."

Stuart looked like he was going to join in the protests, but then he took one look at my face and nodded. "Good idea. I have some things I need to take care of tonight anyway." I'm not sure if he saw the resolve in my eyes or if he was simply backing his wife. Either way, I appreciated it.

"Follow us home?" I asked. We'd arrived in separate cars, as Stuart had come straight from a dinner meeting.

"About an hour behind you," he said. "I want to check something at the house." He didn't mean our house, and all of us standing there knew it. Our heads swiveled in unison to the western edge of the cemetery and the cliff face that led up to the Greatwater Mansion, now owned by Dorsey-Connor Development, though the down payment had been so minuscule, I think it was fair to say the bank owned the house more than my husband or his new business partner, Bernie Dorsey.

They'd owned the place for sixteen days now, the plan being that they'd fix it up, flip it, and make a huge profit. So far, they'd barely dipped their toes in the fix-it-up stage, and even Allie and I had been recruited to help with cleanup and basic upgrades.

Me. The woman who gets flat-head and Phillips screwdrivers confused.

Honestly, there are times when I think that Stuart *still* doesn't know the woman he married.

The mansion had a checkered history, some colorful owners, and ties to the Golden Age of Hollywood. And though it had fallen onto serious hard times, the extent of the work required had ensured the price was right. Now the trick was to get it back in shape without spending so much money that it ate into the profit potential.

"Want to come?" he added.

Tempting, but I shook my head. "I want to get Timmy," I said. "I'll meet you at home." I shot a glance at Eddie. "Need a lift?"

Eddie knows how to drive, but hasn't bothered to renew his license. For a while, I'd been his exclusive chauffeur. Now Tammy had joined the party, and I appreciated the help. Tonight, though, I was guessing he'd taken a cab. His girlfriend hadn't struck me as the pushover type.

"Heck no," he said, waving toward Stuart. "I'm going with your boy. Want to see this shack you two keep chattering on about."

"Can I come?" Allie said. "Please? It's not a school night."

"Fine by me," Stuart said.

I hesitated, remembering that cold inkling of fear. But the truth was that in my life—in my world—fear had become part of the natural order of things.

"It's okay, Mom," my too-wise daughter said. "Go get the Timster. We'll be fine."

Stuart's forehead creased. "Am I missing something? Your Spidey-sense tingling?"

I made a face. "No. I'm fine. I'm just—"

"Being a mom," Allie said, with one of her patented eye rolls. She turned to Eddie. "*This* is why I'm never gonna get a learner's permit. She's terrified the world's gonna come crashing down or something once I'm behind the wheel of a car."

"Or something," I confirmed.

Eddie grunted, then leaned over and scooped up Allie's dagger from where it had fallen to the ground. He handed it to Allie, who slid it easily into the holster at her back. Then he closed his hand over the hilt of his own knife and met my eye. "We're good," said the octogenarian Dirty Harry.

I cast a quick glance toward Stuart, who nodded. "Don't worry," he said, deadpan. "I got their backs."

I suppressed a grin. "Well, okay then. I'll see you guys at home. Don't stay there all night peeling old wallpaper or something."

"And don't you hang back to patrol," Stuart said. "Get Timmy, go home, and get some rest."

In the parking lot, I kissed Stuart and Allie, hugged Eddie, and then watched as they all piled into Stuart's Infiniti. I hesitated, my mood melancholy, before climbing into the Odyssey and firing the engine. They drove out first, and I realized I was smiling. For a moment, I didn't know why. And then it hit me: No matter how many times Stuart had told me he was adjusting to the knowledge of my formerly secret life, I hadn't quite believed him.

Tonight, however, we'd been a family. A real family, albeit one that hangs out in cemeteries. But a family without secrets between us.

And damned if I didn't like the way that felt.

*   *   *

"**At least you know** he's got good reflexes," Laura said. "Oh, to have seen the look on his face."

"He looked a little like he did when I told him I was pregnant with Timmy—terrified, surprised, and secretly proud of himself." I reached for another muffin, smiling in earnest now. What had seemed serious in the cemetery now qualified as coffee-time gossip with my best friend. No one had been injured, Stuart had learned a lesson, and we had a great family story to tell around the table at Thanksgiving. At least on those years that Stuart's parents didn't join us.

"Seriously, though," Laura said as she refilled both our mugs, "is he doing okay?"

"With which? Adjusting to his wife's secret identity? Or learning to be sidekick boy?"

"Both." She slid into the chair opposite me and took a long sip. "For that matter, how are you doing?"

"Under the circumstances, I'm doing just great."

Laura lifted a brow, examining me over the rim of her coffee mug, obviously trying to decide if I was shooting straight or if I was shoving organic fertilizer her way.

"Okay, fine," I said, copping to a little bit of fertilizer. "On the family front things are going really well, actually. Stuart's demonstrating an excessive amount of togetherness, but it's such a novelty that I'm not yet teetering on the brink of insanity. And Allie's actually keeping her room clean and helping around the house."

"Probably afraid that if she doesn't, you'll take away her dagger."

"Whatever works," I said. "Although I am a little concerned about her schoolwork."

Laura nodded sympathetically. "I was afraid of that. Mindy said some things."

Warning bells clanged in my head. "What kind of things?"

"What you'd expect. That Allie's been distracted. Doing her homework, but not doing it well even though she's spending a lot of time in the library." She got up and pushed back from the table, then opened the cabinet above the sink—the one where she keeps the liquor. "Want something with more kick than caffeine?"

"Do I need it?"

"Probably not," she said. "But I do. Hell of a day here, too."

"Oh, hon," I said, the sympathy in my voice real despite the fact that I was not interested in shifting from Allie's problems to Laura's. Not just yet.

Laura laughed, obviously reading my expression, then took down a bottle of Baileys Irish Cream, which happens to be one of my not-so-secret vices. "Don't worry. It's all about Kate until we've exhausted the subject or the bottle. Whichever comes first."

"And then all about Laura," I said, loyally.

"I'll hold you to that." She set the ice machine on her refrigerator door to serve crushed ice, filled two small glasses, then topped them both off with Baileys. About three times the expected serving size, but I wasn't in the mood to complain. And considering the way Laura popped back half the glass, I figure she needed it.

"Doctor Hunk?" I asked, referring to the sexy emergency room doctor she'd been dating recently. She topped off the glass, which suggested to me that I was right, but waved the question away. "Allie," she said firmly. "The problems of a fourteen–year-old outrank minor ripples in my love life."

"Problems," I repeated. Not that any of this came as a surprise to me. Not really. I could see how much work she was doing playing Hunter-in-training. And if I'd actually focused on the issue, I would have come to the rather rational conclusion that between Hunter training and sleeping and the inevitable vegging in front of the television, there simply weren't enough hours in the day for her to be cramming schoolwork in there as well.

"Mindy can't figure out what's up with Allie," Laura said. "That's why she came to me, despite the more traditionally accepted teenage approach of parental avoidance. But she's worried. And, honestly, I think she's pissed off, too. No," she corrected. "Not pissed. Hurt."

"Ironic, isn't it?" Allie had spent hours in a near-fugue state as she tried to decide whether or not to tell Mindy about demons, Hunters, and the rest of it. And, yes, I know it's all supposed to be secret, but I felt a little hypocritical requiring Allie to sign on to the vow of silence plan considering I'd pulled Laura into my confidence. As it turned out, though, she imposed her own closed-mouth policy. The deciding factor was Eric. With Laura and Paul in the midst of a rather acrimonious divorce, Allie decided that the last thing Mindy would want to hear was the news that Allie's father had returned from the dead.

At the time, I'd considered it a remarkably mature decision, and one I really hadn't believed Allie would stick to. After all, she and Mindy had been best friends for years.

But stick she had, and although I was proud of my daughter's ability to keep a secret, I had to concede that there were serious flaws in my daughter's vow of silence. "It's still her decision to make, though," I said, after confessing as much to Laura.

"I know," she said. "And whatever Allie decides to do about Mindy is fine. But the schoolwork's still a problem, Kate. Finals are coming up, and even though they're only freshman, we've got to start thinking about college and scholarships and all that stuff."

I nodded. Now that Paul had walked out, financial woes plagued Laura as much as demons plagued me. Because despite a rock-solid attorney and good community-property laws, Laura was still going to be pinching pennies. Apparently Paul had run their finances deep into the red. Laura would get her share of the pie, but the big revelation throughout the process had been the discovery that what she'd believed to be fancy Boston cream pie had turned out to be not much more than those little apple confections from McDonald's.

The lesson? Everyone lies. Not just Demon Hunters.

"Mindy's going to get loads of scholarships," I said, both loyally and truthfully. The kid earned straight-As and still managed to participate in various extracurricular activities. In other words, exactly the kind of kid Allie was not. "She's going to be fine."

"Thanks," she said, then cocked her head as if saying, *And your kid?*

I sighed and rubbed my fingertips to my forehead. "I get the problem, but the truth is that she's applying herself like never before. Granted, her focus is on demons and theology and mysterious events in ancient history, but the kid's organized and focused and she's doing damn good work. She just needs to direct some of that energy to what the state of California wants her to learn. Manage that, and she'll be golden. At the very least, she'll survive finals." That was my hope, actually: that I could get her focused and applied these last few weeks. Nail her final exams and she'd start sophomore year with a clean slate.

"Maybe David can pull some strings and get her credit for independent study," Laura said. I'm pretty sure she was joking, but the idea wasn't half bad. After all, what good was it for Allie's dead father to have returned to life in the body of one of her teachers if she couldn't even land a decent grade out of the deal?

I frowned and rubbed my temples before taking another

sip of Baileys. Only a few months ago, the mention of David or Eric would have put a warm, fuzzy, slightly guilty feeling in my stomach. Now all it did was scare me.

"Have you figured anything out?" Laura asked, eyeing me with concern. Because she knew as well as I did that the conversation had taken a massive left turn. We'd abandoned the comparatively tame *dead-first-husband-in-living-chemistry-teacher* topic to Serious Stuff. The big-time. The absolute worst of the worst.

"Nothing," I confessed, desperately wishing I had a more satisfactory answer.

"Do you want to talk about it?"

I shook my head. There are just some things you have to be in the right frame of mind to talk about, and the fact that a demon is growing inside your first husband pretty much tops that list.

Apparently that little hitchhiker had been inside my beloved for a long, long time. Dormant for a while, and more recently peeking out from its slumber to make a few bids for control of the body it was time-sharing with Eric. Not that I'd known any of that during our years as hunting and marital partners. And to be honest, I was still coming to grips with this new take on my reality.

Three weeks had passed since I'd learned about the demon inside Eric. Three weeks since we'd defeated Goramesh and Abaddon. Three weeks since Father Ben had died.

The pain still clung to me. The impotence I'd felt in not being able to save him. And now that horrible sense of helplessness was magnified tenfold in the face of Eric's distress. Not only because I didn't have answers, but because Eric had made it clear he didn't want me looking for them.

Not that his wishes had stopped me. I'd been on the phone daily with Father Corletti, but though he'd offered comfort, we'd found no practical solutions. How the demon came to be in Eric, he said, was a story for Eric alone to tell.

He shared with me only what he knew and thought was relevant to our search for answers: that the demon had lain inside Eric since birth. That it had been bound within, but was now peeking out, seeking to merge with Eric. Seeking to become one.

Clinging to hope, Father and I had been in full research mode, plowing through ancient texts in the hopes of finding similar accounts. But to say the situation was rare would be an understatement, and we'd found no precedent, no clues, no secret incantations for either forcing the demon out of Eric or locking him up inside, dormant once again.

My frustration was rising along with my fear. If we didn't figure something out before the demon fully broke free, Eric would be gone, only a demon would be left. And I was a Demon Hunter.

"What does Eric say?" Laura asked. "What's he doing?"

"He tells me he's doing fine. After all, he's known about the demon for years and years," I said, a little more icily than I intended. "Sorry. I get pissy."

Laura's smile was pure maternal, and I have to admit I appreciated it. "You're entitled."

I frowned because she was right. I *was* entitled. Eric had known about the demon throughout most of his life and all of our marriage. And yet he'd never told me. He'd taken the burden on himself, certain he could figure out a way to solve the problem and free himself. The veil of secrecy had been blown three weeks ago, however, when the culmination of a prophecy had proven that there was a demon inside Eric. I knew the truth now, and while I was angry and frustrated that he'd never told me, I was also terrified for the man I loved.

"Can you, um, tell?" Laura asked, looking extremely uncomfortable. "I mean, can you see . . . *it*?"

"Not really," I said. "His temper is edgier, but it would be, you know?"

"Stress," Laura said, knowingly.

"The truth is, he's not letting me see a lot. He tells me he's in control and he's been doing research. He says he's got a plan and there's no way he's letting the demon get the better of him."

"Do you believe him?"

I hesitated. "I want to. Father says that Eric's been looking for a solution for months. Scouring old records and jumping through all sorts of hoops. He even thinks that Eric might have found the answer."

"But?"

"But Eric hasn't officially told *Forza*. Hasn't even unofficially told Father Corletti. And even though we're still patrolling together, he's dodging my questions and shutting me out. Shutting us all out. Me. Father. *Forza*."

She took my hand in sympathy. "It's harder on him than it is on you," she said. "He's all alone. And he's going through a lot."

"Yeah," I said. "And he needs help. It's not like he's got a sinus infection. This isn't going away simply because he hides in the dark and wishes it gone."

She squeezed my fingers. "I'm so sorry."

"I hate that he's not coming to me," I said, my voice thin as we got down to the heart of the matter.

"He probably hates it, too," she said. "But I can see why he's not. You've got Stuart, after all."

I nodded, knowing it was true. Knowing that I was selfish for wanting Eric to still depend on me even after Stuart and I had repaired the rifts in our marriage. I loved him, though, and the thought that he was going through this alone broke my heart.

"Have you told Stuart?"

"Yeah," I said. "I told him last week." I'd hated doing it. Stuart's acceptance of my world was still understandably fragile. But he'd sworn an oath to take me "for better or for worse," and he'd come back to me promising to honor that oath.

Since a demon-possessed ex-husband definitely counted as a tick-mark in the "for worse" column, I had to force Stuart to put his money where his mouth was.

"Exactly," Laura said, when I explained all of that. "Full disclosure. My little girl's growing up."

"It wasn't easy," I admitted. "He left because he was scared of the danger inherent in my job. Now the danger's gotten personal."

"It was always personal, Kate."

Score one for Laura.

"Are you scared?"

"Of Eric?" The idea of being scared of Eric seemed hugely disloyal. "Let's just say I'm worried."

"What about Allie? Is she worried, too?"

"Absolutely not. The demon may be coming," I said, "but it isn't here. Not yet. Eric's still patrolling. He's killing demons side by side with me. He's still Eric," I said, filling my voice with certainty. "And she hasn't got a clue."

"You sure about that?"

I hesitated, my chest tight merely from the suggestion. I didn't want to believe, but more than that, I *didn't* believe. "She never heard the description of who could wield the sword," I said, referring to the vaguely worded prophecy that, ultimately, had proven the existence of Eric's demonic hitchhiker.

"She might have read it. Overheard you talking. Figured it out somehow."

"She would have told me," I said, then frowned as Laura stared me down. I knew what she was thinking without her having to say a word. Allie was fourteen years old. And although I might have an exceptionally close relationship with my adolescent Hunter-in-training, I was an idiot if I thought she confided all to me. I caved. "Or maybe you're right. I'll pay attention. See if I can figure out if she knows without actually telling her."

"Secrets within secrets," Laura said.

"Welcome to my world," I deadpanned. "Completely screwed up, but always interesting."

"Would it help if I told you I was pretty sure my husband actually is a demon?"

I almost cracked a smile but managed to bite it back.

"Didn't think so," she said.

"I can kill him for you," I said. "If he's demonic, it's totally within my province."

"Tempting," she admitted. "But probably not the best idea." She got up and started moving around the kitchen, wiping the squeaky-clean counter down with a damp rag and otherwise telegraphing the fact that she didn't know what to say or how to make me feel better. And the hell of it was, I couldn't help her out. I didn't know what I needed, either, except to have Eric back to normal. And I didn't have a clue how to get there. To be brutally honest, after everything that had happened, I wasn't even sure what normal was anymore.

"They didn't stay too long at the mansion," Laura said, peering through her kitchen curtains.

"Hmm?" I said, my mind on Eric and secrets and the messiness of life in general.

"Your house," she said. "Someone's home."

That got my attention. "No way," I said. I glanced at the clock. "It hasn't even been an hour."

She didn't bother to respond, just stepped to the side, taking the curtain with her so that a triangle of window was revealed. Laura lives one street over, her house backing up to mine, with only a utility easement separating our two properties. From her kitchen window, she had a mostly unobstructed view of our back porch and living room. Our storage shed blocked her view of the kitchen, but at the moment, that didn't matter. Because I saw it, too. The lights on downstairs. And the shadow moving within.

"You'll watch him a little longer?" I said, nodding toward Timmy, who'd been sacked out on the couch when I'd arrived, and hadn't moved once during our entire conversation.

"You're going over there? Call Stuart. Hell, call the police."

I considered that plan for about ten seconds before dismissing it. "If Stuart's home, I'll know soon enough. If it's a demon, I'm more qualified than the cops."

"And if it's a plain, old-fashioned burglar?"

"Then the odds are good I'll scare him off," I said.

"And if not?"

I lifted a shoulder. "I can handle myself."

"Jesus, Kate," she said, but it didn't matter, I already had her kitchen door open, and was slipping my jacket back on. The one with the stiletto conveniently hidden in the sleeve.

"Grab the holy water out of my purse and toss it here," I said. "Keys, too."

She frowned, but complied. "Promise me you won't end up dead," she said.

I stepped over the threshold and onto her back stoop. "I promise," I said. It was an oath I'd sworn innumerable times. So far, at least, I hadn't broken my word.

I figured that had to count for something.

The house was shadow-free as I approached, and I began to wonder if Laura and I were simply being paranoid. Maybe a cloud had passed over the moon. Maybe headlights hitting the front of the house had transformed my wooden coatrack into a wraith.

Or maybe I was engaging in some serious wishful thinking.

Keeping my senses sharp, I moved toward my house.

The lights had been on inside, but I knew that didn't mean the outside was necessarily clear. My intruder could have a companion, and the last thing I wanted was to get jumped on the way to my own ambush. So despite my eagerness to figure out what was going on, I moved slowly and with precision. A good plan in general, actually, considering that the length and breadth of the Timmy-created path of destruction had transformed our yard into a veritable warzone, complete with tiny Timmy toy land mines.

I eased my way around a pile of plastic soldiers, gently kicked aside an inflated beach ball, and skirted the empty dinosaur sandbox.

I moved to my left, edging up against the side of our storage shed, then peered cautiously around the corner, half-expecting a demon to rush me. When none did, I let out a quick sigh and continued forward. I remembered our motion-sensing back-porch light too late, and sprang sideways as it flashed on, hoping it would flash immediately off before my uninvited guest noticed me.

Stock-still in the shadows, I watched the house, frozen for longer than was comfortable until I was certain that I'd remained unnoticed.

Then I edged around the front of the storage shed, my back only inches from the structure, staying clear of the light's effective range until I reached the corner of the house.

We have a picture window in the breakfast area that looks out over the backyard. That window had, in fact, been my re-entree into the world of demon hunting, and I found it ironic that I was now on the outside, hands and face pressed to the glass, as I peered inside, hoping to catch sight of a demon.

And, yeah, I really did hope to see something. To my way of thinking, finding a demon in my house was a lot better than not finding a demon—and spending the rest of the night wondering what the heck Laura and I had seen.

Unfortunately, my prolonged peering revealed no movement, though I did notice that the light at the top of the stairs was on, as was the overhead light in the living room. The second one we left on almost constantly, so that was no surprise, but the light at the top of the stairs had recently shown signs of shorting out, making it necessary to jiggle the switch in order to get any light at all. Because I'm way more afraid of fires than I am of demons—and because Stuart hadn't managed to fix one little switch despite assuring me that he had the skill to tackle an entire mansion—I'd gotten into the habit of making sure the light remained off unless someone was actually going up or down the stairs.

At the moment, that little requirement wasn't satisfied. But whether a demon was breaking my rules or a teenager, I didn't know. Frankly, I considered either possibility equally likely.

Still without evidence of a demonic invasion, I eased toward the porch, less worried this time about the light that burst on at my approach, determined to make me nice and visible to any nearby demons. Fortunately, no attack was forthcoming, and I considered it my lucky evening.

I slid my key into the lock as quietly as possible, twisted, and pushed open the door. In fairness, the creak of the hinges was barely audible, but to my ears, it seemed to ring out like a shot, and I froze in the threshold, senses on alert, ready to take out whatever creature rushed at me.

Since nothing rushed, I stepped inside and quickly keyed in the alarm code, noting with interest that it was, in fact, still armed. Either Laura and I had suffered from a dual hallucination, or my demonic intruder had entered and then reset the alarm behind him.

I glanced around, frowning at the implications. All quiet. No off-putting smells. No heavy footfalls. Not even the eerie scratch of a tree branch against an upstairs window.

As far as I could see, nothing was out of place, either. Stuart's magazines, Allie's schoolbooks, Timmy's entire Thomas the Tank train set. The room was a complete shambles, but it was a homey kind of clutter, and damned if I didn't feel let down.

I was chastising myself for being ridiculous when a sharp, musical twang rang out. I slipped my right hand into my left sleeve, grasping the hilt of my hidden stiletto. With the blade comfortable in my hand, I turned slowly toward the staircase, an admonition to be careful what you wished for ringing in my head.

The sound had come from above, and I recognized it. Timmy's Playskool piano. Clunky colorful keys in a sturdy plastic shell. Virtually indestructible. And loud, too. I should know—I'd banged against it in the middle of the night often enough.

And now, apparently, I wasn't the only one.

I held my breath, watching the stairs and listening. For the most part, our house is well-built, but there are a few creaky places, and the hallway in front of Tim's room is one of them, a fact I learned only too well when he was an infant and I'd tried to sneak away as he'd drifted off to sleep. It had taken only one step on that creaky floorboard for me to learn my lesson.

An intruder, however, shouldn't be familiar with that little quirk.

Except no sound came. No creaks, no footsteps, no evil cackling.

Well, damn.

Whoever this demon was, he was beginning to piss me off.

I climbed the stairs slowly, avoiding the one creaky step and then the creaky board in front of Timmy's room. His Thomas night-light was glowing, casting the room in blue and red shadows. I glanced around, for the first time noticing how menacing Tigger and Pooh can appear in the dark.

A sharp creak sounded to my right, and I shifted as the

accordion door moved ever so slightly outward. The door hadn't been completely closed when I'd entered, but I was certain the gap hadn't been more than three or so inches. Now it was a good seven inches, and growing.

And, honestly, I'd had enough.

"Out," I said. "We either do this now, or you get out of my house and come back after you've made an appointment."

No answer. Which meant that the demon was either ignoring me, or he didn't have a sense of humor. At this point, I didn't much care. The bastard was in my house—in my little boy's room—and we were going to end this now.

I crossed the room in two long strides, then grabbed the door with one hand, my knife poised and ready in the other. One quick pull and the entire closet was revealed to me.

Nothing.

Nothing, that is, except Kabit. The giant fuzz ball blinked up at me, then actually had the gall to yawn before stepping out of the closet and carefully circumnavigating the toy piano as he made his way out of Timmy's room and back toward the hallway.

"*Now* you walk carefully," I said. "You couldn't have stepped a little more lightly a few minutes ago?" I caught up with him at the door and hauled the beast into my arms. Naturally, he didn't have the grace to apologize for interrupting my evening. Instead, all I got was a whiff of tuna-scented cat breath. Nice.

I deposited Kabit ungracefully back to the floor, then made a quick round of the upstairs just for good measure. I wasn't entirely sure how both Laura and I could have mistaken the cat for an intruder, but even if we'd both seen the devil himself walking through my living room, there was no doubt that the beast was gone now. A fact for which I was grateful, as it was after eleven and I was ready to crash.

Upstairs completed, I did another quick round through the downstairs, then headed to the back door.

That was it. I was done. Nothing to see here, folks. Move on. Finis. Good night.

I yawned, then dealt with the alarm box as I fantasized about one more cup of coffee at Laura's. And another Baileys sounded pretty good, too.

I opened the door, debating the wisdom of two shots—after all, it had been a trying day. Then I stepped over the threshold, drew in a cleansing breath of cool night air, and screamed.

Three

I bit the scream back and glared at Eric, now standing right in front of me and looking devilishly amused with himself.

"Dammit, Eric! Don't do that!"

"You're lax, there, Connor," he said, leaning casually on his cane. His mahogany-colored hair glimmered in the porch light, and I saw amusement dance in his silver-gray eyes.

"Not lax," I countered. "Just irritated. I keep getting attacked by demons who aren't really demons."

His face shifted, hardened, and I immediately regretted what I'd said. "Oh, Eric. Dammit, I'm sorry. I wasn't—"

"No," he said. "You're right. Jumped by someone who's *not* a demon. That would be me."

I swallowed, watching his face. Exhaustion cast shadows beneath his eyes, and I could see the tension . . . and the regret.

It was the regret that made my heart twist, because I didn't understand it. Worse, I knew that if I asked, he wouldn't tell me. I knew, because I'd *been* asking. Night after night, patrol after patrol. I'd asked what I could do, how I could help. I wanted to share the burden. I wanted to search for an answer. I wanted to hold him close and tell him it would all be better.

I wanted him to trust me enough to share his pain.

But night after night, he kept his own counsel. And after everything we'd shared, that about broke my heart.

I pushed it aside, willing myself not to sink into an emotional quagmire. "Why are you here?" I heard the harshness in my tone and regretted it. I was angry, yes, but I liked to think I had better control. Apparently I was wrong.

"I needed to talk to you."

I tilted my head up, looking at him through narrowed eyes. "So talk."

His shoulders sagged, but he stayed silent.

"Dammit, Eric, what are you doing here? And why were you in the house?" I crossed my arms and stared him down. "You were in the house, right?"

"I had to make sure you were safe."

"Well, that's something," I said, hating myself for sounding snippy. "Nice to know you still care."

He flinched, and I pushed down a wave of guilt. "You know I care," he said, his voice raw.

"Do I?" I moved closer, my hand going automatically to touch him. I pulled it back, afraid of the connection if I brushed against his skin. Or maybe I was afraid there'd be no spark at all. "You're shutting me out, Eric. In all our years—in everything we've been through together—you've never shut me out before." He'd kept secrets, I knew that now, but he'd never closed his heart.

"Katie," he began, but I shook my head. I couldn't stand to hear another excuse. Another diversion.

"Forget it. You want to keep it businesslike, then that's what we do. Just tell me what's happened. Why do you think I'm in danger?"

He blinked, and I saw confusion in his deep gray eyes. I also saw fear. "Dreams," he finally said. "Impressions. Dark omens. Hell, I don't know. I just had to see you."

I nodded, trying to conjure a supportive smile as fear rose within me, too. *It was happening,* I thought. The demon was reaching out, clamoring for control, and leaving the man to rage against shadows.

I clenched my fists and moved closer to this man I loved, again wanting to touch him but not sure that I should. I wasn't afraid of how he'd react, but afraid of what I'd want. "Let me in, Eric," I said. "Let me help you."

"It's not your problem," he said, his voice unfamiliarly cold. "You made your choice."

I swallowed, my throat suddenly thick with tears. "That's not fair," I said. "We've talked about this. I thought you were dead. I loved you, yes, but I moved on."

"You love him."

"Yes."

"Then you have no business with me. Whatever's inside me isn't your concern anymore, Katie."

"You're the father to my daughter," I said. "What concerns you will always concern me."

"Because of Allie," he said.

"Don't make this less than it is," I said, my voice a hairsbreadth from losing control.

"And what is that, Kate?" he fired back, with vitriol equal to my own. "Are you in my bed? Are you even fucking in my life?"

I stepped back, then kicked one of Timmy's trucks far out into the yard simply because I needed to whale on something. "Dammit, Eric, why are you being this way? You know how I feel. I love you. You want me to shout it from the rooftop? Write you a letter? Sing you a freaking ballad? I will. You know I will. But I have a husband. We have a son. You can't ask me to simply walk away from them."

"Why not?" he countered. "Why the hell not? I need you, Kate," he said, his voice breaking. "Especially now. Especially with what's happening to me. I can't do this alone."

"And yet you won't let me in if I stay with Stuart," I snapped. "That's quite a conundrum. Dammit," I said, my voice softer now. He was in an impossible position. We both were, and right then we weren't making it easy on each other. "Eric, I'm sorry. You know I am. But you also know that I'm married. And I'm not breaking those vows."

"Like I said—you've already made your choice." I could see the pain in his eyes, could hear the loss in his voice. And I wanted to go to him. Wanted to put my arms around him and hold him close and tell him the God's honest truth: that I would always love him—Stuart, demons, and propriety be damned.

But I didn't get the chance, because suddenly he lashed out, the knife that had been sheathed at his side only moments ago now tight in his hand. With the back of his arm, he knocked me off balance. I tumbled to the left, landing hard on a retro-style chaise lounge, the chair and me tumbling backward. I lost my grip on my own blade in the process, the stiletto flying off into the circle of dark that surrounded the porch.

My left arm was trapped between the thick weave of the lounger, and I struggled to untangle myself even as my eyes scanned the porch for another weapon. There was no doubt that I was going to need one. The demon on my porch stood at least six feet tall, with thighs like fence posts. Construction, I thought. Either that or he'd been featured in the WWF. Whatever the beast's former life, he was all demon now, and his beefy face curled into a snarl as he kicked out and up, knocking the knife from Eric's hand before he lunged at me.

I managed to yank my arm free, then scurried backward, crablike, dragging my ass and legs over the fallen lounger, and then giving the entire aluminum contraption a hard shove toward the demon. Not that my efforts did much good. The beast avoided my thrust, instead spinning around and catching Eric hard across the face. As Eric tumbled to the ground on the far side of the porch I climbed to my feet, managing to knock over one of the pots in which I'd tried— and failed—to plant tomatoes last spring. I bent down and ripped out a chopstick I'd used as a stake, figuring it was a better weapon than nothing.

Not by much, though. A fact that quickly became clear when the demon picked up the crumpled lawn chair and hurled it at me, sending me hurtling backward again before the beast himself followed suit, his giant foot aiming down hard toward my throat. I saw the blow coming, planted my feet, and pushed back hard. My shirt rode up, and my back scraped along the concrete, all the gravel that Timmy loved to throw onto the porch digging into my skin. I winced in pain, but mentally cheered in victory, because I'd gained the inches I needed, and that massive foot crunched down on my collarbone and not my windpipe.

A Pyrrhic victory when you considered that I was still on my back with a demon on top of me, but at least I was alive and breathing. And, thank God, Eric was back on his feet and aiming a ferocious crescent kick right at my tormentor's skull, his weak leg firmly on the ground, his weight pivoting off the head of his cane.

To sweeten the deal, the demon spun to look back, which meant that Eric's flying foot connected hard with Dumbo's face. I heard the satisfying crunch of bone and cartilage followed by the low wail of the demon as he backed off, blood gushing from his nose.

"You are not my concern, male," he said, his voice liquid through the blood.

"Oh, I think I am." The leg came around again, but this time the demon was ready. He caught Eric's ankle between his hands and twisted, giving Eric no choice but to shift into the turn or feel his leg snap like a twig. He twisted, which landed him on the ground, momentarily defenseless against the demon's onslaught. I, however, was back on my feet.

Still armed with nothing more than a chopstick and determination, I landed a solid kick at the small of the demon's back, sending him toppling over even as Eric whipped the blade out from inside his cane and thrust it up toward the falling demon.

The demon's wail echoed through the neighborhood, the blade piercing the palm of his hand and extending out the back. A defensive wound, since I was certain that Eric had been aiming for the beast's eye.

Now Eric yanked his blade back, and the demon came along for the ride, ending up nose to nose with Eric.

I was right behind, grabbing for the beast's shoulder, ready to jerk it around and thrust my chopstick deep into its eye, when I saw its back go rigid and heard its low, terrified voice. "Odayne!" it whispered, then backed away, bowing. "Forgive! Forgive!"

From my angle, I could see Eric's face, and he looked as baffled as I felt. An emotion that did neither of us any good, as it gave the demon time to back farther away, managing to both bow and run at the same time. "Do not tell her," it said. "I do not wish to invoke her wrath. Please, sire, do not tell her. Do not tell." And then it turned and faced me dead-on. Its lips curled into a snarl, and before I even had time to draw a breath, it took off running toward the back of my yard. In the dim light, I saw it leap the fence, then race westward along the easement.

I didn't even think about going after it. Tonight, the demon could live. Right then, I had more important things to worry about.

I knelt down beside Eric then took his hand. He met my eyes, only to flinch and look away again, focusing on something over my shoulder rather than on me. "It's out," I said. "It's visible. This demon inside you—he saw it. He *named* it."

Eric nodded, looking as miserable as I'd ever seen him.

"How long?" I whispered. "How long has it been that close to the surface?"

He shook his head. "I don't know."

"What about its name?" I pressed. "Did you know the demon's name?" I was flipping through my mental little black book of demons, trying to remember where I'd heard that name before, or even if I had. After decades of hunting, many of the demon names started to blur together and, in truth, I was always more interested in killing them than inviting them over for tea.

The research and study of particular demons had always interested Eric more, and he and our first *alimentatore*, Wilson Endicott, used to spend hours discussing the various patterns of demons throughout the ages. A demon might manifest in one decade, sliding into the body of a ruler or other important person. The beast could set something vile in motion that would survive even the death of the demon's host body. Then the demon might wait another decade or two to manifest again, sliding into another body and continuing the project.

Eric and Wilson had always found the demon's endgame fascinating. Me, I'd been more interested in my own endgame: getting rid of the beasts and making the world safe for, well, everyone.

Shortsighted, maybe, but at least it kept me focused.

"Eric," I demanded, realizing he hadn't answered my question. "Did you know the demon's name?"

His brow creased, and he shook his head slowly, but there was no firm reassurance. Instead, he looked slightly baffled, as if there was something familiar about all that was happening, but he couldn't put his finger on it.

I frowned, not liking that idea any more than I liked the idea of a named demon living inside him.

I started pacing, ripping the elastic off my ponytail so I could run my hands through my hair. "This is new," I said. "The name's bad enough, but just the fact that Thor there recognized you is bad. New and bad." We'd been patrolling together, and Eric had taken out his share of demons without hesitation or pretense.

And not once during our weeks of patrols had any demon shaken his hand and called him brother.

"What's changed?" I asked, kneeling back down in front of him. "Dammit, Eric, what's changed?"

"Nothing," he said, and I could hear the fire in his temper. Now he climbed to his own feet, paced in front of me. "What do you want me to say? That I have dark, evil thoughts? That my vision turns red? That I stand in front of the mirror practicing my evil laugh?"

"Eric—"

"Because I don't. It's slow and it's subtle and it's terrifying."

I licked my lips, watching him, seeing the changes in him, trying to measure them as the anger began to rage. *That was the trigger,* I thought. At least for now. Anger. Frustration. Maybe even fear. All emotions that brought the demon closer to the surface.

How long did we have before the demon needed no trigger at all?

"Some bastard in a Miata cut me off yesterday," he said, his voice little more than a whisper. "I floored it and tailed him all the way to the county line. Sideswiped him twice. He almost lost control on the narrows," he said, referring to a portion of the Pacific Coast Highway that skimmed a mountain pass, a sheer cliff on one side and a hefty drop down to the Pacific on the other. "Fucker managed to pull it out at the last second. One inch more and he'd be a stain on the rocks beneath PCH."

I swallowed, stayed perfectly still, and tried to gauge the distance between me and my stiletto, still forlorn in our unkempt yard.

He lifted his eyes to mine and I saw both rationality and regret. "I remember that one," he said. "I don't think I remember them all."

"Jesus, Eric."

"Yeah," he said. "I could certainly use His help right about now."

I managed a smile, though I wanted to cry. "Will I do?"

He looked at me, his eyes dark and unreadable. Then he turned and righted the chaise lounge that had been knocked over in the fight. He sat on it, the movement casual, but his expression far from it. "I'd give anything," he finally said, "to keep you away from this."

I flinched, even though I understood the sentiment. He wanted to protect me. To protect my memories of him. I got that. Understood it. And yet there'd been a time in our lives when we'd been everything to each other, and even the worst secrets had been shared.

Or at least I'd thought so.

Without a word, I sank into the chair next to him. "But I am here," I said, "and I'm not going away." I reached over to take his hand. "Let me help, Eric. Bring me in. Don't push me back. Bring me in before it's too late."

He said nothing.

As for me, I pretty much wanted to scream. Instead, I relied on my toddler-wrangling skills, counted to ten, and tried a different tack altogether.

"Her," I said, and saw his head tilt toward me with interest. "The demon said you weren't supposed to tell *her*. That he didn't want to invoke her wrath. Who? Who is she?"

"I don't know," he said, looking at me dead-on. "I swear."

And the horrible, awful truth? I didn't believe him.

The man I'd once trusted with my life. With my soul. With my body and my secrets.

My first love. My soul mate.

I didn't trust him.

And I swear the pain of that realization pretty much ripped me to shreds.

I saw the flare of anger flash in his eyes and knew he'd seen my disloyalty. I cut my gaze away, ashamed. "I told you, Katie. I don't know. I'm not in control here, or had that little fact escaped your attention?"

"You are," I said, believing that with all my heart. What I didn't know was how long he could keep control.

So far, I'd seen only small signs of the demon. Bursts of temper. Unnecessary risks.

I shivered, remembering how he'd almost killed a human recently. Granted, the man had attacked him, but Eric had lost control. He'd reined it in, but that didn't change the fact that he'd gone wild in the first place.

That encounter had been my first clue, actually. My first glimpse of the blackness within.

"What have you learned?" I asked.

He climbed to his feet, then dusted off his pants. "Not enough."

"Dammit, Eric, look at me." I got up, too, shifting around so that I was right in front of him. "You promised me you had a plan. You didn't need help figuring this out, remember? That's what you said."

"I said I didn't *want* help," he said, his voice like ice.

I flinched, but forced myself not to show it. To lose my emotions in objective practicality. "Then what's the plan? What do we have to do to get you back? You. Free and clear." I drew in a ragged breath and cursed myself for the tears that threatened. "Dammit, Eric, I need you. You have to know how much I still need you."

"Oh, Kate." He pulled me close and held me tight, his touch so familiar it made me want to cry. I clung to him, guilty that I still wanted him so badly, and yet absolutely certain I would feel equally guilty if I didn't.

"It'll be okay," I said. "*Forza* managed twice, right?" I said, referring to the fact that, in his youth, the demon had been bound inside Eric. There, yes, but impotent.

At least, that's what I'd been told. When Eric was a small child, *Forza* had locked the demon up, deep inside of him, where it had remained dormant until Eric had unwittingly set it free when he'd used Cardinal Fire to destroy a demon we'd been hunting deep within the catacombs under the city of Rome.

At the time, I hadn't understood how we'd not only escaped from an army of demonic minions, but had also managed to destroy the High Demon who'd tortured and killed the other ten members of our team. A demon who'd been intent on becoming not only corporeal, but also invincible.

I'd been fifteen, Eric almost seventeen. And though neither of us knew it, what happened in the vault that night would color our lives forever.

Afterward, we'd been separated for debriefing. Father Corletti and our *alimentatore* Wilson had asked me the usual array of questions, and I'd assumed that Eric was in the boys' dorm receiving the same careful going-over. As it turns out, it had been a little more complicated than that. Wilson had given Eric the Cardinal Fire as a weapon of last resort, and he'd broken about a thousand *Forza* rules when he'd done so.

The Cardinal Fire, I'd later learned, destroyed the demons in the chamber with us. But because the demon inside Eric was shielded, it wasn't destroyed. Instead, the bindings were, making the demon free to move, to grow, to thrive.

So whereas my debriefing had been tape recorders and paperwork, Eric's had been candles and ceremonies and a dozen priests chanting from ancient texts, calling upon the power of God to bind the demon once again.

It worked. The demon retreated.

But this time, not as deep.

This time, the demon waited, biding time for the opportunity to come forth. And opportunity had knocked when Eric had died when Allie was only nine, his soul and the demon's essence thrust into the ether, still bound together. And it was the demon who had led them back to Earth to now reside in another man's body.

While Eric tried to forge a new life, the demon inside grew ever stronger. So strong, in fact, that the binding rituals used twice before no longer worked. I still held out hope that we'd find some obscure procedure. Some heretical incantation. Something, anything, that would lock back inside the demon that I'd played a part in making stronger.

Because I had indeed played a part—a key part—in accelerating the demon's attack on Eric. After all, I was the one who'd used the Lazarus Bones.

I wasn't proud of the way I'd played God that night, but I couldn't deny what I'd done. After only recently learning that Eric had returned in David's body, I'd been faced with the horror of watching him die again, made worse because I'd played such a vivid role in his demise. Because I'd been the one who killed him.

I'd killed him because I had to. Because he'd begged me to. And I'd done it in order to prevent a demon from moving in and taking over his body.

Ironic, I thought, now that I knew there'd been another demon inside him all along.

I shivered, remembering that night. The way that bitch Nadia had believed she'd won. The way the blood had flowed out of Eric as death approached.

At the time, I'd only just gotten Eric back, and the thought that he was gone again had ripped me apart.

But I'd had the means—I'd had the Lazarus Bones—and so help me, I'd used them. I'd brought him back. Or, as Father Corletti would say, I'd provided the path for Eric to follow back to life.

And he had, guided for a second time back to corporeal life by that demon inside him.

And in returning to the body—in again using that demonic trick—he'd given the demon within a little bit more power.

Father Corletti had told me I didn't cause a demon to be inside Eric, and I knew that was true. But there was no denying that I'd helped the demon gain strength.

That was something I'd have to live with forever.

As if sensing my need, Eric pushed me back and looked me in the eye. "It's going to be okay," he said.

"I want to believe that," I said. "Even more, I want to help."

"You do help," he said. "Knowing you're there. Knowing what I'm fighting for. That's more help than you can know."

I started to shake my head, to argue, to insist that I had to do more, but he brushed his finger against my lips and shook his head, silencing me. He reached up and twisted a stray strand of hair around his finger, then leaned in closer, the warmth of his breath teasing my lips until those lips actually touched mine. I gasped, and so help me, I opened my mouth to him.

He groaned, accepting the unspoken invitation and deepening the kiss.

I melted against him, my fingers knotting in the material of his shirt, every ounce of me desperate for what we'd once shared, longing for the time when we'd truly been partners and he wouldn't shut me out.

Except . . .

I pushed gently away, peering into his eyes. Because I knew now that such a time had never really existed. Not to the extent I'd once believed. I'd opened my life and my heart to Eric—my partner, my lover, my best friend—and I'd assumed that he'd done the same.

He hadn't.

He'd kept secrets from me. Secrets that—if I'd known—might have spared us the danger now lurking inside him.

I closed my eyes and bit my lip, wondering if, had I known, I would have had the strength not to use the Lazarus Bones. Would I have been able to stand there, with Allie looking on, and let her father die?

So help me, I didn't know. And that made me wonder what I would do tomorrow or the next day or the next. What would I do when the demon finally burst free and I had to make the hardest choice of all?

"Katie," he said, his voice cracking. He pressed his hands to my shoulders and his lips to my hair. I closed my eyes, taking some strength from him, but that was all I would take.

I told myself that was all I *wanted* to take. But that, of course, was a lie.

"Don't push me away, Katie."

"I'm not the one pushing," I said. I turned in his arms. "We need to fight this thing, Eric. We need to fight it together."

"Except we're not together."

I shook my head, not willing to let him go there again. "I love my husband, Eric, and nothing is going to change that. I love you, too. But we're in a different place now, and you know it. So don't try to lessen what's between you and me by lashing out against Stuart."

"Fine." He nodded. "Fine. You help. And maybe we'll figure it out before it's too late."

I angled a glance at him, hating myself for suspecting that he was lying, saying what I wanted to hear so that I'd shut up and go away. "Do you know . . . I mean, have you got any idea how long—"

"How much time I have? How long I can fight back the beast?" I winced from the harsh edge of his voice, but nodded. "I don't know," he said. "Probably not long."

I drew in a breath, tried to digest that information. "You don't patrol with Allie anymore," I said. "Not without me."

"You've been enforcing that rule for a while. What?" he added, apparently catching my surprised expression. "You think I hadn't noticed?"

"Fair enough," I said. "But she doesn't go to your apartment, either."

I braced, expecting a fight, but all I got was a simple nod, and that gesture of acquiescence scared me more than anything. Because it set out in sharp relief what we both already knew. The demon was coming closer. The battle was taking its toll. And he didn't want his daughter anywhere near when and if the beast finally burst forth.

We stood silently, both of us acknowledging that unspoken truth, and as we did, I heard a car pull into the driveway, followed by the steady churn of the garage door mechanism kicking into gear.

"You should go," I said, then exhaled in frustration as he crossed his arms over his chest and parked himself on a chair. "Dammit, Eric."

"What? Are we through here? You don't want to discuss strategy? A plan? Research venues?"

"You're being an ass," I said, but I didn't have time to elaborate because Allie came barreling out of the kitchen and into the living room. She hit the brakes, skidding to a stop in front of the couch and turning toward the door, probably noticing the back porch light. That was all it took.

Her high squeal of "Daddy!" rang through the house, and she jumped onto the couch, vaulted over the back, and threw open the door.

"Hey, baby," he said, standing up and catching her as she launched herself at him.

"What are you doing here? It's like the middle of the night."

"It's not like it at all," I said. "It is the middle of the night."

She rolled her eyes. "Mom."

"I'm just saying." I saw Stuart and Eddie in the living room, their heads swiveling in unison toward the back porch. A flash of something harsh crossed Stuart's face, erased in an instant by a now-familiar political smile.

"David," he said, nodding curtly as he stepped onto the patio. "Timmy asleep?" he asked me.

"At Laura's. I was in her kitchen when we saw someone moving in the house," I added. "Or thought we did."

A muscle in Stuart's jaw twitched as he turned to face Eric.

"I don't need to break and enter," Eric said, taking a step closer to me. "I'm welcome."

Considering the level of testosterone flying around, I decided this was a good time to send Allie up to bed. "But it's the weekend!" she protested.

"And a good thing, too. Considering how far in the toilet your grades are, you need the weekend to study."

"But—"

"Go on," Eric said. "I'll call you tomorrow."

I could tell she wanted to argue, but one of the benefits of having her father dumped recently back into her life was that Allie tended to be on her best behavior around him. Which translated into a quick nod, a good-night kiss, and a hassle-free departure.

Stuart waited until she disappeared from view before

rounding on Eric. "Did you come to patrol? To warn us about an imminent demonic threat? To avert the apocalypse?"

"I came to talk to Kate," Eric said evenly.

"It's after midnight," Stuart said. "And last time I checked, Kate's cell phone worked just fine."

"I wanted to talk to her in person."

Stuart took a deep breath, then nodded, as if he was thinking that one over. Honestly, I didn't much like the look of whatever he was thinking, and when he took a step toward Eric, I casually placed myself between the two of them. "Let's be clear," Stuart said, moving in close and putting a possessive hand on my shoulder while he stared down Eric. "Kate's my wife now. And this is my house. I'll admit I was a little freaked out when I learned the truth about you—about all of it—but I came back. I came back," he repeated, "and I swore I'd fight for her. For my family. So don't think I didn't mean it."

"If it's a fight you want," Eric said, "I think we can work something out."

"Eric—" I said, my voice low and my tone fierce.

But Stuart didn't need my help. "Do *not*," he said. "Do not come onto my property and play games with me. I respect that you love my wife. I get that you two have a history beyond anything I can imagine. Most of all, I understand that you lost your family and that you want time with your daughter. I understand it, I acknowledge it, and I even support it. But not like this. You do not show up at my house in the middle of the night to meet clandestinely with my wife. You don't disrupt our household. And whatever personal problems you may have because you landed in some other guy's body or because some badass demon wants to pull your chain, you deal with those somewhere else. Not here. Not in my home."

He took another step closer to Eric. "Are we clear?"

I tensed, waiting for the explosion, but it didn't come. Instead, Eric kept his eyes on Stuart, as if taking his measure, and for the first time finding Stuart adequate. He nodded, short and curt, before turning to face me. "Tomorrow," he said. "We patrol."

"Tomorrow," I acknowledged, then watched as he moved through the dark to the side gate, Stuart clutching tight to my hand.

"I don't want him in my house," Stuart said after the gate swung shut.

"Inside," I said, opening the back door and leading Stuart in before locking it and resetting the alarm.

"I mean it," Stuart said. "He isn't welcome here."

I glanced automatically toward the stairs, but saw no evidence that Allie was snooping. "He's the father to my daughter," I said, keeping my voice low as I led him into the kitchen. "I'm not sleeping with him."

Stuart winced, but had the grace to look chagrined. "You love him."

I closed my eyes. That one, I couldn't deny. And when I looked again at Stuart, I didn't see anger or jealousy. All I saw was frustration, and that directed not at me, but at himself.

"Oh, God, Kate," he said, sinking into one of the chairs around our battered Formica breakfast table. "I'm sorry. I trust you. Hell, I even pity you. Not exactly the typical interaction with the former husband we've got going here. But I gotta be honest. He terrifies me."

"He's not taking me from you," I said.

"That's not what I mean." He pushed the chair beside him out with his toe, and I sat down, facing him, and knowing exactly where this was going. "There's a demon inside him, remember? You're the one who explained it to me. Or have you forgotten?"

"Of course I haven't forgotten," I snapped, though at the moment, I regretted my decision to be quite so forthcoming.

"He's dangerous, Kate."

"He won't hurt me."

"Maybe," Stuart acknowledged. "And maybe not. But what about me? Or Timmy? And even if he doesn't physically hurt Allie . . ." He trailed off, leaving me to draw my own conclusions.

"I'm working on it," I said. "He's working on it."

Stuart looked at me, his eyes seeing more than I wanted. "Whatever you're doing," he said, "do it faster."

Four

"*Mommymommymommymommmeeeeeeeee!* Get up, Mommy! Up! Up! Up!"

I shoved a pillow over my head and rolled over, which was not the way to soothe the savage toddler, who proceeded to march atop the bed humming and screaming and generally making a nuisance of himself.

"Where's your father?" I asked. "Your sister. Somebody, anybody, help me."

"Me, me, me," he said, plunking his little body on my back and aiming a spit-filled whisper toward my ear. "Daddy says up, Mommy. Get up now!"

I rolled over, saw the empty side of the bed, and smelled a rat. "Did Daddy send you to wake me?"

He nodded gleefully, then thrust his arms up toward the ceiling. "Do that, Mommy!"

And despite the fact that I was operating on absolutely no sleep, I tossed my arm above my head, which I considered hugely generous since I knew exactly what was coming.

Sure enough, Timmy leaped on me, his little fingers scratching under my arms in a toddler's version of tickling. I writhed and chuckled and generally pretended he'd managed to hit a tickle nerve. He kept it up for about forty seconds, at which point he couldn't stand it any longer. He flopped back on the bed, arms high above his head. "Do me, Mommy! Do me!"

"I don't know," I said, as if I really had an option here. "Daddy said I'm supposed to get up, not tickle a little boy."

"Yes, tickle!" he screeched, his little face scrunching up and displaying all the signs of an oncoming tantrum.

"Whoa, whoa," I said. "I was just kidding." I looked up at the ceiling. "Wow!" I said, as if amazed. "Look at that. Can you reach it?"

"What?" Tantrum forgotten, he turned big eyes upward. "Right above you," I said. "If you reach really high, you might be able to catch one."

He climbed to his feet, a bit unsteady on the soft mattress and stretched his arms up toward the ceiling, grasping at nothing.

I pounced, pulling him down to the mattress even as my fingers went for his underarms, tickling for all I was worth. He squealed and kicked and screamed and appeared generally delighted with the whole thing. So delighted, in fact, that even when I fell back exhausted on the bed, he bounced and bounced, crying, "Again! Again! Again!" so many times that Stuart and Allie appeared in the doorway.

"You're stuck now," Allie said. "Once he starts, there's no going back. Duh-duh-duh-dummmmmm," she added, in a bad parody of a horror movie soundtrack.

"Thanks," I deadpanned. "You're very helpful. You?" I asked, shifting my attention from my daughter to Stuart.

"Sorry. I got nothing. Except pancakes. How about it, sport? Want to make a trade? Your mother's freedom for a Mickey Mouse pancake with chocolate chip eyes?"

"Pancakes!" he screamed, then leaped off the bed and scurried past his father for the stairs.

"Tossed aside for carbohydrates," I said. "Isn't it always the way?"

Stuart blew me a kiss, then headed out of the room to make good on his promise. I rolled out of bed and headed to the armchair that has never seen a person's tush, seeing as it has throughout our entire marriage served only as a place to hold clothes. I found a pair of sweatpants and tugged them on. I was already wearing a Coronado High PTA T-shirt, so I was now as dressed as I intended to get until after coffee.

I checked the clock, saw that it was painfully early for a Saturday, and decided I had plenty of time before Timmy's ten o'clock social engagement. I also saw that Allie was still hovering in the doorway looking expectantly in my direction.

"Well?"

In response, I shoved my feet into fuzzy bunny slippers. "Ummm?"

"Daddy," she said, rolling her eyes. "Why was he here? Can I hang out at his place this weekend?"

"He was here because we had things to discuss, and not this weekend."

"But—"

"He has to run into L.A.," I lied.

"I could go with him."

I bent down and adjusted my bunny slippers so that my daughter wouldn't see the lie on my face. "I don't think it's convenient this time, kiddo."

"But we can ask him, right? I mean, I could call, and—"

"No."

"What? Why?" Her wail drifted all the way downstairs, and Stuart yelled back up with a curt, "I didn't say anything."

"But why not?" Allie said, trying again with a softer voice.

"Your grades, for one," I said, heading for the door. "Your father and I are both concerned." I told myself I was feeling no guilt. We *were* concerned. That just wasn't my reason for keeping my daughter from her father.

As for the real reason, I should feel no guilt there, either. After all, my first job as a mom was to keep my kids safe. And even Eric agreed that Allie was better off not being alone with him.

That simple fact sat like a dead weight in my stomach, and my fingers itched to pick up the phone and try to reach Father Corletti. We were missing something. Something huge. Something that would save Eric if only we could find it. And now, with the demon inside gaining strength and some anonymous She-Demon out there, I feared we had to find it fast.

I frowned, realizing I hadn't told Stuart about our little encounter with Gargantua the Wonder Demon last night. I glanced toward the door, guilt pooling in my gut. I'd promised Stuart full disclosure, but I hadn't realized how quickly that would become dicey. Demons attacking in the backyard. Demons buddying up to Eric. That was the kind of stuff that could really worry a man. Hell, it worried me.

"Mom!"

"Hmmm?" I turned toward her, but my thoughts were still on Stuart. A short secret, I thought. That's all. I'd gather a little more information, and then I'd tell him everything. At the very least, I wanted to figure out who this She-Demon was. If I had to tell Stuart there was another Big Bad with me in its sights, at a minimum I wanted some information about my enemy. To get that, I was going to need help.

"*Mom!*"

I smiled negligently at Allie, but my thoughts had drifted to Father Ben. He'd been my *alimentatore*—my guide, my helper—and he'd been brutally murdered only weeks before. As always when I thought of him, I felt the stab of regret. I'd been too late to save him, and though I knew in my heart that his death wasn't my fault, I couldn't help but shoulder some of the blame. Those ripples again. He'd come to San Diablo to minister to a parish; he'd become involved in *Forza* because he'd met me. He had, I thought, deserved better. And at the same time, I knew that he would be proud dying the way he had, defending the innocent against the onslaught of evil.

"*Mother!*"

Allie's shriek finally broke through my musings. "Sorry. What?"

"I can study at Daddy's," she said, her exasperated tone matching her expression.

I shook off thoughts of Stuart and Eric and mysterious female demons and focused on my daughter. "Sorry, kid. You study here."

"That's so unfair," she wailed.

"Incredibly," I agreed. "But until you're the mom, you have to live with my arbitrary and capricious rules. That means no applying for your learner's permit until your grades are up—"

"Big deal," she said sulkily, having recently had all her illusions shattered by the previously unknown fact that her fifteenth birthday wasn't the magic day for applying for her permit. That day was fifteen years plus six months. And to a teenager, that extra six months might as well be six years.

"I didn't make the rules."

She crossed her arms over her chest and stared me down. "Maybe not that one."

I tried not to laugh, but I couldn't help it. "Fair enough."

I aimed a finger out the door. "So what's it going to be? Breakfast with the family or sulking in your room?"

"Sulking," she said, then turned to slink down the hall. I'm pretty sure she expected me to call her back, but I didn't have the energy for a fight. Instead, I called after her, reminding her to use the time to study. My response was a frustrated groan and a firm slamming of the door. I'm probably a bad mom, but I couldn't hold back my smile. Because grades and studying and teenage angst had absolutely nothing to do with demons. A tiny bit of normality had snuck into our decidedly *ab*normal life. And damned if that didn't feel nice.

"You're chipper," Stuart said as I slid into my chair at the table.

"Allie's banished to her room studying," I said. "I'm pretty sure I'm on her shit list for the day."

"Shit list!" Timmy shouted, and Stuart cocked an eyebrow while I silently mouthed a contrite, "Sorry."

"Well, I can see why that puts a spring in your step," said my husband the comedian.

"Can't I be in a good mood? Do I have to be sullen just because my daughter is?"

"What exactly is she sullen about?"

I hesitated, our newly established full-disclosure lifestyle at odds with my unilateral decision to postpone the whole full-disclosure thing for a day or two. "I'm not letting her go to Eric's," I said.

"Well of course you're not," Stuart agreed, and I saw the moment comprehension hit. "And she doesn't understand why."

"Sure she does." I smiled. "Her grades suck."

"Suck!" Timmy yelled gleefully, and I took a deep breath and counted to ten. "Party now?" Timmy asked. He bounced a little in his seat, thrilled at the prospect of festivities, even though the child to be feted was a little demon in her own right. Not literally—in my world, those qualifications had to be added. Not that I blamed little Danielle. Her mother, Marissa, had been my arch-nemesis since I'd joined the PTA. And although I'd learned to tolerate her, I didn't see any girlie shopping moments in our future. Her eldest, Joann, goes to school with Allie. Little Danielle, the birthday girl, is closer to Timmy's age. And since Marissa had so generously invited us to the party, I'd shown my respect, love, and admiration by buying and wrapping a handmade Silly String Shooter, the messiest toy I could find.

I might not be able to stake Marissa, but that didn't mean I had to quietly tolerate her, either.

"Now, now, now?" Timmy continued to howl.

"Soon enough," I said. "Let's go get you dressed and we'll head out the door." The party was at ten and it was only eight-thirty. But I figured we'd need a good forty minutes to fight over the outfit. Another twenty to wrap the present (which Timmy had unwrapped yesterday after finding it in the hall closet) and at least fifteen more minutes for me to run into Starbucks and grab the coffee that I'd surely need to get me through this thrilling event.

Once we were both cleaned and dressed, I popped my head into Allie's room and reminded her that cable was off-limits until she'd finished studying. I was rewarded with a grunt, which I assured myself meant that I was fulfilling my parental role. Then I scooped Timmy up and, holding him upside down so that he giggled and squealed and wriggled so much I feared for dropping him, headed down the stairs. Stuart was shrugging into a jacket when we slid to a stop in the entrance hall.

"What's up?" I asked.

"Running into the office," he said, checking his watch.

"On Saturday?"

"Clark wants a meeting."

"Oh." I frowned, processing that tidbit. Clark Curtis was the current lame-duck county attorney and Stuart's boss, although that relationship had turned extremely awkward two weeks ago when Stuart had informed Clark of his intention to back out of the race for county attorney, smearing egg all over Clark's face in the process. "You didn't mention it."

"He called yesterday. I was planning to tell you after I measured the fallout."

I nodded, glad I wasn't the only one hoarding information. "Are you sure you don't want to go back?" So far, only Clark and a few key figures knew that Stuart was pulling out of the race. The handlers had decided to keep it quiet while Clark chose a replacement for my defecting husband.

I thought I saw something wistful pass over Stuart's face, but he shook his head. "Too much time. Too much energy." He leaned forward and kissed me on the cheek. "I have better things to focus on."

I gave him a quick hug, hoping I seemed supportive and not worried. Because no matter what Stuart said, I knew that the bottom line here was unemployment. I couldn't imagine Clark suffering that kind of loss of face and still keeping Stuart on the rolls as an assistant county attorney any longer than was politically correct. Two weeks sounded about right for that purpose, so I had a feeling today was the day Stuart was getting the ax. And since *Forza* doesn't currently offer health coverage—much less vision and dental—I felt a slight stirring of discontent for myself and my two offspring.

But I smiled and hugged my husband and wished him good luck . . . and as soon as he was out the door I said a quick prayer and asked for St. Jude's intercession. After all, every little bit helps.

Since Timmy absolutely refused to let go of Danielle's present, I was struggling to strap him into his car seat with a package on his lap when I heard the front door creak open.

I glanced around and saw Eddie shuffle down the sidewalk in his ratty green bathrobe, his finger held up for attention.

"Hold up there, girlie. You coming straight back after the kiddie fest?"

I mentally ran through my schedule and realized I was. My class on tiling at Home Depot wasn't until two. "Yup. What do you need?"

"Lift to work," he said. "Gotta be there at one. Working the afternoon shift."

I raised my brows. "Work?" This was news to me.

"Been putting in a few hours," he said. "A fellow needs his spending money."

"Oh." I had a sudden image of Eddie working the check-out line at Walmart, and counted the days until he was fired. Somehow I didn't think his generally grouchy attitude fit the corporate profile. Actually, I couldn't think of any jobs where Eddie fit the profile, except Demon Hunter, and he was quite retired from those ranks, his current forays into hunting now focused primarily on announcing how much I still had to learn and how limited *Forza* was in its view of the world. It would be annoying were he not so often right. "So where are you working?" I asked.

"New shop in Old Town," he said. "Doubt you've heard of it."

"Really?" I pondered the possibilities along with the fact that Eddie seemed so reticent to share the details.

"So can you give me a lift or not? If I gotta call a taxi I need to know now. Damn cabs need half a day's notice to get anywhere on time."

I licked my lips as a new thought occurred to me. "Actually, maybe we could trade favors."

His eyes narrowed, bushy eyebrows twitching like caterpillars. "Eh?"

"I need help," I said. "I need an *alimentatore*."

"Ah," Eddie said, all humor draining from his face. "Right."

I swallowed, determined not to cry. "I could really use the help. Please?"

"The Vatican ain't got a spare?" Eddie asked, lightening the mood.

"I'm sure they're working on it. I want you," I added, realizing as I spoke how much I meant it.

"Do you now? Ya wanna tell me why?"

I could have rattled off a hundred reasons, starting with the fact that Eddie had seen things I'd only imagined—and I'd seen my share of the horrific. I could have cited his knowledge and his experience, not to mention his tenacity. I could have even bribed him with a TiVo box.

Instead, I settled on the one thing that mattered to me most of all. "It's because of Eric," I said, and watched as his eye twitched at Eric's name. "You know about the demon," I said. "But there's more." I gave him the quick and dirty overview of what had happened before he and Stuart and Allie had arrived home the night before.

"Ain't it always the way. Some power-hungry demon moves into town and right away tries to take you out."

"It's the job," I deadpanned. "They're all so jealous."

He snorted. "Yeah, there's that. So you want my help tracking She-Ra down."

I did, of course, but it was more than that. "The demon scented Eric. I need answers, Eddie. And I need them fast."

"Heh," he said. "You want an answer? I got one for you right now, free of charge." He poked me in the chest with one bony finger. "Shove a knife through his heart before the demon takes root. Kill the boy now and consider yourself lucky."

"He's Allie's father, Eddie. She loves him." I paused, then looked him dead in the eye. "And so do I."

His shoulders drooped, all the vinegar disappearing from his attitude. "Kate."

"*No,*" I said, shaking my head. "No, you can't say no. You can't walk away from this. I want to help him, Eddie. I *have* to help him. And I need someone who'll see what I can't."

"The demon, you mean. If you're gonna fight it, ya gotta at least say it."

"Fine, then," I said, more harshly than I intended. "You'll see the demon, Eddie. You won't see the man I love. And I need that. I need your perspective. I can't do this without your help."

"And if there is no help?"

"I don't accept that as a possibility."

"And if there is no help?" he repeated.

"Then I'll take a knife and do exactly what you said. I've done it before," I said, steely determination keeping my voice from cracking as I remembered the time not so long ago when I'd had to make that very sacrifice, not then realizing I also had the means to bring him back to life. "If I have to, I can do it again."

This time, we both knew, neither Eric nor the demon would come back.

He raked his fingers through his hair, giving him an even wilder appearance. When he'd finished, he looked back at me. "You giving me that ride?"

"Sure," I said, nodding as I struggled to bring my emotions under control. He'd veered wildly off topic, of course, and I wasn't sure if he was giving me time to gather my wits or if this was the way Eddie negotiated. Either way, I was willing to let this play out however it had to, so long as in the end I got what I wanted.

I took a deep breath and focused on his question. "But why do you need me? Doesn't Tammy usually drive you?"

Eddie let loose with an exasperated snort. "Broke up with

me last night," he said. "Left a message on the machine. What kind of tacky is that?"

Since I thought it was the same kind of tacky as breaking a date because of interrupted cable service, I wisely kept my mouth shut.

"You play chauffeur today, girlie. Just one way. I can catch a ride home with my peeps."

"Your peeps?"

"Coworkers," he said. "You need to pay attention to the lingo, girl."

"Hmmm," I said, not at all sure that *peeps* had made it into the standard employment vernacular. "And tomorrow?"

He waved a hand. "I'm off 'til Monday. I'll figure something out by then."

"You're not going to start driving again, are you?" The idea made me cringe.

"Dunno," he said. "You willing to cart me around? I got work and bingo."

"Yeah," I said, now fully suckered into the big picture. "I already carpool a toddler and a teenager. I think I have room for an obstinate old man."

"Fair enough," he said. "But I'm crotchety. Not obstinate."

"I'll keep that in mind."

"And I'll be your *alimentatore*, girlie girl. But if I'm doing it, I'm doing it right. I want all your debriefing notes. All your Hunter journals."

I stood up straighter, surprised. "Really?"

"I ain't going into the job half-assed."

"All right then, they're yours. Most everything's in the attic and labeled. Whatever you want, you take."

"Okay then." His brow furrowed, and he scuffed his slippers on the pavement. "And just so we're clear—I'm doing it for you and the girl. Not for him."

I nodded. "I know, Eddie. And that's exactly why I want you."

A renegade pirate rushed past me, his hook catching my skirt and jerking me a few steps forward, his bellowing *"Aaaargggh-hhh"* deafening.

I yanked my skirt free, pressed my back against the wall, and sucked in my gut as five fairy princesses stampeded after him, wands waving, their own squeals and giggles almost masking the still-echoing howl of their marauding quarry.

Across the room, the birthday princess pressed her fists against her hips and gave her mother the evil eye. "But I wanna be a pirate! Don't wanna be a stinky princess! I wanna have a hook!"

"Sweetie," Marissa said, kneeling down so that she was eye level with her traitorous daughter. "You're a little girl."

"I'm big!" Danielle insisted. "And I wanna be a pirate." She stamped her foot for emphasis, and I pressed my hands behind my back to prevent me from applauding. For the first time ever, I was not only getting a glimpse of the real Danielle, but I was about to bear witness to my nemesis's meltdown. Toddler birthday parties didn't get much sweeter than that.

"A fiver gets you in the pool," Fran said, sidling up next to me. "Most everyone's betting on Marissa, but I think Danielle's gonna come out the winner."

"Spot me five," I said. "I'm good for it."

"I see my rugrat," she said, nodding toward the far side of Marissa's garage-turned-party-room where little Elena was steering a Playmobil pirate ship over a blue chalk ocean, a pirate patch over one eye, and not one frilly, princessy thing to be seen.

"Fran, I'm shocked. Go slap a tiara on that kid right this minute."

Fran snorted, which was why we were friends. "I'll get right on that," she assured me. "Where's yours?"

I pointed to the opposite corner where Timmy and a boy I recognized from church were going at it with plastic cutlasses.

"Just like his mommy," Fran said.

"What?" I asked, a little too sharply.

"Fighting," she said innocently, as I tried to figure out what she knew and how she could possibly know it. "Self-defense and all that stuff."

"Oh." I exhaled in relief. "You're still coming, right?" Though my demon-hunting expertise was still a secret with the public at large, the fact that I had some fighting skill had leaked out. Cutter's studio is next door to the 7-Eleven near the entrance to our subdivision. Not only does every one of the neighborhood moms visit that store regularly for last-minute grocery items, but most of the kids in the neighborhood take classes from Cutter. And although most of my sessions with the sensei are private, there was no way to keep my workouts secret. And, honestly, no reason to try.

What had started with a few women asking me if Cutter ever did self-defense workshops, eventually evolved into Cutter suggesting that I put together a program and run it out of his dojo. At first I'd hesitated, but Allie and Laura had convinced me that I had a community obligation. "You're a demon magnet, Mom," Allie had gently pointed out. "You think there would be so many demons traipsing through this neighborhood if we didn't live here? At the very least, teach them how to kick the buggers in the balls and run away. I mean, that's something."

I'd gaped at my daughter, decided not to comment on her crudity, and agreed she was right.

And thus began my career as a women's self-defense instructor.

Or, more accurately, that career would begin this evening.

So far, I'd worked with Cutter, going over a plan for what to teach and studying up on basic theories of self-defense for women that didn't involve years of training in martial arts or street fighting. I had fifteen women signed up for tonight's session, Marissa and Fran included.

"Can I bring my mom?" Fran asked. "I told her what I was doing, and she wants in."

"Your mom wants self-defense training?" I'd met Rita once, and was pretty sure that she was capable of eviscerating a bad guy with nothing but sarcasm and a biting wit. That, and the Taser she carried in her purse, which she'd happily thrust at anyone who encroached on her personal space.

"She's always keen to kick someone in the nuts," Fran said. "But mostly I think she wants to see Eddie." A definite twinkle flickered in her eye. "I think she's a little hot for him."

"Good lord," I said. "They'd make a pair." And then, because I figured a woman like Rita would keep Eddie on his toes, I told Fran of his newly acquired single status.

"Will he be at your class?"

"Doubtful. He's working now. In Old Town."

Her brows lifted. "I'll pass the info on to my mom," she said, laughing. "I feel so covert."

"So no class for her? Since Eddie won't be there?"

Fran shrugged. "With my mom, you just never know."

A flash of pink across the room caught my eye, and I looked over in time to see Danielle's wand go flying up toward the ceiling. It narrowly missed the fluorescent lights, then came crashing back down as Danielle jumped and jumped, her giggles mixed with deep-throated "Aarghs" as Marissa handed the pink-gowned princess a black eye patch, a hook, and a skull and crossbones bandana.

"On my hair, Mommy!" Danielle shouted. Looking pained, Marissa knelt down and hid Danielle's perfectly perfect curls under a cap of black bandana.

"I never thought I'd see the day," Fran said, as Danielle took off running, joining forces with four boys who were chasing the princesses in circles around the room.

"Kids!" Marissa called, climbing up on a step stool. "Settle! Settle! It's time to decorate our treasure chests!"

The kids weren't remotely interested. At forty minutes into the party, they'd already participated in a half dozen organized activities, and I imagine their little brains were fried. I know mine was.

Marissa clapped for attention. The princesses continued to squeal and scream. The pirates continued to chase them. Timmy and his sparring partner joined the game, and even Elena got into the spirit, though she kept switching teams so that no one knew if she was chasing or being chased.

Throughout it all, Marissa stood on the stool, her hands cupped at her mouth, and cried out for attention.

After three tries, she gave up and, shoulders sagging, she came over to stand with Fran and me. "She isn't usually like this," she said, her eyes on Danielle who, frankly, looked like she was having the time of her life. Not so Marissa. She had the mortified expression of a gourmet cook who was just outed as having a pantry stocked full of Hamburger Helper

"They're having fun," Fran said.

Marissa's brows knit together. "It's all these other children. Danielle is such an empathetic child. She's tuning in to their volatile emotions and experiencing their need for shenanigans."

"I know exactly what you mean," I said. "Timmy often over-empathizes with his contemporaries following a period of close-knit socialization. It can make parenting so trying."

Marissa's eyes narrowed as she stared me down, obviously not sure if I was being sarcastic or serious.

Fran, much quicker on the uptake, shoved two fingers in

her mouth and let out a wolf-whistle, gaining the kids' attention and saving me from the wrath of Marissa that would surely have descended once she worked her way down to the sarcastic side of the equation.

Marissa shot Fran a look of utter mortification. But Fran smiled sweetly and waved an arm to encompass the garage and all the kids in it. "I think you have their full attention now."

Marissa managed a tiny *har-umph*, and I managed not to burst out laughing. Then she clapped her hands and gestured the children closer. "Pirates need treasure," she said. "So everyone come up here and let's sing the treasure song and get your treasure chest treat!"

I had no idea what she was talking about until she reached down and pulled a clear gift bag out of a cardboard box at her feet. She played Vanna White next, showing off all the fabulous prizes in the bag including Glue Dots, plastic doubloons, gemstones, gold ribbon and plain, cardboard treasure chests ripe for the decorating. Then she did something that made all the other moms in the room cringe: She started to sing.

"*Fifteen gems on a treasure chest! Yo ho ho and we're gonna have fun.* Come on! Everybody sing!" She repeated the song again, shooting a killer glance at Timmy when he bellowed the real "Dead Man's Chest" lyrics, punching extra loud on the bottle of rum.

"I could actually use the rum right about now," Fran said dryly.

I was about to agree when Timmy came running up to me, one hand holding his gift bag, the other holding his crotch. "Gotta go, Mommy! Gotta go!"

"I'd better hurry." I plucked Timmy up from around the waist and hauled him into the house, the design of which was essentially a mirror image of mine. Like ours, a small bathroom was situated just off the living room in the hall leading to the study. I hurried Timmy in that direction, trying not to be jealous at the spotless nature of Marissa's house. I told myself she'd simply cleaned up for the party, but of course I knew better. Unlike me, Marissa didn't engage in the hobby of dust-bunny breeding.

"No, no, no! Me go alone!" Timmy said, when I stepped into the bathroom with him.

"Sweetie . . ."

"I'm big," he said, standing ramrod straight.

"Fine," I said, figuring it wasn't worth the battle. "Don't use nine pounds of toilet paper, and don't close the door all the way."

He flashed me a winning grin and toddled toward the toilet.

I sighed and fought off a moment of melancholy. They really do grow up fast.

Since Timmy can take longer on the toilet that any child in history, I wandered back toward the living room and idly perused Marissa's DVD collection, surprised by the variety I saw there. I'd pegged her as someone who watched only PBS and the BBC as a matter of principle, but the shelves were crammed with action films and raucous comedies side by side with *A Room with a View* and multiple seasons of *As Time Goes By*.

Had to be her husband, because I wasn't about to adjust my impression of Marissa. I'd spent too many years convinced the woman had a stick up her butt.

"You doing okay?" I called out to Timmy, receiving a curt "Yeah, Mommy," in response. "About ready?" I asked hopefully.

A pause, then, "No, Mommy."

With a sigh, I reached into my purse and pulled out my cell phone, checking to make sure I hadn't missed any messages. That task complete, I moved my attention from the DVDs to the pictures hanging in the hall. I was standing there, gazing at a family photo I remembered from Marissa's most recent Christmas card and trying to decide when I could schedule time for a family portrait at the mall, when I caught a flash of movement in the hall leading to the bedrooms.

"JoAnn?" I called, though I didn't actually expect her to answer. Marissa had mentioned that her oldest daughter had escaped the party by scheduling a date with the varsity quarterback to go for ice cream in Old Town. I supposed it could be Marissa's husband, but I knew that he was out of town on a business meeting, and in one of the rare moments when Marissa's facade had cracked, she'd confessed to me that she was furious with him for not figuring out a way to come home on their baby's birthday.

For a moment I wondered if he'd decided to surprise Marissa—not to mention Danielle—but that possibility shattered when the hulking figure in torn black pants and a billowy white shirt stepped out of the shadows and into my view. He had a thick scar across one cheek, and I saw the glint of steel in the knife he held pressed to his side.

His eyes went wide, and his lips smacked as he shifted something in his mouth. "You." He grunted, giving me a glimpse of the red-and-white breath mint. Potent and minty fresh, I knew, to hide the demonic stench of his breath. "Been lookin' for you. Looking for the kiddies," he added, then laughed, as if that was the funniest thing anyone had ever said.

I wasn't amused.

Unfortunately, I also wasn't at all sure what to do next. I could hardly pull out my stiletto and stab him through the eye right there in Marissa's hallway. Unlike in the movies, real-life demons don't vanish with a puff when you kill them. Instead, they exit the body with a *whoosh*, and leave a corpse behind.

I had a feeling Marissa wouldn't be keen on finding a dead body on her cut Berber carpeting.

"Mommy?" Timmy stuck his head out of the door, then turned and goggled at the demon. "Who're you?"

"Arrgh!" the demon said.

And when he lumbered toward my boy, I snatched my knife out of my purse and decided that Marissa would just have to deal.

Five

I rushed forward, giving Timmy a quick shove into the bath-room and slamming the door with a shouted order to "Stay." Without breaking my stride I plowed into the demon, pressing the tip of my stiletto against the soft skin just under his eye, and slamming his back up against the wall.

"Why are you here?" I repeated as Timmy burst out of the door, shrieking for me. "Stay back!"

The demon grunted, and I saw fear in those eyes. An odd-ity among the demon population, but right then I was too on edge to think about it. Too furious that the demon had infiltrated not only my everyday world, but someone else's home.

"Did she send you?" I demanded. "Who the hell is she?"

"I—I just c-come where they s-send me," he stuttered, and that time, my addled brain did process the fear. It also noted the strong scent of rum, not completely hidden by the mint he'd been chewing on.

After that, I saw that the silver knife was a cutlass, and

the hand that held it had a prosthetic hook dangling from the wrist. The black pants resembled something Johnny Depp might wear, and I was pretty sure I'd seen that white shirt on the puffy pirate shirt episode of *Seinfeld*.

In other words, I'd just attacked the children's entertainment.

"Dammit!" I pushed back, switching my knife to my left hand as my right hand rummaged in my purse for the spritzer of holy water.

"Mommy!"

"Kate!" Marissa's voice echoed behind me, but I wasn't going to turn around. Not for her. Not for Timmy. Not until I was absolutely sure.

I held the bottle up, then sprayed him full on in the face. He blinked and sputtered, but he didn't burn, and I managed to shove my knife and spritzer back into my purse before Marissa trotted up.

"What on earth is going on?"

"She attacked me!" the drunken nondemon raged. "Sprayed gunk in my face and got on me with a blade!"

Marissa's eyes went wide. "Kate?"

"He's drunk," I said with disgust, scooping my now crying little boy into my arms. "If you didn't want rum in the song, I figured you didn't want it in the entertainment. And," I added, digging the hole I'd created that much deeper, "he completely upset Timmy!"

She looked from Timmy to me to the pirate with narrowed eyes. Then she leaned forward and sniffed his breath, managing to get in a good whiff despite the fact that Captain Hook slunk back against the wall.

Her nose crinkled and the glare she shot him would have taken a demon down even without a dagger. "Unacceptable," she said, then turned away from him as if he were nothing more important than one of those dust bunnies she swept up so efficiently. "But, Kate," she said, taking my elbow and pulling me toward the garage, "if I don't have a pirate, what are the children going to do now?"

"It's just a suggestion," I said as I hugged my little boy close and dried his frustrated tears. "But why not just let them play?"

"Oh, my God," Laura said, wiping tears of mirth from the corners of her eyes. "That's enough to make me wish I had a toddler. Just to have been there and seen that. And Marissa didn't even wonder why his face was all wet?"

"No," I said, scowling at the piece of ceramic tile our instructor had handed out to everyone in the Saturday workshop. "She called me on it. Told me she didn't believe I'd been worried about a drunk and thought I'd been chasing a demon instead."

"Right," Laura said. "Stupid question."

"At least he really was drunk," I said, abandoning the tile to share a frustrated grimace with my friend. "Which alleviates some of my guilt for attacking a civilian." Not completely, though. I should never have gotten in his face with a knife, and my only excuse was that this whole business with Eric had put me on edge.

"He was drunk, waving a knife, and coming after the kids," Laura said loyally. "And he was sucking on a breath mint."

"So were you fifteen minutes ago," I pointed out.

"But I haven't invaded a dead body. I'm not all demonic and ooky inside."

"Point taken." Demons, as I'd instructed Laura, blend in a little too well with the human population. But there are clues, and sewage-rotten breath is a big one. Of course, not being complete idiots, the demons have tried to alleviate that little hygienic deficiency. And although they can't prevent it, they can work damn hard to mask it. I've known demons to chew parsley, gargle Listerine, and even snack on roasted garlic. Anything to hide the real odor bubbling up from their decaying insides.

"So, does David . . . I mean, with Eric being . . . Never mind." She busied herself by sorting the plastic tile spacers. "I'm not even sure I want to know."

"It's a good question," I said. "And no. His breath is fine."

"You're sure?"

I remembered the kiss we'd shared the previous night. "Yeah," I muttered. "I'm sure."

Being my best friend, Laura knew better than to press the topic. And we were prevented from further delving into the quality of my first husband's breath by the distinct throat-clearing and evil eye granted us by Larry the Tile Guy. Since this was the scoring-and-cutting part of the tile class, I wasn't sure why silence was required, but I knew better than to piss off a tile specialist with a knife in his hand.

Actually, the silence suited me. Laura had raised an interesting point, and I couldn't help but wonder what it meant. Because Eric's breath *was* fine despite the fact that a demon was bumping right on the edge of bursting free. So did it mean that halitosis wasn't the demonic barometer we'd always thought? Did it mean that the demon wasn't as close to bursting free as we believed?

Or did it simply mean that in this—as in so many other things—my beloved Eric was a walking theological and metaphysical enigma.

"You two ladies understand the steps? Everything make sense?" Larry the Tile Guy asked, interrupting my musings.

"Absolutely," I lied to him, unwilling to admit that my demonic mental meanderings had kept me from focusing fully on his tile lecture.

"Why don't you give it a whirl?" He dragged over a board

with Saltillo tiles already laid in, with the exception of a rectangular void smaller than the area of a single Saltillo tile. "Cut me that puppy there from one of the bigger tiles. I'll be back in a jiff to see how you're doing."

"Right," I said, as he marched to a newly married couple who'd recently passed around photos of their new home. I eyed Laura for help.

She held her hands up and leaned back on her heels. "I'm not the one being drafted to remodel. If knowledge comes my way, I'll take it. But I'm not actively seeking it out."

"Terrible attitude," I chided.

"Isn't it though?" She pointed at the bulky gizmo on the floor between us. Earlier, Larry had demonstrated how to use the contraption to score tile, then snap it along the line to form a smaller piece with straight edges. In other words, the machine helped break things. How hard could that be?

"Right," I said, scowling at the thing. I scooted over to the tiled board and started to measure the empty space. "I can do this." Since Laura said nothing, I took that as tacit support and made a quick mark on my tile with the provided pencil. "So what about you?" I asked, after I'd made three marks and was rolling in the satisfaction of a job well done. "Since I had to go tackle yet another demon in my backyard, I didn't get the chance to send appropriate sympathy your way."

"Maybe you can get something to spread around your lawn," she said. "Forget Miracle-Gro," she added, with an announcer's affectation. "Get some Miracle Go!"

"It would be a miracle if they did go," I said, feeling rather surly about the topic. *Reasonable,* I thought. After all, it had always irritated me when Stuart brought his work home with him. "But maybe Allie's relic-and-holy-water mixture would work," I said, thinking of the cemetery. "I'll ask Father Corletti, and if it does—"

Laura held up a hand, stopping me. "I've been a good

friend and put up with a lot, but I really don't want to hear about you spreading crushed up saint bones in your backyard. You end up going to those kinds of extremes, do me a favor and just don't tell me."

"That's what you get for changing the subject," I said. "I was all set to lavish sympathy upon you."

"You don't even know what's bothering me," she said.

"True," I admitted, erasing one of my pencil marks and squinting at the damn tile, which seemed determined to trip me up. "But I'm an equal opportunity sympathizer. And you don't have the Paul-drama spark in your eyes," I said, referring to her soon-to-be ex-husband and the murderous look that crossed her face whenever she thought of him. "I'm gonna go with Dr. Hunk."

"Yeah, well you'll be going far and fast," she said grumpily. "He dumped me."

"Oh, sweetie," I said, abandoning the tile to grab her hand and give it a sympathetic squeeze. "If he dumped you, he must be evil."

She managed a wobbly smile. "He didn't seem evil."

"Do you want me to take care of him?" I asked. "Stiletto through the eye. Drown him in holy water? I can do Paul at the same time and call it a two-for-one special."

She rolled her eyes, but she also smiled, and I looked down at my marked-up tile, secretly pleased with myself. Being a best friend might not be as flashy or dangerous as demon hunting, but the job was just as rewarding, if not more so.

"What do you do now?" she asked, and at first I thought she was talking about her potentially demonic ex-doctor. I quickly realized she meant the tile, however.

"Score it?" I frowned, trying to remember Larry's list of instructions. "Right," I said, positioning the tile on the contraption, so that when I ran the slider thingy down, a slight cut would be made on the line I'd drawn. "Here goes nothing."

I pulled back slowly, wincing a little at the sound of the blade cutting through rock. Laura peered over my shoulder as I did, the ends of her hair falling into my field of vision. "You know, if I pay attention, I could redo the entire house. Wouldn't even look like the same place Paul ever lived."

"It's an idea," I said. "But if you have the urge to tile, I'm hoping you'll head to the mansion. Trust me when I say I can use all the help I can get."

"Mmm," Laura said. "I think I'm going to limit my help to the nonphysical. Research. Moral support. That kind of thing."

"Wise," I said. "You can start with my She-Demon."

"No ideas at all about who she is?" Laura asked, although she already knew the answer. We'd been over that ground and more during the drive to Home Depot.

"Nothing so far. I told Father Corletti what happened, and he's looking into this Odayne demon, but so far he hasn't gotten back to me with anything useful. Actually," I amended, "he hasn't gotten back to me with anything at all." I flashed a bright smile her way. "But that's okay, because I have you. My super-research gal."

"If I'm your gal, I guess that makes Eddie your guru," she said. She rocked back on her heels, her expression thoughtful. "And he's really going to do the *alimentatore* thing?" she asked. "He's not just pulling your chain?"

"He was sincere," I said. "He's not going to break promises that will end up hurting Allie."

"Well, this should be interesting," which pretty much summed up my feelings. She pointed to the tile. "So now you snap it."

I nodded, pressing down on the padded lever to hold my main piece of tile in place, then using my other hand to press down on the overhanging portion. I'd lined up the score with the edge of the metal box, and as I pressed against it, sure enough—*snap*—I found myself holding two pieces of tile.

"Nifty trick," I said, shifting the tile to make another score line perpendicular to the first one. I took a few moments to look around the room. Except for a sandy-haired college-age student, everyone seemed to be moving at about the same pace. Which made me feel somewhat better at being both a novice and pathetically slow.

Our work area was near the entrance, and a few people slowed to watch as they came into the store. I saw a tall woman with gorgeous auburn hair holding the hand of a toddler with an orange carrottop and freckles. He looked about Timmy's age and was yanking on the woman's hand, seemingly desperate to get on with their day. She sipped idly on a Starbucks cup, hesitating near the automatic doors. For a moment, our eyes met, and I smiled, the solidarity of a shopping mom. She looked back blankly, though, and I began to wonder if she'd even seen me. Probably mentally running shopping lists in her head.

"So where do you think he's working?" Laura said. Since we'd rode together to Home Depot, we'd both seen Eddie head off down Fourth Street, the local car-free promenade near Main Street. Unfortunately, Fourth Street curves sharply, and unless we got out of the car and actually followed him, we couldn't pinpoint his destination. We'd actually considered that as a plan, but since that would make us late for tiling class, we'd decided to leave it to another day. "Maybe he's doling out ice cream at Baskin-Robbins."

I tried to picture Eddie in a uniform asking kids if they wanted a cherry or sprinkles. "I'm thinking no. Besides, he said it was a new shop."

She frowned. "My old phone had a web browser. I probably could have figured it out by now. But I gave it up for this old thing." She tapped the outer pocket on her purse, which held your standard-issue, telephonically functional phone. "It doesn't do a damn thing."

I squinted at it. "It doesn't make calls?"

She rolled her eyes, looking remarkably like my daughter in the process. "Kate, sometimes I wonder about you."

I ignored that, my thoughts having shifted to my missing teenager and toddler. "Do you see Timmy and Allie?"

She craned her neck and peered around, then shook her head. "Are we worried?"

I hesitated, then shook my head. "I think it's okay. Allie said she was going to entertain him, so I'm sure they're off doing something entertaining. Probably playing in tubs in the bathroom fixture section."

"Or plucking the petals off flowers in the garden section."

"Or emptying the bags of play sand all over the aisles," I said.

I lasted a good twelve seconds before I reached for my own telephonically functional phone and managed to call my daughter despite my lack of Internet and text-messaging capabilities.

"Can we go yet?" she asked, answering on the first ring.

"About fifteen more minutes. If you want to start heading this direction, that would be great."

"So you were just calling to check on us?" I stayed guiltily silent. "Come on, Mom! We're in Home Depot. Even if some demon was stupid enough to jump me here, it's not like there's a shortage of weapons. I'm looking at a screwdriver, an ax, and a sharp pokey thing right now."

"Hardware aisle," I said to Laura. And then to Allie, "Is that really the place for Timmy?"

"Mother."

"Fifteen minutes," I said, and hung up. So long as the kid was entertained . . .

"Does she know about She?" Laura asked. I must have looked baffled, because Laura clarified. "Does Allie know about the 'She' that your backyard demon went on about?"

"Not yet. I haven't had the chance to tell her. And I

haven't figured out how to tell her without mentioning her dad's little problem."

"How about Stuart? Told him?"

I shot her a frustrated look.

"Just saying," she said. "You need to tell him."

"I know. I will. But I want information before I do." I flashed her a wide grin. "That's where you come in."

She looked like she had more to say on the subject, but Larry the Tile Guy showed up. "Excellent work," he said, peering down at my cuts. "Set it aside and we're all going to mix some mortar. I've got tiles over there for everyone to pick from, so go on and get dibs on a pattern."

We headed that direction along with all the other tile warriors. "Does Eric know?" Laura asked. "Who She is, I mean."

"If he does, he's not telling me." I spoke flippantly, but I could tell from Laura's expression that she wasn't buying it.

"You okay?"

I wasn't entirely sure that I was, but I managed a smile. "Peachy."

She looked like she was going to argue, but she didn't get the chance because all of a sudden a huge clatter rang out through the room, accompanied by the dispersal of hundreds of ball bearings across the floor. And there, in front of it all, was my little boy, racing pell-mell for the automatic doors at the front of the store.

"Timmy!" I shouted, trying to vault over the pile of tile.

Allie's own shouts echoed my own, but when she stepped on one of the bearings, her feet went flying out from under her and she landed on her rump, a half dozen onlookers standing stock-still to stare at her, no one offering a hand because of the minefield that was the floor. "Timmy!" she cried. "Stop right now or no ice cream!"

The threat didn't work. Not so much because the kid was being disobedient, but because he was freaked. The noise, the people yelling. My kid was no stranger to a high decibel level, but usually in smaller quarters. And without a cadre of employees and customers converging on him.

"Mommy! Mommy!"

"Timmy! Right here!"

But he couldn't see me, and those automatic glass doors opened wide, and as Laura and I sprinted forward, all I could think about was my little boy stepping out into that busy parking lot and—

"Come here, kiddo! Let's go see your mommy."

I positively froze in relief. The redhead I'd noticed earlier had scooped him up about six inches beyond the door, and was holding him close, pointing in my direction with a hand holding a Starbucks cup. I got there in a second, which was about a second longer than I wanted. She passed my boy to me and I clutched him close, my heart pounding in my ears, the roar of blood starting to die down around me.

"Big noise!" Timmy said. "Big noise!"

"Mom! Oh, God, Mom, I'm so sorry. There was a box and then he pulled it off the shelf, and those things went everywhere and—" Allie rubbed her rear, tears streaming down her cheeks, and as much as the fear that still coiled within me made me want to lash out, I pulled it back. All was well, I told myself. All probably would have been well even if he'd made it to the parking lot. I would have caught him in time. Nothing to freak out about.

And yet there I was, freaked, and desperately grateful to the stranger who'd waylaid my son.

I squeezed Allie's hand, a silent promise that all was okay. To the woman, I turned my full attention. "They can really get away from you, can't they?" she said, smiling down at her own toddler, before I had the chance to say anything.

"They can and they do," I said. "Thank you so much."

Larry sauntered over and ruffled Timmy's hair. Delighted at being the center of attention, Timmy beamed. "We all okay over here?"

"We're good. I'll be right back. I'm sorry for the disruption, and we'll pick up those bearings and—"

"Nah, it's cool. We got it." And I could see that they did. Already a crew was clearing the aisle of the mess created by one small boy.

"Can I buy you another coffee? Lunch? A small continent?" I asked the redhead.

"Australia would be nice. Thanks." She cocked her head to the side, eyes narrowed in thought. "You look awfully familiar. I thought so earlier, but—oh, I know! Cutter's studio! You're going to teach that women's self-defense class!"

"Do you train there?"

She shook her head. "I'm in that 7-Eleven all the time." She reached down and hauled her boy up to her hip. "I'm pretty sure he eats baby wipes and Kleenex when I'm not looking," she said, and the little boy lifted his eyes toward the ceiling and shook his head in mock exasperation, an affectation so funny on a toddler it had me smiling.

"I know the feeling."

"Listen, I've been meaning to pop in and ask about your class. I'd love to sign up. Does it start soon?"

"I've got a class at four, actually, if you want. Three Saturdays, and then I'll start a new session." Technically, the class was sold out, but I figured Cutter would give me a pass if I squeezed one more student in.

"Oh, could I?" She bounced junior on her hip. "I think about him, you know? And I just want to be safe."

I squeezed my own little boy, clinging to my neck like a monkey. "Yeah," I said. "I know exactly what you mean."

"Best thing to do's just grab 'em in the nuts," Rita Walker— Fran's eighty-six-year-old mother—announced to a smattering of applause. "That'll show him who's boss."

"Actually," I said, "Rita has a point." The class was scheduled for two hours each Saturday over the course of three weeks, and though I'd originally planned to open the class with a discussion of theory, basic awareness, and how to not project yourself as a victim, I soon realized that this group was keen to jump straight into the middle of things. Which left me altering my lesson plan on the fly. "And we'll come back to that in more detail, but for the moment, let's go with it." I signaled to Cutter. "Want to give us a hand?"

Rita snorted. "Ain't his hand you're gonna be mangling now, is it?"

"Guess I'm glad I wore a cup," he said.

"But did you wear shoes?" I asked, with an evil grin.

His brows lifted, and he cocked his head, knowing full well what was coming. "Well, hell," he said.

I laughed. "You're the one who suggested I play teacher."

"But I never suggested I play victim."

"You're not," I said. "That would be me." I turned my attention to the ladies. "Okay, now here I am, foolishly standing outside my car rummaging in my purse for my keys. What's the first thing I did wrong?"

"You should have put them in your hand before you left the store or your house or whatever."

"And you should check under the car. Could be some whack-job on his belly with a knife."

"Both right," I said, continuing to pantomime a frustrated shopper. "And here comes the bad guy."

I couldn't see him behind me, but from the cackles of laughter, I assumed Cutter had pasted on a Snidely Whiplash expression and was creeping toward me on tiptoes. I continued to frantically rummage in my pretend purse until I felt his arm snap around my neck, pulling me close.

I reached back and clamped down hard at his groin, thankfully not doing any damage—or embarrassing either of us too fully—because of the cup he'd had the foresight to wear. "That's not it, though, ladies. You'd think it would be, but——" I stepped back and down, smashing the instep of Cutter's left foot and eliciting a howl from my injured-yet-helpful sensei.

I turned, flashed him a smile, and let the applause slide over me.

"Okay, ladies. Partner up and you try it. Don't grab tight, and stomp down on the mat, not on your partner's foot. I don't want any genuine injuries."

"Now you're concerned," muttered Cutter.

I made a rude noise and rolled my eyes. "Come on, Sean. Be a man."

"If you'd grabbed me any tighter, I don't think I would be anymore."

"I'm not terribly worried." As examples of the male species went, Cutter was a prime specimen—a blackbelt several times over, former military, and loyal to a fault. He's also damn good-looking, a little fact that I think played at least some part in my sold-out class tonight. "Buck up and help me make rounds," I added with a grin.

We spent the next ten minutes circling the practicing women, correcting form and helping them get comfortable grabbing and pounding with all of their strength. Yelling came next, and for that I actually recruited Allie from the children's room. Since child care is often an issue with women, I'd convinced Cutter to let Allie and Mindy come in and babysit. I needed the help, but I'll also admit that I was blatantly manufacturing reasons for the girls to get together. And as I poked my head into the kids' room, I had to say that my evil plan seemed to be working. Mindy and Allie were sitting in a circle with the kids, clapping and singing about the farmer's dog named Bingo.

Allie popped up when she saw me, letting Mindy take the spotlight. "Whatcha need?"

"Come yell for me," I said. When Allie had first started

her own training, I'd demanded she work on her yell first. Most women think they can yell, but when actually put in the position, they manage little more than an anorexic squeak. With practice, however, you can learn to bellow on command. And not only does a nice, loud yell prepare you for fighting, it has the added benefits of potentially scaring your attacker, letting your attacker know you're not going to give in easily, and it alerts your Demon Hunter mother who is hopefully nearby and ready to beat the crap out of any demon who even looks at you funny.

We explained all of that (well, the relevant parts, anyway) to the class, and then had Cutter sneak up on Allie. In addition to whipping around and catching him with a solid crescent kick to the shoulder, she burst out with a yell loud enough to wake the dead.

Both moves earned her vigorous applause, even from Mindy, who I saw watching from the doorway.

"So there you go," I said. "Grab your partner and start blasting eardrums."

It was during that cacophony that the redhead from Home Depot rushed in, her eyes going wide at the spectacle. Her little boy smacked his hands over his ears and scrunched up his face, and since I feared for an imminent tantrum, I hurried over. "Sorry! You walked in during the craziest part."

"And the loudest," she said. "Is there a place for John-John?"

I smiled down at John-John and held out my hand. He made a face, but took it, and I nodded toward the back room where the toddler karate classes were usually held. "We've got teenagers amusing the natives," I said. I nodded toward Allie. "Including mine once she quits doing the Rebel Yell."

"She's good at it," the woman said.

"I'm sorry," I said, sticking out my free hand. "I'm Kate. And I know John-John now." I flashed him another smile, but he scowled and looked away. Honestly, I was thinking I'd found little Danielle's date for the prom. "But I don't think I ever caught your name."

"Lisa," she said, her wide smile more than making up for her boy's less-than-rosy personality.

I led her and John-John back to the children's room, with Allie following on our heels. I noticed that Lisa sent the kid away without much fanfare, and decided that was another oddity with the child. Though they were about the same age, Timmy's partings were much clingier than this little carrottop and, I have to admit, I think I preferred Timmy's way. As much as there were times that the Velcro-child phenomenon could be an annoyance, at the end of the day there wasn't much I loved more than my kid holding me tight in a never-ending hug.

Class moved fast after the yelling session, covering basic things like using whatever is near you as a weapon, to me going through a quick "don't try this at home" sparring session with Cutter simply because Laura egged us on.

"I missed the groin foot-step thing you were talking about," Lisa said when Cutter headed next door to grab a few more bottled waters, making sure we had enough to go round when class was over. "Could you run through it with me?"

"Sure," I said, then pointed to the mat. "You're heading to your car, thinking about your groceries or something equally mundane, not paying attention to your surroundings, when out of the blue—"

I broke off as I wrapped my arm tight around her neck, pressing just hard enough so that she'd know the fear of that pressure on her windpipe, but not so hard as to cut off her ability to breathe.

"Mom!"

"Mrs. Connor!"

Allie's and Mindy's cries rippled through the room, but

I had no idea why because as I loosened my grip so that I could turn toward the problem, Lisa slammed her fist back into my crotch, grabbed the inseam of the loose-fitting khakis I'd selected for class, and slammed me down onto my back. She was on top of me, her face right in mine, before my brain even had time to process what was going on.

And, with her mouth that close, there was no way to avoid the stench of serious halitosis hidden under the bitter scent of coffee laced with breath mints.

She pressed forward so that her mouth was almost at my ear. "Fight back, and my consort will thrust that pencil through your little boy's brain."

"Who the hell are you?" I hissed, keeping my voice low and hopefully out of earshot of the shocked members of my class.

"Odayne is hers," she said, making me blink. Under the circumstances, I'd made the snap assumption that Lisa was the She-Demon. Apparently, I was wrong. "Hers? Whose?"

But she didn't answer, instead thrusting a blade up high, and then bringing it flashing down toward my chest.

At the same time, I burst up, head and knees rocking forward as I jerked to the side, managing to off-balance her so that the knife that had been aiming for my chest instead sliced my sleeve and drew a long line of blood.

I howled, a loud, raucous noise, and my head seemed to split open into flashes of red and white as Lisa leaped off me, looking around wildly at the crowd. She kicked out and got me in the ribs, knocking me back as I was trying to rise, all the while screaming for John-John to join her as she sprinted toward the exit.

He raced forward, limping slightly, the irritated toddler face now clearly revealing the malice of a fully grown man.

Or, rather, a fully grown demon.

Dear God, Timmy.

I was up in an instant, racing to the kids' room, realizing

as I flew that the red and white lights in my head weren't from a concussion but from the fire alarm that someone had tripped.

I had no idea who, but I was desperately grateful, especially when I found my little boy screaming in the back room, complaining about the big noise, and his sister fighting back tears as she clutched him in a bear hug. "He had a pencil shoved in his ear and a thumb against his eye," Allie said, switching her hug to me as I clutched tight to Timmy, my insides gone to liquid. "He was just a little kid, Mom. A baby."

I closed my eyes and breathed in the scent of my own baby's hair, trying to stop the trembling inside me. "No," I said. "He wasn't a baby. He was a demon. And we're all lucky to be alive."

Six

"**Do you believe her?**" Laura asked, as she moved around my kitchen, randomly opening and closing drawers and straightening whatever out-of-place utensils got caught in her sharp, obsessive gaze. "That Lisa isn't the She-Demon, I mean?"

"Considering she was about to kill me, I don't really see the point of lying," I said, with a glance toward Timmy, who was amusing himself by whapping my clean silverware on the floor. "So yeah, I'm thinking she's only a minion."

"A scary, horrible, freakish minion with a toddler consort. Ick. Major, major, major ick," she added, putting her back into the scrubbing now, so much so that I almost reached out and made her sit down—her constant motion was making me jumpy—but I understood the reason for her movement. Nervous energy. And Laura, for better or for worse, didn't get the chance to work hers off with a stiletto or a crossbow.

At the same time, Laura wasn't the one with her arm

stinging from disinfectant. I scowled and rubbed my hand over the bandage, still more than a little amazed that not only was I alive, but that all of the women in our group believed my off-the-cuff story about how Lisa was a plant to prove the point that even people who are skilled in self-defense (that would be me) can get their ass kicked if they're not constantly on guard. The lesson was so creative and brilliant, in fact, that the group gave us a standing ovation.

In reality, Laura had realized the knife was real, completely freaked out, and had raced to Cutter's office and yanked down the fire alarm, thus accounting for the red and white flashing lights I'd seen. The ladies, thankfully, had believed that was part of the fun.

As for Cutter, he'd come back after all the drama was over, but when Laura was still hyperventilating. "She okay?" he'd asked, and I'd responded with the completely irrelevant comment that Laura was thrilled we were doing the class since it gave her the opportunity to work out her aggressions.

"Divorce," Cutter had said knowingly.

I'd nodded. "That and the guy she's been seeing. Broke up with her," I added, in response to his questioning expression.

It may have been my imagination, but I thought I saw a flash of interest. Since my thoughts were more in tune with attacking female demons and their toddler consorts, however, I'd paid it very little mind.

Now in my house with my thoughts free to roam, I had to wonder if there wasn't a little spark between Cutter and my best friend.

I didn't have time to ask Laura, though, because two sets of footsteps pounded on the stairs, and I heard Allie call out for Mindy. "Would you just wait? Mindy! Come on—"

"Come on what?" Mindy retorted, her tone sharp. "Come on and wait around while you make up some stupid story? I'm not an idiot, Allie. Something's up around here, but if you don't want to tell me, that's fine. That's just fine," she repeated, since obviously it wasn't fine at all. "I'm tired of the whole stinking thing."

"Mindy!" Allie said, clomping after her. "It was just some freak. The kind of freak that's the reason Mom's having the classes in the first place."

I caught Laura's eye. Wasn't *that* the truth.

"Just stay, okay?" Allie continued. "We've got finals soon and you promised to help me with algebra."

"You know what would help?" Mindy shot back. "Studying. Wild and crazy, I know, but maybe if you studied instead of whatever else you're into lately, you wouldn't need me to cram with you at the last minute."

Last minute? I mouthed to Laura, but I could see from her innocent expression that she'd been impressing on Mindy that even months out from finals was last minute as far as she and their scholarship plans were concerned.

"But you have fun with whatever it is you're doing. I already told you, I'm going to the movies with Bethany and Emily." And with that, she slammed the door, just as Allie skidded to a halt in the living room, in full view of me and Laura, the misery on her face making my heart break a little.

"Allie," I said softly. "Tell her." I swiveled to look at Laura, who nodded once, then managed a watery smile.

"It's time," Laura said.

"Then you do it," Allie said, surly. "She doesn't want to hear it from me."

"You're exactly the one she wants to hear it from," Laura said kindly.

Allie shifted from foot to foot. "She's going out. The movies. And she's gonna be pissed."

"That you're doing something she's not?" I asked.

"That I didn't tell her," Allie said.

"The longer you wait, the more pissed she'll be," Laura

said. "And I think she'll understand. At least give her the chance."

"Yeah. Okay," Allie said. But instead of running after Mindy, she ran upstairs.

I caught Laura's eyes. "That went well." I drew in a breath. "You'll be in the doghouse with her again, too," I added. Laura had recently felt the wrath of Mindy when she and Paul had decided to delay news of their impending divorce until after the holidays. It hadn't been pretty.

"It'll be okay," Laura said firmly. "This isn't my secret to share. It's yours and Allie's. She'll understand that." She moved to the refrigerator and yanked open the door, then pulled out a sticky ketchup bottle and began to rinse it in warm water. "I think."

I sat back at the table, feeling no guilt that my best friend was cleaning my kitchen. We all work off our stress differently, and I figured that not pitching in was my little contribution to Laura's mental health and well-being.

After a few moments of scrubbing, she broke the silence with a sigh. "That kid." She shivered. "That little boy."

"I know," I said. "But you need to remember that he's not really a little boy. Not anymore."

Laura's eyes cut to Timmy, who was still making music with forks and spoons. "I know. But knowing and believing aren't always the same thing."

I pushed out of the chair and went over to my kid, who gleefully passed me a serving spoon so I could join the band. I whacked listlessly a couple of times, then couldn't stand it anymore. I hugged him close and was rewarded with his chubby little arms going tight around my neck. "I like you, Mommy," he announced, making me laugh. "I like you sooooo much!"

"Good to know," I said. "I like you, too, Sport."

"At least you have a lead now, right? You can figure out where they're playing house, hunt them down, beat them up because you know you want to, and then learn everything you can about this She-Demon."

"Not a bad plan," I said. Laura certainly had right the part about wanting to beat them up. "But I don't have a clue where to start looking."

"I do," Allie said from the doorway, making both me and Laura jump. "Jeez. Antsy much?"

"Something like that," I said, then plunked Timmy back onto the floor. He blew me a big kiss, then toddled off to wreak havoc in the living room, the spoon still tight in his hand. I debated between following him to render safe my personal possessions or staying and listening to Allie's demon report.

I chose the demons, and hoped I wouldn't regret it.

Allie slapped a printout from the computer on the table in front of us with dramatic flair. "*L.A. Times* Metro section. Page five. Two weeks ago."

Laura grabbed the paper before I did, and since I couldn't stand not knowing, I got up and walked around to stand behind her.

Their deaths warranted only two paragraphs, though I supposed that if the world knew they were actually dead, the story might have been bigger. As it was, the reporter had simply transcribed the facts as he knew them. Apparently the real Lisa and John-John had been hit by a drunk driver in a Hummer going eighty in a thirty-mile-an-hour zone, sending the minivan into a violent rollover. The airbags deployed, presumably saving the mommy and kid despite the rollover and ultimate high-velocity crash into a utility pole. All of which would have been good news if the airbags really had saved them. But despite those fabulous safety features, I knew the truth. Mom and baby had died. And two demons had decided to take up residence.

None of which was reported in the article, of course. Instead, the newspaper reported that a nurse in the following car rushed to assist, found no pulse on either of the victims, and called 911 even as she began CPR. Her efforts, of course, were successful, and the paper lauded her skill and Good Samaritan attitude.

Me, I knew they would have come back even without the breaths and compressions.

"Treated for minor abrasions and released," Allie said. "The thing is, they were San Diablo residents. But the local paper didn't report it." She shrugged. "So we missed it."

One of my habits is to review the daily paper looking for potential new demons. If I find any, I make it a point to try to track them down on patrol. Since I didn't know about Lisa and John-John, they hadn't been on my hunting radar.

"Anyway," Allie went on, "I guess when they got back to San Diablo they dug in and played good little soldiers until it was time to go shopping for a fight."

Despite the seriousness of the situation, I couldn't help but smile at Allie's tough-guy Demon Hunter persona. I might have hesitated to get her involved—might still be hesitating for that matter—but there was no denying that she had the skills and the attitude.

She clasped her hands in front of her on the table, corporate-meeting style. "But what I don't get is how can that little boy be a demon? I thought they could only use grown-up bodies."

"Why'd you think that?" I asked, channeling Father Corletti and Wilson and any of a half dozen other teachers I'd had during my years of training at *Forza*.

"Well, because, because babies are—"

"Innocent," Laura said. "And you told us that the souls of the faithful fight. That's why demons don't slide into every dead body that comes along."

"Faith and innocence aren't the same thing."

"Dear God," Laura said.

"I don't know the mechanics of it," I said, speaking

briskly so that my thoughts didn't shift to my own little boy. "Maybe children aren't strong enough yet to fight. All I know is that it happens. But that dead little boy's soul is gone and safe, even if his body is being used. And that's what matters."

"But if little kids can't fight, then why don't more demons use them?" Laura asked.

I shrugged. "Limitations of the flesh, I'd think. The demon's essence is stuck with the body it goes into. It gets some of that preternatural strength, sure, but it's stuck in chubby little limbs with an inconvenient center of gravity. And even if the demon can articulate and think and reason better than your average twenty-six-month-old, if it does any of that in public, there goes any hope of blending in."

"So why'd this demon slip into John-John?"

"I don't know. They're obviously a team. Maybe those were the only bodies available."

"Or maybe the intent was to get Timmy all along, and this was their top-notch evil plan." That from Laura, who was pouring a cup of coffee even while looking so seriously at me it made my stomach twist. "Kate, why would they want your little boy?"

"To hurt Mom," Allie said, and I knew that no matter what, I wasn't underestimating my daughter's reasoning skills again.

Laura's eyes met mine. "Whoever she is, she wants you bad."

"She?" Allie repeated. "The She-Demon you guys were talking about when I came back in?"

I met Laura's eyes, then took a sip of my coffee and nodded.

"So who is she?" Allie asked. "Does she have anything to do with Odayne?"

I barely managed not to spit coffee all over the table. "Odayne?" I repeated. "What do you know about Odayne?"

"Not much," she said. "Eddie called and asked me to start some research for him. A demon named Odayne."

I made a mental note to string Eddie up by his toenails. "Did Eddie say why?"

"He said the demon's one of Daddy's old enemies. Was he giving it to me straight?"

"As an arrow," I said, pleased to at least not have to concoct a complicated lie. "So what have you found?"

"Nothing. But Eddie did say that Odayne has ties to some female demon, so when you were talking about this She-Demon, I thought maybe there was a connection."

"Probably so," I said, then decided to bite the bullet and give her a bit more of the truth. "There was a demon in the backyard last night. We'd sent it screaming right before you guys got home. But it mentioned Odayne and the She-Demon both."

She tossed her head back and groaned as only a put-upon teenager can. "For crying out loud, Mom, why didn't you tell me? We're supposed to be all open with the demon stuff now, remember?"

"I remember, and I was going to tell you as soon as I had the chance." I managed a half-shrug. "It's Stuart I'm keeping the secret from."

Her brows lifted. "You're going to be in so much trouble."

"Probably," I admitted. "But it's my decision. Don't rat me out, okay?"

She lifted her hands in surrender. "You're the boss. I only work here." Her eyes narrowed. "But that's it, right? It's only Stuart who's secret boy? I've got the full deal? Because if you want me to be able to do research I need to know—"

The phone rang, and I jumped up, thrilled to avoid answering that particular question. I snatched the cordless, then sagged with relief when I heard the dulcet tones of Father Corletti's thick accent. "Katherine, *mia cara*, can you speak?"

"Fran! Hey, yeah, it was quite a trip today, wasn't it? Listen, can you hang on? I left that paperwork you gave me in the bedroom." *And the lies, they just keep on coming.*

"Of course," he said.

I signaled to Allie and Laura, both of whom looked uninterested, then took the phone with me as I jogged up to the master bedroom, locked the door, and then, for good measure, headed all the way through the room and into the bathroom. I knew Allie wouldn't listen in on an extension—why would she eavesdrop on a conversation with Fran—but if she passed by my room, I didn't want her to overhear anything incriminating.

Secrets within secrets within secrets again . . .

"I'm sorry to keep you waiting," I said once I was perched on the closed toilet lid, the phone pressed to my ear. "Did you learn something? About this Odayne dude?"

"I did," he said, and I could tell from his voice that it wasn't good.

"Tell me," I said. "Just tell me and get it over with."

I heard his long sigh, and could picture him taking off his cap and massaging his fingers over the downy tufts that covered his mostly bald head. "Odayne is one of the oldest demons, and unique among the demon realm," he began. "For one thing, his origin is shrouded in mystery."

"His origin? I don't get it." As far as I knew, no one really knew where demons came from, though they had to come from somewhere since we knew that some were older than others. But the *where* and *how* of demon creation had never been satisfactorily explained.

When I said all that to Father, he grunted in agreement. "This is true. But there are suggestions in the ancient texts that whatever the normal birthing procedure for a demon is, Odayne circumvented it."

"Okay," I said, accepting that tidbit even if I didn't understand it. "So that makes him different. Maybe that's why he's keen to bind up with Eric. What else?"

"We've discovered a most disturbing fact," Father said. "Even killed in his true form, Odayne will not die in the manner that other demons do."

"But—" I began, then immediately closed my mouth, realizing I didn't know what to say. Father's pronouncement went against everything I knew about demons. When they were in a human body, a demon could be stopped but not actually be killed. When you pierce them through the eye, the demonic essence is sucked out of the body. The body turns back into a corpse, but the demon himself isn't dead-dead. Instead, it's simply returned to the ether, hovering silent and invisible as it waits for the next unwitting newly dead body to open up.

Since the process of body occupation isn't simple—and since time moves differently in the demonic realm—the dead demon can't just turn around and two seconds later pop into another dead body. Instead, a demon has to wait, bide his time. Which means that although there is a certain amount of futility to my job, the benefits of destroying corporeal demons outweigh the downside that the demons will eventually come back.

But it's not all an exercise in futility. The holy grail for a Demon Hunter is to kill a demon in its true form—when the demon walks the earth not as a human, but as the scaly, slimy monster that populates Hollywood films. The movies, in fact, do such a good job representing demons that I have to believe a few Hunters have moonlighted as Hollywood consultants over the years.

Kill *that* beast, and the demon is really gone. *Poof*, end of story. There's no coming back for a demon killed in its true form.

That was one of the basic truths of my world, and now Father Corletti was telling me it wasn't true at all. "Explain," I said, needing to hear him walk me through it so I could get the ramifications straight in my head.

"Odayne can live among the ether with his brother demons," Father began. "And our archives include records documenting his entry into the newly dead."

"Okay," I said, dubiously. So far, Father hadn't cited anything unusual. "But that's not what's happened with Eric, right?"

"Eric is experiencing the manifestation of Odayne's true form."

I cocked my head. I didn't much like the sound of that. "Start at the beginning," I said. "And go slowly."

To his credit, he did. Apparently, Odayne's true form gestated within a human host, merging and binding with it over the years as host and demon aged and grew. In youth, the demon's influence was minimal, segregated within the host's body and soul as a sort of demonic embryo. Then, in youth, that embryo could even be controlled—frozen, as it were—and the demon would remain in stasis. But if the stasis was broken, as happened in Eric's case, the demon would gain power with each passing day, becoming harder and harder to push back or control.

As its demonic adulthood approached—as was apparently happening with Eric—the demon manifested more and more until it merged completely with the human, creating a vile and dangerous hybrid.

"To be trapped and tied up with evil," Father said, his voice infinitely sad. "I do not think there could be a worse fate."

"No," I agreed, my throat thick as I spoke the word. "I don't either."

Neither of us said it, but we both knew that Eric was on his way to that very fate. I wouldn't—*couldn't*—let it get there.

And if I failed? If I couldn't find a way to bind the demon or banish it from Eric's body?

I shivered, knowing only too well what would have to be done.

I closed my eyes, and I asked the question I had to ask. "Why didn't you tell me? All these years, and I never knew."

"Katherine," he said, releasing my name on a sigh. "How I wish things had been different. I cannot say why you were not told at first, other than it was Eric's wish. I was not told either, and I am having my own troubles coming to terms with the decision of my superiors to leave me uninformed. I find strength in my faith, of course, but I am still human, and to certain things I would like practical answers."

In my bathroom, thousands of miles away, I nodded agreement.

"I was never told the name of the demon—I am not sure that anyone, even Eric himself, knew the beast's name. So your information tonight was essential. As for the more basic question of why I did not tell you once I knew the truth? I can only say that I at first withheld the information because I believed the demon to be bound. And later, when you gave your life to another man, there seemed no point in telling you things about a man who was dead and gone, and whose memory you cherished."

"And when he came back?"

"When he came back, you had another family, did you not? And Eric's secrets then were truly his own."

It was my turn to sigh. I didn't like his answer at all. Didn't like it, but I did understand it. And I still had questions about how the demon got into Eric in the first place, and about who at *Forza* knew it was there.

"Again," Father Corletti said, "those are questions for Eric himself. You and I will work together to eradicate the problem at hand. The problems of the past? Those are between you and Eric."

I closed my eyes and nodded, once again not liking the answer. But I knew I couldn't change Father's mind, which meant I had to take what I could get. "Okay, then. Let's talk about now. How will I know?" I said. "How will I know when the line's been crossed and the demon's out and there's no coming back for Eric?"

"Ah, *mia cara*, that I cannot tell you. The most recent archival account of Odayne's growth was recorded in the year five hundred and twenty-seven. It is sketchy at best."

"They always are," I said wryly. "You said Odayne doesn't die when killed in his true form. What did you mean by that?"

"Apparently, he returns to an embryonic state," Father said. "And he will find a new host."

"New," I said. "You're certain?"

"Nothing is certain, but that is what the archives suggest."

I started pacing my room, trying to get this all straight in my head. "I can live with another host," I said, probably selfishly. "It might never happen, right? Or he might float around in never-never land for three centuries before landing in someone."

An unsuspecting child, I thought, then fought a shudder. I needed to concentrate on the problem in front of me, not a potential problem that might not even be an issue for centuries.

"So we get it out of Eric," I said. "We focus on that. Forget binding, that's a dead end. We get it out, and we kill it, and we send it back to the demon nursery to start all over again."

It was a solid plan, I thought, except for the getting it out of Eric part. I was determined to remain confident, though, telling myself that we would find a solution despite the fact that *Forza* had been working on that very problem for decades, and so had Eric. After all, we had a kick-ass team now. Me, Eddie, Laura. Even Allie if I could figure out a way to set her up as a research drone without letting her know why. And we all worked well under pressure.

"Katherine—"

"Hang on, Father," I said, in my groove. Eddie had to have contacts from his old days. Maybe some of them would have an idea. At the very least, it was worth investigating. And then I could—

"Katherine."

I blinked. "Yes?"

"There is a way."

"What?"

"A way," he repeated. "There is a way to kill the demon in its true form. Forever dead, never to leech upon another human. Never to grow within another innocent child."

I bit back a curse, remembering just in time who I was talking to. "But that's great. Why didn't you say so before?"

"It is a weapon," he said, "though we have as yet been unable to locate it. We are hopeful, and our research and archival teams are searching for it. Priority one," he said, and I drew in a breath, duly impressed.

"A weapon," I repeated. "What kind? How does it work?"

"A dagger with a dual blade, the hilt in the middle. One thrust from either blade and the demon truly dies."

I felt a little trill of excitement that we had a solution, but that quickly burst when the horrible ramifications tumbled down around me. "Wait," I said. "Wait a minute. *The body.*"

"This demon must not be allowed to continue. If the means exist to eradicate it, we must do so before it claims another innocent."

"Wait, wait, wait," I said, pacing frantically now. "Just a damn minute. What about the body? The demon is inside Eric's body."

"Yes," Father said, his voice infinitely sad. "Use the dagger to destroy the demon, and you will destroy the man as well."

Seven

"Dear God," Laura said, then lowered her voice to a whisper. "If what you're saying is right then there's no way to get Eric clear without killing him."

I nodded miserably as I pulled my knees up to my chest and hugged them tight against me. Allie had gotten bored with waiting and had gone upstairs to research. Since I wanted away from prying ears, Laura and I had adjourned to the back porch. While we sat in the nylon-woven lawn furniture, Timmy dumped handfuls of pea gravel from underneath his Playscape into little plastic tubs.

"What are you going to do?"

"I'm going to find another way," I said. There had to be an alternative. I couldn't bring myself to believe that in order to save Eric I had to kill him.

"Did Father say there was something else you could do?"

I shook my head. "The archival references are so old that it's hard to get any real information, but he did say that some of the really ancient documents actually reference stories of Odayne walking the earth."

"People like Eric," she said.

"Yeah. But they got clear somehow. They managed to break out of this entanglement. And that's key," I said, "because we already know that Odayne and Eric are attached spiritually, not physically. So even if I kill Odayne—really kill him—there's no guarantee that's gonna break Eric free." Just the opposite: I feared that if I truly killed Odayne, then Eric would be trapped in some sort of dead-demon realm for all eternity.

And that was a reality I couldn't comprehend.

Laura leaned over and gripped my hand, hard. "If those people got free, then Eric can, too. I mean, they didn't even have the Internet. We've got Google. We'll figure it out, Kate. I promise."

I managed a smile. "I like the sound of that. Where do we start?"

"With what we know." She got up and started pacing. "We know the demon's name is Odayne. And we know that some missing dagger takes him totally out of commission." She frowned, a little vertical crease appearing above her nose. "Actually, how does he know this dagger's going to do the trick? I mean, it can't have been tested, right? 'Cause if it had been, then we wouldn't be worrying with this Odayne demon today."

I conjured up a wisp of a smile. "Faith, Laura. Plain, old-fashioned faith."

One elegant eyebrow raised. "Personally, I'd rather have a warranty."

"Yeah, well, that would be good, too."

She bent down to pick up Timmy, who had rushed over, giggling, and thrust his arms into the air, shouting for her to "Pick me! Pick me!"

"How did it start?" she asked, bouncing Timmy on her

hip. "I mean, how did this Odayne dude get inside Eric in the first place?"

"I don't know," I said, steeling my resolve. "But Eric's held onto his secrets long enough. When I see him tonight, he's telling me the truth."

I couldn't tell from Laura's eyes if she believed me or not. But that was okay. Right then, I wasn't sure if I believed it myself.

From the front of the house, we heard Stuart's car pull into the driveway. "Are you going to tell him?"

I shook my head. Laura's lips pursed together in disapproval, but she had the good grace not to say anything. Instead, she passed me my son, who clung like a monkey, giggling and laughing. Then she headed inside, returning a moment later with her purse and Stuart at her heels.

"So, anyway," she said, sounding almost bored. "Come over after you patrol tonight and you can borrow those knitting needles." As I gaped in confusion, she waved a hand. "Hi and bye, Stuart," she said. "I'm out of here."

"Knitting needles?" Stuart asked, heading back inside. I followed him, even as I fished madly for an explanation to Laura's completely unexplainable excuse to get me to her house later for a full debriefing. Considering we saw each other regularly for absolutely no reason at all, saddling me with such a lame lie was really bad form. It would, of course, cost her.

"Laura used to knit," I explained lamely.

"And you're going to start?"

"Weapons," I blurted. Then I thought about it, and since that wasn't such a bad idea, I repeated myself. "Weapons," I said firmly.

"Uh-huh," said my clever husband, not in the least convinced. "I've seen the armory you keep in the attic. You want to explain why we're adding knitting needles to the arsenal?"

"We're hunting with knitting needles?" Allie asked, coming down the stairs with a yellow pad covered with scribbled notes. "Why?"

Stuart pointed at her, as if she'd justified his very existence. "Thank you. See?"

"What do you mean 'see?' I never denied they were an unusual weapon. And I also never said they were for here."

Allie and Stuart exchanged glances, and I used that few seconds to rack my brain for a more detailed lie and curse my best friend, not necessarily in that order.

"Not for here. For the mansion."

"We're going to knit at the mansion?" Allie asked. "What? In front of the fire?"

"Very funny. We'll keep them there. In a basket or something. With yarn. And other knitting accoutrements."

"Because?" Stuart prompted.

"Because a basket full of stilettos and daggers and holy water might make Bernie curious."

That clicked with him, and I saw when understanding filled his eyes, followed by a slight curve to his lips I didn't quite understand. "What?"

"I'm just wondering what you're going to do when Lila asks you what you're knitting."

"Lila?"

"Bernie's wife. I'm sure she'll come over once or twice. And Kate, darling," he added, "I've seen the afghans she knits."

I frowned, but Allie collapsed on the couch in peals of laughter. "No worries," I said. "I'll tell her it's Allie's hobby." A neat little trick that not only saved me from learning a new skill, but had my daughter remembering just who was the mom in this family.

"No fair!"

"Nope," I agreed. "Not fair at all. And speaking of not

fair," I added with a nod to her little brother, "could you go give him a bath before dinner?"

"You're gonna bathe him before dinner?" she asked.

"No," I said calmly. "You are."

She shot a glance toward Stuart and—thankfully—cut off further argument. Most likely, she assumed I was going to tell Stuart about the demon in the backyard. But the truth was I wanted to talk about much more mundane things. Grown-up things. Normal family things.

And I wanted the time alone with my husband.

As she headed up the stairs I made a mental note to catch her before she came down again. I needed her to stay mum on the backyard demon. For now, at least, I was tangling my daughter in my web of lies. And the truth? I'd been living with lies for so many years that that indiscretion caused me no guilt, only the slight twinge of fear that one day Allie, too, would be able to lie like a pro. Even to me.

I closed my eyes against the image, simultaneously proud of my daughter for what she was taking on, and horrified by what I was getting her into.

Stuart tapped my elbow, and I opened my eyes to find a glass of red wine in front of me. "Life saver," I said.

"Rough day?"

"Class," I said. "The women. Some of them just get to me."

"Too dainty?"

I couldn't help the laugh. "No. Nothing like that." I saw the curiosity on his face, and knew he was about to ask the details of my day. I waved it away. "I don't even want to talk about it. Tell me about your day. You're the one who probably really needs the wine."

"The parting was surprisingly amicable," Stuart said, taking a seat at the kitchen table.

I took a sip of wine. "Really?"

"Amicable, but unavoidable."

I searched his face, looking for regrets and second thoughts. I found none, but still wasn't soothed. There was no doubt he'd done this for me—for us—and I loved him all the more for it. The guilt, however, weighed on me. "You're okay?" I asked.

He nodded, then reached out his hand for me and settled me on his lap. "I'm fine. I wanted this, remember?"

"You wanted the county attorney job," I reminded him.

He nodded. "Do you remember why?"

"So you could be a big-shot political lawyer dude?"

He chuckled. "That was my primary goal, yes. After that, I wanted to help. To make a difference." He stroked the pad of his thumb down my cheek. "I think I can make a difference helping you, too."

"All right," I said, still not completely convinced he was cool with this change in circumstances. "But you're sure you're okay?"

This time, he outright laughed. "I'm good, Kate. Really. And now I have more time for the things that are really important to me." With a low growl, he bent me back and started nibbling on my neck. "Like remodeling the mansion," he murmured.

I sat up and smacked him. "Thanks a lot. I know where I rank."

"At the top, sweetheart," he said, his eyes seeing only me. "Always."

I started to feel all warm and fuzzy inside, and it wasn't because of the wine. I shifted on his lap, sighed when his arms tightened around me, and leaned in close. "Does the top include health benefits?" I asked, my sexy murmur mimicking his earlier one.

As I'd hoped, he laughed. But he also nodded, which surprised me. I sat up straighter and stared him down. "Really?"

"It's me, Kate. I'm not going to do something stupid that leaves my family unprotected."

"Oh." I frowned, trying to figure this out. "So what did you do?"

"I'm *of counsel* for Pete Tomlinson's firm. Real estate transactions, handling enough hours to ensure benefits, but not so many I can't work with Bernie. And fight a few demons."

"You've been busy." Apparently I wasn't the only one in the family who kept secrets. First the house speculation, which I'd known was out there as a vague "maybe someday" kind of thing, but had never imagined that he'd been working to bring "someday" into this year, much less this month. Now I find out he's been wheeling and dealing to land soft at a new job. I wasn't sure if I should be flattered he was so meticulous about not upsetting our household bottom line, or frustrated because he hadn't let me in on his plans.

In the interest of self-preservation and fairness, I went with flattered.

"Pete knows it may be a temporary position, too. So if the development company takes off, there won't be any hard feelings when I quit to jump in with Bernie full-time."

"I'm really impressed."

"It gets better. He's actually thinking of investing."

"You're kidding?"

"Not kidding, but it's not definitive. He knows real estate's a tricky investment in this market, and although he knows me, he doesn't know Bernie."

"Bernie's a great guy," I said, thinking of the teddy bear of a man who'd been friends with Stuart for years. "Take the two of them out to dinner, serve margaritas, and then sit back and let the investment checks roll in."

He leaned forward and kissed me on the nose. "I'm so glad you said that."

I looked at him, not sure I liked his tone of voice. "Should I be worried?"

"No," he said, but he said it a little too casually, and he appeared to be examining the ceiling closely instead of looking at my face.

I slid off his lap and stood facing him, my legs about shoulder distance apart, my hands loose and ready. I was, I realized, in fighting stance.

Flustered, I stepped back and tried to relax. "What?" I demanded. "What did you do?"

"Nothing. I told you." He got up and went to the counter to pour himself a fresh glass of wine. "I just invited Bernie and Pete over tomorrow night."

That did sound like nothing, which meant I was missing something, or Stuart was holding out on me. "And?"

"And their wives," he said, almost sheepishly. "Nothing fancy, though. Just cocktails. Snacks. That kind of thing."

"Are you completely insane?" I asked, my left arm going immediately out to my side to point toward the living room. "Have you *seen* the state of our house? And I haven't cleaned the guest bathroom in over a week, and Timmy's been using it regularly, so if you think—"

"I'll clean the bathroom," he said, far too reasonably.

"Damn right you will," I muttered.

"And the rest of the house," he added. "I've got tonight and tomorrow. It's no big deal. Really."

"Yeah," I said, thinking about demons lurking in the bushes. "It is."

"Why?"

"Because . . ." I sucked in a breath, frustrated that I'd walked into that one. "Because you don't just go and foist cocktail parties on people. I mean, it made sense when you were running for office, but you're not anymore, and you didn't even think to call? Maybe I have plans tomorrow night."

"Do you?"

"That's not the point!" His lips quivered, which really

wasn't the way to get on my good side. I poked him in the chest to accent my ill temper. "And why do we have to have this shindig here? What's wrong with Bernie's house?"

"I'm the connection between Pete and Bernie," he said reasonably. "But if you don't want to have guests over, I'll work something out."

I closed my eyes, wallowing in guilt.

"Dammit, Kate. What's wrong?"

"It's fine," I said. "Honest. Bad day. Grumpy mood. It's fine. It'll be fine." Chances were good the demon wouldn't come back, right? And I could always make sure Allie and Eddie were paying attention while I socialized.

"Be fine?" he repeated, his voice rising with speculation. "And you don't want guests? What aren't you telling me, Kate?"

I started to deny it, but didn't. My husband wasn't an attorney for nothing. "This just isn't the best time to have people over, okay?"

"Not okay," he said. "Not until you tell me why."

"Fine. All right. Okay. A demon showed up. Yesterday, before you got here. And today. At Cutter's." I cringed a little and waited for the explosion. Instead, I got icy calm.

"And you were going to tell me this when?"

"I was," I promised. "I swear. But yesterday we were so focused on David that I honestly didn't think about it, and when I realized I hadn't told you, I wanted to wait until I had some answers."

"You didn't think I might want to help you find those answers?" Still flat. Still ice.

"I'm sorry," I said, knowing I deserved the dressing down and wishing he'd raise his voice. Anger, I could battle. This calm unnerved me. "I didn't think."

"No," he said. "You didn't."

He drew in a long breath, then put his wine down so that he could rub his temples. "I stayed, Kate. I stayed because

I love you. Because I want to make our life work, no matter how surreal it might be." He met my eyes, his firm and demanding. "You shut me out once. Now that I know the truth, don't think you can do it again."

I swallowed and nodded. As dressing downs went, that one was relatively painless.

He kissed my cheek. "We'll make blintzes," he said. "We'll do it together tomorrow afternoon. It'll be fun."

I looked up at him, this man who was using the words "blintz" and "fun" in the same sentence, and all I could think was that even after all my deep confessions, he still didn't know me at all.

"You should have called me, Kate," Eric said, his tone harsh and clipped, anger hiding hurt. "A woman and a demon child approach you, practically befriend you, and then try to kill you? I think that warrants a call."

"Eric—"

"Don't even say it. I'm at your side until this goes down, and right now, I'm still me. And I intend to do whatever the hell is necessary to stay that way." He turned and met me dead-on. "I'm not losing, Katie. I fought for this body, and I'm damn well staying."

I nodded, though his words sent ripples of worry down my spine. *He'd fought for the body.* Because the body wasn't his. And someone else wanted to take control now. Someone who just might end up having a hell of a lot more strength than Eric. Literally.

"Goddamn it," he said, to no one in particular.

"I wasn't trying to shield you," I said. "And you're the one who said you weren't my partner. Remember?"

A hint of a frown touched his lips. He'd come back from a debriefing at *Forza* without having signed back on as a Hunter. At the time, I'd wondered why. Now, of course, I knew the reason. Equal Opportunity Employer or not, *Forza* wasn't inclined to have a demon on the payroll. Even a dormant one.

"They had you on before," I murmured, opening the door for Eric to tell me the full story. The story he'd kept from me during our years as partners, our years as lovers.

He said nothing though, just picked up the pace, his eyes searching the dark.

I cursed under my breath and sped up. This night wasn't ending until we'd talked, he and I. But I could wait. I didn't like it, but I daily counseled my little boy on the virtue of patience. Far be it for me to make a hypocrite of myself.

We were a few blocks away from the Old Town shopping area, just off Main Street, on a street lined with wooden-frame bungalows with cheerful gardens and brightly painted front porches. We both knew the neighborhood well, as we were only one street over from the house we'd moved into a few months before Allie was born. We'd spent countless hours walking these streets, pushing a stroller and talking about nothing. Nothing and everything. And never—well hardly ever—talking about demons. Instead we'd planned Allie's future. We'd pondered the possibility of getting a dog. And we'd had long, involved discussions about what color we should paint the living room.

I'd thought we were so normal, like we'd climbed over some wall and left it all behind.

Obviously, I'd been wrong.

But we weren't here tonight to reminisce. Instead, we were looking for a mother and her son. Two demons that I wanted to have a few words with. And then, yes, I wanted to drive stakes through their eyeballs.

Sometimes, it's the simple things in life . . .

Stuart had wanted to come, had wanted to confront the woman and child who'd attacked his wife and baby. But as he hadn't yet joined me on regular patrols, there was no way I would agree to walk him into what I truly hoped would turn into a combat situation. He wasn't happy, but he'd agreed, and I had to wonder how many such arguments we'd have in the future, and if I'd ever be comfortable hunting with him the way I'd always been comfortable hunting with Eric.

"This is it," Eric said, nodding at a pale blue house with a six-foot privacy fence. We were in the alley behind the house, and I climbed up onto a recycle bin to peer inside.

"Dark," I said. "Probably rabbited."

"They're probably crashed in a motel somewhere. We can check the flops along the highway after we patrol here."

I nodded vaguely, then hopped off the bin and tried the back gate. Open.

"Come on," I said as I pushed inside and moved slowly to the back door. It wasn't locked either, and we went in carefully, falling easily back into old rhythms as we checked the house, covering each other as we made sure the structure was secure.

"They're not here," he said when we'd circled back to the living room. "Let's go."

"Wait," I said. I wanted to take a look around. If they'd been living in the house for two weeks, it was possible they'd left something behind that could help us. Information about the She-Demon, or possibly even a forwarding address. You never knew. Demons, like humans, got sloppy. And the longer a demon lived in a human shell, the more human it became.

Without warning, I thought of Eric, wondering if the demon inside him had been humanized. And, too, wondering if Eric's humanity would come through should the worst happen.

But no. The worst wasn't going to happen. Not on my watch. Not if there was anything that I could do to prevent it.

"What are you thinking?" he said, his eyes fixed on me.

I considered dodging the question, but that wouldn't help either of us. Instead, I faced it head on. "I need to know, Eric," I said. "Everything that happened to you. I deserve the whole story. I can't help you—not really—unless I know everything."

"What do you know?" he asked, so calmly that I had to clench my hands into fists to keep from lashing out at him. Because what little I did know hadn't come from him. I'd had to hunt it down on my own, pry it from other people, while the man I'd once loved with all my heart and soul stayed as quiet on the subject as he'd always been.

"I know what Father Corletti's told me," I said. "About how it's been inside you all along. And about how the Cardinal Fire unbound it. The later stuff, mostly. The early stuff—like how the demon came to be inside you—he said that's for you alone to tell me." I drew in a breath. "It's time, Eric. Tell me what I need to know to help you."

We were in the kitchen, and he looked around, as if he hoped Lisa and John-John would leap from the cabinets and put a stop on this conversation.

I took his hands, pulled him until he had no choice but to shift on the bench and face me. "It's me, Eric. It's Katie. Whatever you tell me, it will be okay."

For a moment, his eyes searched my face. Then he nodded, one quick jerk of the head before pulling his hands free and pacing in front of me. "It wasn't an accident," he said, his voice flat, controlled. "There was nothing surprising to them about the fact that there was a demon in me. Just the opposite, actually. It's what they wanted. It's what they planned." He spit the last word out with such vitriol I closed my hands into fists by reflex alone.

"Who?"

He faced me, and the pain I saw in his eyes about broke my heart. "My parents."

"*Your parents?*" The words hung there between us, vicious

and surreal. "But that's— But you don't know your parents. Don't know anything about them?" Obviously he did, of course, but reality was about two steps behind my mouth.

"I did," he said. "I do."

"Dear God. Why didn't you ever tell me?" I hadn't meant to ask. I didn't want to sound whiny or needy or hurt. Especially considering we were no longer married, my hurt feelings hardly compared to the pure hell—literally—that Eric was going through.

"Why didn't you tell Stuart?" he asked.

It was a rhetorical question, of course. Eric knew perfectly well why I hadn't told Stuart about my demon-hunting days. I'd married him as Kate, an ordinary widow with an ordinary suburban life. That was the woman Stuart had fallen in love with, and I didn't want him looking at me and seeing another girl.

Yes, that had probably been extraordinarily neurotic of me, but the heart can't always be controlled.

"But I knew," I said. "I knew about demons and things that go bump in the night."

"You knew about evil," he said. "You knew what it did and how it could hurt." He stopped pacing long enough to take my chin in his hand. "And I couldn't bear the thought that you'd look at me the way you're looking right now, with the knowledge that something dark is inside, that it was put there by my parents, and that one of these days, it's going to come out."

"That's not how I'm looking," I said, forcing my eyes to stay on him.

"Isn't it? It's what I think when I look in the mirror every day."

"You're not your parents any more than you're the thing inside you," I said, moving to him and holding his face in my hands so he had no choice but to look into my eyes. "Whatever is inside you, it's not you. You can beat it back, Eric. You can and you will."

A troubled expression passed over his face. "I used to think so, Katie. I really did. Do you think I could have lived with you, had a family with you, loved you if I believed that somehow I was putting you in danger? And I kept looking, even when we were living here, for a way to make it stop. That's why I kept in contact with *Forza*. Why I met with Father Oliver and worked with Father Donnelly to become an *alimentatore*," he added, referring to other secrets he'd kept that I'd only recently discovered. And now I knew a little bit more about why he'd done it.

He drew in a breath and continued. "And doing all of that made me feel safe. Like I had it under control. I had to believe that, you know, because I could never have done anything to do you harm. Even after I died," he added, clenching his fists at his sides and then drawing in a deep breath. "Do you think I would have sought you out after I came back if I didn't believe I could fight it down? That's what I used to believe. That's what I *had* to believe."

Something tickled on my cheek, and I brushed it away, felt the wetness, and realized I was crying. "Used to think so?"

"It's winning, Katie," he said simply. "I try—I try so hard—but it's winning." He lashed out, kicking a cabinet so hard it not only made a dent, but made me jump.

"Try harder," I said, angry now, too. "Dammit, Eric, you've beaten this thing back before. You can do it again."

"Every damn day I try. Every. Damn. Day." He drew in a breath, and I saw real fear in his eyes. "I go to Mass now, and it hurts, Kate. It hurts inside like a fire is ripping through me."

I swallowed, not wanting to hear this. That was bad, very bad.

A demon can walk on holy ground, but it hurts like hell, and the longer they stay, the more it hurts. That's one of the best tests, actually, for determining if a creature is a demon. Certainly it's more accurate than breath, which could easily be present in a human simply because of poor hygiene.

In the past, Eric had no problems entering the cathedral, but if it now caused him pain . . .

I shook my head, wanting it to all go away. Wanting to fly back in time to the year Allie was born, when we were safe and Odayne was bound up tight, not causing trouble. Not doing anything.

But there was no going back, and even if we could, would I want to? Yes, I'd been blissfully ignorant, but the truth was that even then, Eric was tainted, his soul entwined with a demon.

What if he had lived to a ripe old age? What if we'd grown old, had grandchildren, and one day died peacefully in our sleep? I believed in heaven, believed in the tenets of my faith, and I believed that despite my lies and my secrets and my multitude of sins, that upon my death, my soul would go to heaven. And though I'd never actually sat down and considered the parameters of my afterlife, I think I'd always believed that Eric would be there with me. He was my first love so how could he not?

I knew now that I'd been both blind and naive. Nothing in this world is a given, and that is true times ten when you walk in the shadow of demons. Eric wouldn't have met me in heaven. He was bound to Odayne, to the demon realm.

Bound to hell, unless we could find a way to untangle Eric's soul from the demon.

"We'll find a way," I said. "I don't care if I have to fight until my fingernails bleed and research until my eyes fall out. We're going to get answers, and we're going to save you."

"I wish I was as confident," he said.

"I'm confident enough for the both of us."

That sad smile touched his mouth again. "I'm glad to hear that. But you're setting yourself up for disappointment."

I started to shake my head no, but he took my chin in hand. "Yes," he said. "I know it. *Forza* knows it. And Katie," he said, the knife edge coming back into his voice, "even your parents knew it."

"What?" The words seemed to swirl around me, a thick, viscous soup of nonsense. "I'm not—what?"

He turned away so that I was facing his back, and though I wanted to see his face, my legs didn't seem to be working. So I sat and let his familiar voice wash over me, telling me things I'd never known and had never imagined. "I was six, maybe seven," he began. "Not when the demon first came inside—that was before. That was at birth, maybe even conception. But there were things that had to be done. Rituals that had to be performed to bring the demon out, to infuse him through me. To make us one." His shoulders shook as a shudder passed through him. I wanted to go to him, to hold him, but I couldn't move. I could only listen and hope that it wasn't going to be as bad as I feared.

"I don't remember much, but I remember candlelight. And chanting. And the ritual cuts made into my back. They wanted to scar me, Katie," he said, finally turning around. "They had to scar me in order to mark me, and I can still feel the sting of the blade digging in, ripping off flesh, and the feel of the salt in the wounds to ensure the scar remained."

"I've seen your back, Eric," I said. "There's no scar."

"They finished only part of it," he said. "A serpent's head, fangs bared, forked tongue lashing out."

"It's not there," I insisted. "Eric, there's no scar."

His smile was thin. "It's there," he said. "Even if you can't see it, it's there."

"Eric—"

But he held up a hand, cutting me off. "No. Let me finish. Because they *didn't* finish. They didn't bring it out, didn't twine it with me. Not fully, anyway. And not for lack of trying. But they were stopped. The ritual interrupted."

"By who?" I asked, though I feared I already knew.

"Your parents," he said.

"They were Demon Hunters?"

"Not with *Forza*. I don't think anyone ever really knew where they came from or how they got a bead on what my parents were up to. But they did, and they came, wandering the streets of Rome posing as a young couple on vacation. And they tracked my parents down and they burst into the ritual."

"Intent on killing your parents," I said, following the story although I felt numb.

"No," he said. "Intent on killing *me*."

"But—"

"But nothing," he said. "They came in. They tried to take me out. My father wasn't having it, and they fought. I don't remember it. I only know what they told me. But at the end of it, my father and your parents were dead."

"And your mother?"

"Lived three days. Long enough to come out of a coma and tell Wilson everything," he said, referring to the man who would later become my—our—first *alimentatore*.

"Were they with a cult? Did she tell *Forza* who they were?"

"She didn't have to," he said. "He knew them. My parents were Hunters, Kate."

"What? No. That's impossible. Why would they do that?"

"They thought they were doing good. They'd been working with Father Donnelly, and they thought they'd made a breakthrough. A giant step in this centuries-old game we play." He paused and drew in a long breath. "They thought they'd figured out a way to castrate the demon and yet steal its strength. They didn't know what they were doing to me," he said, and I knew he had to believe that. Had to believe that his parents had only wanted the best for him because otherwise it was too painful to look at what they did to him, no matter what they'd hoped the endgame would be.

"You were supposed to be some sort of Super-Hunter," I said. "Stronger, faster, able to anticipate their every move." I frowned, realizing that some of what his parents had planned had actually come through; Eric had always had an uncanny knack for anticipating a demon's next move. We used to joke that it was our secret weapon. Apparently, we'd been right.

"It wouldn't have worked, of course," he said, "and your parents stopped it before the ritual was complete. But the demon was still inside me, and *Forza* needed to make sure it wasn't going to come out. There were rituals. Binding rituals. And they trapped it inside. Bound it tight. Suspended animation, just like in the movies."

"How did they know what to do? Did your mom tell them?"

"Wilson knew," he said, his eyes dark. "He'd worked with my parents, but pulled out at the end, tried to convince them they shouldn't go through with what they planned before I was born. And then when I came along, he said I seemed like such a normal baby that he assumed they'd taken his word. Decided they couldn't do it. He was wrong. And before my mom died, she told him everything."

I cringed, both from what his parents had done to him as from the hand that Wilson had played in it. I'd trusted Wilson. Believed in him. And I'd never once had even an inkling of a clue that he knew secrets about Eric. Or about me, for that matter.

"And my parents?"

"*Forza* tried to identify them, never managed. But they did track them to a shabby hotel, and apparently they found something that suggested they were traveling with a child."

"But they didn't find me?"

"You were found exactly where they told you. Wandering the streets of Rome."

"And Father Corletti? How much of this did he know?"

"None, Kate, I swear. All he knew was that a child was found, an orphan. And he took you in. He didn't even learn the truth about me until after the mission in the catacombs. After I used the Cardinal Fire." He met my eyes, his sad. "That's when I learned, too. Because the demon was trying to get out, and *Forza* had to shove it back in. Bind it tight again."

"But they did bind it," I said.

He nodded. "We've been over this ground. The demon's stronger now."

"Maybe," I muttered, my thoughts in turmoil. I stood and began pacing. "You were so young, and you carried so much. You should have told me, Eric," I said. "Everything we were to each other—everything we are. You should have told me. You shouldn't have gone through it alone."

"I didn't want to, Katie," he said, his voice raw. "I loved you, and I was so afraid I would lose you." He moved closer, only inches from me, and I took a step backward until my rear pressed against the kitchen countertop of Lisa and John-John's tidy little house. "I was afraid," he repeated. "Afraid you wouldn't want me."

The breath hitched in my throat. "Never," I whispered. "How could you think that?"

"Kate," he said, and before I could think, his arm hooked around me and pulled me close.

"Eric, no—"

But he kissed me, hard and deep and long, and with such pure need that I thought I would drown in the desperation of that moment. My hands knotted automatically in his shirt, and I opened myself to him, all while my head was screaming for me to stop.

I didn't. I took comfort in the kiss. Comfort in the familiarity, and comfort that this wasn't a demon in my arms.

It was my husband.

Except it wasn't.

My senses rushed back to me, and suddenly mortified by what I was doing, I moved my hands to his shoulders and pushed back. He murmured a protest and pulled me closer, a move that I countered with flat hands against his chest and a forceful shove. "No, Eric. We can't."

His eyes, soft and warm, flashed with fury, and I watched, strangely fascinated, as he reined it in.

"We need to go," I said, moving sideways along the counter away from him. "Let's finish the patrol." I needed to get outside and get some air. Mostly, I needed out and away, and I went, not caring if he was following.

I was a block down the alley when he fell into step beside me.

"We were married, Kate. You don't have to be ashamed."

"I'm married now. Yes, I do."

I heard him sigh and expected an argument, but none came. Instead, we walked in silence, moving through the streets and weaving down alleys.

Nothing jumped out at us. Probably good, considering my mood. I hated myself for my weakness with him, but even when I tried to shove that aside, I was left staring at the bombshell that was my parents. For so long, they'd been ghosts to me. Eric's news drove home that they'd been real people. People with names and purposes and a little girl who I could only hope they had loved.

I was sniffling when Eric stopped.

"What?" I asked, my voice low. "Do you see something?"

"Look," he said.

I followed the direction of his gaze and gasped. *Our house.* We'd circled through the neighborhood and ended up at our house.

"It's for sale," he said, nodding at the realtor's sign. "Think anyone's living in it?"

"Let's look," I said, though I knew we shouldn't. We crept closer and peered in the windows. Empty. No furniture. No people. Barely even any dust left behind.

Eric grinned, so quick and playful it tweaked my heart. "Let's go in."

"Are you nuts?"

"Probably," he said, then moved swiftly to the back of the house. He used his elbow to break a pane of glass, then reached in and flipped the lock, all while I stood there, mortified, not quite able to believe we were really doing this. "I want to see it again," he said. "I need to."

He stepped inside, and since I wasn't going to hang out on the back porch by myself, I stepped in after him.

The place was as I remembered it. The big kitchen with the glass-front cabinets. The huge pantry that we'd rarely filled, being young enough to eat out more than we ate in. The black-and-white tile floor that had at first seemed so silly, but had soon grown on me.

I crossed through to the living room, and there my breath hitched. Eric was sitting on the window seat, grinning like a little kid. "Wanna look?"

"There's nothing there," I said, unable to keep the laugh out of my voice.

"You never know. The elves might have come while we were gone."

I shook my head, but moved closer. "Fine. Let's look."

He hopped off the seat and lifted the wood to reveal a compartment probably designed for linens. We'd lived in the house for two months before we even knew the compartment was there, so good was the craftsmanship. Once we'd found it, we'd acted like giddy children and left presents for each other at disgustingly sappy intervals. "Nothing," he said, peering inside. "Damn."

I smiled despite the fact that we'd found no hidden treasure, because it reminded me of all the silly secret games we'd played. Eric had always loved to share secrets—it had even become a special game with Allie—and it hurt to think now about the huge secret those smaller ones were shielding.

"Kate?" He was looking at me, watching my face, and I shook my head, forcing my expression back to normal.

"Did you try the loose board?" I asked. One of the floor-boards inside the compartment had come loose, and one Christmas I'd hidden his present inside.

He reached in and tugged the board out, then looked in the small space. "Nope. Nothing."

"Bummer," I said, then sat back on the seat next to him once he closed up the compartment.

There may have been no presents, but the adventure had cleared my mood, and now that we were inside, I knew that I'd needed this little excursion as much as Eric had. We'd been a family in this house, and although I once again had a family I loved, it was nice to remember where it had started. After growing up with dorms and living in ratty hotels or even on the street when we hunted, this little house had seemed like a gift of normalcy. Hard to believe I'd gone from being a street urchin in Rome to a suburban mom. But I had.

How, I wondered, had I gotten to Rome in the first place?

"My parents," I said, the topic bubbling back to the surface. "Someone saw them. Someone knows them. Someone at *Forza* touched their things. A hotel owner spoke with them." I looked at him, saw the sadness on his face, and knew that despite everything happening to him, his heart was breaking for me a little, too. "Do you think it's in the archives? Their stuff, I mean. Do you think *Forza* kept it?"

"I don't know," he said. "I really don't. Why don't you tell Father what you've learned? It'll help you to know." What he didn't say was why it would help. If I was losing Eric, it would be nice to gain some history. To have some other piece of my life returned when one was amputated.

I managed a quick smile, though I didn't really feel like smiling. "I'll do that," I said, although I wasn't certain I ever would. A part of me was curious, yes. But another part felt kicked in the gut. I'd never been one to fantasize about my parents, but what little imagining I'd done had cast them as loving people who'd wandered astray during their tourist days in Rome and gotten mugged. Probably injured while trying to save me, and then there I was, alone and lost.

Never once had I imagined they'd left me alone to go off playing superhero. It was one thing to fight, I thought. Another completely to risk making your kid an orphan.

I frowned, realizing that I did that, too. I did it every single day. Maybe my kids wouldn't be orphaned, but—

I pushed myself to my feet, maternal instincts warring with the need to protect, to fight, to do what I was trained to do. What so few people *could* do.

What was it Allie had said when she'd first found out I was a Demon Hunter? That I was like a cop. Or a soldier.

And she'd been right.

What I did—what I was doing every single day—was right.

But if that was true, then why did it hurt so bad? Why did it feel like the parents I never knew had kicked me in the gut, said a big *screw you*, and run off to get themselves killed.

"Shit," I held up a hand, warding off Eric's questions and sympathy. "I think we're done here." I stood to go.

"Katie." His voice was so soft. So *Eric*. And damned if the tears didn't start flowing.

"Don't do this," I said as he stood, too. "I don't want to go there. I don't want to cry on your shoulder. I don't want to cry at all."

He moved a step closer, his eyes dark and full of purpose. "What's wrong with my shoulder?"

I managed a whisper of a smile. "It's not mine anymore." If I was going to cry on anyone's shoulder, it should be Stuart's.

"You're not your parents," he said, moving closer and backing me against the wall.

I couldn't help my smile. "How do you do that? How do you always know what I'm thinking?"

"You're part of me, Katie," he said. "You always have been."

And because I saw him leaning closer—because I saw what he wanted and wanted it myself—I shook my head. "No."

"We're not connected?" he asked, his lips brushing mine. "You can't say no any more than you can stop breathing."

"Eric," I repeated, *"no."*

"Hush," he said. And then he took my mouth in his, his lips soft but firm.

I pushed him away, shaking my head, not willing to go there again. "I said no."

"And I said yes," he spat, then jerked me closer. I gasped, surprised by the fierceness of his touch. "Dammit, Kate, you're mine." And then he was on me again, his mouth crushing against mine, his teeth tugging at my lip, biting and claiming, and his hands owning me, touching me.

I tried to speak, tried to find words, but I couldn't, and when his hand dipped under my shirt and found my breast, I gasped not in arousal but in fear.

I bit down hard on his lip, then yanked my head back when he groaned. "Let me go," I said, my voice firm, my fear absolutely hidden.

"The hell I will," and then his leg was behind mine, pulling me off balance, knocking me to the ground. His shirt had come untucked from his jeans, and as he twisted around, I saw a flash of red, angry scar—and it was in the shape of a serpent, fangs bared and tongue forked.

I couldn't even gasp, couldn't process that horrible image, because he was on top of me, his hands at the button of my jeans, and all I could think was that this was not happening.

It was *not* happening.

I kicked up, not catching him as hard as I wanted in the balls, but managing enough of a whack that he jerked up, and I got a good look at his face.

I gasped as I looked into his eyes.

I gasped, because I'd expected to see the beast, the demon.

But it wasn't there. The man looking at me—the man attacking me—was Eric.

Eight

For the first time in my life, I was terrified of this man, and I rolled over, clawing at the ground as I tried to scoot out from under him and climb to my feet. I caught another glimpse of his face and the shock I now saw there calmed me some. I'd fought Eric before, and although I'm strong, he's stronger, and the one thing—the single thing—that kept me from smashing a punch into his jaw and sending him hurtling into unconsciousness was the fact that I knew that if he wanted to, he could take me down in an instant.

He'd stopped, though, and now he was backing off, his eyes dark and lost and telling.

But that didn't mean I felt safe. On the contrary, I felt sick. Nauseated and, yes, afraid.

He moved forward, something dangerous flaring again in those beautiful eyes.

"Get back," I hissed. "Pull back, or I swear to God I will end this now." Despite my jumbled emotions, I pulled out the very blade that Eric had given me on our third anniversary. I watched him, forcing my hand to remain steady, as I searched his face, desperate for even a glimmer of the Eric I knew.

He took another step toward me. "Back!" I cried again, but this time I followed with a dose of holy water from the vial in my jacket pocket. Eric howled in pain, his body bucking so hard I feared he would break. But that wasn't really what caught my attention. No, what intrigued me was the telling fact that not a millimeter of his skin was scarred or in any way marred by the holy water.

"I'm sorry," he wailed. "I'm sorry, I'm sorry. I'm so damn sorry."

"Eric," I whispered, horrified, but he pushed past me, running out of the house blindly toward the street. I followed, my mind whirling, my only goal to stop him. To let him know that I knew the truth—that it hadn't been him, but the demon inside.

At the core, Eric was still Eric.

How much longer he would stay that way, I didn't know. I feared that now that it had started, the change would come faster and faster, spinning him round and round like a whirlpool until Eric and the demon were one, individuality lost along with any hope of getting back the man I loved.

I frowned, the mental image of the demon and Eric's increasingly frenetic spinning dance playing at my mind. We'd been trying so hard to find a way to bind the demon or force him out of Eric, and while that definitely needed to be our game plan, maybe we should spend some time searching for a way to simply slow the process. Because if we could gum up the works and keep the demon's tentacles from tightening faster and faster, then maybe we could buy some time to find answers.

It was worth discussing with Eddie, I thought, as I raced

after Eric, stumbling to a halt as I reached the playground where we used to take Allie.

He had settled into a swing, his heels lost in the sand as he swung mildly back and forth. He turned as I approached: I saw nothing of the demon in his eyes. Instead, I saw regret. And fear.

"Did I hurt you?"

I took his hand, pressed it tight in mine. "No," I said firmly, then followed it with a smile, because I knew he needed that. "Absolutely not. Although if your balls feel a bit black-and-blue, I'm afraid you've got me to thank for that."

"Thank you," he said, with such sincerity it made me wince.

"Eric—"

"No." He climbed to his feet. "I mean it."

"There's nothing to thank me for."

"Under the circumstances, I think beating the crap out of me would be completely justified. A smack in the groin hardly seems sufficient."

"You remember?" I asked.

"Every lousy second." He inhaled deeply through his nose, pressed the heels of his hands to his temples as if warding off a killer headache. "It's like being trapped in a dream you can't wake from, only it's much worse than seeing yourself walk around naked. There's no control. There's only consciousness. And impotence." The air between us seemed to hang silent and heavy before he spoke again, and when he did, it was with infinite regret. "I would never hurt you, Kate. You know that, right?"

"I do," I said, though I feared that in the end, Eric would be the one who hurt me most of all. "We really should go," I said, hesitant this time, as my last attempt to leave had ended with me pressed against a wall, panting.

He nodded, then started moving toward the street, his cane tapping the way.

We walked in silence until the weight of the quiet turned unbearable and I had no choice but to speak. "What are we going to do, Eric?" I considered telling him about the dagger, but the truth was that I couldn't bring myself to. If it came to that, then I suppose I would learn whether or not I had the strength to wield the thing. But I saw no reason to torment Eric with the knowledge that the people he loved were now spending their time searching for a weapon that will kill him, even though it wouldn't save him.

Apparently, though, my worry was for nothing, because it was Eric who raised the subject, surprising me with his soft, whispered declaration that, "There's a dagger, and it can end this for me. For us both."

My breath hitched. "Do you have it?"

He stopped walking to look at me, his face bland. "I've spent years looking for it, and I haven't found a single clue. I don't even know what it's supposed to look like, much less where to search for it. For all I know it's a myth. Maybe it doesn't even exist at all."

"I almost hope it doesn't," I said, my words a whisper as I moved on.

He matched my stride. "If it comes down to it, you can't do that."

"Do what?"

"Feel sorry for me. Fight foolishly for me."

"I'm not a foolish fighter," I said lightly, but he grabbed my arm, pulling me to a stop and looking at me hard, his eyes burning, and not with the light of demon fire.

"I mean it, Katie. If it comes to it, you end this thing. With the dagger, with a sharp stick, with a fucking car key. It doesn't matter. But you end it."

"Eric—"

"Promise me."

"Eric, please—" I knew I had to, but the thought ripped me to shreds.

"You've done it before," he said, and he was right. At the time, though, I'd been confident that he'd be free, his soul leaving this plane and finally, thankfully, coming to rest in heaven.

Now, I knew differently. Unless we found a way to untangle Eric from the beast, he would have no reward. He would, for all intents and purposes, become a demon himself. And what would that do to him? I wondered. Over decades, over millennia? Though his soul might start out pure, and though I believed in Eric's strength, I didn't know if that strength would last for an eternity. And the thought of Eric sliding into the abyss—the thought of the father of my daughter becoming truly evil—it was more than I could bear.

Eric didn't see all that on my face, of that I was certain. But he saw enough, and his own expression softened. "You can't make this about me," he said.

"I'm not making it anything," I countered. "It is about you."

"I mean it, Kate. You can't let the demon live because you think that sometime, down the road, you'll find a way to separate us. You kill that son of a bitch. Kill him, and let me worry about how I'll get free. Because I will. Somehow, eventually, I'll find a way."

I nodded, my throat too thick to talk. I didn't believe him—hell, I didn't know what I believed—but I knew that he needed to believe I was there, his backup plan in case his internal struggle against the demon failed.

The hell of it was, though, I didn't want to be the backup. I couldn't, in fact, think of anything I wanted less. "You fight, dammit," I said. "You fight, and you don't stop fighting."

"What do you think I'm doing?" he said, and his grin was so very Eric that I couldn't help the laugh that bubbled out, only to be cut off in a strangled sort of yelp as a small torpedo rocketed at me from around a shrub and knocked me onto my ass.

Except, of course, it wasn't a rocket. It was a toddler. A demonic toddler to be exact, and its strong, stubby fingers gripped me tight around my neck even as I tried to get my arms under it so I could thrust up and out and break its hold on me.

"Off!" I tried to shout, but it sounded more like a strangled "Urlf!" Not that I was worrying about my personal sound track; I was more inclined to worry about breathing. The fact that my attacker was a toddler didn't even faze me right then—when hands are closing off your windpipe, the age of those hands is not at the forefront of your mind.

But once I'd managed to get some leverage and pry him off with a huge shove that sent him hurtling back onto the sidewalk, the similarities between him and Timmy washed over me. The little bastard was wearing a Disneyland T-shirt, for God's sake! I'd put Timmy in one exactly like that this morning, and while I had my knife ready, and my mind was telling me to take out the lying little bastard, those damned maternal hormones were slowing my hand.

Eric, I saw, had no such compunction.

He leaped, tackling the toddler with every ounce of strength in his body, and then beating on the thing with fists that wouldn't stop no matter how much I yelled out for him to do just that. His shirt rode up as he pummeled the kid, and the scar I'd seen earlier seemed to pulse in the thin light of the streetlamps.

My eyes scanned the area as lights came on from nearby houses, and I feared that we'd soon hear the shrill siren of police cars, and see the red-and-white flash of lights filling the alley.

"Dammit, Eric! Stop!" Though right then, I wasn't at all

certain whether I was speaking to Eric or the beast inside him.

I was in tears by the time he'd finished tormenting the demon, and finally did what he should have done right off—slide the razor-sharp point of his favorite stiletto into the demon child's eye.

He let go of the body, watching with flat eyes as it dropped to the ground. He toed the body over so that it lay facedown, and I shivered, colder still when he lifted his face to look dispassionately at me.

"Eric," I whispered. "Please. It was a child."

"It was a demon," he said. And then he turned and walked away, leaving me alone with the body and my thoughts.

A California coastal town, San Diablo boasts both beaches and mountains. Or, more specifically, beaches and craggy foot-hills of mountains. The town's origin dates back to the California missions, and even before San Diablo took that name, the cathedral sat tall and proud at the top of the cliffs, a focal point for what later became the rather artsy, sleepy town of San Diablo.

I'd hoped to see Eric at Mass, as his presence there would mean that the demon had fully retreated inside of him. And that, of course, was the reason I kept twisting in my seat to scour the crowded pews. After the third such acrobatic move, Stuart elbowed me and asked me what I was up to. Since I didn't want to remind him of Eric's condition (not that I expected him to forget) I muttered an apology and fixed my eyes on the bishop.

The truth was, though, that I'd rather be distracted than listen to Mass. Not a particularly devout state of mind, I'll admit, but not one I could shake, not when I used to sit on these very pews and listen to Father Ben celebrate the Mass and deliver his homily. I closed my eyes tight, and felt Allie squeeze my hand. Even Timmy hugged me, his little hands pressing against my face, and though I held my breath and waited for the tantrum, it didn't come.

Little miracles, I thought. They were around me every day.

But it wasn't a little miracle I needed in my life right then.

It was a big one.

And since I was in a church, I closed my eyes and prayed.

After communion, Timmy's good behavior wore out, little miracles being limited by their very definition. Fortunately, the tantrum didn't come, but the squirming did. Along with the kicking and the whispering and the whining. In light of a few rotating heads giving me the evil eye (the nondemonic sort), I decided to take Timmy out. I hauled him up so that he clung like a monkey, walked gingerly over Allie's feet, and made my way up the aisle, quietly shooshing my little boy, who now insisted that he didn't want to leave.

The moment I stepped through the heavy doors and into the narthex, I saw Eddie, lounging by a bulletin board announcing a fellowship brunch after Mass in the Bishop's Hall. Though Catholic, Mass hasn't been tops on Eddie's priority list in a long while, definitely not since I've known him. My immediate reaction was fear, and I hurried to him with a "What? What's happened?"

"Don't get your panties in a wad," he said. "Just trying to do my job. Both of 'em."

"Both of them?"

He hooked a finger toward the parking lot. "Got Rita out there. She's gonna give me a lift to work."

"Rita? You mean Fran's mother?"

"Don't know any Fran, but Rita said she was in your class yesterday. Dropped by the shop after. Said she was window-shopping, but didn't buy anything." He leaned in closer, his brows waggling. "Personally, I think she just wanted to pick me up."

I agreed, but didn't tell him so.

"And now she's giving you lifts around town? You two only met yesterday."

He snorted. "At our age, you think we want to waste time?" He waggled his brows. "Gonna take her for dinner and a walk on the beach after. So don't wait up."

I swallowed a laugh, but had to give Rita credit. The woman knew what she wanted, that was for sure.

Ushers pushed open the doors to the sanctuary, and the parishioners started filing out. I eased closer to Eddie as Timmy wiggled to get down, then spread his arms wide and started zooming around me in an impression of a jet. "So what have you learned?" I asked, because as fascinated as I was by both Rita and Eddie's mysterious new job, I was primarily interested in his new employment as my *alimentatore*.

Eddie, however, wasn't talking. At least not to me. Instead, he addressed the air over my shoulder, telling "Blintz boy" to head on outside and take the rugrat with him.

I turned to find Stuart standing behind me, a scowl on his face. "I asked Eddie to be my temporary *alimentatore*," I explained.

"And I got business to discuss with your lady. And a schedule to keep. You want to get a move on?"

"Kate—" Stuart began.

I pushed Timmy toward him. "Just—please."

I'm not sure if it was the plea in my voice, the exasperation on my face, or his irritation with Eddie in general, but Stuart kissed me on the cheek, scooped up Timmy so that his plane became airborne, and headed toward the main door to shake the bishop's hand. I crossed my arms over my chest and silently dared Eddie not to get straight to the point.

"This dagger," he began. "*Forza*'s just started looking for that, right?"

"Right," I said. "Father Corletti told me that they didn't know the name of the demon within Eric until now. And apparently this dagger's unique to Odayne. So no one would have been searching for it before." A problem, of course, since millennia-old daggers don't tend to be easily discoverable on eBay. Not that I particularly wanted the dagger—I still wasn't convinced I'd be able to use it—but I was smart enough to know that no matter what was going to happen, I at least needed to have every known weapon in my arsenal.

"But that's the thing, ain't it?" Eddie asked.

"Thing?" I repeated, playing back the conversation in my mind as I wondered where we went astray. "What are you talking about?"

"Eric," he said. "Just because *Forza* wasn't looking doesn't mean Eric wasn't."

"Looking for what?" Allie said, making me jump a mile.

"I thought I saw you go out with Stuart," I said, sounding more accusatory than I meant to.

She shrugged. "I came back. What's the big?"

There was, I assured her, no "big" at all. But as for what we were talking about, I had no clever response. Eddie, however, was winning big-time *alimentatore* points. "That demon that's been dogging your dad," he said. "Apparently there's a dagger that'll take the bugger out for good."

"Odayne," Allie said. "So far I haven't found anything about him." She shot me a smirk. "I've got homework that has to come first."

"Actually, this one may be hot," I said. "Bump it up for a week, and if we haven't made progress, you'll still have time to cram."

"Wait. What? My mother? *My* mother is telling me to blow off studying?"

"Not blow off," I said. "Just reprioritize." Grades and school and all that stuff were important, of course. And while I had no desire to sacrifice her grades or her college chances, I also wasn't willing to sacrifice her father.

More than that, I knew that she wouldn't be willing to, either.

And while I may not have told her why she was researching, if she did know, I was certain she would shove schoolwork aside in a heartbeat. Which meant that if she later found out the truth about her dad, and learned that I hadn't prioritized this work, then I'd be in even more trouble.

I sighed, absolutely stymied. I'd promised my family open and honest, but right then I simply didn't see the way to pull that off. Not without breaking young hearts that didn't deserve to be broken.

Allie was still looking at me with arms crossed over her chest and eyes narrowed in disbelief.

"What?" I demanded.

"You tell me."

I closed my eyes and drew in a deep breath, suddenly tired of the whole thing. "I want answers, Allie, is that so hard to understand? And as much as I wish it weren't always true, you're better at finding them than Laura."

"But school," she pressed. "There's something else going on, Mom. You need to tell me. You know I'm going to figure it out, and—"

"Just stop it," I snapped, making both her and Eddie jump. "I already told you the demon's important to your dad and may be back in town. And if that's not reason enough for you to think it should be priority, then I'll just take the assignment and give it to Laura and you can spend the next week redoing all your homework for the year so that you nail your finals cold. But if you want to help, then do it. Don't question it. Don't analyze it. Just do it. Because I need answers, Al. I'm not going to be late again. I'm not going to lose someone else on my watch."

The words flooded out, along with the tears. And although I managed not to raise my voice, we still caught a few looks from stragglers in the narthex.

To my shame, Allie looked completely chastised, and as she moved to put her arms around me, she glanced through the now-open doors to the altar. She was, I knew, thinking about Father Ben. And although I'd started my speech only hoping to convince her to drop her line of questioning, I'd ended up there, too, only realizing after the fact how much of the truth I spoke.

I missed him terribly, and I'd known the man for less than one year.

I'd lost him. I was the Demon Hunter in town, and he'd died on my watch.

I felt responsible because I was responsible.

And there was no way in hell I was losing Eric, too.

I couldn't.

I *wouldn't*.

Problem was, I didn't know how to save him.

"I'm sorry, Mom. I wasn't thinking."

I returned the tight hug she'd wrapped me in. "It's okay, baby. Sometimes it's raw all over again." I felt her nod, and kissed the top of her head. "Head on out and help Stuart with Timmy, okay? I'll be just another minute."

"'Kay."

"And tell Rita I'll be right there. She's in a red Miata convertible," Eddie said as Allie's eyes widened. "Can't miss her."

"The Padre wasn't your fault, girlie," Eddie said, once Allie was out of earshot. "And Eric ain't neither."

"I know that."

He worked his mouth as he considered me, then blew out a loud breath. "We need him. Hate to admit it, but we're gonna need that boy's help."

"No," I said, despite the weight of disloyalty in my gut. Nothing would ever change the fact that I loved Eric, but after what had happened last night, I no longer trusted him. And I certainly didn't trust his ability to keep things secret from Odayne. "If we are plotting Odayne's downfall, we're going to do it without Eric looking on."

I saw respect in his eyes when Eddie nodded at me. "Finally getting to the truth, ain't you, girl?" I started to answer, but he waved me off. "I said we needed Eric. I didn't say we were going to call him up and have him come over for a planning session."

"What then?"

"He's known about this for how long? His whole life, almost, right?"

"Since we were teenagers. Since the Cardinal Fire unbound the demon the first time."

"And Eric's a smart boy, right? He'd be looking for ways, keeping his eyes open, studying myths and legends and hoping to find facts. Hoping to find a way to get rid of the demon inside."

"Sure."

"Interesting career he chose after quitting the hunting life."

I cocked my head, finally clucing in to where Eddie was going. Because Eric had worked as a rare books librarian, filling the San Diablo County Library—not to mention his den—with fascinating and unique works, all of which he'd handpicked.

And if we were lucky, one of his handpicked books held the answers we needed.

Nine

"But if the answer was in his books, wouldn't he have already found it?" Laura asked.

We were back at the house, with Allie tucked away upstairs and Stuart and Laura at the kitchen table. Laura was looking thoughtfully at me while Stuart had his nose buried in the newspaper.

"Not necessarily," I said. "Eric bought a lot of books. I don't think there's any way he could have gone through all of them."

"And even if he did," Stuart said, peering at us over the top of the paper, "it's possible he missed it the first time around."

"Eric was pretty good at this research stuff," I said, feeling foolishly overprotective of my now-demonic first husband's skills.

"I meant he might have been made to overlook it," Stuart clarified. "We have no idea how far the demon's influence reaches."

"Leave it to the lawyer to suggest the worst-case scenario," Laura said with a grimace.

"Way worst-case," I said. "The demon was bound back then. It only started to get some serious power after Eric came back inside David, and then even more when I used the Lazarus Bones to bring him back." I clenched my hands at my sides, determined not to kick myself any more about that. My ass was already black-and-blue, and as everyone from Stuart to Father Corletti had told me, Eric's present circumstances were not my fault.

"But not bound tight," Stuart said. "Right?"

"Maybe," I said, feeling surly because he was right.

I heard a *clomp-clomp* on the living room floor, and tensed, because it didn't sound like any noise that would normally be moving through my house. Laura saw me, and clutched the edge of the table. "What is it?"

I shook my head, and put my finger over my lips as I stood up, then moved around the table so that I could see into the living room.

What I saw, just about laid me out flat on the floor. But this time, with humor, not fear.

My little boy, completely naked, except for a pair of black pumps, one of my evening bags, and a smear of red lipstick over his mouth. He looked up at me and smiled. "I go shopping!" he announced even as I heard a rap at the back door.

I turned and saw Mindy, her hand over her mouth to hold back a laugh. I gestured for her to come in, and she did, her eyebrows midway up her forehead. "It's a good look for him, Aunt Kate," she said. "Maybe you should tie a red bow to his little—"

"Mindy!"

She had the good grace to look embarrassed. "Maybe not."

"Honestly," I said, refusing to admit out loud that her suggestion was extremely camera-worthy. For that matter, I was deeply regretting not having my own camera handy and charged up. If nothing else, this would be the perfect photo to pull out on prom night.

"You looking for your mom?" I asked, as Timmy started shaking his butt and announcing that he was dancing.

"Allie," she said. "If you think she'll—"

"Allie!" I called up the stairs. "Come on down here."

Her "Just a sec!" floated toward us, followed by the elephantine pounding of feet as she clambered down the stairs, skidding to a stop midway across the living room. She shoved her hands in her pockets. "Hey."

"Hey." Mindy stared at the floor. "So, um, I was thinking that since your parents are having this party thing tonight that maybe we should bribe my mom to let us rent something from Blockbuster and eat popcorn and Chips Ahoy." She looked up at me. "I mean, if it would be okay with—"

"Fine," I snapped off, mentally crossing my fingers. "Totally fine." I hooked my thumb back toward the breakfast area, then headed that way. "I'm just going to go check on the stuff," I said lamely, then disappeared, Allie's eyes burning a hole in my back.

Since you can't see the part of the living room where the girls were standing from the breakfast table, eavesdropping was easy, as Laura and Stuart had already figured out. Both were absolutely silent and leaning slightly toward the wall, and as much as I wanted to take the moral high ground and give them both a dressing down for not giving the girls their privacy, I couldn't do it. I was too curious myself. And so we all sat silently, listing slightly toward the wall, as our daughters' voices slowly rose in pitch and volume.

"But your mom said it was okay."

"Yeah, but that's because she's not thinking, she's already told me my priority needs to be—"

"What?" Mindy demanded. "Oh. School, right? Was she totally pissed about the grade on your—" Her voice dropped, as if she remembered that we could hear everything, and I had to wonder what new project Allie had given short shrift.

There was a long pause as they batted around a few conversational volleys that we couldn't hear, and then Mindy's voice rose again. "—how I'm supposed to understand if you won't tell me what you're doing?"

"I'm researching demons, okay? Is that what you want to hear?"

I froze, and I saw that Stuart and Laura had done the same. We looked at each other, not breathing, and waited for the other shoe to drop.

When it did, it was hardly the explosion I'd expected.

"God," said Mindy, "this is your big secret? That you're into those stupid Internet role-playing games? I mean, just because they're not my thing doesn't mean you have to hide them from me. I mean, God, Allie. You want to give me a little more credit?"

"Maybe you need to give me more credit," Allie shot back. "And it's not stupid. If you knew anything at all about what I do—"

"Fine. Then show me. Let me log on as Morgana the fairy princess and you can show me what you're doing in your spare time now that's so freaking important you blow off your friends. 'Cause you are, you know. I wasn't even going to come over today, but I miss you, and you're being a total bitch, and I'm tired of it."

I could hear the tears in Mindy's voice and moved my hand to cover Laura's, who looked about ready to leap up from the chair and go comfort her offspring.

"You want to know more about what I'm doing? Fine." I heard the stomping of feet, and then Allie's voice from farther away. "So, are you coming, or what?"

When they'd both trampled upstairs and we heard the door snap shut, I breathed again. "Think it'll do any good?" Laura said.

"I guess we'll know soon enough." I cocked my head, half of me expecting Mindy to run terrified down the stairs, the other half expecting to hear her indignant cry that Allie was a royal bitch for playing with her.

But I heard nothing. And I honestly couldn't decide if that was good or bad.

"Cookies," Laura said, standing up and going to my freezer. "I think the occasion calls for them." Laura has a tendency to bake when she's nervous. Considering she was in my poorly stocked kitchen rather than her own, though, she was obviously willing to settle for slice and bake. She pulled out a cookie sheet, then opened the freezer and started rummaging for dough while I remained at the table, a dozen things on my mind.

Frustrated, I smacked at Stuart's newspaper with my fork. "Well?"

"Well, we have a plan," he said. "You've got some of Eric's old books in the attic, right? Laura and I can start perusing them, and—"

"You and Laura? What about me?"

"As much as I hate to say it, I assumed that you'd take the more direct approach and talk to Eric himself. At the very least, you need to be out patrolling. No matter what Eric did to the little boy, the mother's still hovering."

"She's not really the mother," I said with a shudder even as my eyes cut involuntarily to the picture window in our breakfast room. The thought that Lisa might be out there right now, sneaking silently around my backyard, both creeped me out and pissed me off.

"Here's something interesting," Stuart said, laying the paper down and tapping a headline in the Metro section.

I peered over, and skimmed the article upside down. Mr. Albert Preston, one of the residents of the Coastal Mists Nursing Home, had a heart attack during an organized shopping trip to the mall. The paramedic who arrived on scene had been about to call time of death when life "miraculously shuddered" back into the old man. Naturally, everyone was thrilled.

I grimaced, but Stuart only beamed. "Sounds like a demon, doesn't it?"

"Yeah," I conceded, "it does." I'd hunted more than a few demons bred at Coastal Mists. For a while, the place had been a veritable demon factory. That had slowed down, thankfully, and more recently my visits to the nursing home on the cliff had been tame. I still kept a presence at the place—I went in regularly to read aloud to the residents and get a whiff of their breath—but lately nothing had gone awry.

"So we go tonight?" Stuart said, as I goggled at him.

"Tonight?" I repeated, trying to decide the most politic way of telling my husband he wasn't ready for the real thing. "In case you forgot, we have company coming. And what's with the 'we?'"

"Is this going to be a domestic dispute?" Laura asked. "Because if it is, I'll just go read a magazine until you're done."

"Not a dispute," I said. "A calm, rational discussion about the fact that we can't go patrolling tonight, even if I wanted to, because my husband invited over guests." I shot a winning smile at Laura. "Apparently, we're making blintzes."

She turned toward Stuart, her expression suitably amazed. "With Kate? You're making blintzes with Kate?"

"I am nothing if not optimistic," my husband the comedian said. "I firmly believe Kate is a woman of many hidden talents."

"And I firmly believe I married a—"

My rude comment was cut off by the chime of the front doorbell, which caused Timmy to come squealing—still naked—into the kitchen to announce the arrival of "peoples." Chuckling, Stuart stood and pointed to me. "I'll go meet the peoples. You try to come up with an insult that doesn't involve an obscenity."

I flashed him a simpering smile and silently seethed. The things I put up with . . .

"More coffee?" I asked Laura as Stuart headed away.

"One more cup. And then I should get home. Theoretically, I have things to do."

"Theoretically?"

"Laundry, vacuuming, dusting," she said, ticking them off on her fingers. "But I'll probably end up researching for you."

"Good girl," I said, half listening as Stuart greeted someone at the door. I could hear the deep murmur of his voice, followed by higher-pitched tones. A woman, though I couldn't make out what she was saying.

What I *did* make out was Timmy's high-pitched yelp and Stuart's controlled shout for me to get my ass in there.

It took me about two seconds to arrive, but that was two seconds too many. Lisa was inside, her hands tight on Timmy's head—hands I knew were strong enough to snap his neck with no effort at all.

"I'm sorry," Stuart said, talking to me though his eyes never left Lisa.

"You didn't know what she looked like," I said.

"I should have figured it out."

"Hush," Lisa said, pushing Timmy ahead of her as she urged us all toward the living room. I wanted to fight back, to attack, but until I could figure a way to keep Timmy safe through all of this, I was in total cooperation mode.

"I should kill him right now," Lisa said. "Retribution for your destruction of John-John."

"Kill him, and there's nothing shielding you. How long do you think you'll last in here without my little boy to hide behind?"

"I'm not worried about a pitiful attack from a human," she said. But she made no move to harm Timmy, and I could only hope that she realized just how much she needed him to keep her alive in that body.

Behind her, I saw Allie step quietly along the upstairs hall to pause at the top of the stairs. She turned and signaled for Mindy to stay back and quiet. I couldn't risk looking at her more directly, not so long as I wanted to keep her presence a secret.

I did, however, risk a glance toward Stuart. He also stood facing Lisa, which meant he was facing Allie as well. I sent him silent instructions to be careful. To keep his eyes on Lisa and to only watch Allie in his peripheral vision.

Fortunately, Allie's movements were big enough. She thrust her arms out, mimicking Lisa, then used one arm to smash the other away. I pressed my lips together, terrified of the plan she was suggesting, made all the more dangerous because it required both Stuart and I, and I had no way of knowing if he was understanding Allie's spastic gestures.

"Such a nice little boy," Lisa was saying, her thumbs stroking his hair. "And now that my John-John is gone, I do require a replacement. I think he'll do very nicely."

"Not in a million," I said, even as Allie counted down with her fingers. Three, two, one—

She screamed, the sound so high and piercing I'm amazed glass didn't shatter. It didn't need to, though, because the scream itself did the job, causing Lisa to jerk around, loosening her grip on Timmy.

At that moment, I slammed into her at the elbow, then immediately grabbed Timmy by the waist, pulling him down out of Lisa's hands as she grappled for him, a split second too late.

As I did that, Stuart tackled her, his high school football days coming in handy. She slammed backward on the floor, and I heard Laura cry out. "Stuart! Here!" and then a kitchen knife was skidding toward him along the wooden floor. He snatched it up and then thrust it down toward her eye.

But Lisa cried out, "No!" and damned if Stuart didn't hesitate.

That was all it took. She twisted, knocking him off and then bending his wrist back until his hand opened and she could snatch the knife.

I let go of Timmy and was moving in their direction, but Allie got there first. And as Lisa thrust the knife toward Stuart, Allie kicked out, sending the blade skittering back across the floor toward Laura. Then she reached into her back pocket and pulled out a yellow pencil. With a warlike cry, she thrust it forward, slamming it into Lisa's eye before leaping back and breathing hard.

Lisa's body wavered, and then flopped sideways off of Stuart, who kicked his way out from under the body and sat there staring at it as the familiar shimmer broke the air—the demon escaping back into the ether.

"Oh my God. Oh my God!" Mindy pounded down the stairs, her eyes wide. "It's true," she said, as I moved back to Timmy, to gather him in my arms. "It's really true."

"It's true," I confirmed. I looked at Allie. "You okay?"

She rotated her shoulders, then glanced toward Lisa. For a moment, she looked vaguely ill, then it cleared and she nodded. "She was going to kill Timmy and Stuart. Yeah. I'm fine."

Mindy looked between Allie and me, her own expression shifting between horror and fear and amazement. From the kitchen, Laura called to her, and she bolted in that direction, losing herself in her mother's embrace.

"How about you?" I asked Stuart.

"Not so good," he admitted. "Maybe I'm not ready to go patrolling."

"Maybe it's time I worked harder to make you ready," I said.

"I couldn't do it." I could hear the tinge of self-loathing in his voice. "She would have killed Timmy. She's a creature from hell. I know all of that, and I still couldn't manage to shove a knife through her eye."

"It's hard," I told him. "Harder than you think it will be." I exhaled loudly and caught Allie's eye. "You did good, kid. Made me proud."

A wisp of a smile touched her mouth. "Told you I can handle myself." She cocked her head. "And if we start saving now, I can handle myself with a car when I'm sixteen."

"Dream on," I said, but I'll admit I was smiling.

"So what do we do about the body?" Stuart asked. "We've got company in just a few hours."

"Well, Stuart," I said. "Fortunately, we have a really big pantry."

In the end, we decided that the trunk of Stuart's car was a better demon hiding place than the pantry, and with help from Laura and Allie, we had Lisa wrapped up in an old sheet and dumped in the car in no time.

Mindy offered to help—which I considered a good sign that we hadn't scarred her for life—but we all declined her offer. There are some things you don't need to be doing the first time you learn that demons are real, and disposing of the body is one of them.

After dealing with the body, Laura and the girls headed over to Laura's house, taking Timmy with them, because my best friend is a saint. Once the house was empty, Stuart and I turned to the next matter on the agenda, something significantly more scary than demons, at least in my book: cooking.

"Do you want to tell me again why we're doing this?"

"Two reasons," Stuart said easily. "One, I want my new boss and my partner to know each other socially. It makes it easier if I have to divert time from one of my obligations to another. Makes them seem involved. Like they have a stake in my success in both arenas. And, of course, I want them to know my wife."

"I already know them both."

"And now they'll know you better."

"Are you sure you made the right decision quitting the campaign?" I asked. "You're a born politician."

"I'm not entirely sure that's a compliment."

I only smiled, figuring it was best not to comment.

The corner of his mouth twitched knowingly.

"And the second reason?" I asked.

"Normalcy," he said. "This is what normal people do. They have friends over. They drink coffee and eat blintzes and sip wine."

"I don't think I've ever had a blintz at someone's house."

"Trust me. Blintzes are mandatory. Along with bad jokes and gossip about coworkers."

"Patrolling for demons after dark?"

"Usually not."

"Regular weapons training?"

"As a rule, no."

I shrugged, feigning nonchalance. "Sounds like a dull existence, but I suppose we can try it for the night."

He slid his arms around my waist and nuzzled my neck. "How many of these have we had, with only you knowing what kind of evil might decide to crash the party?"

"Several," I admitted.

"And I never knew." He stated that as fact, without a hint of regret or disapproval. Nonetheless, I stiffened, my own mind voicing his unspoken accusation.

"I'm sorry," I said. "I did what I thought was best."

"And tonight?"

I drew in a breath, knowing he was worried. So was I, but I had no intention of letting it show. "Tonight, I have you to help me."

"Does that make it better or worse?" he asked. "I don't

have your skill. I'm a liability, not an asset." He paused, and I saw the muscle in his cheek working. "I'm not Eric."

I drew him close, kissed him hard. "You're not," I agreed. "And I love you."

"You say the sweetest things," he teased, but I was pleased to see that he looked genuinely relieved.

"Does that mean I can have a reprieve from cooking? I can put out plates and cups and napkins. I'm a great napkin putter-outter."

"Togetherness," he said. "Trust me."

As it turns out, the cooking extravaganza wasn't quite the horrific ordeal I'd expected. Stuart had gone a little crazy printing recipes from allrecipes.com, which I thought was incredibly cute, a fact that embarrassed him enough that he refused the apron I teased and taunted and tried to tie around his waist. After that playful interlude, though, we got down to business, and by the time we went upstairs to change for the evening, we'd managed not only blintzes but tiny little quiches, a selection of cheese and fruit, and cheesy biscuits with sausage that just about melted in your mouth.

I fully intended to abdicate kitchen duty altogether. There is no shame in passing the job off to the more prepared partner. Especially if it means we'd have meals more interesting than meat loaf and pot roast on a semi-regular basis.

I was dressed and ready and trying to convince myself not to dig into the little quiches when the first guest rang the doorbell.

At least, I assumed it was the first guest. After this morning's debacle, I wasn't taking chances, and I peered through the peephole before opening the door to Bernie. I gave him and Lila quick hugs, then sent them back to Stuart as I waited for Pete and his wife to park their car and walk up the drive to the front door.

Beyond them, on the far side of the street, a woman

leaned against a sleek black Ferrari. She had dark hair and wore black pants and a black jacket. I couldn't see her face in the dim light, but I didn't need to. I knew her build and the way she moved.

Nadia Aiken.

I frowned, then forced my expression to clear as I welcomed Pete and his wife, now introduced to me as Angie, into my home. I did the kiss-kiss greet-greet thing, and when I turned to look back, the Ferrari and the woman were gone.

"Something wrong?" Pete asked. A reasonable question as I was still standing in the threshold, the door open wide.

"Sorry. Mind wandering." I plastered on a smile and followed them in, wondering if I could have been mistaken. Why would Nadia come back to San Diablo, after all? A Demon Hunter turned bad, she'd messed my life up pretty good a few months back, and managed to get out of town before I could stop her, much less before I could drag her kicking and screaming into *Forza* for adjudication and punishment.

Surely the woman in the street must have been someone else.

But no matter how hard I tried to convince myself, the image of Nadia remained, dogging me through the evening despite my efforts to push her out of my head.

"Here's something I think you'll all find interesting," Bernie said, when we were all settled in the living room with coffee and brandy. He reached into the tote bag filled with paint chips, fabric samples, and scale drawings of various rooms, then emerged with a small black book. "One of Theophilis Monroe's journals," he said. "He lived in the house, you know."

I did know, actually. The mansion itself had been built in the twenties by a silent film producer. At one point, Theophilis Monroe, a rather nasty black-magic aficionado with ties to San Diablo's founding family, had moved in and done some heavy remodeling, some of the details of which had played a key part in our recent defeat of Gora-don. What surprised me was that Bernie had one of Monroe's journals. I'd been under the impression that they'd all found their way to the cathedral archives.

"Monroe incorporated all sorts of demonic symbolism into the house once he got his hands on it," Bernie was telling Pete, who clearly wasn't aware of the bad apple on the founding father's family tree. "The guy was into black magic. A total nutcase, of course, but it's fascinating to read about."

"Where did you find it?" I asked, flipping through the little book.

"Under the floorboards of the eastern bedroom," he said. "We were working in there this afternoon. Who knows how long it's been there."

I glanced up at Stuart, then back down at some of the drawings and phrases that popped out from the page.

"My wife's first husband was a rare books expert," he said, with that political smile. "And she's developed a bit of an interest along those lines, too. Mind if we keep it for a while? We can skim through it and see what we can pull out to go in the ultimate sale brochure."

"Sure, sure," Bernie said affably.

"You're going to push the black-magic connection when you put the house on the market?" Angie asked, her nose wrinkling.

"Don't knock it," Pete said, patting her hand. "The more they push it, the more inclined I am to invest."

She laughed, but I could tell that Bernie realized Pete was serious. He leaned in closer and spoke directly to Angie. "You probably don't believe in that kind of stuff, but trust me. People get a whiff of demons and danger, and prices start soaring. All that spookiness just makes a thing more interesting." He shifted his gaze to take in me and Stuart. "Don't you agree?"

I met Stuart's eye and that was all it took. We burst out laughing, leaving Pete, Bernie, Angie, and Lila to stare at us and wonder what exactly it was about demons we found so funny.

If only they knew.

"I don't think I've been so uncomfortable since I first decided to run for office," Stuart said. "All I kept thinking was that there was a body in the garage. Did it show?"

"You were the epitome of cool," I said. We'd changed into black slacks and T-shirts and called Allie back from Laura's, since I wasn't going patrolling with Stuart without backup. I'd left Timmy with Mindy and Laura with a promise to call me if so much as a stray dog ran into the yard. And, yes, to call Eric if for some reason they couldn't reach me.

Eddie was a no-show on this adventure, which I assumed meant that his and Rita's date had gone well. Now Stuart and I were creeping along the western edge of the Coastal Mists Nursing Home, while Allie was doing the same on the eastern side. "I'll have Eric come by and pick the body up tomorrow."

"I'm not entirely sure that's the best idea," Stuart said.

I shrugged. It wasn't as if I had a lot of options. "So you choose. We dump it in the landfill, sneak into the crypts, or pass it off to Eric." Now that Father Ben was dead, I was no longer able to easily hide dead bodies in the crypt under the cathedral. Fortunately Eric—or rather, David—had been able to step up to the plate. As the chemistry teacher at Coronado High, he had developed a foolproof way to dispose of the bodies. A way, frankly, that I didn't care to think too much about.

I aimed a smile at Stuart. "Landfill or Eric. Your decision."

"You're cocky when you're right," he said, but he said it with a smile.

"I'm also right that you don't need to be out patrolling tonight, either. You need more training before getting in the field." We'd had this argument at home once already, but Stuart had won by pointing out that any newly made demon was undoubtedly going to be drawn into the service of Odayne and the She-Demon. While he'd been right about that, I'd been less inclined to agree with his assessment that he should help me track down and terminate the new demon.

In the end, though, I'd given in. I didn't want to go alone, and I didn't want to call Eric. And, yes, Stuart could use some practical training. And since newly made demons are more easily slain than their counterparts who'd had time to settle into a body, I figured this was as good a practice case as any.

"I know you're worried about me," Stuart said. "Don't be."

"You're that confident?" I asked.

He shrugged. "Flexible," he said. "If we don't meet any demons, we can pick a spot with a view of the moon on the ocean and I can make out with my wife." He nodded toward the rolling lawn that extended beyond Coastal Mists, ending at a sheer drop-off overlooking the Pacific.

"I can tell you're going to be a very productive patrolling partner."

"Depends on your definition of productive," he said, and planted a kiss on me. "If we make out with our eyes open, the demons can't sneak up on us."

I laughed, feeling only slightly uncomfortable. Having never been on an official patrol with Stuart before, I hadn't really known what to expect. But if this was a preview of coming attractions, I had to admit I liked the scenario.

The walkie-talkie on my hip buzzed, interrupting the moment. I snatched it up, still amused by the fact that Allie had presented it to me in the car and insisted I wear it. "We'll be in constant communication," she said. "And it even has a GPS chip. You know. In case we get separated."

"Where'd you get this?" I'd asked, but she'd only smiled.

"Mom, do you copy?"

I gave a little shake of my head, amused by the military tone. "Roger," I responded, my voice low. "Do you see something?"

"Negative," Allie responded.

"Well, then what happened to radio silence?" I asked. "It's hard to sneak up on a demon who can hear us coming."

"You really think he's outside? I figured we were gonna go in and wander the halls. You know, skulking in the shadows and stuff."

"Skulking is on the agenda," I admitted. "For me, anyway. I want you and Stuart to wait out here." This, naturally, raised a protest from both my protégés. "Hey," I demanded, eyeing Stuart and hissing at Allie. "Who's in charge here?"

"Fine. Whatever. And that's not why I buzzed you, anyway."

"It can wait," I said. "Radio silence, remember?" We'd arrived at the rec center window, and since I wanted to have a peek, I passed the walkie-talkie to Stuart, then pressed my face up to the glass and peered around. Not surprisingly, the room was entirely empty, the facility completely quiet.

"So I was reading through some of the notes that Bernie brought," I heard Allie say over the tinny speaker, making me grit my teeth and shake my head in exasperation. "And it's the coolest thing. Did you know the house has a safe room? An honest-to-God safe room."

I stepped back from the window, frowning at both the

walkie-talkie and the expression of bafflement on Stuart's face. "Ask her what part of 'radio silence' she doesn't understand," I demanded, but he merely waved my words away. Honestly, was I the leader here or wasn't I?

"What do you mean 'safe room?'" Stuart asked. "The place was built almost a century ago. Safe rooms weren't a standard feature."

"Not for home invasions," she said, the trademark Alison Crowe eye roll coming through just fine orally. "A Theophilis Monroe—style safe room. You know. To keep out demons."

That perked me up, and I tried to snatch the walkie from Stuart. He scowled and held it tight. "What are you talking about?" he said.

"I guess he wasn't as keen on the demons as everyone thought. Either that or he wasn't as cocky about keeping control of them as we thought."

I tried again and this time managed to snag the walkie. "A demon-safe room? As in consecrated ground."

"Relics. Holy water. Everything blessed by the pope. Pretty cool stuff."

"Which room."

"That room down the hall from the kitchen. The one we figured was servants' quarters that's only got a bed in it," Allie announced, and I could practically hear the grin in her voice. Honestly, I had to agree. Theophilis Monroe, the big bad black-magic aficionado, running and hiding under the bed when the demons got out of control.

"You're right," I conceded. "That is a cool fact. But right now I need you focused and right here. I want you and Stuart watching each other's backs while I do a round inside."

"Roger that," she said, but before she clicked off, I heard her sharp, terrified intake of breath.

"Go!" I yelled to Stuart, and we both hauled ass around the side of the building toward the thick stand of trees where Allie had been hiding.

"Dammit!" I yelled, when I saw her standing next to Eric, his arm tight around his daughter's shoulder. "Dammit, Allie, you scared me to death."

"What?" She glanced down at the walkie. "Oh. Sorry. I squealed, huh? I just wasn't expecting to see Daddy."

"No," I said dryly, looking at Eric. "Neither was I."

"I saw the article in the paper," he said. "I figured you'd be hunting."

"And you thought we needed help?" I asked, my arms crossed over my chest.

"I wanted to tell you not to bother. He came after me earlier. I took care of the problem."

"You go, Dad!" Allie said.

He grinned and kissed her forehead as my chest tightened. I so desperately wanted Allie to know her dad. To hang out with him and be pampered by him and listen to all of his stories. But right then, at that moment, I wanted her the hell away from him.

And I couldn't say a word.

"What's with the walkie-talkies?" he asked.

"I got them from Eddie," Allie said.

"Apparently he's taking the control and coordination aspects of his new position seriously," I added.

"I wondered what he was doing in Eyes Only," Eric said.

I blinked. "Where?"

"Eyes Only. It's a new shop in Old Town. Spy equipment."

"You're kidding?" I examined his face, saw only amusement, then shared a grin with Stuart.

"Eddie with spy equipment," Stuart said dryly. "We're going to have to start watching what we say around the house."

That got a laugh out of everyone, including me, and in that brief moment, life seemed normal, even good. We were a family, albeit odd and extended. A team.

Then Eric cocked his head and took my arm to pull me aside. "Hold up there, buddy," Stuart said. "This isn't your party."

"More mine than yours," Eric shot back. "The party, that is. Not the woman." Though it was clear from his eyes that he meant me as well. "I need to talk to Kate."

Stuart took a step forward, and I stepped between them. "It may surprise you to know that the alpha wolf game isn't helping. And I do need to speak to Eric." I looked at Allie. "You and Stuart can get in some more training."

I thought Stuart was going to argue, but I stared him down. He must have seen the plea in my eyes, because he nodded, then moved toward Allie. "Looks like we've got no targets," he said. "What kind of practice can we squeeze in on the lawn of a nursing home?"

Allie grinned wide, and as Eric and I walked away, I heard her laugh. "Well, I could tell you to drop and give me twenty, but . . ."

"What is it?" I asked when we'd moved out of earshot. "What really happened?"

"He knocked on my door, Kate. Knocked on my door, and when I opened it, the bastard bowed and told me he was there to serve."

"Did you question him? Ask him about Odayne, get any details at all that we can work with?"

"I invited him in, shut the door behind him, and slid a blade through his eye," Eric said, sounding more danger- ous than I'd ever heard him. More dangerous, even, than I'd recently seen him.

"Dammit, Eric, you should have held him. Should have called me." Interrogation wasn't my strong suit, but I could manage it when I had to. And, honestly, if I was interrogat- ing some badass demon that was somehow involved in drag- ging Odayne out of my husband and into the world, then interrogating his ass would be a pleasure.

His face darkened, and I was on the verge of revising that earlier observation on his dangerous appearance, because right then he was close to outdoing even himself. Then he seemed to pull it together. "I know," he said. "Believe me, I know. But I couldn't. Dammit, Kate, I couldn't stop myself."

I nodded, hoping I looked businesslike and determined rather than worried and shaken. This lack of control was bursting forth more and more frequently, and so far, we'd found nothing to slow it down. Worse, we had no hints, no leads. No anything.

"There's more," he said, and I looked up at him, certain the worry was written all over my face. "I'm remembering my dreams."

For the longest time, he could remember only that he'd had them. That they were dark. That they were filled with the demon. Impressions of evil and danger. But no specifics.

"Are you okay?" I asked, taking his hand and hating the thought that he was privy to whatever vile machinations went on in a demon's subconscious.

"So far it hasn't been too bad," he said with a wry grin. "Though I feel a bit like a teenage boy."

I scowled. "What are you talking about."

"Sex," he said. "Violent and brutal, but also hot. Very hot."

Despite the fact that this was only a dream, I felt a knot of jealousy skip into my stomach.

"That's two demons now, coming to me as if I'm part of the team." I could hear the torment in his voice, could see it in his eyes. "And now these dreams. Wild, sexual dreams." He reached out as if to touch me, but pulled his hand away. "I wish I could say it's you in them, but it's not." He reached out and brushed my cheek, my heart fluttering merely from the touch of his hand. "Katie, I don't know who she is, but she's there, with me. And the demon inside. Dear God, he wants her."

I'm not sure if it was jealousy or prudence that made me speak then, but I took that opportunity to tell him that I thought I'd seen Nadia.

"Nadia?"

I laid it all out for him. How I'd opened the door and seen her standing in the distance.

"You're sure it was her?"

"No," I admitted. "But I have a feeling it was. Especially after hearing about your dream."

"She wasn't in my dream," he said stiffly, and I was petty enough to rejoice a little about that.

"If she's here," he said, "we'll find her. And whatever she's up to, we'll stop it."

He reached down and grabbed my hand, the support entirely Eric, and the wash of relief that flooded through me was overpowering. And why not? I needed him on my side and on his game. Because Nadia was bad news for both of us. The last time she was in town, after all, she'd used Eric for demon bait, then strung him up and tried to bleed the life from him. I'd taken it a step further, of course, and shoved a knife through Eric's heart.

I'd brought him back to life, but that didn't change the fact that Nadia—a former Hunter gone bad—pretty much topped my shit list.

Ten

As it always does, Monday arrived on the heels of Sunday, and after what I could only think of as a wild and unpredictable weekend, we fell back into routine. Better than routine, actually, because now that Mindy and Allie were walking the best-friend path again, I didn't have to drive Allie to school. Laura gained that honor.

"We need to start the carpool up again," Laura said, but I shook my head and made a sign of the cross as if warding off evil. For years, we'd had a neighborhood carpool going, but little by little the riders were dwindling away, schedules altered by pre-class band practice or post-class musical rehearsals. After several rocky attempts at coordinating, I pulled out, practicing what all those self-help books recommend: the power of saying no. Considering that I had a toddler, a teenager, and a constant flood of demons, I had more than enough juggling on my hands, and driving my own daughter—and only my daughter—to school seemed like a fair and reasonable decision.

Naturally, I'd felt like a selfish, guilty bitch.

At the time, Mindy had been going to school early and coming home late. Not only had it driven Laura crazy, but it had meant that our girls hadn't ridden together. Once Mindy was past rehearsals for the musical, the rift between them had widened and they still weren't riding together. Now that the rift had healed, I wasn't sure what I was more happy about—that my daughter had her best friend back, or that I no longer had to drive her every single day.

Laura, thank goodness, had that honor today, and although I'd asked her to come over and help me research after she dropped the girls off, she'd said she couldn't this morning.

Actually, she'd gone a bit pink, looked down at the cup of coffee we were sharing while the girls got themselves organized, and said she had some things she needed to do beforehand, but that she'd meet me at three-thirty to help with Allie's party planning.

"What's going on?" I'd asked, and she'd blushed even pinker.

"Nothing. Honest. It's nothing. If it turns into something, I'll tell you, but until then, I'm— Oh, hell, I'm going to go take the girls to school." And then she'd left, leaving me baffled. I ran through a mental list of possibilities, and decided the odds were that she was getting back together with Dr. Hunk. And although I was desperately, pruriently curious, I also knew she'd tell me in her own sweet time.

In the meantime, my focus needed to be on demons. And on toddlers, I thought, smiling down at the little boy playing with his trucks on the kitchen floor. My *clean* kitchen floor, which was amazing in and of itself. But, yes, the house was still spotless, having been scrubbed clean with Stuart's help yesterday before the party. Well, the downstairs anyway. The children's rooms and their bathroom were still a wreck, but since we hadn't reached a point that would require the health department to step in, I decided not to worry about it.

Stuart had left early for the office and then a run-through of the mansion, so I was on my own watching Timmy. I tossed some of his trucks in a laundry basket, then picked up both the basket and the boy and headed upstairs.

Our attic is of the *Brady Bunch* variety, the kind that is accessed through a door and stairs rather than some annoying pull-down ladder. The room is finished as well, with drywall over the insulation, though we'd never bothered with paint or anything other than plywood flooring.

For years, I'd secretly kept my old hunting trunk up there, with my additional equipment tucked away in the storage shed. Now that my secret was no longer secret, my entire arsenal of weapons and books was up here, with the added bonus that they didn't have to be concealed.

I spent fifteen minutes moving daggers, crossbows, and swords back into locked cabinets so that Timmy would have a nice safe area in which to drive his trucks, and then I opened one of the boxes of Eric's old books. Allie had already been up here, and she'd taken an entire box down to her room. Her reports so far had been limited to an announcement that she "couldn't find a dang thing," and I hoped that I'd have better luck.

The leather-bound books were musty and fragile, and as I pulled out the top one, tiny bits of desiccated leather stuck to my fingertips. I sat the book carefully on the floor and began to slowly flip pages, forcing myself to concentrate on the words and not let my mind wander.

Research had never been my strong suit; that had always been Eric's thing, and now I had to wonder if he really had enjoyed research, or if he'd simply been desperate to find his own answers.

Answers that weren't, I realized, in the book I was reviewing.

I carefully pulled out another, and then another, both of which I managed to review before Timmy got restless and begged for me to play "truck" with him. Since truck requires me to lay flat and still and pretend to be a massive highway system, this wasn't the kind of game I could play while multitasking. And though I tried to convince him that he really didn't want to play that game, he was not to be deterred.

"Ten minutes," I said, and he jumped up and down, holding up both hands, fingers splayed, and shouting, "Ten, ten, ten!" at the top of his lungs.

Five minutes into it, I heard Eddie's familiar tread on the stairs into the attic, then grimaced as he peered into the room, his grin wide, as Timmy drove a truck up my arm, over my chest, and then down toward my belly button.

"Heh," Eddie said, as I scowled in his general direction.

"Take my place," I said. "And then let's see if you laugh."

"You're missing the humor, girl," he said. "What's funny is that you're down there and I'm not." He whipped off a little salute. "And now I'm off to work. Tonight we can talk about whatever you find in those books. Assuming you ever get off your back and look again."

"Very funny. Now go."

He went, and I heard his chuckle all the way down the stairs.

I gave Timmy an extra five minutes of using Mommy as a highway, then sat up, to his extreme and vocal displeasure. "Mommy's gotta work, kiddo."

"NOOOOOO!!" he wailed "Play truck. PLAY. TRUCK!"

At which point I had to either give in and play, or stick to my guns and work.

I chose the middle ground and carried him downstairs for a bribe of a banana and Teddy Grahams.

"I love you, Mommy," he said, trucks forgotten now that his face was all smeary with fruit and chocolate crumbs.

"I love you, too, munchkin," I said, hauling him from his chair into my lap. I wrapped my arms tight around him and buried my nose in his thick mop hair. I breathed deep of the clean scent of baby shampoo and tried to rid my mind of the memory of that bitch holding my baby's head. Honestly, I couldn't bear it, nor could I stomach the thought that she might be gunning for my family.

"Too tight, Mommy!"

"Sorry, kiddo," I said, and loosened my grip. But I had an idea. A little idea, but it might give me some peace of mind.

"What we do, Mommy? What we do?" Timmy asked as I stood up.

"We're getting dressed," I said. "And then we're going to go have a chat with our friendly neighborhood James Bond."

Eyes Only sits at the southern end of the Promenade, between a coffee shop and a candy store. Timmy and I hit both of them, coffee to fuel me and candy to fuel the kid. Then we pushed open the mirrored door to the spy shop and found Eddie standing behind the counter, his eyes going wide when he saw us.

He recovered quickly enough and snorted. "Look who's here."

"So it's true." I looked around, took in the various spy accoutrements.

"Oughta be a detective," he said. "What you doing? Tailing me?"

"You gave Allie the walkies," I said. "And Eric saw you in here one day. Wasn't too hard to figure it out."

He shrugged.

"Why didn't you tell me?"

He snorted. "Man's gotta have his secrets, right?"

I blinked, baffled. "Out of everything we know about each other, you're keeping secret the fact that you work in a spy shop?"

"I'm old and eccentric," he said. "You need more explanation than that?"

"No," I admitted. "I think that about covers it."

"So you here because you got curious? Or 'cause you need something."

"Both," I said, then pointed to Timmy. "Can you track him?"

"What? You mean like put something on him? Have him swallow a radioactive isotope. Direct a satellite to this location?"

I blinked, not certain if he was serious, or if he'd been watching too many movies on his new television.

"Ha!" he said. "Gotcha."

"Very funny. Seriously, I want to know my kid's safe. You got anything like a LoJack for kiddos?"

"That I can do," he said. He came out from behind the counter and moved through the store with more efficiency than I'd ever seen him move through the house. After a few minutes, he'd put quite a little pile on the counter and gestured me over for a closer look.

"All of these will work," he said. "This one here's designed for kiddos," he said, holding up a small pin shaped like a ladybug. "Designed for if you lose your kid in the store, though, so it's not got much range. This one's not as cute, but it's probably more like what you want." He pulled out a black bracelet. "Whaddya think, kiddo? Wanna wear jewelry?"

Timmy's arm enthusiastically shot out, and as soon as I gave a nod, Eddie fastened it onto Timmy's arm. "There you go," he said, then passed me the other half of the kit and showed me how to work the various controls in order to trigger a panic alarm and a GPS locater. By the time I shoved everything into a complimentary Eyes Only tote bag, I was feeling both high-tech and confident.

"You getting one for Allie, too?"

"Allie's a badass Demon Hunter, Eddie, or hadn't you heard? And badass Demon Hunters don't agree to be tagged."

"Whoever said she had to agree?" He disappeared under the counter and came back out with a tiny box that he opened to reveal a minuscule metallic dot. "And whoever said Hollywood got it wrong?"

I looked down at the little dot, met Eddie's gleaming eyes, and smiled.

The Palace Theater is four blocks from Eddie's spy shop, and I filled the distance with a leisurely stroll, stopping in various stores, including a jewelry store where I found a beautiful silver and glass pendant onto which I could stick the microdot without it being visible. I tucked it away, planning to present it to her on Friday at her birthday party.

As soon as we neared the theater, Timmy yanked his hand out of mine and raced forward, screaming for Allie, who had just barreled out the front door with Thomas Marks, the manager, strolling behind her, his expression both tolerant and amused.

"Mom!" she cried, swinging Timmy up onto her hip. "It is so cool. I didn't have any idea how cool when I picked it, but it is so freaking cool!"

"Considering we've already put down the deposit, I'm glad to hear that. Tom, it's good to see you again," I added, extending my hand to his to shake. "Thanks for letting us come by. I wanted my friend Laura to see the inside, too, since she's my decorating guru. She'll be here any minute."

"Not a problem," he said. "We love showing off the theater. And you lucked out, too. Usually, we provide a two-hour window before events for decorating, but in your case, we'll have a work crew in here on Thursday afternoon, which means you can pick up the key anytime after five and take your time fixing the place up."

"This is so totally going to rock," Allie said, stepping back until she was actually in the street between two parallel-parked cars.

Built during the Hollywood heyday, the theater was a showcase for all the bells and whistles, pomp and circumstance that had been included in moving picture venues back then. The exterior boasted an art deco style with accents ranging from Egyptian (hieroglyphs etched into marble columns) to Gothic (the gargoyles that peered down from the rooftop). A stand-alone ticket booth sat flush with the sidewalk, its gold highlights gleaming in the sun. Someone on Thomas's team had put a mannequin in the ticket taker's seat, a jaunty usher's-style hat in red velvet with gold cording on her head, the design matching the uniform in which she'd been dressed.

Above the ticket booth—and just under the gargoyles—an old fashioned marquee announced the theater's availability for private parties. On Friday, though Allie didn't yet know it, that marquee would be filled with a special birthday message, and I couldn't wait to see her eyes when she saw her name up in lights.

An outdoor waiting area filled the space behind the ticket booth, customers kept out of the elements while they waited for the previous show's patrons to exit by a black marble overhang dotted with tiny lights, so that at night the illumination from the lights simulated a starry sky. Those stars shone down on San Diablo. Or, more particularly, on the map of 1924 San Diablo laid out in marble under the waiting patrons' feet.

And, of course, on either side of the patrons were walls of glass display cases, showing past and upcoming movies. Thanks to Laura and her computer-goddess best-friend qualities, by Friday evening those cases would be filled with posters of Allie, each showing her at a different age, from babyhood up to just shy of fifteen years.

My step hesitated as the reality struck me—my baby was growing up.

"I always knew they'd only grow in one direction. I just never expected fast-forward."

I turned to find Laura standing beside me, with Mindy bounding past to catch up with Allie. Thomas was holding one of the glass doors open, patiently waiting for me to get with the program. I did, matching Laura's step as she headed inside. "I could just ground her until she's twenty-one. Keep her inside. Keep her my baby."

"You could," Laura agreed mildly. "But you don't really want to."

No, I didn't. My little girl was growing up, and doing it well. And damned if that didn't make me proud.

It also made me want to cry, which was a little embarrassing with Thomas looking on.

"Right," I said, snapping out of it. I turned to Thomas. "You've got things to do, and we need to get the lay of the land and figure out what to buy for decorations. Do you need to stay with us, or can we wander?"

"Wander all you want," he said. "Let me just show you a few highlights." We started in the lobby, with Thomas pointing out the main entertainment center, from which we could pipe music into the rest of the theater. "And, of course, you can use the concession stand however you want." It was empty now, but I saw from the gleam in Laura's eyes that she had big plans for it.

"What?" she said, catching me eyeing her. "Put out a few party favors, some extra snacks. We could even sell them. Optional, of course," she added when she saw my raised eyebrows.

"But that's a great idea," Allie put in. "'Cause I already told everyone that I didn't want presents and that we were gonna put together a basket for charity. I'm thinking literacy, you know? So if we sell extra snacks and silly party favors, then all that money can go to the literacy fund, too." She nodded firmly to Laura and then turned to me. "What do you think?"

"I think you're an exceptional kid," I said, feeling a little like the Grinch when his heart swelled in the end.

"Exceptional enough to get a car on my next birthday?"

"No," I said, "but nice try."

She harrumphed, but her heart wasn't in it, and she and Mindy flounced off to explore the rest of the theater.

Laura and I followed more leisurely. The inside was exceptional, with gold leaf over plaster carvings showing angels and lions and birds surrounding the stage, which was set up for either movies or live performances. Six boxes protruded over the audience, three on each side, and in the back a balcony looked down on the action. Once filled with seats, the balcony area was now a dance floor, and Stuart and I had arranged for a DJ to be tucked in a corner and play the days' popular music, as well as a few oldies to satisfy the grown-ups.

While Laura wandered around taking snapshots, I headed onto the actual stage, looking up at the intricate system of flies and counterweights. Allie and Mindy were in the audience, and though I couldn't see them, I could hear them, currently engaged in an involved discussion of the proper proportion of games to disorganized mingling required for the ultimate party. That quickly shifted to the guests, and Allie's excited announcement that Charlie had agreed to come.

I frowned, trying to remember if I knew Charlie, and couldn't help but smile when Allie trilled on and on about how he'd actually asked her to tell him her favorite color. I was still smiling when something lashed out and caught me across the neck, slamming me back against the wall. An arm. And it was attached to a woman.

"Hello, Kate," she said. "You're looking well."

"Hello, Nadia," I said, slipping my hand into my purse and curling my fingers around my knife. "I'd say it's nice to see you, but I'd be lying."

She stepped back, her laughter low and silky. She looked much the same as she had the last time I'd seen her—sexy as hell and absolutely lethal.

"Shall I call Allie back here? Give her a little kiss, too? Honestly, it's hardly been any time at all, but already she's so grown up." She leaned in close, her mouth close to my ear. "But here's the big question for you. Is she more like Mommy or Daddy? Darkness or light?"

"Any closer, and you're going to feel my knife in your eye," I said, hatred pounding in my chest. "You hang with the demons, you damn well better bet I'm going to treat you like one."

Her hand went to her mouth, fingers covering pursed lips. "Why, Kate, I'm shocked. Such strong language. What would your children think?"

"You want strong language? I'll be happy to demonstrate some for you," I said, taking a step closer, and gratified to see she took a corresponding step back.

"Tsk-tsk," she said, her eyes burning into mine. "So serious. Calm yourself, dearest. There's no need for fisticuffs. Not yet, anyway. I'm only here to deliver a message."

"Is that a fact?" I shifted, my knife hand at the ready. "What's the message?"

Nadia glanced down at my knife, sighed a little. "After all we've been through, and you don't trust me. It saddens me, Kate."

"Message, Nadia."

"It's for Eric," she said. "Not for you. Tell him she's waiting. Tell him she's wanting."

"Who?" I snapped. "Who is she?"

"Tut, tut, Kate. Aren't you the inquisitive little one?"

"I'm warning you, Nadia."

"You? Warn me? I'm shaking. I'm positively petrified." She leaned back and smiled. "But there's no need to threaten. All will be revealed in good time. And until then, I think we should avoid playing Twenty Questions, don't you?" I remained silent, seething, and she cocked her head, as if just realizing something. "Isn't it ironic that when I was here last I was trying to put a demon inside him. Silly of me, since there was already one in there with him." Her brow furrowed even as my hand tightened around my knife. "I wonder if they would have duked it out in there. Bam! Bam!" she said, jabbing out with her fists. "Honestly, it would have been something different in the demon trade. Usually all we see is the same old, same old."

"Not true, Nadia," I said. "I get to see pathetic, simpering bitches like you, who've taken the skills *Forza* gave them and turned them on their ass, and for what? Some fake sense of power? You're an idiot, Nadia. And more, I don't like you."

"Oh, now I'm hurt, truly, and on so many levels. Honestly, how do I respond? Let's try this," she said, her voice hardening. "One, I do not simper. Ever. Two, my power is not fake. Three, my IQ puts me significantly higher than the idiot range, and I'm confident I've made the most of my superior intellect. As for the bitch comment, I'll cop to that. It's part of my charm."

"Whatever you're up to," I said, "you're not going to manage."

"Is that a fact? And I suppose you have time to stop me while you're running around like a headless chicken trying to figure out how to save Eric from something he doesn't want stopped anyway."

"Get out," I said, her words pissing me off more than they should.

"Does darling daughter know? Maybe I should tell her." She took a sideways step, as if she was going to call out for Allie, and I took a forward step, to keep her from doing just that.

What I hadn't expected, but should have, was the leg that whipped out and caught me across the chest as I approached. She knocked me back, then was on top of me before I could blink. She grabbed me by the collar, pressed a kiss to my forehead, and then shoved me back so hard I was certain a Kate-shaped imprint would show in the backstage wall.

"Mom!" Allie called as I bounced forward, determined to get in a blow of my own. But she was gone. She was gone, and I'd been whipped, but good. *"Mom!"* Allie called again, rushing toward me. "What happened?"

"What?" I scoped out the room, searching for Nadia, but she'd disappeared.

"Your forehead," Allie said. "Is that blood?" She rubbed her finger on my forehead, then looked at it, her brow crinkling in confusion. "Lipstick?"

I considered making something up, then decided she had the right to know. She had a history with Nadia, after all. The bitch had started out as hero material to my daughter and nosedived to a position of utter contempt. If anyone deserved to know that Nadia was back, I thought, it was Allie.

She tensed when I told her, her entire body going stiff and her hands clenching into fists at her sides.

"Who's Nadia?" Mindy asked.

"The queen bee bitch of all time," Allie said, and when I didn't bother to chastise her about the language, Mindy's eyes went wide.

"Wow. So it's, like, personal, huh?"

"Yeah," I said. "You could say that."

"It makes sense, though," Allie said. "I mean if anyone's going to work for some hotshot She-Demon, it would be Nadia."

"You have a point," I agreed, as thoughts of Eric and Nadia and vengeful She-Demons filled my mind.

Honestly, I missed the days when all I had to do was go out and hunt demons.

Nowadays, everything was too damn personal.

Eleven

I spent the rest of Monday alternating between reading through Eric's old books and trying to get in touch with the man himself. Unfortunately, I was having absolutely no luck on either front. And although the inability to find anything in the books bothered me, the lack of communication with Eric was making me positively frantic, especially now that I knew the She-Demon was "waiting" and "wanting." For all I knew, she wasn't waiting anymore, and Eric was being quiet because the demon inside had taken over, and now it was off on holiday with She-Ra.

By Tuesday morning, my nerves were positively raw, and although I told myself I needed to keep the faith, I feared that I'd lost Eric before we'd even had a chance to save him.

"Give it a rest," Eddie said, as I dialed Eric's number for the five hundred and seventy-fifth million time. He downed one last slug of coffee as Rita honked three times outside our front door. "He's probably out boinking some other woman. Probably Nadia, eh? She sure as hell wanted to boink him last time, and what red-blooded male wouldn't want to take a bounce on her?" He glanced toward Stuart as if for help. Stuart, being the smart guy that he is, ignored Eddie, turning instead to me.

"If this is it," Stuart said, "we'll deal with it. We'll figure it out. And you will be okay."

I nodded, not worried about me, but about Eric. Worried that if this was it, then I was going to have to shove a dagger through the eye of a man that I loved.

And, yes, worried that if that was what I needed to do, that I'd be unable to bring myself to do it.

"You're going to worry yourself sick," Stuart said, getting up and brushing a hand over my hair. He kissed my head, then tilted it back so he could look in my eyes. "Don't make it worse in your head than it really is."

Good advice. The same kind of good advice I'd probably dish out to my kids. And yet I was finding it damn hard to take it.

With a promise that I could reach him anytime, Stuart rushed out, hurrying to meet Bernie and a bevy of craftsmen who were descending on the mansion with a flurry of bids

Allie had already left for school with Laura, Timmy was parked on the sofa watching *Dora the Explorer*, and I was lost in the kitchen with my fears and Eric's phone numbers on speed dial.

To distract myself, I returned to the attic and brought down a stack of Eric's books. I spread them out over the table, making silent deals with myself—review one hundred pages and make a call to Eric's cell, another hundred pages and I could call his home. Finish a stack of five books and I'd call from Stuart's private line in the study. The one with the caller ID block, just in case Eric was avoiding my phone numbers.

By Tuesday afternoon, I'd dialed Eric's home and cell phone numbers so many times and from so many phones my speed-dial finger had a callous, and my voice was raw from leaving pleading messages for him to call me.

Completely frantic, I finally broke down and called Stuart to tell him how worried I was, and the fact that Stuart didn't hesitate before dropping whatever project he was working on at the mansion was a testament to how much the fear had crept into my voice. It was he who suggested we drop Timmy at Laura's and then go by Eric's apartment. "We'll look," he said, reasonably. "And maybe then we'll know what's really going on."

Neither of us spoke on the way; how could we with the thickness of my fear sucking up all the useable air in the car? And as soon as Stuart pulled up in front of the building, I was out the door and running up the stairs.

"He's not answering," I told Stuart when he joined me outside Eric's door. I'm not entirely sure why that surprised me. I hadn't really figured he'd be in. After all, Eric was a thorough man, and if he was avoiding me, I would expect him to do a good job of it.

"Do you have a key?" Stuart asked. I nodded, then saw a flicker of something that might be pain flash in his eyes.

"He gave it to me for Allie," I said, pushed by a need to explain.

"It doesn't matter," he said. "Just open the door."

I wanted to argue until the chill left his voice—even red-hot anger was better than the ice I heard—but now wasn't the time. I slipped the key in the lock, tried to turn it, and found that it didn't do a damn thing.

I looked at Stuart and shrugged. "Apparently I was mistaken. I don't have a key after all."

"Back door?"

I shook my head. "Sliding glass, no outside lock, and we're on the third floor."

"Then we break the window," he said. "And hope he doesn't have an alarm."

He took off his shirt, wrapped it around his hand, and smashed in the side window. Then he carefully pushed the shards of glass away, unlocked the window, and shoved up the sash. "Back in a minute," he said, then disappeared inside while I stood there alternating between feeling extraneous and being impressed with Stuart's breaking-and-entering skills.

He opened the door for me and I stepped inside. The apartment smelled musty, as if it had been closed up for days after someone cooked onions, and my nose wrinkled as I poked around, rifling through Eric's papers as I tried to find something—anything—that would give me a sense of where he was right then. And of how far out the demon had pushed.

Unfortunately, Eric was not in the habit of keeping a diary about his battle with his demonic internal foe, which meant that I did not find a conveniently detailed story. Nor were there clues scribbled on pieces of paper left casually by the bedside.

In other words, I found not one of the types of clues that were regularly discovered by heroes and heroines on television and in the movies. Feeling cheated, I began to look deeper, digging through his clothing drawers and poking my fingers between his mattress and box spring.

"Anything?" Stuart asked.

I started to shake my head, but as I did, I noticed a floor vent with a loose screw and very little dust on that part of the floor. "Hang on," I said, then bent down to peer at it. "There's something in here."

As Stuart bent down beside me, I loosened the screw with my fingers and pulled off the vent cover. A spiral-bound notebook was inside, like the kind a student might use in math class.

"What's in it?" Stuart asked.

I flipped through the pages, my mouth going dry as I did.

Page after page was covered with intricate, detailed sketches of a double-bladed dagger, an ornately carved hilt in the middle. "It's the dagger," I said, looking up to face my husband. "It's Eric's sketches of a dagger he swore that he'd not only never seen, but that he'd never even discovered a clue as to its looks or its whereabouts."

"Huh," Stuart said, glancing at the spiral with what could only be described as false casualness. "From the looks of that, I'm inclined to say he lied."

"Yeah," I said, wishing desperately for another explanation, but finding none. "I know."

"It doesn't necessarily mean he has the dagger," Laura said. Stuart and I had spent another hour trying to find either Eric or more clues. We'd failed, and I'd put on a facade of false cheer so that he wouldn't feel compelled to hang around and hold my hand. Instead, I waited until he was back out the door, let the facade drop, and headed over to Laura's to retrieve my little boy and wallow in coffee and sympathy. So far, the wallowing was working well, and the grape Popsicle Timmy was sucking on was keeping him quiet and happy.

"Maybe he's seen it in dreams," Laura continued. "You said he has them sometimes, right? And he can't remember them?"

"Lately he's been remembering," I said, thinking about the sexual dreams he'd described to me.

"But not all. Maybe he doesn't even know about the vent. Maybe you snatched the demon's notebook and Eric doesn't know about it at all."

"Maybe," I agreed. "Or maybe he knows damn well what's going on and he's holed up in a cheap motel somewhere screwing Nadia's brains out as they walk through every one of those dreams he's been having lately." I balled up my napkin and tossed it across the room. It landed softly, without the kind of crash and blast that would have eased off some of my frustration.

"Want a brick?" Laura asked.

"If I thought you'd let me," I admitted, "I'd say yes."

"Sorry. I'm probably going to redecorate, but I'm not for certain. Maybe later we can go to the mansion and demolish a countertop or something."

At that I did laugh, and that simple act alone had me feeling better. "Do you think he is with her?" I asked. "With Nadia?"

"I don't know what to think," Laura admitted. "It is weird, though. Why didn't Nadia kill you? I mean, she had you, right? You said she jumped out of nowhere and surprised you. So why'd she even talk? Why not just whack you?"

"Thanks," I said. "Just the kind of thing I want to think about."

"It's a legitimate question," she said with an apologetic shrug. "I may not be able to whack the demons, but I do what I can. And that includes asking the hard questions."

"So it was either for old times' sake," I said, "or for some specific purpose."

"Keep you alive for something," she said. "But what?"

"You're the research gal."

"Probably a ceremony. Every time we turn around, there's a ceremony. I'll see what I can figure out."

I glanced at the clock and frowned, amazed at how much of the day had already flown by. "I promised Stuart I'd go by the mansion and put in a few hours, and Allie's meeting us there after her session with Cutter. Want to come, too?"

Pink tinged Laura's cheeks. "No thanks. I'm, uh, busy. But Mindy's going. They've totally crossed back over the bridge to normal."

"I know. Thank goodness. I'm not sure about the rules. Would we have been allowed to stay friends if our girls were feuding?"

"Absolutely," Laura said with a wicked grin. "We'd each be spies for the other side."

I laughed, then pushed back from the table. "I better get going."

"Hang on," she said, then jumped to her feet. Before I could ask what was up, she trotted out of the room, then trotted back a few minutes later with a mailing tube. "This is only the first one, but I wanted you to see it."

"Me see! Me see!" Timmy reached out as Laura opened the tube and slid what looked like a poster out.

"Not with purple Popsicle hands you don't," I said as Laura yanked it up and out of reach.

His little face turned red with displeasure. "Me. See. Too!!!"

"Go wash your hands and then you can see," I said, to which he responded by licking the purple off his fingers.

"All done!" he said, holding out his hands, fingers splayed wide.

"I don't think so, buddy," I said, then scooped him up around the tummy and hauled him over to the sink. He laughed and clapped and shoved his fingers under the stream, managing to splatter the front of my shirt with water. I plunked him on the floor, handed him a towel, and we both headed back to the table.

Laura had unrolled the poster and was using a salt-and-pepper shaker along with a creamer bowl and a trivet to hold down the four corners. I took one look at the poster and gasped. "Laura," I said. "Oh my God. You're wonderful."

"You think so?" she said, cocking her head to examine her handiwork. A full-size poster with a pink background and a collage of images. My little girl, from her first day in the hospital to a recent shot of her in Cutter's studio, her leg up in the air in the perpetual capture of a crescent kick, and two dozen photos showing stages in between.

I dragged my fingers over Allie's face, and looked up at

Laura feeling sappily sentimental. "Fifteen years," I whispered, even as I sat down and pulled Timmy into my lap, only half-listening as he started humming. I never thought my kids could outdo the fascination and love I'd felt that first time I'd held each of them, but every day, it grows. "Hard to believe what children can do to you," I said to Laura. "And it's almost scary how much your heart is at risk."

"Definitely scary," Laura said. "But worth it."

I hugged Timmy so close and so tight that he stopped his rendition of the *Wonder Pets* theme song. Soft arms went around my neck and he hugged me close. And, because I'm a sentimental sap, I started to cry.

"I did it!" Mindy screeched as the dagger flew from her hand to lodge in the drywall of the mansion's entrance hall. "Did you see? Did you see? I totally did it!"

"That's great," I said, while Allie gave her a hug. "Keep practicing and you'll be able to do it every time." That, I thought, was saying a lot, especially when you considered they'd been at this for an hour, and Mindy had managed to lodge only one knife in the drywall. More often, the hilt had banged uselessly against the wall, and then the blade had fallen harmlessly to the ground.

"Just remember," Allie added, trotting over to pull the blade out of the dented and sliced wall, "it's all in the wrist." She aimed and let the dagger fly, landing it neatly in the middle of the circle they'd drawn on the drywall with one of Stuart's work pencils.

"Wow," Mindy said. "This really is pretty cool."

I turned away, smiling at the pleased expression on Allie's face, then moved to the far side of the foyer to check on Timmy in the library. The room that had been empty only an hour earlier was now filled with an assortment of toy cars and building blocks, and there was my little boy, passed out on the floor amid what appeared to be an abstract artist's rendering of the Los Angeles highway system. He had Boo Bear, his bedraggled blue bear, clutched tight in his arms, and I could hear his soft little snores. I smiled, then stepped back quietly in time to see Stuart coming down the stairs, a clipboard in his hand, and a frown on his face.

"Problem?"

He shook his head absently. "Water leak in the master bathroom. We're going to have to replace the pipes, the dry-wall, and probably retile the floor."

"Oh." Since I had no idea if that was in or out of the budget, I wasn't sure what else to say. "Um."

He laughed. "It's okay. I'm just doing an inventory of the work. So far, there's a lot of it."

"Ah," I said, glancing toward the seriously battered wall that had become the focus of target practice.

"Don't worry," he said. "I already told them it's okay."

"Good," I said, as Allie rolled her eyes.

"Like we'd just run around throwing knives at things without asking first."

"I apologize for impugning your good sense," I said, causing another more dramatic eye roll from my daughter.

"At any rate," Stuart said, doing a valiant job of ignoring us, "I wanted to run through some paint swatches with you."

"Yeah?" I said, mildly pleased. "With me?"

"I'll get a second opinion on whatever we pick out."

"Thanks a lot," I said, but not really insulted. Considering I had no confidence in my overall decorating taste, a second opinion was a damn good idea.

He held the paint chips like a hand of cards, then held them up toward the wall. "Something off-white for this room, I think," he said, and I nodded. The entrance hall was magnificent, with a gray marble floor, a polished mahogany staircase, and floor-to-ceiling windows. A crystal chandelier above broke the light into thousands of dancing dots of color.

"Off-white works," I said. "Anything more would take away from the room and the light."

He kissed me on the nose. "Perfect."

"So when are we going to paint?"

"We're not, actually. I took the liberty of hiring someone."

I gaped. "But Stuart. The budget."

"He's working for a flat two hundred a day. Painting. Tiling. Whatever we need. All we need to do is provide the materials."

I gaped at him. "You're kidding, right? That's practically theft. And you checked the guy out? Maybe he's a demon looking for a sneaky way to infiltrate himself into our lives." Okay, that was stretching. Demons weren't that sneaky as a rule. And while the idea of a demon laying tile might amuse me, the idea didn't reek of reality.

"Not everything has to do with demons," Stuart assured me. "This is about giving a young guy a solid start. He works on a house like this, it's going to help make his reputation. And I told him he could put a sign in our yard. *Tile and Woodwork by Joe* kind of thing."

"His name's Joe?"

"Joe Martin," he said. "He's Pete's nephew. Nineteen years old, spent the last year working odd construction, wants to angle his way into high-end remodels, general contracting. I told him that if the price was right, I'd help him out."

"And the price was definitely right," I said.

"Don't knock it. He's getting fair compensation. At his age, advertising and word-of-mouth are everything."

Behind us, the entrance doors flew open. I whipped around, my free hand reaching for the knife hidden in my jacket sleeve, then stopped when I saw Lila Dorsey, looking much like Dorothy from *The Wizard of Oz* with a picnic basket over her arm.

"Look at you all! Working so hard. I brought snacks," she said, setting the basket down on the tiled foyer floor. "Where's Bernie?"

"L.A.," Stuart said. "He found a discount flooring supplier, and he's gone to check out the quality."

She sniffed and shook her head. "Honestly, the man carries a cell phone. You'd think he could use it to call me every once in a while. Never mind. He'll just miss out."

She whipped a thin blanket out of the basket and spread it on the floor, then started pulling what appeared to be an endless supply of fruits and cheeses and sparkling waters out of the basket. "Well, come on. It's time for a little break."

Allie and Mindy needed no further prodding, and I have to admit that the thought of something cold and sparkly to drink was more than appealing.

"Do you knit?" Lila asked, glancing toward the basket of yarn and knitting needles that I'd completely forgotten about.

"That would be Allie," I said, my sweet smile toward my daughter earning me one very firm scowl.

"How nice," Lila said. "And I'd be happy to teach you, too, Kate."

"Mom would love that," Allie put in, before I had a chance to decline Lila's invitation. "She's always telling me how much she wants to learn."

"My mom, too," Mindy said, as she and Allie caught each other's eyes and then burst out into peals of laughter.

Lila looked at me, confused, and I managed a bright smile. "Teenagers," I said, as if that explained everything. From the knowing look on Lila's face, I began to think that maybe it did.

As Stuart settled in beside me, I noticed a shadow pass

in front of the door that Lila had left open. I tensed, then exhaled with relief as Eric stepped into view.

Beside me, Stuart remained tense, and I had to silently admit that I'd relaxed too soon. Eric had been missing for more than a day. For all I knew, he wasn't even Eric anymore.

Wary, I climbed to my feet, shooting glances to Stuart that I hoped made clear that he needed to stay down and silent.

"What's up?" I asked, aware of Lila's silent curiosity. I slid my hand over the back of my jeans, reassured by the presence of the switchblade I'd tucked into my back pocket even as I felt guilty for wanting protection from this man.

Eric met my eyes, and for a moment I was certain he could read my mind. Then the moment passed, and I saw a glint of humor. I exhaled slowly in relief, cautiously optimistic. Perhaps we hadn't lost him yet.

He looked from me to Stuart. "I thought one of you might know someone who could repair a broken window," he said. "Seems I had a break-in."

"That's unfortunate," Stuart said smoothly. "But don't worry about it. We're happy to help you get it fixed."

"Good," Eric said, his eyes no longer on me but on my husband. "I figured you could help."

"So if that's it—" I moved forward and took Eric's arm, turning him and aiming him toward the front door.

We stopped cold.

Because right there in the doorway was my old buddy Thor, the World Wrestling Federation demon reject who had attacked Eric and me that very first night.

"I am here," Thor said, with a deep bow to Eric, "to serve you."

Eric's arm tightened protectively on mine, even as he twisted around to face Stuart. "Go," he said.

"I don't think so," Stuart answered, his eyes darting between Thor and Eric.

"Eric?" I asked, my eyes darting from Stuart to the girls, who were standing stock-still on the far side of the room, Allie positioned in front of Mindy, the knife they'd been throwing tight in her hand. Behind them, I could see Timmy, asleep on the library floor.

Not good. This was so very not good.

"It's okay," Eric said. "It's okay, I swear. Trust me."

I drew in a breath, saw the confusion on Lila's face, and made a decision, hoping to hell it wasn't the wrong one. "Didn't you have something you needed to show Lila upstairs?" I asked Stuart, forcing a smile. "Why don't you go on? I can deal with this contractor by myself."

"Kate."

"Contractor?" Lila asked.

"Highly recommended," I said, forcing a smile. "Go on. Bernie would be so upset if you didn't show that thing to Lila."

He wanted to argue, I could see it on his face. But I shook my head and broadened the smile so much my face hurt. "I've got it under control."

He nodded, and helped Lila to her feet. "She's right. I totally forgot, but Bernie wants your opinion on one of the upstairs rooms, and if we hurry, we can probably still catch him before he leaves the supplier."

"But—But—" Lila sputtered, but she was no match for Stuart who had her up the stairs and out of there. And, bless him, he grabbed a pair of knitting needles on the way. Though how he intended to explain *that* to Lila, I didn't know.

I had my knife in my hand now, and though I kept my eyes on Thor, I spoke to Allie. "Safe room." She wasted no time, just grabbed Mindy's hand and took off.

"Master," Thor said, with a low bow to Eric.

"Out," Eric said. "You can serve me by leaving me the hell alone."

"I serve you," Thor said once again. "And I serve your beloved as well."

Eric cast a sideways look in my direction. "She wants you out of here, too."

The demon's bland, subservient expression shifted into a sneer. "Your *true* beloved, sire. This one is merely a distraction. This one," he said, lunging toward me, "must die."

His motion was so fast, so unexpected, that I barely managed to get clear. As it was, his fingers grazed my shirt as I darted out of his way even as Eric moved in front of me to block the beast.

"Get out of here," Eric said to me. "I've got him."

No way. Even if Eric had been one hundred percent, there was no way I was leaving Timmy. That simply wasn't an option, and so instead of leaving, I shifted on my heel and switched direction, running back toward them, Eric's curses echoing through the foyer. The demon lashed out, knocking Eric out of the way, though he apologized loudly as he did so. Then he dove at me and managed to catch me around the ankles. I went down with a splat, my knife sliding out across the slick marble floor.

I cursed and clawed at the floor, trying to get purchase, but the demon was hauling me back toward him. I relaxed, planning to attack anew once he'd pulled me closer, but before that happened, he let go of me. I flipped over, and realized that Eric had tackled the beast. They were on the floor now, each one struggling for the upper hand.

"Blade!" Eric shouted. "Kate, kick me your blade!"

The knife I'd dropped was right at my feet, and I hesitated only a second. And then, praying that I wasn't reading Eric wrong—praying that this wasn't a demonic ruse to gain my trust—I thrust my leg out and sent the knife skittering across the floor to Eric.

His fingers closed tight around it, and even as Thor screamed out Odayne's name, Eric slid the blade home.

"Don't call me that," he said with a sneer. "The name's Eric. And if you can't remember that, you lousy son of a bitch, you can call me David."

Then he pushed the body off of him, laid back on the tile, and sighed.

I took the time for one quick glance toward the library, saw that Timmy had managed to sleep through the whole thing, then slid across the floor to rest my head in the crook of Eric's arm.

"Thanks," I said.

"You would have handled it."

"Yeah," I agreed. "But I'm glad you were here to do it." I rolled over and propped myself up on my elbow. "I've been worried that I'd lost you."

A sad smile touched his lips, but he shook his head. "Maybe for a little bit you did," he admitted. "I don't really remember."

I hesitated, but knew I had to ask. "Was it Nadia?"

His brow furrowed. "She's really here then?"

"Gave me a message for you." I met his eyes. "She's waiting. And she's wanting." I sat up, then took his hand. "Do you know who? Who this She-Demon is?"

He shook his head, and when his lips curved around the word *no*, I was both disappointed and relieved. Relieved that he hadn't fallen that much further into the abyss, but disappointed he had no new help to give us.

Beside me, he shifted, and I sat straighter, suddenly wary. "What?"

He didn't meet my eyes. "I don't know who she is," he repeated. "But I think I've been with her. Kate, I think that's where I was."

"Oh." I swallowed, hoping he could see how much his words shook me. "Well. That's—"

"Troubling," he suggested.

I almost lied, but knew that I couldn't. Not to him.

"Yes," I said. "But you found your way back." I squeezed his hand hard, pushing down my own fear. "You found your way back, and you're going to hang on."

"I'm back," he admitted, but I didn't like his tone or the way his silver-gray eyes skimmed over me.

"Eric? What is it?"

He didn't have a chance to answer me, though, because Stuart's overly loud voice echoed down from the upstairs. "I'd really like to show you a few more rooms."

"Later," Lila said. "Bernie's not even answering his phone. We'll have our snack, and the upstairs will keep."

"Get him," I hissed to Eric, nodding toward the body. We dragged it toward the kitchen as Stuart's and Lila's footsteps echoed down the stairs.

"I think I left some cutlery in the kitchen the last time I was in here," Lila said, and I sighed with exasperation and looked helplessly at Eric.

He, thank goodness, kept his cool. He opened the cabinet doors under the sink and shoved Thor's head inside. Then he crouched down and started muttering about pipes and fittings.

Lila stepped in, opened up a drawer at the opposite end of the counter, and looked curiously toward Eric.

"Plumber," I said brightly. "We've got a leak."

"We have a lot of them," Stuart said, stepping into the kitchen and immediately into his role. "After he finishes under there, maybe we can have him take a look at the upstairs."

"Great," I said, with a huge smile toward Lila. "I think the girls got distracted. You head on back to the picnic and we'll be right there."

Her smile matched mine, and with a handful of silverware now in her hand, she practically bounced back to the foyer. I sent Stuart a desperate glance, and he followed her out.

"Bring him," I said to Eric, who followed me toward the

safe room, dragging Thor behind him. He dumped him at the threshold, only jumping slightly when Allie squealed "Daddy!" and shot off the bed to hug her father.

I stood there with a body at my feet, no useful help, and a slightly nosy woman in the foyer. "Mindy," I said. "Come give me a hand."

As Allie clung to her dad, Mindy and I dragged the body into the room and then shoved it under the bed. "Sorry," I said to her. "But thanks."

"Are you kidding? That was the coolest. I got to hide a demon. I mean, like wow."

"Wow indeed," I said with a smile. "Come on girls, back to Lila before she gets curious."

Allie nodded, then broke away from Eric, still standing just outside the entrance to the safe room. I frowned, suddenly uncomfortable, and I kept my eyes on him as I stepped out of the safe room as the girls rushed ahead for snacks.

"Thanks," I said, watching his face.

"Not a problem."

"Thor definitely had it in for me." A shadow seemed to cross his face, his silver eyes darkening. "What?" I asked. "Eric, what is it?"

"Nothing," he said, his voice remote. "But he didn't understand."

I swallowed, feeling suddenly cold. "Understand what?"

He smiled, then reached out to stroke my hair. "That you're not to be harmed. That we don't want to harm one single hair on this perfect head."

And then he leaned forward and kissed my forehead. And so help me, for the first time in my life, I shuddered under Eric's touch.

I didn't sleep. Instead, I lay in bed, my forehead seeming to burn under Eric's kiss, and my heart twisting in fear. He'd told me that "we" didn't mean me any harm, but who was "we?" Eric and Odayne? Odayne and his beloved?

And why were they allowing me to remain safe? Out of Eric's love for me? Or was there some other, more nefarious reason?

My fists clenched in the sheets, my mind whirling. What was I supposed to do now that the demon was truly mixed up with Eric? Maybe not completely, but there was no denying that Eric's soul was poisoned, and I was no longer sure there was a way back.

I tossed in bed, and at some point sleep must have come, though it was filled with dreams of fire and knives and Nadia bending close over Eric's naked body. And Eric turning his head to look at me, telling me they wouldn't harm me and that I had to watch, watch, watch as he descended to rule in Hell.

I woke up with a scream caught in my throat, then almost released it when I saw the faces looming over me.

"Dammit! What are you two doing?"

"Nasty dreams?" Eddie said.

"Are you okay?" Allie asked at the same time.

Beside me, Stuart stirred, and I could tell the moment he realized we had company. He stiffened, then sat up. "Kate," he began. "Why is half the household standing over our bed?"

"I haven't got a clue," I said grumpily, but I plumped up the pillow behind my back and sat up to hear the answer to that very question.

"It's Lilith," Allie said. "Lilith's the She-Demon."

I swallowed a gasp and looked at Eddie, who nodded seriously. Lilith is one of the world's oldest and most powerful demons. A creature who existed even before the world was formed. A vengeful female who legend said mated first with Adam, then cursed all men when he bound himself to Eve. "Are you sure?"

Allie nodded. "I've been doing all sorts of research, and I finally found a reference to Odayne and a lover."

My gaze shifted back to Eddie, and he shrugged.

"*Forza* doesn't know anything about this," I said.

"Yeah. I know. I found it in some online role-playing games."

"Allie!"

"No, it's good information," she protested. "I contacted the guy who plays under Odayne's name. And he's like some theology buff. Got a Ph.D. and everything. And he did all this research and found these love poems. Only they weren't really poems. They were more like prayers. But not to God. They were to Lilith, and he said he found them in the archives of some disbanded satanic cult. At least that's what he thought, but it turned out not to be satanic at all. It was goddess worship. Only not a benevolent god. It was a cult that worshipped Lilith."

I was staring open-mouthed at my daughter. "You found all this out by going to online gaming sites?"

She shrugged. "*Forza*'s not the only group out there that knows stuff about demons."

"She's a smart kid," Eddie said, giving her a gruff hug.

"That she is," Stuart muttered.

"So what did these poems or prayers say?"

"That's just it," Allie said. "They were prayers for the safe return of her beloved."

"I thought Lilith's whole thing was that she had no use for men," I said.

Allie shrugged. "Guess she found one she could stand, 'cause the poems were more like love songs, you know? About how Lilith and her mate were one, and each was the heart and soul of the other. Sappy stuff, but creepy, too. And a little bit sad, even, because he was gone, you know? Trapped. I'm not really sure how, but bound I guess. Like the time Andramelech was bound in Solomon's Stone," she added, referring to a vile demon who had been trapped inside a stone that God had once given to Solomon. The stone had eventually been cut down and placed in a ring, and now that ring was safe inside the Vatican. "But the poems mention her mate's name. And it's Odayne. And I guess Lilith is, you know, like really in love with him."

"Lilith and Odayne," I said, as ice-cold fear shimmered through my veins. This was worse—much worse—than Eric merely having a demon trapped inside. Now he had a demon inside that one of the most vile and powerful demons in history wanted released.

"You did great work, sweetie," I said, smiling despite my fear. "Amazing work."

"Thanks," she said, preening.

"Now I need you to go check on your brother."

Her smile faded. "Why?"

"Because I think I hear him."

"I don't."

"Then I think you need to go get dressed for school," I said.

"It's still early."

"Allie." I injected a warning into my voice.

"God! If you want to get rid of me just say so!"

"I want to get rid of you," I said, then saw the temper flare in her eyes.

"That's so unfair!" she wailed. "I figure this stuff out and I don't even get to hang for the planning session. I'm not a kid! I'm fifteen!"

"Not until Friday, you're not."

I waited for her to make some sarcastic comment, but none came. Instead, she stormed away, muttering.

As soon as she was out the door, Eddie turned serious eyes on me. "We need to find that dagger," he said. "And we need to find it soon."

"Forget the dagger," Stuart said. "If we can't find it, we

take that demon out the old-fashioned way. A knife through the eye."

"He'll just come back," Eddie said. "Born into someone else."

"Forgive me if I'm more worried about my family than someone else's future problem."

Eddie nodded. "We look for the dagger," he said. "And if we don't find it, we do it your way."

"Either way, Eric's dead and trapped," I said. "His soul will be tied to this demon for eternity. There's got to be a way to unbind them," I said. "We just haven't found it yet."

"And we're running out of time. Kate—" Stuart began, but Eddie held up a hand to cut him off.

"With these two, there's no halfway," he said. "Lilith's evil. And Odayne's the mate of the first evil. And now that power's waking up inside your boy. You willing to risk that? You willing to risk your kids?"

I closed my eyes and shook my head. Of course I wasn't. No matter what—even if it meant sacrificing Eric—my kids had to come first.

"You find that dagger, and you use it," Stuart said. "And if you don't, you can be damn sure that I will."

Twelve

After the announcement of Lilith's descent into San Diablo, I'd assumed the day couldn't get any worse. I was, of course, wrong. And as I stood in bare feet amidst a sea of dishwasher bubbles, I listened as Laura rattled off fact after fact after fact about my new nemesis. I'm not sure if a broken dishwasher is really on the same par as a vile uber-demon, but in my current mood, both seemed equally horrible.

"She's a badass, all right," Laura said, frowning at her laptop.

"That's a given if she's come to San Diablo," I said dryly. "All we ever seem to get are badasses." I dropped another towel on the floor and moved it around with my toe, trying to sop up some soapsuds. I don't know what Timmy shoved into the dishwasher, but after an expensive service call, I'm sure the plumber would be more than happy to tell me when he finally fit me into his busy schedule.

In the meantime, I was more energized than ever about finding a way to unbind Eric from Odayne, and while Laura researched Lilith on the computer, I finished going through all of Eric's books in the attic.

By the time I closed the last book, my head was pounding, my eyes were swimming, and I was mightily discouraged.

"Nothing?"

"Not in these," I confirmed. "Nothing that seems to even touch on Odayne or unbinding a demon from a soul. And as if those questions aren't enough, I can't stop thinking about what Eric said. About how they didn't want to hurt me. It doesn't make sense."

"Eric loves you," she said. "He'd fight to keep you safe."

"Maybe," I said. But I wasn't sure I believed it.

I caught Laura glancing up at the clock. "You need to go?"

"Sorry," she said.

I brushed off the apology. "As much as I like the idea of having my own personal research minion, I know that you have a life beyond demons. That is, of course, why I'm training Allie."

"Damn," Laura said. "I'm about to be outsourced."

She tucked her computer under her arm and promised to spend some time researching later. Every little bit helped. If anything, Allie and her online gaming research had proved that point.

I left not long after she did, hauling a screaming, cranky little boy around to various errands that I'd been ignoring. Home Depot for Stuart and the grocery store for the family being tops of my list. "Cap'n Crunch!" Timmy wailed in the cereal aisle. "Please, Mommy! Please, please, please!"

And, because I am a sucker with a fondness for those crispy little orange-colored bites, I caved, earning myself a tight hug and a firm, "I love you, Mommy."

Sugary cereals. The way to every child's heart.

When we finally got back home, I settled Timmy in his room for a nap, and began unloading the car. Three hours of shopping and two dozen bags and I still didn't have any new clothes. Somehow, it just didn't seem fair.

I was shoving two Snickers bars into the freezer when Allie and Mindy came barreling inside, backpacks flying as they tossed them onto the kitchen table. Then they both fell into chairs and demanded ice cream.

"Hello? Do I look like your personal serving wench?"

"A little," Allie said.

"Around the eyes," Mindy added.

"Here." Allie reached into her backpack and pulled out a report covered in clear plastic.

I took it, then smiled when I saw the cover. *Lilith. Bitch Demon from Hell. By Allie Crowe and Mindy Dupont.*

"We had free periods today," Mindy said. "And access to the computer lab."

"This is great," I said seriously, flipping through the pages. They'd included various images of Lilith they'd located online (though how they accessed sites relating to demonology from the school I didn't know, and figured I shouldn't ask). More important was the history section, which included a few accounts of possession by Lilith herself.

"It's not common," Allie said when I mentioned the reference to her. "But it's happened before. And the really interesting thing," she said, moving to stand by me so she could point to the relevant sections of the report, "is this right here."

I started to skim the language myself, but Mindy chimed in. "Every time she's possessed someone, there have been hints that Odayne's burst out in some poor sap. That's what he does," she explained. "He grows inside humans and then when he's like a grown-up demon he takes over and the person is just buried inside."

"It's nasty stuff," Allie said, while I made fascinated noises and hoped that they couldn't tell that not only did I already have this information, but that it worried me greatly.

"You've done terrific work, girls," I said, closing the report and trying to change the subject. "But school is for schoolwork. I don't want your grades to suffer. Especially yours," I said, aiming a stern glance toward Mindy. "Your mom's counting on scholarships."

They both rolled their eyes at that, and then Mindy shook her head in a gesture I recognized as Laura's when she'd reached the point of exasperation.

She tugged her backpack toward her and started pulling out folders. "All done," she said. "And we even did extra credit work. We're totally on the ball, Aunt Kate. I swear."

"Honest," Allie confirmed when I glanced her way. "Me, too. All caught up."

"Well," I said, then stayed silent since I didn't know where to go from there. Homework done before reaching home was a new precedent in my household. And if this was the boon from getting Mindy involved then I couldn't help but wish that Allie had shared our deep, dark secrets months ago.

"So since we're all caught up, can I sleep over at Mindy's?"

"Mom's got a date coming over, but it's just Cutter, and we'll totally stay out of their way."

"Cutter?" I repeated.

The girls exchanged glances. "You didn't know?"

I hid a frown, wondering why Laura hadn't mentioned it and trying not to feel slighted or jealous. Daily, I seemed to be learning how little the people most important in my life shared with me. "No, no," I said. "My mind was just somewhere else. And if you're sure a sleepover's okay with Laura then it's okay with me."

"Awesome," Allie said. "And can we go patrolling tonight?"

"Not tonight. I've been checking the paper. No new leads."

"You don't have to come. Just Mindy and me. I want to take her. And a slow night's a good one to start on, right?"

I aimed a severe look in her direction. "Are you insane? Of course you're not going patrolling on your own."

"But—"

"No. Now go get your stuff for tonight before I change my mind. Honestly, Allie! Patrolling? What on earth are you thinking?"

She didn't tell me what she was thinking. Instead, they both skulked away, leaving me alone in the kitchen with thoughts of Lilith and Odayne and Cutter and Laura. In other words, a mishmash of thoughts sufficient to spur a headache in the strongest of women.

Which was why I didn't feel in the least bit weak when I went to the freezer and snagged one of my candy bars. Not only did I need it, I deserved it.

I was finishing up my second Snickers when the girls clambered back down the stairs. I got a quick kiss from Allie, and then they were gone. I watched the door slam shut behind them, and fought a sense of loss. For a moment, I considered calling Laura, then I remembered her date.

With Cutter.

Honestly.

I started pacing, needing to get my mind off my friend and back onto the more serious problem of my first husband. And since I had no brilliant new ideas on that front, I decided to head upstairs and see if my trusty *alimentatore* had figured anything out. I was halfway up the stairs when I remembered that Rita had come by earlier, and they'd headed out to the movies. For a Wednesday night, romance certainly seemed to be in the air. And, yeah, I was feeling a little sorry for myself when the garage door opened and Stuart walked in.

"The dishwasher's dead, Eddie's at the movies, the girls

are sleeping at Laura's, and she's got a date with Cutter," I announced. "How was your day?"

"Good," he said. "I've got a deal closing on Friday."

I examined his face. "You're liking it?"

"I am. But don't think I like it so much that you're going to convince me to stop training."

"I'll keep that in mind," I said.

"So should I go change?" he asked. "We can go out tonight."

I shook my head, suddenly realizing I had a much better idea. "Not a good night for patrolling," I said, moving closer to him and closing my hand around his tie. "So I'll just give you a tip today, okay?"

"Fair enough," he said, keeping his eyes on mine.

"Dagger. Eyes. And only the eyes. Don't forget."

"I won't forget," he said. Or, rather, he tried to say it. I caught him in a kiss that effectively cut off his words. I could tell I surprised him, but my husband's a big-shot attorney, and he recovers from surprise quickly. He deepened the kiss, making my entire body weak and tingly. "Upstairs?" he asked.

"Here," I said, then grinned when I saw his brows lift.

"Really?" he asked.

"Damn right," I said, kissing him again, backing him toward a wall and fumbling with his clothes.

He got with the program quickly enough, and while I'd like to say that Stuart knows how to follow directions, "here" quickly became "there," and we ended up sweaty, satisfied, and naked in the living room, rolled up in each other's arms on the floor, half-covered by the afghan I keep on the sofa.

"Well, that was a nice welcome home," Stuart said. "Where's Timmy?"

"Either asleep in his room," I said, "or getting an eyeful at the top of the stairs." We both glanced that direction, relieved to find there was no small child peering down at us.

"I love you," I said, then kissed him, this time warm and sweet rather than hot and desperate.

"I know," he said. "I love you, too." He pulled me close, and we stayed like that, the wood floor beneath us growing more and more uncomfortable, but neither of us wanting to get up and break the spell.

The phone, however, managed that.

I sighed and climbed to my feet, frowning when I saw that it was Laura. "I thought you had a date," I said.

"Oh." I heard the guilt in her voice. "Right. About that. I was going to tell you, but—"

"It's okay. Really. But is it true? You're dating Cutter?" I tried to decide how I felt about that. I had nothing going on with the man—nothing—but I'd always had the impression he was a little attracted to me. So was I going to be jealous now that he was hot for my best friend?

I told myself I wasn't, and hoped that I meant it.

"No!" Laura said, but then qualified it with a soft, "Well, maybe."

"You're not sure?"

"I'm working for him," she said. "His office manager quit, and since I used to do administrative stuff for Paul, I offered to fill in until he found someone. And now he's hired me officially."

"And tonight? Was that admin stuff?"

I could practically hear the blush over the phone.

"Don't answer," I said, managing to keep the chuckle out of my voice. "And I'll only say this. I know Cutter. I like Cutter. And we already know he's not a demon. I figure those are some serious points in his favor."

"Yeah," she said. "And he kisses great, too."

"Laura!" And that time I really did laugh.

She did, too. "Listen, I didn't call to talk about the man in my living room—"

"He's still there?"

"I need to talk to Mindy," she said as a knot of fear settled in my gut. "Her dad wants her to come on Wednesday, but—"

"Laura," I said sharply. "Mindy's not here."

"What? Did you let them go to the mall?"

"No," I said slowly. "I let them go to your house."

"Shit," she said. "I can't believe it. I can't believe they'd do that."

"They wanted to go patrolling. I said no."

"You don't think they'd go by themselves, do you?"

I considered it, remembered too clearly what Allie had asked. But I couldn't believe she'd actually go through with it. "No," I finally said. "Allie knows she's not a match for a demon. She wouldn't put Mindy in that kind of danger. She'd only go patrolling if I was with her. Or," I added, realizing the awful truth, "if her dad was with her."

"Allie has no idea why Eric's dangerous," Laura said.

"I know." Stuart was beside me, the fear in my voice having brought him over. He clung tight to my hand and watched my face. "Get over here," I said. "And in the meantime, I'll call Eric."

I dialed Eric's cell as I climbed back into my clothes, and both Stuart and I managed to be dressed by the time Laura and Cutter arrived at my house. "Straight to voice mail," I said. "His home phone and his cell."

"What do we do?" Laura asked, clinging hard to Cutter's hand. To his credit, he didn't ask one question, though I knew he had to be baffled.

"You and Cutter go back to your house in case they come back. Stuart stays here. And I'm going to go see if I can find Eric."

Her eyes were wide and worried, but she nodded.

"Be careful," Stuart said as I slipped on my jacket, checked my stiletto, and made sure I had enough holy water in the vial in my purse.

"Trust me," I said. "If he's out patrolling with them, the only one who has to worry tonight is Eric."

I kept trying, constantly pushing the redial button on my phone as I sped over the San Diablo streets toward the beach.

"Hello?"

"Eric?" I almost slammed into the back of a Mercedes I was so surprised to hear his voice. "Where the hell are you?"

"At home. Why?"

"Mindy and Allie. Are they with you?"

"No." He said, his voice sharpening. "Why?"

"You're sure? Dammit, Eric, if you've taken them out patrolling, I'm—"

"I said they aren't here. I'm not him. I'm not Odayne. And still you don't fucking trust me."

"Trust?" I snapped back, remembering his words at the mansion. Remembering the look in his eye. "Dammit, Eric, you've been lying to me."

"What the hell are you talking about?"

"Never seen the dagger? No clue where it is or what it looks like? You've got drawings of it, Eric. A whole notebook of drawings and notes."

"The hell I do," he said, but the force had gone out of his voice, and I stayed quiet, realizing that he needed to process the words. "Jesus, Katie. I didn't know."

I drew in a breath and gripped the steering wheel tighter, desperately wanting to believe him, but not knowing if I should. And, yes, knowing that even if what he said was true, that in and of itself was terrifying.

"You really don't know where the girls are?" I asked, this time more softly.

"I don't," he said. "But I'll come over. I'll help you look."

"Thanks, but—"

My phone beeped and I pulled it away from my ear long enough to look at it, then let out a relieved breath when I saw that the call was coming from Allie.

"It's her," I said.

"If there's trouble, call me."

I promised I would, then clicked over to my daughter, and was immediately blasted by a stream of "I'm sorry, I'm sorry, I'm sorry!"

"They're safe," Stuart said, taking the phone from Allie. "Come home."

I did, cutting over the streets in record time to find both girls sitting quiet and forlorn on the sofa. Laura and Cutter had come back, and now they were pacing the living room with Stuart.

"We weren't going to patrol on our own," Allie said the moment I came in. "Honest. And so we headed to Daddy's."

I saw Cutter's brow furrow at that, but decided that now wasn't the time to worry about it.

"I talked to him," I said, anger rising. "He swore he hadn't seen you."

"He didn't," Allie said, quickly rising to his defense. "We saw him."

"And Nadia," Mindy added.

"They were going upstairs. You know. To his apartment."

"And we didn't figure it would be a good idea to interrupt."

"No," I said, forcing my voice to stay calm. "I don't expect it would be."

"So we came back."

"How?" Stuart asked. "Neither of you has a car."

"Joann," Allie said. "She was going to the beach to meet some guy, and we tagged along. And then when we said we weren't staying at Daddy's, she brought us back. I think she decided to blow off her date."

"Good," I said, wondering if all the teenagers in town had gone insane. Maybe there was a full moon or something.

"This conversation isn't over," Laura said to Mindy. "Home. Now."

"And you," I said to Allie. "Upstairs."

As soon as they all left, I looked at Stuart, my head shaking. "It's all spiraling out of control," I said.

"You need to tell her," Stuart said. "She needs to understand the truth about her father."

"I know," I said, rubbing my forehead. "But it's two different issues, isn't it? And even if everything was peachy keen with Eric—hell, even if none of us in this house knew a damn thing about demons—she still shouldn't have done this. She shouldn't have gone out on her own. She knows better," I said, thinking back to the last—and only other time—that she'd snuck out of the house. A time when she'd nearly gotten killed.

"I know," said Stuart gently. "But keep in mind that she came back on her own. Allie's a good kid."

At that, I raised my eyebrows.

"The operative word being *kid*," he admitted. "But she reined it in. That's more than a lot of fourteen-year-olds would do."

I nodded, but I didn't say anything. Because the truth was, that was what worried me. Because fourteen became fifteen and that became sixteen.

And with each year came more independence. More defiance. And definitely more danger.

I woke to the sound of someone moving stealthily through the house, and without even realizing I was moving, I was out of bed with my stiletto in my hand.

"Whasgoinon?" Stuart mumbled as he pulled my now-empty pillow toward him.

"Just getting a snack. Go back to sleep." If there was a demon downstairs, Stuart would be pissed in the morning. But I'd rather deal with his irritation about missing the action than have to watch his back while I checked out our house.

I moved slowly down the hall, avoiding the creaky spot as I peeked my head in Timmy's room. He'd managed to maneuver himself completely upside down, and now his feet were on his pillow, and Boo Bear was clutched tight in his arms. He snored softly as he slept, sounding a little snotty and wheezy, and I made a mental note to put him to bed to-morrow with a humidifier and some Vicks VapoRub. Until then, I'd cover him with an extra blanket, but I'd do it after I checked the rest of the house.

I pulled the door closed and moved on to Allie's room, which was bathed in the soft pink glow of the wall flowers she'd picked up from Ikea. Plastic blooms with lights be-hind them, six of which now outlined her window in stark contrast to the opposing wall with its martial arts posters and display cases for swords and knives. The latter were new, as Allie had only recently started haunting thrift stores and flea markets for bits of antique weaponry. On the whole, I had no objections; after all, if she wanted to be a Hunter, I wanted her to be the best, most focused Hunter she could be. The combination of focus and training and interest translated to skill.

But at the same time, I'll admit I missed the posters of the boy band of the moment and the hours on the telephone in the evening talking with her friends about absolutely noth-ing. I'd never had the high school experience; I'd never re-ally had the chance to be a teenage girl. And I'd desperately wanted my daughter to have a different kind of childhood.

Sometimes things don't turn out the way you planned.

And though I mourned my daughter's lost innocence, I'm honest enough to admit, privately, to a hum of self-satisfaction and pride, that she wanted to be like me.

Right then, I feared she might be doing exactly that.

She wasn't in her bed, which meant that either it was Allie I had heard moving quietly through the house, or else she'd heard the sound, too, and had slipped out of bed to go battle our intruder.

Not an option I cared for, and I was back out the door and moving quietly down the stairs even as the possibility occurred to me. I told myself she was simply restless; after all, the alarm hadn't tripped, and I was certain I'd set it. Probably she was curled up on the couch reading a romance, or sitting at the kitchen table stuffing her face with forbidden ice cream, and when I saw her I was going to feel downright foolish for getting so worked up over nothing.

That was it, I told myself. Nothing major. Just a teenager.

Even so, I moved with care, watching my back as I slipped through the living room, peering into shadows as I made my way toward the darkened kitchen.

Not one light was on downstairs, the only illumination coming from the light under the stovetop vent hood that I keep on as a matter of habit. It glowed a muted yellow, the anorexic light barely illuminating the kitchen beyond.

Still, I saw nothing moving in the dark and heard nothing rustling in the shadows. And as I moved closer, my worry spiked. My daughter wasn't in her bedroom, she wasn't in the living room, and the kitchen was too dark and too quiet.

Shit, shit, shit.

I told myself it was nothing. That I was unreasonably worried. That I would have heard a struggle if a demon had broken in and gotten to my daughter.

And I was damn certain that she wasn't going to be

sneaking out again. Not after what had happened earlier in the evening.

So what was going on?

I didn't know, and that scared me, the tempo of my heart accentuating my fear. Training, however, took over and I moved with purpose and stealth into the breakfast area.

I was, honestly, prepared for anything.

Anything, that is, but what I saw: my daughter, head down at the table, shoulders shaking with muted sobs.

I was at her side in a heartbeat. "Allie." I put my arms around her and she jumped, her eyes wild, then focused as she looked at me. She gasped, then threw her arms around me, pressed her face to my chest, and cried and cried and cried.

I'd stooped to hug her, and now I balanced on my heels, one hand holding the side of the table so that we both wouldn't topple over. With my free hand I stroked her hair while I made soothing mommy noises, all the while mentally racing through the various possibilities that had brought on such histrionics.

This, I knew, was more than the fact that she'd gotten into trouble earlier. True, Allie was a good kid and rarely got into the kind of trouble she'd seen last night, but she also had a thick skin. More than that, she was smart enough to know when she deserved the trouble that came her way. If she was mad about her dressing-down, it was because she knew she deserved it. But these weren't the sobs of a kid who was angry at herself. These were the sobs of a breaking heart.

I remembered the conversation I'd overheard at the theater, and wondered if I needed to go out and kick Charlie's butt. But even that didn't feel right. This wasn't about a boy.

And as my heart twisted in my chest, I had the low, sinking feeling that I did know why her heart was breaking.

"Allie." Gently, I pushed her head off of me and scooted back, releasing myself from her hold. I took her hands in mine, then tugged another chair out with my foot. I sat down, still holding her hands and looking into her miserable, tear-streaked face. "What is it?"

"You shoulda told me, Mom," she said, then wiped her dripping nose with the sleeve of her baseball-style jersey. "God, Mom, why didn't you tell me?"

I winced, wanting to pull her close again and tell her I'd kept secrets only because I wanted to protect her. But I couldn't go there yet. Not without knowing exactly what was upsetting her. "What is it you think you know, Allie? What haven't I told you?" I swallowed, praying she didn't know the truth about her father.

But even before she spoke, I knew from the pain in her eyes that my prayers would go unanswered today. She knew.

So help me, somehow, she'd learned the truth about Eric.

"Allie," I repeated, this time with more urgency. "Tell me."

"It's Daddy," she said, her words sucking all my hope from the room. "There's a demon inside my dad." The words came out barely intelligible, strangled with sobs, and she was back in my arms again, my hands stroking, my voice murmuring, and my mind thinking murderous thoughts about Eric's parents for what they had done to their son. For what they were doing to my family.

I don't know how long we stayed like that, me holding her, stroking her, loving her. And wishing like hell I could make the hurt go away. When she was little, I'd nursed her with kisses, smiley-face bandages and Bactine. Somehow, I didn't think that would work tonight.

When her sobs finally gave way to sniffles and then struggled, gasping breaths, I leaned back, one hand still touching, but trying to give her some space. She looked up at me with red, puffy eyes that held nothing but sadness.

"You knew all along," she said, her voice as flat as cardboard. "Why didn't you tell me?"

A thousand lies sprang to mind, but I settled for the truth. "This," I said, nodding at her. "I wanted to spare you this."

"How? It's there. It's in him."

"Maybe not forever," I said, and saw the tiniest bit of hope in her eyes. "Maybe not if I can help it."

"And me," she said. "You have to let me help."

"Could I stop you?"

That earned me a smile. "No way."

"Didn't think so." I brushed her hair out of her eyes and forced myself not to pull her close again. She was growing up, my girl, and she'd proved numerous times that she could stand on her own. "How did you find out?"

"I guess I didn't really know until right now. But it was all there, you know? I'd seen all the signs, but I hadn't really started putting them together until I was doing this research. But it made sense. Daddy's temper lately. It's kinda sharp, you know?"

I did know. I wasn't certain that Allie had noticed, but apparently, she had.

"And you didn't want me to patrol with him alone, and every time I said I was going over there, you freaked."

"I didn't freak," I said indignantly.

"Like, duh. You so totally did."

"Maybe a slight discomfort," I said, "but not a freak-out."

She shrugged. "And then I started this research, about Odayne. And there's all this stuff about how he's bound inside a person until the time when he bursts forth. And I thought about the *Alien* movies, and how the creature bursts out and how in the last one it was like Ripley was the creature's mom or something and——"

I held up a hand. "Allie, sweetheart, I haven't got a clue what you're talking about."

She sighed, and I felt like the most clueless mother on

the planet. "There's Odayne," she said curtly. "Bound in a human. Then there's Daddy. And his temper, your freak-outishness, and it all just came together." She blinked owlishly at me. "But I still wasn't sure. I still didn't really *know*. And I hated myself for even thinking it. But now . . . you're here . . . and you said . . . and there's no way to avoid it. Because it's true. Oh, God. It's really true."

It was my turn to sigh. "Oh, baby," I said, stroking her hair. "I'm so sorry." I managed a small smile. "But there's one thing you got wrong. I didn't freak out."

She rolled her eyes. "Delude yourself all you want. You totally freaked."

"Maybe a little," I admitted. "Don't tell? It'll tarnish my kick-ass Demon Hunter persona."

"My lips are sealed," she said, following that up with the genuine smile I'd been hoping for.

We sat in silence for a moment, watching Kabit stalk around, probably wondering why no one was hopping up to get him a kitty treat.

"How?" she asked. "How can he have . . . you know . . . inside him?"

I considered telling her that I didn't know and that it didn't matter, but I couldn't manage it. Instead, I got up and went to the freezer, then returned with two frozen Snickers bars.

"It's bad, huh?" she asked.

"It's definitely not good," I agreed. "And I don't know everything. But I do know that it started with Eric's parents. With your grandparents," I said. And then I drew in a breath and told her exactly what I knew.

She didn't speak a word while I told her the story I'd parsed together from what Eric had told me, from Father Corletti's input, and from my own experience. And when I finished the story, she dried her tears, nodded, and whispered, "Thank you."

I held tight to her hand. "Are you okay?"

"Yeah. I mean, no. Not really. But I guess I will be. I guess I don't really have a choice, do I?"

I shook my head, more proud and more sad than I could ever remember being. And never had I felt more exhausted.

"It's not even four," I said, after I was pretty certain the tears had passed and weren't coming back. "You can still catch a few hours before school."

She nodded then pushed back from the table and stood. I pulled her down for a quick kiss, but stayed there as she moved toward the living room. She stopped in the doorway and turned back to me. "We'll save him, right? Odayne's not going to win, is he? We're going to get Daddy back?"

I felt the tears well in my eyes as I looked back at my daughter, wishing I could lie and tell her that I knew everything would be all right.

I couldn't, though. Not to Allie. Not anymore.

So I said the truth, which was the best I could do.

"I hope so, kiddo. We're going to try like hell, and I really, really hope so."

I found Eddie already in the living room recliner when I stumbled, blinking, down the stairs. I hadn't gotten nearly enough sleep, but the dishwasher repair guy was supposed to be coming sometime between eight and noon, and if I wasn't awake, he'd be there at eight. If I was awake, of course, he'd pull into the driveway at eleven-fifty. That's why I prefer demons; with repairmen, you can never win.

The pull of coffee was dragging me toward the kitchen, but the little black-and-white composition book in Eddie's lap snagged my attention and halted my progress. And why wouldn't it? The little book contained my notes; all the experiences I'd had as a Demon Hunter in San Diablo.

"Light reading?" I asked, dryly.

He glanced up, peering at me from half-moon reading glasses. "I never talked to my Rice Krispies," he said, giving the page a thump with his thumb and forefinger. "Defamation of character. That's what this is. Talk to my cereal. Phhhbt."

I stared at him for a moment, considered arguing with him, and decided that without coffee, I'd only lose the battle. So I left him and continued on.

Not surprisingly, he shuffled into the kitchen after me. "Honestly, woman. These reports read like a diary. Where's the detail? The analysis?"

I pulled out the carafe and found it empty, which caused me to silently curse my husband. He'd rolled out of bed and into the shower at seven, and I'd heard the garage door rise forty-five minutes later. He'd had plenty of time to make coffee, but did he? Noooo. Probably planning to drive by Starbucks, which was all good and well except that it would have been nice if he'd made a pot for me.

I stomped to the freezer to pull out the bag of ground coffee as Eddie droned on about the lack of quality in my accounts. Neither the lack of coffee nor Eddie did much to improve my mood. I tend to wake up needing an infusion of caffeine. Couple that with a lack of sleep, and I'm pretty much a walking nightmare until the first brewed cup.

I shuffled back to Mr. Coffee, dumped the grounds into the basket, and pushed the button to start, then turned around and faced Eddie, who was muttering about my "embarrassing lack of details." Fueled or not, I figured I didn't have a choice. "In case you forgot, I'd been retired for fifteen years when I put that report together." I'd only done it out of habit, too, pulling a composition book out of the box of miscellaneous school supplies I pick up every August on the cheap. "I didn't even consider it a report. More like notes to myself. Besides, it's not like you weren't there for most of that stuff."

"Ain't even like you were keeping accurate notes." He snorted. "Rice Krispies, my fanny."

I hid my smile, both amused by his reaction and also pleased that he truly didn't seem to recall just how loopy he'd been when I'd found him drugged up in the Coastal Mists Nursing Home.

"Don't know what you're smiling about," he said, and I made a valiant effort to wipe the smirk from my mouth. "Now this here's a bit more helpful," he said, holding up a more recent book.

I groaned. "You're actually reading all of my reports?"

"Hey now, girlie. As your *alimentatore*, I have to warn you that impudence will not be tolerated."

"I'll make a note of it."

"And damn straight I am. Every single one of them. We got a situation here with Eric, and nobody in the world's closer to that boy than you are. So I'm reading and I'm learning." He tapped the composition book, then tapped his head. "It's all bubbling away in here, mixing together like a soup. If there's a link, a fact, something we overlooked, I'll find it. You can count on Eddie."

I believed him. Despite the fact that he looked absolutely harmless standing there in faded blue flannel pajamas, his chin as bristly as a cactus and his eyebrows like caterpillars about to crawl away, I absolutely believed him. And to prove it, I tossed my arms around him and gave him a big hug, satisfied when I pulled away to find him blushing.

"You're distracting me, woman," he said. "I got questions for you."

"Shoot," I said.

"Right here," he said, flipping pages and finally tapping the pages. "This bit about you and Eric tied together. What did Father C mean by that?"

I frowned, remembering how Father Corletti had dropped that little bomb on me. "Remember when I was afraid that maybe I'd opened the way for a demon to move into Eric by using the Lazarus Bones?"

He snorted. "I remember. Not much to worry about after all, seeing as the beastie was already inside him."

I grimaced. "Yeah, well, Father Corletti told me that I didn't open the door for anything new and bad to come back down into Eric. But he did tell me one thing that happened. And it's a big thing."

"Tied together," Eddie said, tapping the page. "Spit it out, girl."

"It's just what it sounds like," I said. "Or at least Father Corletti says so. We're tied to each other. Or, rather, he's tied to me. It's like I made him a part of me or something. If I die, he dies."

Eddie leaned back in his chair, looking smug. "And there you go."

I gaped at him, confused. "And there I — Oh! Why didn't I see it before?"

"You really do have a free pass, girlie girl. They kill you, they kill your boy, too."

"But why would they care? The demon can still live in Eric's body, right?"

"Didn't before," Eddie said. "Eric died in San Francisco. Body was buried and Eric's soul and the demon shot out into the ether."

I frowned, because he was absolutely right. "But the first demon tried to kill me. So did Lisa."

"Maybe they weren't following the party line. You said yourself Eric told you he didn't want a hair on your head harmed."

"Yeah," I said. "But he's Eric."

"Is he? Was he that day? Right then?"

I licked my lips, not wanting to answer. But Eddie was right. No matter how much I twisted it around to look at it, there was no escaping the fact that Eddie was right. I told him as much, too, then watched his smug expression broaden. "But you did talk to the Rice Krispies," I said, unable to resist.

He snorted. "Don't mean nothing. You're only crazy if they talk back."

"Who?" Allie asked, bounding into the kitchen in a knee-length T-shirt.

I glanced at the clock. Ten past eight.

"Cereal," Eddie said.

"Oh," she said, then looked to me for help.

I wasn't biting. "Why aren't you at school?"

"Hello? Up like half the night, remember? You were with me." She eyed the hissing coffeemaker. "Is it ready?"

"Get in line," I said. "Honestly, Allie, you can't just decide to stay home and—"

"I've got a bead on Lilith," she announced, effectively shutting me up and causing Eddie to put down the composition book he was undoubtedly about to begin cross-examining me with.

"Say again?" I said.

"Lilith," she said, looking firmly at me and Eddie in turn. "I figured it out. I know where to find her. I know exactly who she is. More important, I know exactly what she wants."

Thirteen

"**She wants to be like** her lover," Allie said. "Like Odayne. Can I have a Pop-Tart?"

"Come again?" Eddie said, but I got it. I got it, and I didn't like it.

"She wants humanity," I said. "Not simply to be in a human body, but she wants a taste of a human soul. Oh, God."

Allie nodded, and since I was making no progress toward her breakfast, she got up and went to the pantry herself.

"Nadia," I said, feeling more than a little sick. "She's time-sharing with Nadia."

"That's what I figured, too," Allie said, from inside the pantry. "Don't we have strawberry ones?" I ignored that, knowing that her mind wasn't going to stay on tasty breakfast treats for long. "You said she was really strong in the theater, right?"

I grimaced and absently rubbed my shoulder. "I assumed she'd been working out. Apparently she was being a little more industrious than that."

"But it's not the same, right? She's not inside Nadia the same way that Odayne's inside Daddy?"

"No," I agreed. "She's not."

When a demon possesses a human, there's a Linda Blair/ *Exorcist* thing going on. Spinning heads, frothing at the mouth. The whole Hollywood spiel. But if a human willingly allows a demon to move in and share the body, then there's no external sign. Cooperation is key. It's different from what was happening with Eric—his soul was involved, not the body—and Lilith and Nadia weren't actually one. Not yet anyway.

"Time-sharing isn't going to be enough for Lilith," I said, standing and starting to pace. "She's been around since before time began. She doesn't understand humanity, but she wants to. And she's not going to want to do it by halves."

"She'll want to merge. Entwine her essence with Nadia's soul."

"Nadia doesn't know. She couldn't possibly have gone willingly into this arrangement if she believed she was going to lose herself."

Allie rolled her eyes. "Mom. Please. This is Nadia we're talking about. For one, the bitch is totally delusional, and probably figures it'll only turn out good for her. And for two, if there's power at the end of it, she's gonna be all over it."

Once again, my kid was right. Rough around the edges, but right.

"How, though?" I asked, thinking aloud. "How would she manage?"

"Ceremony," Eddie said. "What else."

I gawked at him. "You know of a ceremony like that?"

"Hell no," he said. "But you been around as long as I have, you learn one thing's for certain. Someway, somewhere, someone's gonna come up with another damn ceremony."

I smiled, remembering that Laura had said something very similar.

Eddie shoved back from the table as the sharp beep of a horn sounded. "That's Rita. You two get on that."

"Us? You're the *alimentatore*."

"So I am, girlie. But it's your man's ass on the line, and between you two and the bitch, I think it's personal." He paused, his attention turning to Allie. "Call *Forza* first, though. Let 'em know what you got."

"*Forza*," I repeated. "You, the Lone Ranger of *alimentatores* is actually pulling *Forza* into the loop? On purpose?"

"Like I said when this started, this ain't for me. It's for the kid. And if *Forza*'s got a bead on this ceremony Lilith's got planned, then we need to know. And that was some damned clever hoops the kid jumped through. *Forza* ought to know the kid's got the goods."

"The kid's sitting right there," I pointed out.

"So she is," he said, and a wide smile split his face. "You're doing damn good there, kid. Course I wouldn't expect anything less from my granddaughter." He winked, then turned and headed for the door, leaving Allie and me shaking our heads in wonder.

"So should I? Call, I mean?" She glanced at the clock, as if it held answers. "What time is it in Rome now?"

"Just after five in the afternoon," I answered automatically. "Go ahead and call. If you can't get Father Corletti directly, ask him to call back as soon as he can. Tell him it's urgent."

"Shouldn't you call?"

"Go on," I said, as the doorbell rang. "And go in Stuart's study. That's probably the dishwasher guy."

As it turned out, I was right; it was the dishwasher guy. Or, at least, it was a guy wearing a brown work shirt with *Mr. Appliance* embroidered on it. Under the circumstances, I didn't intend to take any chances.

I led him through the house to the kitchen, and once he was peering into my dishwasher, I took a vial of holy water out of my purse and poured it into one of Timmy's plastic Dora the Explorer glasses. Then, feeling only slightly foolish, I marched over beside Mr. Appliance. "See anything?"

"A sword," he said, which was so utterly completely off the beaten dishwasher path that I immediately tensed, certain I'd invited into my home a demon with a sense of humor.

"What?" I said, and when he pulled his head out of the mechanism, I tossed the contents of the cup on his face, then watched as he spit and spluttered, but absolutely didn't burn.

Okay, time for me to be more than a little embarrassed.

"I'm so sorry! I tripped," I lied. "And now you're all wet. Oh, dear." I passed him a towel, all the while silently chastising him for mentioning a sword. I mean, honestly. What was the man thinking? "Are you okay?"

"Fine," he said, drying himself off. "Usually it's a burst hose instead of a customer dousing me, but I'm used to getting wet on the job." He rocked back on his heels and pointed to the inside of my dishwasher. "You got yourself a little army in there," he said. "Plugging up the drain."

"I do?" I leaned over and peered in, for the first time noticing the green plastic arm extending up, waving a sword as if about to launch an attack on the silverware. "I see," I said. I cast a backward glance toward the living room, where my own little demon sat innocently watching the *Backyardigans*. "I have a feeling I know how that happened."

"Oh yeah," he said cheerfully. "See it all the time. You want I should fix?"

I half-considered dumping the job on Stuart, who I firmly believed should have found the army when I'd first complained of escaping bubbles. But I owed Mr. Appliance for a service call anyway, and I didn't think it would take too long to free the army. Besides, if I didn't get the thing fixed, I'd be spending another day or two washing dishes by hand, and that was something I really wasn't looking forward to.

Once he was happily disassembling the dishwasher, I headed out into the living room to check on Timmy, who was singing along merrily about a Yeti. I gave him a kiss, found myself thoroughly ignored in favor of Nickelodeon, and continued on toward Stuart's study. Allie was hanging up the phone as I came in, grinning broadly. "You got through to Father?"

"He told me I did really awesome work."

"You did," I agreed. "Does he have any ideas about the binding ceremony between her and Nadia?"

"Not yet, but he's going to check the archives and get back to us. But Mom, he said I should come to Rome! He said I'd like looking over the resources and that he'd totally love to meet me."

"I know he would," I said, smiling.

"No, Mom. You don't get it." Her eyes were bright and excited. "He didn't say it because he has to ask you first, but I'm positive that he was gonna tell me I could go there and train. He thinks I'm good, Mom. He says I take after you."

My smile broadened. "Did he?"

"Uh-huh. And Daddy, too, only I know he meant the nondemon stuff, you know?"

"I'm sure he meant the nondemon stuff," I said, once again struck cold by the fact that throughout our entire relationship, "the demon stuff" had always been hidden under the surface.

"So can I?"

I blinked. "Can you what?"

She rolled her eyes and sighed, deeply frustrated with her idiot mother. "Can I go to Rome and train?"

"Oh." The question caught me off guard, and I sat down.

"'Please, please, please! I mean, I should, right? That's what Hunters do, unless they're rogue. Isn't it?"

"It's what Hunters do," I admitted. And although I couldn't believe I was even letting this conversation progress, I heard myself asking, "Is it what *you* want to do?"

"Are you kidding?" She looked at me with the same bafflement and amazement I would have seen if I'd asked if she wanted her own car. "I mean, duh."

Not the most articulate, but she got the point across.

"You're sure? No hesitations? Just duh?"

Her brow crinkled, making a line appear above her nose. "Well, yeah. I mean, I want to do this. Is that bad?"

Is that bad? The question rattled around inside me as I considered my answer. What should I tell her? What did I wish someone would have told me, all those years ago?

Not that I'd had a choice, not really. I'd been raised in the life. For the life.

But it was nice to live in a fantasy world where I had a say in deciding my destiny.

"Mom? It's not that complicated a question."

I wasn't sure I agreed with that, but I caught the undertone of teenage impatience and abandoned my own musings. "Tell me this," I said. "Why?"

She blinked. "Why? Why what?"

"Why do you want to go to Rome? Why do you want to be a Hunter?"

"Are you kidding? Why wouldn't I?"

I could think of a lot of reasons, not the least of which was the fact that if she walked away—if she went to college and got a job in a bank—the odds were good that no one she knew would ever again have a demon inside them, she wouldn't spend her life fearing for the next attack, and she'd most likely survive to see her own grandchildren. I could have said all that, but I didn't. Instead, I simply said her name. She heard the rest in my voice. Like I've always said, I've got a smart kid.

"I can't walk away simply because it scares me," she said. "I mean, could you?"

"I *did*," I reminded her. "Your father and I both walked away because we wanted a family. Neither one of us thought this was a good life for kids."

"Well, see?"

"See what?" As far as I knew, I hadn't just brilliantly bolstered one of her arguments.

"It doesn't matter what you do, Mom. It finds you. It finds you, and it sucks you back in. And the second time you didn't walk away," she added, pointing a stern finger in my direction. "You didn't have to sign back up with *Forza*, right? But you did, and you told me why. Do you remember?"

"Not specifically," I said dryly. "But I'm sure it was profound."

"It was. You said you had the ability to fight evil, and that meant you had the responsibility, too."

"You're right," I said, touched that she'd not only listened so well, but had taken my words to heart. "That was profound."

"More than profound, Mom. It's true. This is big stuff, you know? The biggest. And most of the people out there don't even know what's going on. It's like a secret war, you know? And for whatever reason, I got drafted."

"You could dodge," I said. "Head up to Canada."

"Ha-ha. Forget drafted. I enlisted. Signed up with eyes wide open because I think this is important. And yeah, I get the risks, and yeah, I know you might not get grandkids. But it's *good*. It's good versus evil, and it's not sponsored by Nintendo, and evil keeps getting her claws in, you know? And if I can help stop that—if I can do even the tiniest little thing—then I think it's worth it. And oh, God, Mom, you're crying!"

"I am not," I lied.

"Do you really think it would be a terrible mistake?"

I shook my head. "No. On the contrary, I think that was one hell of a mature speech from a girl who doesn't even have her learner's permit."

"Yeah?" She preened a little. "Cool. So I can go?"

"I'm not saying no," I said. "But I am saying that I think you're too young."

"Too young! But you were only fourteen!"

"And I didn't have a family," I said. "Give it some time, see if you still want it."

"I will," she said grumpily.

I laughed. "Allie, give me a break. I'm not saying no. But I don't want you to rush it. And I also want to see what your dad thinks about it."

She swallowed, then licked her lips. We both knew that I wouldn't be asking her dad anything about her soon.

"One or two more days," I said firmly. "One or two more and then we'll go to his apartment and ask him together."

"Okay," she said, her voice small. Then she seemed to buck up as she turned to grin at me. "Maybe he'll think fifteen's not too young."

I sighed. Loudly.

"There is one other reason I want to do it, you know."

"Yeah? What's that?"

"Being a Hunter is just too dang cool."

"I think that's the last of them," Betty Lackland said, plunking five more musty, leather-bound books on the table where Laura and I had settled ourselves in the San Diablo County Library. We'd come here after dropping Timmy at day care and Allie at school, armed with the appropriate note from her mother to excuse her tardiness.

We weren't only in the library, though. We were in the rare books room, a section that was both well-stocked and well-renowned, due in large part to Eric's efforts when he worked here.

I, of course, had assumed he was happily ensconced in your average, everyday rare books librarian job. Pulling in items of interest, cataloging them, slapping Library of Congress or Dewey Decimal numbers on them, or doing whatever it was that librarians did.

Naturally, I'd assumed wrong.

My husband had been using his acquisitions budget to acquire rare books and manuscripts that touched on his situation. That maybe even documented similar situations. More important, one that maybe documented a way out.

At least, I hoped he had. I'd already reviewed all the books he'd acquired personally. If we didn't find a clue in the library, I feared I was running out of ideas.

"So we're hoping he either didn't get around to reviewing all these books, or whatever cure he found didn't work right the first time, right?" Laura said as Betty left the room. "It still seems like a long shot to me."

I nodded; we'd been over this ground before. If Eric had figured a way out of his unwanted relationship with a tagalong demon, he would have done whatever was necessary to put that information into effect. The fact that Odayne was still with him meant he hadn't found the answers in his books. Either that, or it meant he'd tried the answer and it didn't work.

"All this ceremonial stuff, it has to happen in just the right time and in just the right way," I said. "If he tried it and something didn't go the way it was supposed to, it's possible he wrote it off as a bogus ceremony."

"And trying again could do the trick," she said. She scowled at the mile-high stack of books Betty had brought in. "You want the top of the stack or the bottom?"

"Let's just grab and go," I said, then watched as she pulled a book from the top and carefully opened it. I followed suit, only to discover that my selection was in Latin.

"Great," I said. "If the answer's in here, we'll never find it." Unlike the books at home, which Eric could have filled with bookmarks and marked with sticky notes, these public books would have to be marked less obviously.

"Look for bits of paper between the pages," she suggested. "He might have marked a page and forgotten. He might have even written in the book with pencil."

I lifted a brow, thinking of my bibliophile husband. "Probably not," I said. "But I'll keep my eyes open." Figuring that any book with a solution to our problem would have been opened, poured over, and possibly photocopied, I closed the book and examined the side, looking to see if there was any place where the pages didn't slide together just so, any place where the spine seemed stretched. Any indication at all to indicate that a book had sat open and developed even the slightest hint of a crease.

Naturally, I found nothing. Not surprising, considering it was not only my first book to examine, but that I'd picked it from the stack at random. Still, hope springs eternal. Since there were apparently no shortcuts, though, I flipped slowly through the musty pages looking for anything—annotation, marking, even creepy illustrations—that might suggest we were on the right track.

I found nothing. And five books later, I'd still found nothing. My nose, however, tickled from the dust.

At least this wasn't like searching through old records in the cathedral archives. Those boxes were kept in the basement and, at least until reviewed, not kept very tidy. Dust wasn't my problem then, bugs were. Libraries, thank goodness, were blissfully bug-free.

"Anything?" I asked Laura as she closed a leather-bound volume with fancy gold writing.

"Not a thing. Are we wasting time?"

I frowned. "I guess we won't know that until we're done looking."

She glanced up at the clock. "You staying or coming with me?" Since Laura was working that night at Cutter's, our plan was for her to pick up Allie and Mindy and take them with her. Convenient for me since Allie could get in an extra class. As for Mindy, she could either cheer her friend on or do homework.

"I'm staying," I said. "I'll pick up the girls after class and take them to my house after we pick up Timmy. If you want Mindy to stay the night . . ." I added, letting my voice trail off into suggestiveness.

"We're not that serious yet," she said. "Honestly, I still can't figure out why he's interested in me at all."

I shrugged. "Brains and good looks," I said. "After all, you can balance his books. And you do look cute in a *gi*, even if your crescent kicks are for shit."

Laura laughed, which was just the reaction I was going for.

"Fine. Okay. I'm off." She nodded at the still tall but significantly less intimidating pile of books. "I'll expect a full report in the morning."

"If my eyes don't fall out from the strain, you'll have it."

An hour later, I was beginning to think that I hadn't been exaggerating. My eyes were dry and sandy, and no matter how many times I blinked, I couldn't seem to clear them. My throat felt scratchy, most likely from the mustiness of the old books. And I was absolutely certain that the windowless walls of the rare books room were closing in on me.

In other words, I wanted the hell out of there.

There were, however, only three books left. At least in this batch. Betty had come bounding in twenty minutes earlier to inform me that she'd forgotten to tell me about five titles that had been shipped down to UCLA as part of an inter-library loan. She'd requested the books' return and promised she'd call me when they were in.

Oh, yay.

In the meantime, in the spirit of thoroughness, I had to look through this last trio of tomes. I pulled the top book off and turned to the first page. When I saw that it was in Latin, I almost put it aside, but, honestly, I was too afraid of missing something important. So I flipped pages, looking for familiar Latin words or clues that Eric had found something interesting in the book. About two-thirds of the way in, I found what I was looking for—a page, completely missing. It had been ripped free, leaving a scar of jagged, yellowed paper behind. And although my Latin is for shit, I could at least catch the gist of the words on the surrounding pages. The section was talking about trapping and binding evil. And if the missing page was specific to Odayne, then I'd just found what we were looking for.

Too bad it had gone missing.

Frowning, I made a note of the book, then left the rare books room and headed for the circulation desk. "The rare books don't circulate, right?"

"That's right," Betty said. "I'm sorry it's inconvenient, but it's the only way we can ensure the integrity of the material."

"Right. No problem. I totally get it. But is it possible to tell me whose pulled a particular book?"

"Well, now, I don't know." She pressed her fingertips to her mouth, and I could just imagine her head filling with concerns about policy, privacy, and the First Amendment.

"I just don't want to duplicate work with my team," I said, hoping that made sense despite the fact that I'd never given her specifics as to why I wanted to look at Eric's acquisitions, much less laid out for her the duties of my imaginary team. "If I can review the list for this book, I can rule things out quickly enough."

Her lips pursed as she checked the computer, then relaxed as she looked back at me. "I don't suppose I can do much damage telling you one name, now can I?"

"Just one? Since when?"

"Since Eric died, dear. These books don't get that much use. Fine collection he pulled together, don't get me wrong. But it doesn't get much practical use, you see."

"Right. So, um, who looked at the book?"

"David Long." She peered up at me. "Do you know him, dear?"

I nodded, smiled bright, and tried not to let her see that my insides were churning. "Oh, yes. He's on the team, all right. How long ago did he request the book?" I expected her to cite a date that corresponded more or less to Eric's return in David's body. After all, surely he would have come straight here and started to research the problem again.

So I wasn't at all prepared when Betty beamed owlishly at me from behind her silver frames, then firmly announced that David had been in only three short days before.

"That recent?" I asked. "You're sure?" I was leaning against the counter, trying unsuccessfully to lean in and see her computer screen.

"Of course, dear. Is something wrong?"

"No," I said, trying to convince myself as much as Betty. "Of course not. Thanks so much for checking." I started to step away, then thought of another question. "Has Mr. Long been to the rare books room often?"

"You are a hard taskmaster, aren't you?" she asked as she tapped keys. "But it's good to check up on your employees. Hmmm." She peered up at me. "I hope your Mr. Long isn't supposed to come regularly, because the last time he was here was—goodness—four years ago."

I swallowed. David was still David four years ago.

"And when he was in the other day," I asked, "did he request any other books?"

Her eyes scanned the monitor as her fingers clicked. Then she shook her head. "No, just this one." She peered at my face. "You're sure there's not a problem?"

"Positive," I said. But I couldn't escape the reality that something was very, very wrong. Yes, it was possible that David was simply continuing the research he'd started as Eric. And it was possible he'd decided to do that by focusing on one random book.

More likely, though, was the scenario that played through my mind. That the page in question held my answer—and the demon inside Eric didn't want me to have it.

The possibility turned my stomach, because if the answer lay on a page out of a rare book—a page that had been stolen—I had no way of getting that information back. It wasn't as if I could run down to Barnes & Noble and pick myself up another copy.

"Dammit, Eric," I muttered. "Couldn't you have fought?" My fear, of course, was that he couldn't. That he was through fighting, and that I'd run out of time.

"I'm sorry, dear?" Betty said.

"Nothing. I'm wondering, is there a way to find out if other copies of that book exist?"

"Well, let me see." She began tapping at the keyboard, her rhythm more or less in tune with the rhythm of my own tapping foot. "I can only access copies that have been databased online, and—why yes. The Harry Ransom Center at the University of Texas has a copy, there's a facsimile copy in Prague, and—oh! The Vatican library has a copy as well." She looked up at me. "With a book this old, I wouldn't be surprised to learn those are the only copies in existence," she said, but I was no longer listening. My mind had stopped working at the mention of the Vatican.

Right there. The information was right there at Father

Corletti's fingertips and they'd missed it. Most likely because the binding spell was unique to Odayne, and until a few days ago, no one had realized it was him we were dealing with.

"Betty, you are a saint," I said, then leaned across the counter to give her a quick hug. "I need to run, but I'll be back." I was gone before she had a chance to answer, my cell phone out, and my finger already pressed over the speed-dial button for Father Corletti.

Before I pushed, the phone buzzed in my hand. Irritated, I saw that it was Allie. "Not now, honey. I've got to call—"

"*Mom!* Oh, God, Mommy!"

Instantly, my heart was pounding, and I was racing for my car. "Are you all right? What's happened? Where—"

"Cutter's," she said. "I'm fine. We're fine. But, oh God, Mom! Get here fast."

Fourteen

I found the closed sign on the door when I got to Cutter's, and the door locked. I was on the verge of smashing a rock through the glass when Laura rushed forward, looking both frazzled and exhausted. "Thank God you're here," she said after she'd unlocked the door and ushered me in. "Cutter wanted to call the police, and he thinks I'm crazy for—"

"What happened?" I interrupted, but by that time, I didn't need to ask. We'd passed the partition that blocked part of the view of the workout area from the front doors, and I could see for myself well enough.

What happened was that a demon had died, stabbed through the eye with a Maybelline mascara wand.

I turned and found Allie, who shrugged and looked slightly green. "Mindy was doing her makeup," she said. "It was handy."

"Dammit, Kate," Cutter said. "I'm calling the cops. I should have called fifteen minutes ago. I don't know what the hell I was thinking."

"No." I'd been looking at the demon—the old man from Coastal Mists that Eric assured us he'd killed. His face was now scarred with what I realized were holy water burns. Allie had been thorough, I thought, and felt a quick stab of pride. Now I looked up at Cutter and shook my head. "You have to trust me on this, Sean, but this isn't a matter for the police."

"In case you hadn't noticed, there's a body on my floor."

"Yeah," I agreed. "Under the circumstances, that's going to be inconvenient."

"The crypt?" Laura suggested. She was crouched on the ground near Mindy, who sat with her back to the wall, hugging her knees to her chest.

"Are you okay?" I asked her.

Mindy managed a quavering smile. "I told Allie I thought all of this was cool. Now, I'm not so sure." She looked at me with big brown eyes brimming with tears. "It was gonna kill us, Aunt Kate. It was absolutely gonna kill us, and Allie stopped it."

"That's the only reason I haven't called the cops," Cutter said. "Jesus, Allie. What's going to happen to her?"

Laura gave Mindy's head a kiss and then moved over to Cutter, getting right in his face. "Allie's going to be fine," she said. "She didn't kill anyone."

I saw Cutter's eyes shift to Allie, who shrugged and nodded. "He's not a person, Cutter. I swear to God."

"But he's a body," I said firmly, trying to keep my mind on the problem. Cutter we could deal with. The body, we needed to get rid of. "And the crypts are out of the question. The bishop doesn't know about the demons, and now isn't the time to tell him."

"Demons." Cutter's single word came out on a breath, and while I heard surprise, I also thought I heard a wisp of understanding. Or, maybe I was imagining things.

"Should we take the body to Daddy?" Allie asked.

I shook my head. "Eric's not going to be able to help us this time." I toed the demon, reining in the desire to kick the shit out of the corpse for attacking people I loved. "He came in here? Attacked you?"

Allie nodded. "Said he was going to kill me and then all the rest of us. He meant it, too. Cutter went after him, and the demon knocked him all the way back there," she said, pointing to the far wall. "Musta really hurt, but it gave me time to get my spritzer bottle out of my backpack, because I remembered what you said about not assuming anything."

"Someone's in the process of killing you, you defend yourself and worry about the demon/human thing later," I said. "But good girl for remembering."

"Yeah, well, I got him in the face, you know. And the water burned the shit out of him."

"Water?" Cutter said. "That wasn't mace? Acid?"

"Holy water," I said, keeping my eyes on Allie. "Then what?"

"I started whaling on him while he was clawing his face, and I shouted for Mindy to toss me something pointy, and she did and, well, there you go."

I couldn't hold the professional veneer any longer. I pulled her close and squeezed my eyes shut, afraid that once I started crying, I wouldn't be able to stop.

"He's dead, Mom," Allie said. "It's over, and we're all safe."

I nodded, snuffled, and pulled my head up. "He's dead, all right," I said. "And apparently for the second time."

"What?" Laura asked, but I could tell from Allie's expression that she already knew what I was going to say.

"This is the man from the paper. The one we were going after at Coastal Mists."

Laura frowned. "But I thought David told you that he'd killed it."

"David?" Cutter asked. "David Long?"

"Apparently he lied," I said, ignoring Cutter.

"You're right, then," Laura said. "We can't ask him to do something about the body. Landfill?"

I shook my head. "Too dangerous. Hang on. I've got an idea." I pulled out my cell phone, preparing to call Father Corletti and beg for a disposal team. I'd been denied them in the past—with *Forza* having all sorts of economic cutback problems, there simply weren't teams available—but in the past I'd had other options.

"Wait," Cutter said. "Just wait a damn minute. What in the name of God is going on?"

"He's got that right," Allie said, then started laughing so hard that I had to write it off to post-trauma hysterics.

"Demons? Bodies? Holy water? Answers, Kate. And this time, I really want them."

I nodded. For a long time, I'd known the day would come when I'd share the truth with Cutter. And why not? I liked him. More than that, I trusted him.

"I mean it," he said, apparently taking my silence for hesitation. "Tell me what's going on." He reached out and took Laura's hand, pulling her slightly closer to him as he spoke.

I looked at the two of them and, in spite of everything else, I smiled. "Go ahead, Laura," I said, as I moved across the room with my phone. "Tell him everything."

"Nobody leaves, nobody moves," I said, pointing to the cluster of people now in my living room. It was after six now, and I'd insisted Stuart come home with pizza, which was now getting cold on the kitchen counter as everyone waited for me to finish running through my instructions. "I'm only going to be gone an hour or so, and I want everyone inside, safe and sound, when I get back."

"We can't live like this every day, Kate," Stuart said. "And the demon is dead."

"There are always more demons," I countered. Suddenly tired, I sank down on the couch next to him. Everyone important to me was in that room. Stuart, Eddie, Allie, Timmy. Then Laura and Mindy and Cutter. The only one missing was Eric, and the fact that he wasn't in the room—was no longer welcome in the room—had thrown off my equilibrium.

"Please," I said, all of my exhaustion flowing into my voice. "Just for tonight. Don't argue. Eat pizza. Play stupid board games. Just let me have this one night of knowing you're together and that you're safe."

"And what about us worrying about you?" Stuart said.

I drew in a breath and shot Eddie a quick glance. "They're not going to kill me."

"I'm still not understanding why that is," Laura said, an admission that Allie immediately seconded.

"I don't understand how it works, either," I admitted. "All I know is what Father Corletti told me, and considering Eric confirmed that they don't want to kill me, we have to assume it's true."

"That you're tied to Eric. Or at least to his soul," Stuart said, speaking through near-clenched teeth. I didn't blame him. Hard enough to know your wife still had ties to another man, and worse still if that man was turning out to be a demon.

I nodded, trying to keep my thoughts and demeanor in professional debrief mode. "Right. When I brought him back from the dead—"

"*What?*" That from Cutter, but I chose to ignore it, figuring Laura could add in that detail later.

"—the magic worked a connection. If I die, he dies."

"He-Daddy? Or he-Odayne?"

I met my daughter's eyes, and had to smile when I saw that she was standing straight and tall, using the same tricks I did to remain objective. Or, at least, as objective as possible. "Honestly, I don't know. The connection's with Eric, so it makes sense that he's the one who would die."

"But that must kill Odayne, too," Laura said. "Otherwise, I don't think they'd much care. I mean, they're just interested in getting him a body, right? Him and Lilith. A matching set."

I had to agree. "Right. They're being careful with me, because if Eric dies, then it's San Francisco all over again," I said, referring to Eric's death back when Allie was nine. "Eric and Odayne would be back in the ether, and they'd have to wait for another chance to pop into a body. And that could take years, even decades."

"The ether?" Cutter asked, and this time I took pity on him.

"It's where most demons are. Think of it as another dimension. They're only a problem to us if they manage to become corporeal. You know, get into a body."

"A dead body," he said, this time looking to Laura, who nodded confirmation.

Mindy lifted her hand, as if she was in class. "So you're safe right now because if they kill you, then Eric dies and Odayne goes poof with him?"

I nodded. "Looks that way."

Stuart moved to my side and took my hand. "They may not be able to kill you, but they can hurt you," he said.

I managed a watery smile, knowing all too well that the hurt he referred to wasn't physical. At least not to me. "Yeah. I know." I swallowed thickly, afraid the tears would start up again if I looked at Allie or Mindy or Laura. The tears had already flowed once, when we were still at Cutter's waiting for the disposal team that Father Corletti had ordered up from Los Angeles. They'd made great time, actually, and I think the sight of the team, in their matching scrub shirts and with their white cargo van, so efficient and controlled, had driven the truth home to Cutter. The shocked look on his face had vanished, replaced with a ferocity I knew only too well. He might not be trained at hunting demons, but he was one of the best fighters I knew, and if anything happened while I was gone, I felt better knowing he was there to fight.

I pushed up off the couch. "Enough," I said. "It's time." I couldn't put it off any longer. There were too many things about which I had to confront Eric. The dead demon. The missing page. "Lock the doors. Don't let anybody in. Be safe."

"Mom," Allie said, but this time without the eye roll. "We know."

"Call me if Father Corletti calls back," I said. He'd promised to go straight to the archives and look for the book with the missing page. With any luck, we'd have a binding spell for Odayne by morning.

"Okay," I said. "I'm off." I headed toward the garage, Stuart's *I love you* floating after me.

I paid attention as I backed the van out of the driveway, carefully watching to make sure no one managed to sneak inside the garage as the door was open. I saw nothing, and thought that was, at least, something. Now, alone in the car, I could finally let myself go. I didn't cry—I didn't have the time for that sort of luxury—but it felt like the tears were flooding my insides. Fear and worry and utter horror that my dangerous world had intruded so far into the real world.

Except it was all real, wasn't it? Demons and monsters and things that wanted to hurt me and my family and my friends. All real and all horrible, and what had happened today at Cutter's only underscored how impotent I really was. Even with all my training, all my knowledge, all of my secret peepholes into the messy netherworld. None of it mattered. Not really. Not when the demons were going to use the people I care about to get to me.

I wanted to say that I was a strong enough person that I could withstand their dirty tactics, but I wasn't sure that I was. They'd gotten to me this time, and the one person I needed to pull me back to center wasn't going to be able to help me. I knew that—was absolutely certain I'd lost him—but damned if I wasn't going to try to get him back. Because if I could save him, then maybe I could save all of us.

"Hang on, Eric," I said, not realizing how tightly I was holding the steering wheel. "Dammit, *fight*."

I called his apartment from the road and got no answer. That was fine. If he was screening my calls, I'd confront him when I saw him. And if he really was gone, well, that was fine, too. I'd break in and search his apartment. With any luck, I'd find the page from the book. With even more luck, the part of him that was still Eric had left it there for me to find.

My fear was that I wouldn't find it and that Father Corletti wouldn't find it.

My fear was that the page was gone for good, the binding spell lost to the sands of time.

And without that spell, then there was no way to bind Odayne. No way, at least, that I knew of. Though I had to admit that my knowledge of binding demons was limited. I was much more of a kill them and be done with it kind of girl.

And, of course, binding Odayne wasn't my only problem. The truth was that Lilith was as big a problem as Odayne, if not bigger. Odayne was simply more personal because he'd moved into my husband. But Lilith was not the kind of demon I needed gunning for me and my family, and if I did manage to stop Odayne, I was going to have to deal with her wrath, and that would really, really, really not be pretty.

Too bad there wasn't some way to bind *her*. Some sort of two-for-one special would be good, actually. Something. Anything.

But nothing brilliant jumped to mind, most probably because this really wasn't my turf. For that matter, until this whole mess with Eric, the only bound demon I'd ever really had to deal with was Andramelech, trapped inside Solomon's Stone. Then again, I corrected myself, that had to do with Eric, too. He'd trapped the demon, after all, unknowingly sacrificing himself in the process, his soul getting sucked out of his body even at the instant the demon was sucked into the stone.

Wait.

I played that back in my head, my eyes narrowing as I thought about what I knew about Solomon's Stone. It could be used to trap a demon. All the person doing the trapping had to do was jam their finger—the one wearing the ring—into the eye of the demon. But the person trapping it had to be willing to make the ultimate sacrifice—their soul sucked out and up into the ether.

What would happen if Eric wore the stone and jammed his finger into Lilith's eye?

Suddenly excited, I dialed my house, then waited impatiently until Stuart put Eddie on the line.

"Sounds like a damn fine plan for trapping her, but it makes Eric your scapegoat. He's gonna get stuck back in the dead zone."

"What if we combine the attack on Lilith with an unbinding ceremony? Then wouldn't Eric stay and Odayne be sucked out?"

"Don't know," Eddie said. "Don't really know."

"Can we research it? I mean, it's an idea, right? And it's a way to get rid of Lilith. She's dangerous, Eddie. And she's never going to give up. She's going to go after my family."

"I'll call Rome," he said. "I'll get the stone here. At the very least," he said, "it's a weapon. And we need all the weapons we can get."

I hung up feeling slightly ill, because I couldn't imagine sacrificing Eric back to the ether. If we could find an unbinding ritual, then maybe it wouldn't come to that, but I had to confess that I was losing hope. My options seemed to be closing in around me, and my goal of saving Eric was beginning to waver against the bigger goal of keeping my children safe and alive.

I hated having the choice thrust upon me, but I also knew which way I was going to choose. For my children.

Always, always for my children.

I drew in a breath as I turned on Eric's street and prayed that it wouldn't come to that. I wanted to unwrap Eric from Odayne and fight side by side with him to nail Lilith and her demon lover. And all I could do was hope that Eric was still enough inside David's body that he could help me make that wish come true.

It was perhaps a foolish wish, but I couldn't get it out of my mind. No matter how many secrets he'd kept from me, I knew that one thing was true—Eric loved me. And if there was any way—any way at all—for him to help me on this quest to save him, I knew damn well that he would find that way.

I found a spot right in front and pulled in, then raced up the stairs to his apartment. I pounded on the door, got no answer, and tried the knob. It turned easily, and I pushed the door open.

Then I froze.

The scene before me reeked of déjà vu. Nadia on Eric's lap in the chair nearest the door. Eric's hands on her, his eyes blind with passion.

The last time I'd walked in on such a scene, Eric had been mortified. This time, I don't think he even noticed me as Nadia impaled herself over and over and over on him, her fingernails digging into his shoulders.

I should have looked away—I wanted to look away—but somehow I couldn't. And because of that, the smug smile on Nadia's face when she turned to look at me hurt that much more.

"We have company, darling," she said, pushing Eric back

as he bent forward to suckle at her naked breast. His head turned slowly, and I saw his eyes widen as he looked at me. I saw more, too. I saw recognition. I saw *Eric*.

No. That wasn't him. That wasn't the man I loved. It was Odayne and only Odayne, and with my chin high, I took a step inside the room. "Odayne," I said. "He won't let you stay, you know. Eric's a fighter. More than that, he's a winner."

At that, the body I knew as Eric only laughed. "What makes you think he hasn't already won? I am victory. *We*," he said, in that painfully familiar voice. "We are victory."

He rose then, his back displayed to me, and I saw the bulging, horrible scar on his back. The serpent, and it seemed to be staring right at me.

I shook my head and, unable to bear it any longer, shifted my gaze to Nadia. "I'm going to kill you," I said, slowly and softly. "I'm going to take you out, watch you die, and then I'm going to dance on your hollow, lifeless body."

"Temper, temper," she said. "And don't even think about it. We are very strong. And if we choose to, we will crush you like a bug."

"We," I repeated. "You and Lilith."

"What a good little student you are. Of course. We are one now."

"Not completely," I said. "Not yet."

"Do you think you can stop us? You cannot. We are strong. We are timeless. And we are ever so patient."

"You're evil and you're vile, and I'm going to end you."

"How?"

I stayed silent, and she laughed, the sound surprisingly girlish. "You enjoy your heroic fantasies, darling. The rest of us will live in reality."

I took another step closer, my fists clenched tight at my sides.

"Ah, ah," she said, and suddenly there was a knife in her

hand, its tip pressing into the flesh over Eric's heart. I froze. Eric, I noticed, smiled.

"You won't kill him," I said. "You want him too much."

"Clever girl," she said. "But killing him won't send my darling away. Not this time. He's twined enough inside the body now. Not fully. Not yet. But close." With her free hand, she stroked his cheek, the gesture so gentle, so loving, it made me sick. "Kill the flesh and the demon will still live, here, inside this body."

"And Eric?" I asked, hating myself for asking, and fearing that I already knew the answer.

This time, Eric's head turned to look at me. "He will be with us, of course. He is always with us."

"It makes the human in me happy," Nadia—or, rather, Lilith—said. "She likes him, you see. And I think you already know that he likes her. Likes her very, very much I believe."

I couldn't stay. Couldn't watch the two of them anymore, couldn't listen to the horrible things Lilith was saying. Or that Odayne was saying through Eric's mouth.

And as much as I wanted to, I knew I couldn't take them on. Not and survive.

And if I didn't survive, then neither would my family.

I turned away, my back to them before either could see the tears, and pulled the door open. I hurried out, Nadia's laughter echoing after me.

I'd hoped to get away. To at least get into the car before the tears came, but my control wasn't cooperating, and I stumbled down the steps with tears streaming down my face. I cried for Eric, trapped in a body he didn't want to be in. And I cried for myself, unable to erase the picture of my beloved Eric with another woman, even though I knew it wasn't really Eric at all.

I cried because I wanted to save him and I had no idea how.

And I cried because I was tired. I was so damn tired.

"You're a fool," Nadia said, and I whipped around to find her behind me, now wearing one of Eric's shirts and nothing else.

"Careful," I said. "You'll catch cold."

"Stay away from me, Kate. Don't get ideas. Don't think you can play the hero and win this round. You've won too many times, darling. You've used up your quota." She leaned in close, her face only inches from mine. "It's my turn, sweetheart. It's my turn to win."

I tried to think of a snappy comeback, honestly I did, but my mind wasn't sharp enough. My reflexes were a hell of a lot sharper, and I kicked up with my knee at the same time I smashed forward with my head. I caught her hard in the crotch at the same time I smashed her nose. A second later, I had her by the shoulders and sent her tumbling down so that her bare ass skidded hard on the rough concrete sidewalk.

Her face curved with fury, and she stood, eyes black now, the whites totally gone.

I stepped back, realizing I'd crossed a line. Realizing for the first time that Lilith was no ordinary demon and that I'd just fucked up, but good.

"You won't kill me," I said, praying that Eddie was right. "You *can't* kill me."

"The hell I can't," she said, her voice seeming to reverberate throughout me. "But you are right. I won't. Do you know why?"

Something squeezed at my throat, and I realized it was her hand. I blinked, not at all sure how she'd moved that fast. My body was icy with fear, but I fought it. Told myself to steady. I wasn't dying today. Not now.

A small comfort considering there were lots of ways to hurt me. Lots of ways to make me beg for death. And lots of ways to punish me without ever giving me that sweet release.

"Do. You. Know. Why?" she repeated.

"I die, he dies," I said, working hard to speak with my throat held so tight. "And all this work is for nothing. They're both gone. Back to the ether. And your precious Odayne will have to start all over again in some other body."

Her brows lifted. "Aren't you the clever one? But you're wrong. So very wrong."

"The hell I am."

"Something like that," she said with a smile. "The truth is that if you die, *Eric* dies. Eric dies, but Odayne stays, warm and cozy in that body I like so much."

I swallowed, trying to process what she was telling me. Because what she was saying—what I was hearing—was that *my death* was the unbinding spell I'd been looking for.

"That's right," Nadia said, apparently reading my thoughts. "Odayne is within the flesh now, and there he will remain."

"You lie," I said. "If that were true, you'd be trying to kill me right now." Yet even as I spoke the words, I knew that she was telling the truth. And I also knew why she wouldn't kill me—why she wouldn't release Eric's soul from Odayne. It was for the reason Allie said—Lilith wanted that brush with humanity, and she wanted her lover to have a bit of humanity as well.

"You understand," she said. "I see it in your eyes. I want my beloved back. Is that so hard for you to understand, Katie-kins? Is it so hard for you to see how we are alike? You should be supporting me, not hunting me. For that matter," she said, with a flick of her wrist, "you should be down on your knees worshipping me."

And then I was. She'd tossed me down like so much garbage and the hand that had been on my throat was now on the top of my head, grasping my hair, tilting my head back so that I had no choice but to look at her.

"I have her in me now, the Hunter who vexes you so. Her

humanity flows in this body that I now fill. We are not yet one, but we will be soon enough, and when that happens I will be open to all the pleasures of your world. I will wish to share them with my beloved. And for that, he must feel the sting of humanity, too. For that, he needs his counterpart. The human soul with which he has been twined lo these many years."

"It was an empty threat, then," I said. "Inside. When you threatened Eric with the knife."

She laughed then, and her hand shook as it did, jerking at my hair and making me wince. "Not at all. Kill the flesh, and the soul lives inside. Once Odayne is fully bound to the flesh, the death of Eric's body will not break the bind between them."

I licked my lips, my mind racing. I had no reason to doubt what she said, but at the same time, she *hadn't* shoved the knife into Eric's heart. There could only be one reason why she held back, and that was that Odayne still wasn't yet fully bound in the flesh. He was emerging, but the game wasn't over yet. Which meant—or at least I hoped it meant—that there was still time to save Eric.

"But killing me is different than killing the body," I said. "The Lazarus Bones tied my soul to Eric's. Kill me, and you free Eric's soul. And your lover loses his grip on humanity." I managed a smile. "Quite the conundrum, I'm sure. It must really irk you not to be able to kill me."

"Not at all. I'm a patient woman, after all. After so many millennia, patience comes quite easily to me. And once Odayne and Eric are fully bound, the ties between you and your husband will be broken. He will no longer be yours; he will be fully mine. And once that happens, dearest, I assure you that I will kill you without hesitation."

"He's fighting it," I said. "I don't care what show you put on for me in there. Eric's fighting it."

"Yes," she said. "He is. But that hardly matters. He's losing the battle. He's tiring. He's weakening. And even if he weren't, I'm unwilling to take chances."

"You're going to do something," I said, thinking of all those ceremonies Eddie was talking about. "Something to fuse Odayne and Eric."

"Clever girl. I merely intend to hurry the process along."

"How? When?"

"Such curiosity! But it doesn't matter. There's nothing you can do to stop it. And once it's done, I promise I'll put you out of your misery. You can thank me for that later."

"You'll never touch me," I said, but considering she had me by the hair, I'm certain my words lacked their full impact.

"Oh, I assure you I will. And in the meantime, dearest, I may not be able to kill you, but I know how to hurt you. You, and those you love."

And with that, she hauled back with her free hand. Lightning fast, her fist flew at me, and with her other hand holding my head in place, there was nowhere to go. I screamed when she made contact, the world turning red, then gray, then black.

And as my head hit the pavement, I was vaguely aware that she was gone.

And after that, all was black.

Fifteen

The light tap at my bedroom door startled me, and I lifted my head from the pillow, my fingers still stroking Timmy's hair. I'd been lying there for an hour, my little boy asleep beside me, and I'd been watching him. Just watching. And trying hard not to think.

"Hey," Allie said, poking her head inside. "Daddy called."

That got me moving, and I sat up, angering the headache that was pounding against my eyes. I don't know how long I'd lain unconscious and sprawled out on the sidewalk in front of Eric's apartment, but it was long enough to make my muscles stiff. I'd gone home and moved straight for the bedroom, taking Timmy with me, only giving Stuart the barest overview of what had happened as he taped up my broken nose.

"What did he say?" I asked, and saw Allie wince at the nasal quality of my voice.

She came over slowly and sat on the edge of the bed, careful not to wake her sleeping brother. "He said to tell you he was sorry," she said, and I felt the tears start to well. "And that you shouldn't give up on him because he's going to beat this. He says he doesn't know what happened. That it was important for me to tell you that he doesn't remember any of it. That it was Odayne, and he was inside, but he was lost and he couldn't get out."

"But he's out now."

She nodded, her own eyes brimming. "And he said that he loved me. And that I was supposed to tell you that he loves you, too." She drew in a deep breath. "Mom, what happened?"

I shook my head. Never was I going to tell her that truth. "The demon," I said simply. "The demon is taking over, and Lilith is right there moving it along."

"And Nadia?"

"As far as I'm concerned, they're one and the same."

She licked her lips. "Can we really stop her? I mean, she's, like, hugely powerful."

"We have to," I said, refusing to harbor any doubts. "It's the only hope your dad has. Stop Lilith, and he can fight Odayne. Buy some time. But if we can't stop her, she's going to do the binding ceremony, and Eric really will be lost." I reached over and squeezed her hand. "I need to talk to Stuart and Eddie, okay? Don't you have some research to do?"

"Tons," she said. "Does that mean I don't have to worry about homework?"

"No school for you tomorrow," I said. "Or Friday."

"Next week?"

"This will be over by next week," I said firmly. "One way or another, it's going to be finished."

She stood up and moved to the door, then paused and looked back at me. "I called everyone and canceled my party."

"Allie!" It was, of course, the right thing to do. I'll confess, though, that I was amazed that she'd done it.

"They're trying to hurt you through us. I figured they wouldn't hesitate to go after a bunch of my friends. Slaughter a bunch of innocent teenagers, and—" She broke off with a shrug. "Well, you know."

"You're absolutely right," I said, coming to a decision. "And you're still having the party."

She frowned. "Are you nuts?"

"Not with your friends. But with us. The family. Laura. Mindy." I tried to smile, but stopped when it made my nose hurt. "You deserve it, and we won't be in any more danger in the theater than at home." And though I didn't say it, the truth was that we were probably in less danger. After all, home had a multitude of windows and doors whereas the theater had only the main entrance and one fire exit. And if nothing else, it was another evening during which I would know everybody's exact location.

"You really mean it?"

"Absolutely," I said. "We'll bring extra holy water, stock away a few weapons, and pray," I said. "It'll be smaller than we planned, but it'll still be a party."

"Yes." She made a pumping motion with her fist, then flashed me the kind of grin that assured me I'd made the right decision. "And, Mom? Sorry about your nose."

My fingers automatically rose to brush my battered nose, and I winced. "That's okay," I said. "I was getting tired of seeing the same reflection every time I looked in the mirror. Stuart and Eddie," I reminded her. "Can you get them for me now?"

"Right."

She scooted out, and a few moments later my husband and Eddie trundled in. Stuart immediately came to the bed and put his arm around me. Eddie paced, hands shoved deep into his pockets.

"The stone's supposed to arrive on Friday. I talked to Father Corletti this morning."

"So that's the plan, then," I said. "We get the stone, we corner Lilith, and we hope for the best."

"How are we going to corner Lilith?" Stuart asked.

"Eric," I said. "We use him as bait." I looked up, met my husband's eyes. "She loves him, you see. We get him away—make her think he's in danger—and she'll come. She'll come, and we'll be ready."

"That she-bitch is wicked strong," Eddie said.

"So's the stone. It held Andramelech. It'll hold her." I spoke firmly, but I couldn't help the way my confidence wavered. "Won't it?"

Eddie drew in a breath, then nodded. "I think so. So long as we can get through the ceremony before she rips the skin from our bones. And so long as Eric's willing to jam his finger into the queen bitch's eye. So, yeah. Except for those few minor points, then yeah. I think it'll work."

I swallowed. "Good," I said, with more confidence than I felt. The truth was, I didn't feel much at all except numb. I'd taken a beating, both emotionally and physically. And what I wanted right then more than anything was for this all to be over. "What about the book?" I asked.

"Gone missing from the Vatican library," Eddie said. "Last time anyone saw it was right around the time Eric went back to Rome to work through some of his issues."

"Shit," I said, and heard both Eddie and Stuart grunt in agreement. I looked from one to the other, and my feeling of being at loose ends dissipated. No matter what, I wasn't alone in this. "Thank you both," I said.

"For what?" Stuart asked, while Eddie harumphed and turned a bright shade of pink.

"For helping. For understanding. I don't know," I said, suddenly flustered. "Just for being there."

Stuart sighed and took both my hands in his. "I don't

know Eric. Not really. And what I know, I don't much like. No, don't say anything," he added, when I started to protest. "It's jealousy, and I know that. But I don't have to like the guy to know that I would never, ever wish what's happening to him on anyone. Worst enemy or my wife's first husband. I love you, Kate, and you love him. So there's no question. Of course I'll help."

"Thank you," I said, then shot a sad smile toward Eddie. "Are we pretty sure that it'll be Odayne who's sucked into the ether?"

He shook his head. "Mildly sure. But it could be Eric. Or it could be both of them. As far as we know it's never been done before, but if we do the ceremony in the safe room, then the demon is going to want to leave—it's gonna want to get the hell out of there, no pun intended. And Father Corletti agrees that that'll increase our odds." He shrugged. "It's the best we can do. It's a risk, though. For all of us, and mostly for Eric. You willing to take that risk, girl?"

I nodded. "I don't think we have a choice." I took Stuart's hand and tugged him down next to me on the bed. "I need to talk to Stuart for a minute, okay?"

"You're doing good, girl," Eddie said, looking me hard in the eyes. "Damn good."

I managed a smile, then cringed because the movement hurt my nose. He chuckled, then headed out of the room.

"There's another way," I told Stuart as soon as Eddie was gone. "If we screw up and can't bind Lilith and she gets the ceremony started to twine Odayne and Eric together, there's still one way left that can save Eric's soul." I licked my lips, hating what I was about to say. "If I die, Eric not only dies, but his soul goes free. Lilith pretty much admitted that little loophole."

"Wait, wait, wait." He stared at me as if I'd gone insane. "There is no way you're—"

"No," I agreed. "I'm not. I can't." I pressed my palm

against his cheek. "I *won't* do it." But I looked away then, tears filling my eyes. "I feel so guilty. There's a solution. A way to save a man's *soul*. A man I love, and Stuart, I really do love him. It's right there, and I can reach out and touch it. But I can't take it. I can't."

"Of course you can't," Stuart said, holding me close as I clung to him. "You can't," he repeated. "And Eric wouldn't want you to."

About that, though, I wasn't so sure. Because there'd been a time in my life when I would have willingly gone into the abyss to save Eric's soul, and when I was certain he would have done the same to save mine.

But I wasn't that girl anymore, and my future now lay with the man who now held me in his arms, gently stroking my hair.

I would try to save Eric, yes. But I wasn't going to sacrifice my life or my family to do it.

Federal Express delivered the ring with Solomon's Stone Thursday morning with advertised swiftness. All good and well, but the stone was useless to us without both Eric and Lilith.

"So what's the plan?" Allie asked, bouncing Timmy on her lap and popping dry Lucky Charms into her mouth. "I'm only eating these 'cause I need the sugar for energy. Next week, I'm totally going back to Kashi."

"Mellow!" Timmy said, picking out a green marshmallow. "Wanna eat mellows!"

"Get your own bowl, twerp," Allie said, but she reached across the table to fill her own bowl up higher to share.

"Don't feed him that," I said automatically, but the odds of me pursuing that particular point were slim. My mind was too occupied with other things to worry about basic childhood nutrition. "Since I'm not going to be with you,

I want all of you to stay at the mansion today," I said. "For that matter, I want you in the safe room. Laura and Mindy and Cutter, too," I added, picking up the phone to call Laura's house.

She answered on the first ring, and I told her what I wanted. "Hang on a sec," she said, then came back to the phone not two minutes later. "We'll meet you there," she said, and I couldn't help but smile.

"Tell Cutter I said *good morning*."

"We were just going over some figures for the studio," she said, but I could hear the smile in her voice.

"I've got work," Stuart said, then he caught the expression on my face. "Fortunately, I've already put a wireless router in the mansion. I'll have one of the paralegals e-mail me the agreements to review."

"Rita'll keep," Eddie said. "Hate to break our first date, but sometimes allowances gotta be made."

I collapsed into an empty chair nursing my cup of coffee. "I love you guys. We pull this off, and Lilith's history."

Allie looked at me, her blue eyes wide and innocent. "Yeah," she said. "And there's a good chance that Daddy's history, too."

I held out my hand, and she took it, squeezing hard. I hoped that only Odayne would be thrust into the ether when Lilith was bound in the ring, but I couldn't guarantee it.

"He's smart, your daddy," Eddie said. "And he loves you. He'll find his way back. He did it once before."

"He had help then," she said. "He got to piggyback on the demon."

"It is done, though," I said. "Father Corletti said so. Not often, but it's done. If anyone can do it, your father can."

"He'll be someone else. He might be in China or Russia or the South of France. And he could be in the ether for decades. Time's different there, right?"

"But he'll be back," I said more firmly. "Back and without

a demon. His soul his own." I swallowed, my throat suddenly tight with second thoughts, even though I knew this was for the best. More than that—it was perfect. The only clean solution. Or as clean as it could be considering we had to get Eric to cooperate and Lilith in the trap.

When I thought about it that way, the solution wasn't so perfect. On the contrary, I had to wonder if we were screwed.

"There's no other solution," I said, as much to them as to myself. I pushed back from the table, unable to sit still. "We need to get going."

Allie and Stuart exchanged glances, but didn't argue. They both headed out of the kitchen to gather their stuff, Allie passing Timmy off to me on the way.

I plopped him on the counter and peeled a banana, trading bites with him as we waited.

"You don't have anything you want to take?" I asked Eddie.

He patted the pocket of the oversized shirt he was wearing. "Ian Fleming. Seeing as I'm working in the intelligence trade now, I figure I gotta know the literature."

I laughed. Couldn't argue with that.

"We ain't gonna live like this forever, girl."

"This works the way I want it to, and we won't have to."

We took the van, figuring if they needed to leave for some reason—and I warned them that they'd better not—they could take Laura's car. In fact, Laura and crew were waiting for us when we got there, not having had to waste time gathering toddler toys the way I had, remembering at the last minute that there was no way Timmy was going to last in an empty house without a variety of amusing distractions.

At the mansion, I waited until they were tucked away inside the safe room, and then I kissed my family good-bye and promised to be back soon.

"Be careful, Mom," Allie said. "They can't kill you,

but . . ." She trailed off, as if saying it would make it come true.

I brushed my fingertips lightly over my bruised and swollen nose. "I know," I said, and then I left the family I loved to go try to save a man I loved.

Sixteen

I couldn't find him. I went all over San Diablo, checking the fancy hotels and the dives, Eric's apartment, and Nadia's old digs.

I walked the beach. I roamed the parks. And I found no sign of him.

When I got back to the mansion, I found my family and friends camped out in the safe room.

"Stay or go?" Stuart asked.

"Home," I said.

Allie frowned. "Do you think that's okay?"

I nodded. I couldn't be certain, of course, but instinct told me that Nadia would want to keep herself and Eric as far away from me and mine as possible until after she'd bound herself to Lilith and until after Odayne was bound to Eric. Any other scenario, and Eric might try to break free, might fight her and help me.

Which at least explained why I'd had no luck in that department. But the tiny bit of good news was that—assuming I was right—we were all safe for the night.

I told everyone my thoughts, and they agreed. "Damn good reasoning," Eddie said. "Course Lilith's a crazy bitch and you can't predict crazy, but I'd say the odds are in our favor."

Not a completely rousing endorsement, but it was good enough, and we piled back in our cars and headed home. I'd asked Cutter and Laura to stay at our house, but Laura had declined. Cutter, however, promised to stick close by. And that, I figured, was something.

Timmy was asleep by the time we got home, and I tucked him gently in bed, with Stuart looking over my shoulder. "Allie needs you," he said. "And then I need you, too."

I kissed him hard and long. "A promise," I said. "I'll see you in a few."

He pressed a soft kiss to my nose, and I headed down the hall for Allie's room, where I found her already curled up in bed.

"Hey," I said, climbing in beside her and pulling her close. "You okay?"

"He's in there, Mom," she said, her voice barely a whisper. "He's in there and he's fighting, and we have to find him and get him out. Promise me. Promise me this is going to work."

I drew in a noisy breath. "You know I can't promise that, baby."

"Do it anyway."

I felt the ring in my pocket press into my hip. The stone that was going to solve our problems. The panacea that was going to make Lilith go away. "I promise," I said, and I damn sure hoped I wouldn't have to break it.

"Sleep here with me tonight?"

I thought of Stuart alone in our bed, and knew that he would understand. "Absolutely," I said, and held her tight. The last time she'd snuggled in my bed, she'd been nine, and we'd just learned that her father had been murdered. She'd slept with me for three solid months, and then she'd announced one day that she was doing okay, and that she needed to be a big girl and go back to her own bed. She hadn't backpedaled. Not once.

I'd been proud of her then for knowing it was time to grow up.

And I was proud of her now for being grown up enough to ask me to be there for her.

"We're going to stop Lilith and we're going to free your father."

"I know you are," she said. "I love you, Mom."

"I love you, too, baby," I said, and then I fell asleep with wisps of tears on my eyes.

Friday arrived as an oasis of sanity in a week gone mad. I'd fallen down on the job with regard to Allie's party preparations, and that meant that today I wasn't going to worry about Eric's whereabouts or fear an imminent attack from Lilith or Nadia or whoever the hell she was today. Instead, I was going to run around to grocery stores and party-supply stores. I was going to buy fancy little cupcakes. And I was going to desperately, frantically wonder what on earth the mother of the fifteen-year-old birthday girl was supposed to wear to a party.

Because even without all her friends there—even without her father as part of the crowd—I still wanted to make this the best birthday possible for Allie. I wanted, at least a little, to live inside the illusion that not only would everything be okay, but that it was already fine and dandy.

Foolish, I know, but for a few hours I needed the foolishness. Honestly, I think we all did.

Before all of that, however, I had to see the birthday girl

herself, and so I tiptoed into her room with a wrapped package under my arm and a toasted bagel in my hand, a single candle stuck atop a schmear of cream cheese. Despite the fact that my wide and varied talents do not include singing, I belted out "Happy Birthday," causing my normally groggy-in-the-morning daughter to sit bolt upright, a smile wide across her face.

"Hey," she said. "I'm fifteen."

"I know," I said. "I was there when you were born."

She smirked and held out her hand for the bagel. "Do I get to make a wish?"

"Absolutely," I said, and although she didn't tell me what she wished for, I knew. I was wishing for the same thing, even without flaming breakfast products.

"So," she said casually, after taking a bite from her birthday bagel. "Is that for me?"

I pulled the package out from under my arm and looked at it, feigning surprise. "Huh. Now where on earth did that come from?"

"Gimme!" she squealed, and bounced on the bed in pretty much the same manner as when she was six.

"Stuart and I got you some more presents that you can open tonight at the party," I said. "But this one's from me."

"Yeah?" She hefted the box, which I'd wrapped in the Sunday comics since I could find no wrapping paper in our house. About fourteen inches long and five inches wide with a depth of about two inches. And she was examining every bit of it. "Hmmm," she said, pressing her ear close and shaking it. "A dagger," she said smugly. "I knew it."

"Allie," I said, with a shake of my head. "You won't know for sure until you open it."

"Good point," she said, and ripped into the paper with a laugh. In seconds, she was down to the box, which she sat on her lap as she tugged the lid off. I fought a smile as she looked at the beautiful necklace with the silver pendant.

The one I'd bought at the jewelry store near Eddie's spy shop. "Oh, wow," she whispered. And though I knew she was expecting a different present and was desperately hiding her disappointment, she drew it out and hooked it around her neck. "It's amazing. Thanks."

"You're welcome," I said, still trying not to smile. "I thought the colors would coordinate nicely with the leather of the sheath."

"Oh," she said, confused. Then her eyes narrowed and she peered up at me. "Sheath?"

I shrugged and nodded toward the box. With a scowl, she lifted it, her face lighting up as she realized that the weight was a bit more significant than an empty box would be. She tugged out the paper on which the necklace had rested and revealed a pearl-handled steel dagger tucked into a rich, brown leather sheath.

"Wow," she said, taking it out and stroking a finger reverentially over the finely crafted handle. "Really? For me?"

"Got your initials and everything," I said, motioning for her to turn it over. There, engraved on the blade, were the initials AEC—Alison Elizabeth Crowe. "It's yours, baby. You earned it."

She caught me in a huge bear hug and, thankfully, had enough presence of mind to leave the knife on the bed when she did so. "This is awesome, Mom. And this is going to be the best birthday ever."

I smiled and hugged her back, but I saw the shadow in her eyes. Not quite the best birthday, I thought. But for today, at least, maybe we could all pretend.

Actually, it turned out that pretending wasn't really required. The day passed so swiftly with preparations—and so safely without signs of brooding or attacking demons—that none of us thought of much other than getting everything ready at the theater. "We really don't have to go all out," she said, over and over. "I told everyone I'm sick, remember?

That the party's off. So it's not like we have to fix the place up still."

"Actually, we do," I said firmly, and when I saw the smile bloom on her face, I knew that I'd said—and done—the right thing.

The day passed in such a demon-free haze that after a few hours I couldn't help but second-guess Allie's decision to disinvite her friends from the party. Certainly, it was shaping up to be a demon-free night.

More than that, though, the lack of activity on the demon-front was starting to make me nervous.

After all, if Lilith was busy harassing me, that meant they didn't have time to plan for this massive binding spell. But she wasn't harassing. She wasn't even watching from afar and sneering creepily. She simply wasn't there.

And neither was Eric.

And, yeah, I was worried. Because how did I know she hadn't already performed whatever ceremony she intended to perform? A ceremony to speed up the bond between Eric and Odayne; a ceremony about which I still knew no details despite days of searching.

"There's nothing you can do," Stuart said as he held up the end of a Happy Birthday banner. "But if it helps, I don't think it's over. I think we still have a chance to save him."

"Why?" I asked, needing to hear reason and not merely hope.

"Because if it were over, Lilith wouldn't stay away. She'd come to gloat. And," he added, his eyes flat and hard, "she'd come to kill."

Despite that cheery prospect, Stuart's analysis made me feel better, and I finished the party preparations in a reasonably good mood, my Eric/Lilith problems tucked as far away in my mind as possible.

We finished fifteen minutes before Laura arrived with Mindy and Cutter. I let them into the concession area through the ornate front door, and was about to lock up again when Eddie arrived with Rita on his arm. I drew in a worried breath and shot him a fierce look over Allie's head, but he just shrugged without looking the slightest bit remorseful or worried about bringing another person into the fold.

"This looks so totally awesome, Aunt Kate," Mindy said, looking around at the lobby decorated with streamers, Happy Birthday banners, and well over fifty helium balloons. We'd inflated another ten with old-fashioned lung-power, and Timmy was busy racing around, bopping the balloons with his fists and head as he tried to keep them airborne.

"What? No praise for your mother?" countered Laura, and I had to laugh. She'd finished the posters documenting Allie's fifteen years on the planet, and they filled each of the ten display cases, four inside the theater, and six outside surrounding the ticket office.

"Mom," Mindy said, with an eye roll I was sure she'd learned from my daughter.

As she and Allie wandered the room, looking at all the posters, Rita shuffled up to them, then thrust a present into Allie's hand. "Nice girl like you," I heard her say, "gotta have one of these. Ain't no two ways about it." And though I couldn't see what was in the box, I did hear Allie's delighted laugh after she opened it. She hugged Rita, then tucked something black and squarish into her back pocket before following up with a second hug.

I cast a glance toward Eddie, but he only shrugged.

Across the room, Mindy had grabbed Allie's hand. "The posters are a blast, but did you see the marquee? I mean, how awesome is that? You got a picture of it, right?"

"Marquee?" Allie turned to look at me, and I realized that she hadn't yet seen it. We'd come in through the fire door off the alley in the back.

"Come on," I said, leading everyone out through the glass

front doors. We gathered near the old-fashioned ticket booth and looked up at the marquee that protruded out over the sidewalk. The sun had set, the only illumination now from the streetlights and the white glow of the backlighting on the marquee, highlighting the words we'd ordered for the occasion: *Happy Birthday, Allie! Congrats on Fifteen Fabulous Years!*

"Oh, wow!" she squealed. "That's so cool. That's so totally awesome." She flung her arms around me, then around Stuart, who hugged her back enthusiastically. "Can we get a picture? Can you fit me and the sign in?" she asked, jogging over to stand beneath it.

"Sure," I said, lifting my camera to my eye. But when I looked through the viewfinder, Allie wasn't smiling in my direction. Instead, she was looking across the street, her expression somehow both wistful and scared. "Allie?"

Her eyes darted toward me, then back across the street. I turned and saw nothing at first. Then a truck that had been blocking my line of sight moved, and I saw Eric standing there.

"Daddy?" The pain in Allie's voice coupled with the raw longing seemed to grab me by the heart and squeeze.

He kept his eyes on her, moving slowly into the street, ignoring the horns and curses from drivers who had to slam on their brakes to avoid hitting him.

"Eric!" I called. "What are you doing?"

He didn't look at me, but he did lift his hands, as if in surrender. But rather than reassure me, the gesture made my blood run cold.

I think he must have realized the move was a misstep, too, because a split second later he burst into a run, practically launching himself from street to sidewalk. And Allie, so desperate to have her father back, stayed put one second too long, so that when she finally did turn away and start to run back toward me, his fingers were close enough to reach, and his hand closed around the back of her shirt and pulled her, kicking and screaming, close to him.

Around me, pandemonium broke out, but it seemed like white noise to me. Everything was happening in slow motion. I'd lunged forward when Eric was still in the street, and so I was close to them now, the blade I'd kept in my back pocket already in my hand.

Eric was ready for me, though, and he grabbed Allie around the waist, then used her as a human shield, twisting her so that the force of her legs thrust out in front of her caught me across the waist, knocking me to the ground, and sending my blade flying.

"No!" Allie screamed.

Behind me, everyone rushed forward, then stopped when Eric yanked Allie's new dagger from the sheath at her waist and thrust the tip against her jugular. "I wish to spend time with my daughter on her birthday," he said, in a voice far removed from Eric's. "I very much suggest you don't make a move for your fallen knife."

On the street, cars honked and people stared, and I was certain it was only a matter of time before someone called 911 and the police came. Fine with me, actually. Right then, I was happy for any distraction I could get.

"Eric, no!" I called, but he only smiled at me.

"Names are important, Katie. If you wish to speak to me, call me by my proper name."

"I am," I said, calculating whether I could take another step forward.

He grabbed her tighter. Allie yelped, and I froze in place. "My name is Odayne," he said. "Say it. *Say it.*"

"Odayne," I whispered, then felt the slow trickle of a tear sliding down my face.

"Excellent." He leaned down to speak closer to Allie's ear, still loud enough that I could hear him. "Now you be a good girl and come spend time with Daddy," he said. He took a step backward, and I could see that the pressure of the knife against her neck had loosened. He had her walking backward, and Allie kept her eyes frozen on me, just as I kept mine on her. Behind me, my friends and family might as well have evaporated. Right then, my whole world centered on my daughter. On saving her.

Too bad I didn't have a clue how to do that.

They took another step backward, and I could see the fear on Allie's face. She stumbled, reaching out for her father for balance, then jerking her arm away quickly as if realizing who she'd reached for. I heard him chuckle, as if he realized, too.

And then I saw something else. I saw Allie, quick as lightning, thrust her hand into her back pocket, as if she'd planned the move all along, as if she'd stumbled on purpose. Even as she did, I heard Rita's sharp intake of breath behind me, and before I even had time to process that oddity, Allie's hand was back out, and the black box Rita had given her was tight in her hand, and it was pressed against Eric's body, and he was shaking, screaming, his eyes wide with pain.

"Taser," Rita breathed even as Stuart called out for me to catch.

I turned just in time to grab the knife he'd sent flying. I snatched it out of the air, positioned it in my hand, and as my daughter dived sideways and down to the ground, I sent the blade hurtling through the air toward Eric, then raced forward toward my daughter.

He dodged the knife, but it still struck him, slicing deep into his upper arm.

His yowl of pain echoed around us, and for a moment, I feared he would go after Allie again. We'd reached each other, though, and now I thrust her behind me, then stood facing Eric.

A split second of indecision crossed his face, and then he

raced once again into the street. I hesitated, and then broke into a run after him, snatching my fallen knife as I went.

I didn't catch him.

A delivery truck in the road slowed me down, and by the time I reached the opposite sidewalk, he'd slipped between two buildings. I followed to the alley, but he was gone. I could search for him, I knew, but I abandoned that plan quick enough, certain that the more prudent option was to go back to my family. To stay with them and keep them safe and whole.

By the time I got back, a uniformed officer was on the scene, summoned apparently by a passerby who'd seen Eric with the knife to Allie's throat.

We told him what had happened, leaving out the demon parts, of course. And also leaving out Eric's identity. The story, as relayed by us, centered on an attack by an unknown man on a fifteen-year-old girl who, thankfully, had a Taser handy. My knife-throwing skills didn't come up, and the officer had no evidence of any blade other than the one the Good Samaritan had reported at Allie's throat.

Although the officer urged us to make a formal report, we begged off, assuring him that Allie was fine, that the encounter was nothing more nefarious than your average mugging, and that the best thing for Allie was to get her mind off the mugging by returning to her birthday celebration.

Back in the theater, I locked the door behind us, sagged against the glass, and let the tears I'd been holding back flow.

"Turn it off, girlie," Eddie said, even as Stuart held me close. "You gotta turn it off if you're gonna fight him."

I lifted my head and met Eddie's eyes. He was right, of course, but what he advocated was easier said than done.

As I pulled away from Stuart, nodding reassurance when his brows rose in question, the ringing of Allie's phone shattered our uncomfortable silence.

She answered, and I could tell from her expression who was on the other end of the line.

She listened, her mouth open a little, and by the time I reached her side, she had ended the call, having not spoken one single word.

With eyes brimming with tears, she looked up at me. "Daddy," she said. "Not Odayne. That was really Daddy."

My heart fluttered in my chest. "What did he say?"

"That he was sorry. That . . . That I should try to have a happy birthday. And," she added, her breath hitching as she fought sobs, "that I should remember that he loves me, and he always has." Her eyes met mine. "When he hung up, he said good-bye. And I think it was more than just hanging up the phone, you know? But he was back. *Really back.* He'd gotten free. Somehow he'd gotten loose long enough to call me. Only now . . . now, I'm scared."

I understood the sentiment; I was scared, too.

"Can you go?" she asked. "Can you go get him now? Now, before Odayne comes back?"

Beside me, Stuart took Allie's hand. "I'm not sure that's such a good idea."

"They won't kill you," she said. "You're the only one who can get him."

"If she's right," Eddie said, "and he's gotten free of Odayne, now's the time. Maybe the last chance, too. If Odayne keeps taking over, we're gonna lose the chance to get that ring on Eric's finger. And if we lose that chance, then there ain't no way of stopping Lilith."

"We don't have a way to unbind him," I said. "If Odayne goes into the ether, Eric goes with him."

"Please," Allie said. "I know Daddy. And he'd rather be incorporeal with a demon than alive on Earth with us dead."

The truth of her words cut through me, and I nodded, knowing that she was right.

"We'll go stay in the safe room so you don't have to worry about us. But please, please. You have to try."

Stuart squeezed my hand, but whether it was in fear or reassurance, I didn't know. And, I suppose, it didn't matter. Because Allie and Eddie were right. If Eric was Eric, then I had a small window of opportunity to bring him into our plan.

I had no choice.

It was time to ask him to use the ring with Solomon's Stone.

It was time to ask him to sacrifice himself in order to save the rest of us.

Odayne.

I wanted to kill him.

I wanted to kill him for putting Allie's life in danger. For breaking her heart.

And I wanted to kill him for sneaking into the man that I loved and hiding him away, piece by piece.

I wanted him gone, and the ring that could accomplish that was snug inside my pocket. The ring that could bring an end to this if only I could make all the pieces fit together. Send Odayne back to the ether. Trap Lilith. Destroy everything she'd worked for. Destroy everything she loved, if a creature such as her really could love.

And in doing so, I'd be condemning Eric's soul to be bound to a demon. But there was no other way. The ritual to unbind him from Odayne was lost, ripped from the book by Eric's own hand. Or, to be more accurate, by Odayne.

We were, I realized, all out of options.

I moved through the night fueled by hate and, yes, by fear, too. Lives were on the line now. The lives of people I loved. My children. My family.

And somehow, someway, we were going to end this. And soon.

First, I had to find Eric.

He wasn't at his apartment. Fortunately, neither was Nadia, and I counted that as a blessing even as I feared that Odayne had surfaced again and had gone to her.

I told myself not to believe that.

Eric had to be alone because I needed him to be alone, and I refused to accept any other possibility.

So I stalked through his apartment, trying to think where he would go. If Eric had any semblance of control, he'd go someplace where I could find him. Someplace he had a connection to. The high school. A hotel we'd stayed at. Someplace we'd shared. Someplace where he'd been only Eric and the demon hadn't yet intruded.

Someplace like the house.

As soon as the thought entered my mind, I knew I was right. Not only was the house standing empty, but I knew it was on his mind. I raced out of his apartment and stumbled blindly to the car, making record time to our old neighborhood. I slammed on the brakes in front of the house, skidding half off the driveway and onto the tidy lawn.

My stomach tightened as I saw that there were no other cars and the house was dark. If he wasn't there, I was seriously screwed, as I was all out of ideas. But once I got to the front door, I knew that I was right. The realtor's lockbox had been ripped off the door, and the frame had been busted. The door swung open easily, and I stepped inside, wary.

"Eric?" I called, but heard only silence in response.

I moved through the house, checking the rooms, feeling more and more despondent as I found each room empty.

I didn't really know despair, though. Not until I got to the bathroom.

Not until I opened the door and found Eric in the bathtub, his slit wrists flowing blood into the inky red water.

"*No!*" I cried, and bounded across the room in one gigantic leap. I pulled the drain on the old clawfoot tub and slapped his face, relieved when he blinked at me, then more relieved when I saw his eyes focus. "Shit, Eric. Shit, shit, shit."

I wore a denim jacket, and now I used my knife to slice it to ribbons, binding his wrists tight to staunch the flow of blood.

"What were you thinking?" I shouted, as tears streamed down my face. "What the hell could you possibly be thinking?"

"Without blood," he whispered, "the demon will be weak. At least for a while. Time enough for you . . . Time enough for you to fight. And she can't bind me without blood. The ceremony," he said. "The ceremony to bind me to Odayne. To speed the process. It requires my blood. Gotta get rid of it. Flush it away. Make it go."

"*No,*" I said again. "Without blood, you die, you stupid, stupid man."

He was fading on me, and I smacked him hard in the face again, then took him by the shoulders and shook him. "Don't you dare die on me, Eric. Don't you dare."

I checked his wrists again, saw that the bleeding had essentially stopped. The water was out of the tub, and he was shivering now in wet clothes.

"Wait here, and if you even think about taking those ties off your wrists I will kill you with my bare hands the second I get back. Do you understand me?"

He didn't answer, but his lip curved up, just slightly, as I stood and raced from the room back to the car. I grabbed a couple of Timmy's blankets along with a package of juice boxes and my workout bag, then practically flew back inside, fearing the worst. But Eric was just how I'd left him, and I started to breathe again once I saw him.

"How long? How long have you been sitting here bleeding?"

"Not long," he said, his voice weak. "Had to. Allie. I hurt—"

"That wasn't you," I said sharply. "That was Odayne."

"That was me," he said firmly. "Or it will be soon enough."

"It damn well will be if you kill yourself," I said. "Dear God, Eric, you'll be twined with him forever."

"But I won't know, Kate. I won't know. It's not consciousness like we have now. I've been there, remember? And trust me Kate: I won't know."

I closed my eyes. "But I will."

"I can't do this," he said as I started to wrangle him out of his wet clothes. I had a T-shirt and the pants from a *gi* in my bag, and I was determined to get him in dry clothes and out of the bathroom. "I can't stay like this and risk hurting Allie. Risk hurting you."

"You won't," I said, although I didn't believe it. I'd been at the theater, after all. And, of course, he knew that.

"Dear God, I almost destroyed her."

"You didn't," I said. "She's safe and you fought your way back out."

"This time," he said. And neither one of us spoke the horrible truth: that it had been close. And if Allie hadn't had Rita's Taser, she could well be dead.

"There won't be a next time," I said, my voice firm. "We have a plan. We know how to end this."

He looked at me blankly, then shook his head. "Some things. Some things I've been able to keep from him. To hide. I've had to fight, because when the demon comes out, he knows. He gets into my head. But there are a few things that I know. Things he won't let me tell, but still secrets that I keep."

I shook my head, not understanding. "What secrets? What does the demon know?"

"He doesn't want me to use it. It would be the end of him."

My eyes went wide. "The dagger! Eric, you do know where the dagger is? Tell me. Where is it?"

His face contorted in pain, and I saw the scar on his back begin to bulge.

"No," I cried. "Don't even think about it. Forget the dagger. We don't need the dagger. We have another plan." I swallowed, and held his hands close. "We can get rid of Lilith—do her in forever. And she's vile, Eric. You know how bad. So that's a huge thing. Because if we don't get rid of her, she's never going to leave us alone. Never going to leave *Allie* alone."

I waited, expecting him to speak, but he stayed silent.

I hesitated only a moment longer, and then continued. "And although we can't kill Odayne, we can make him start all over." I drew in a shaky breath. "It's going to be hard, but not any harder than this. Not any harder than what you planned to do." I licked my lips, looked him dead in the eye, and told him the plan to use the ring with Solomon's Stone.

"So I end up dead," he said after I had explained. "Dead and still tied to that beast. I thought you said you had a solution."

"Dammit, Eric, it's the best solution we can find. The ceremony to unbind you from Odayne has been lost," I said, resisting the urge to blame him. "But you'll come back. Odayne's going to grow inside another body, you know he is. And while he's growing, you can be searching for a way out. And maybe the next time you can find your way free."

"Maybe," he said, his voice harsh, angry. Not that I could blame him. The solution was hardly the best.

"There's another way," he said.

"How? If there is, then tell me."

"Do you love me, Katie?"

My heart hitched. "You know that I do."

"Then come with me. Take me. Your life and mine."

I opened my mouth, certain I'd misunderstood him, and just as sure that I hadn't. "Eric . . . You can't ask me that. Allie. Timmy."

"We're bound, Kate," he said. "Did you know that they are, too? Odayne and Lilith. She created him for herself. Couldn't abide the thought of any other male except one she'd rendered on her own. So she created him, breathed life into him. Loved him. Loves me."

His voice had gone a little singsong, and I shivered. "Eric. Stop."

"It's almost poetic."

"Stop," I shouted, and saw with satisfaction that the dreamy look in his eyes cleared. "Don't talk like this."

"About their love? Or about ours? I thought you loved me, Katie. I thought we were soul mates."

"This isn't something you can ask."

"Why not? You love me?"

"Of course I do," I said, tears falling freely.

"Then this is the solution. You know it as well as I do. We're bound, and we always have been."

I shook my head, horrified that he'd ask me to take my own life, to toss away what God had given me and sacrifice my children in the process . . .

Although I knew that it had to be the demon talking, I still couldn't bear it, and I stood up, moved to the far side of the room and watched him with my back against the wall. I tried to speak, tried to tell him how, and tried to tell him why, but I couldn't find the words. And in the end, I simply stood there, watching him, and slowly shaking my head.

He watched me a moment. "Are you going to die for me,

Katie?" he asked, as I watched the scar on his back begin to pulse with life.

I shook my head. "No. And the Eric I know would never ask me to."

"Funny," he said. "The Katie I know would never say no."

Seventeen

"In the safe room," I said to Eric. "You have to go in."

"No," he said. "I can't. The pain."

"You have to," I said, feeling close to hysterics. "You know it's the only way. You're still weak, the demon will retreat inside, and if you're in the safe room, it'll keep him at bay."

We were back at the mansion, the tension between us thick, and we hardly had the time for a heart-to-heart or to exchange warm fuzzies.

In the end, Eric had agreed to wear the ring. He'd agreed to the plan. And although it broke my heart to know that this was the last night I'd see him on this earth, I comforted myself with the knowledge that he really was Eric. Because only Eric would have made the decision to sacrifice himself for Allie and me. More, I knew Eric was a fighter. He'd find a way out of the ether again, and he wouldn't give up until his soul was free.

"She'll come for you, right? She'll come here? She can find you?"

"She'll come," he said. "I told you, they're bound."

"Then the safe room makes even more sense. If the demon's in pain . . ."

I trailed off because there was no need to finish.

"I know," he said. "I know I have to." He drew in a breath. "I can do it," he said, twisting the ring he'd already placed on his finger. "I *have* to do it."

"I'm right here," I said, and I think he knew that I meant more than the merely physical.

Since he was still unsteady, he had his arm around my shoulder, his other hand holding his cane. He stumped forward, then stopped when the safe room came into view. The door was open, and Allie was on the floor, peering out as if she'd been keeping vigil, her face streaked with tears.

"Daddy?"

I watched him close his eyes, then hold out his hands for her. "I'm sorry," he whispered. "I'm so, so sorry."

She took a step forward, as if ready to run from the room to him, but I stopped her with a curt warning.

"But, Mom!"

"You don't leave the room," I said, my eyes going from her to the others. "None of you." I turned to Eric. "Go on, then."

He hurried to Allie, his arms held wide, his face revealing a hint of the pain he felt entering the room. He buried it, though, and when she hesitated only a moment before rushing into his arms, the pain on his face evaporated completely, replaced by a wistful sadness that both broke my heart and filled me with relief.

Mindy, I noticed, remained in the far corner, her back to the wall and her eyes never leaving Eric.

Allie stepped back, her eyes on his wrists, bound as they were in strips of denim. "What did you do?" she asked.

"I never meant to hurt you," he whispered. "I'd rather

die than hurt you," he said, as more tears spilled down her cheeks.

"This room . . ." His hands clenched into fists, and through the thin, white T-shirt I'd given him, I thought I saw the scar on his back writhe beneath his shirt.

"Eric?" I whispered.

He turned to me, his face tight, his skin pale. He clenched his hands into fists, and there was no denying the struggle going on inside this man. "She's coming. Dear God, she's practically here."

And, yes, she sure as hell was.

It started slowly. So slowly that I thought at first Eric was wrong. That a heavy truck was rumbling up the street. Or that we were feeling the first rumbles of an earthquake.

But trucks couldn't shake down a mansion, and earthquakes didn't go on for eternity.

And as we stood there, huddled in the safe room, the world around us began to rumble, the walls of the mansion shaking, and dust filling the air.

Around us, the walls seemed to scream as the foundation and framing were wrenched apart, the power of Lilith cutting a path in front of her, and we watched as the flooring in the kitchen and the hallway leading up to the safe room seemed to split, tiles bursting and flying, the walls cracking and shaking.

I slammed the door to the safe room shut and gestured for everyone to get in the middle of the room. The walls and floor and ceiling had been imbibed with the bones of saints, but that didn't stop the room itself from shaking as she tore through the rest of the house. And even as the world shook around us, my stomach clenched from the fear I saw on the face of everyone in that room with me.

Everyone, except Eric. There was no fear there. Only despair. And pain.

And then, with one horrible, dusty explosion, the door

to the safe room exploded, splinters flying as I shouted for everyone to get back.

Allie jumped immediately, scooping up Timmy with one hand, and grabbing Mindy with the other even as Cutter jerked Laura and Rita to the far wall. Stuart moved to stand beside me, but Eddie hauled him back by the elbows, and I shouted out, crying for him to go, because I couldn't split my focus by worrying about my husband even while I worried about our plan.

I stood side by side with Eric, my hand clasped tightly in his even as the walls of the safe room began to crack and split.

And still, we hadn't seen her.

"She is among the first of the demons," Eric said, his voice holding a soft, almost sensual reverence that had me looking at him sharply. "She is strong."

Quite the understatement, I thought, in light of what she was doing to the house. And the truth was, I'd never run across anything like this. Never met a corporeal demon with the power to destroy. In true form, yes. But as a human, never.

Lilith was a rare creature. Rare and terrifying and as she walked into view, the floor popping and churning and bursting apart as if blazing her path, I squared my shoulders and forced myself not to show my fear.

"Eric?" I whispered, desperate to know that it was still the man I knew beside me, and not the demon I despised. Because if Odayne had returned— if our plan was over before it had even begun—then I really would be afraid.

"It's me," he said, and I exhaled in relief. "He's trying, but I'm winning. For the moment. But, Kate," he added, "if—if this is the end—I want you to know—"

But he never got to say it. Because suddenly she was there. Right there, larger than life and filling the doorway.

And with a single hand extended in invitation, she called to him.

"No," I said, stepping in front.

Her eyes barely even cut in my direction, and she surely never touched me, but it didn't matter. I was thrown backward, landing so hard against the back wall of the safe room that the impact cracked the plaster.

"Mom!"

"Kate!" Stuart was at my side in an instant, but I was already struggling to my feet.

"Now!" I cried to Eric. "Now, before it's too late!"

And as I held my breath, he stepped out of the room and then, as her lips curled up in a victorious smile, he thrust his finger up and fast, going straight for her eye.

I held my breath, as I knew everyone around me was doing. It was going to work. It *had* to work.

And as we watched, the ring shattered, shards from the stone suddenly flying everywhere, the dust of the destroyed gemstone seeming to sparkle in the light.

I heard screaming, someone calling out, "No!" at the top of their lungs. And it was only when my throat hurt that I realized it was me.

Our chance to stop her had failed, the ring destroyed and useless. And as she smiled at me—as the bitch moved to the very edge of the safe room and actually *smiled* at me—I couldn't suppress the wave of revulsion that swept through me.

Odayne stood beside her now, the light inside that I knew was Eric slowly dying. He turned his head to look at her with such adoration it made my heart break, and when he turned to me, I could barely see through the tears. "It's there," he said, the words coming out in a croak as if he was having to fight to force them past his lips. "With the hidden. Like a secret. Find it. Use it."

And then the light faded, and he turned dead eyes on Allie. "Come with me."

She took a step back, fear and revulsion and utter sadness on her face.

I moved to stand in front of her. All of us moved to stand in front of her. "We're okay. They can't come in the room." I looked at Eric. "Even he can't come in the room anymore."

"Well said, Kate darling," Lilith said, her voice seemingly amplified in the small room. "And so true. Fortunately, entering won't be necessary." She held out her hand. "Come, child."

"Never," Allie said, the strength in her voice making me proud.

"Come, child," she repeated, and this time, Allie took a step toward her.

"Mom? Mom, what's happening?" The panic was unmistakable, as was the fact that she was moving forward, with slow, deliberate steps.

"No," I said. "No, no, no." I held on to her arms even as Stuart and Cutter and Laura grabbed on to her legs and Eddie held her around her waist.

"Pitiful," Lilith said, and with one violent jerk, Allie was ripped from us.

Her screams seemed to sear my brain as she flew through the air to Lilith's waiting arms. I raced forward, but was thrown back again, as was everyone else. And by the time I'd climbed once again to my feet and raced out of the safe room, they were gone.

Just like that, they'd gone.

My knees went weak, my legs collapsing beneath me, and suddenly I was on the floor, Stuart's arms around me, his voice telling me we'd find her, we'd find her, that we were going to find her.

"How?" I forced the word out past the despair I felt Allie and Eric. I couldn't bear it.

"The tracking dot," Eddie said, crouching down beside

me. "That's what you bought it for, right? Don't tell me you forgot to use it."

"Got it," **Eddie said,** doing something to a tiny computer screen that he swore was tuned in to the microdot I'd placed on Allie's necklace. "They're heading for the national forest."

"On our way," Stuart said, steering the car into a sharp U-turn. It was the three of us alone in the car, chasing an electronic beep, desperate to find my daughter. At first I'd told Stuart not to come, but he'd refused, then casually reminded me that we'd be wasting precious time by arguing. "She's my daughter, too," he said, and there was no way—no way in hell—I was arguing with a statement like that.

We'd left the rest behind, Cutter and Laura and Mindy and Rita in the safe room with Timmy. It was an illusion at best. If Lilith wanted my son, we'd just learned well enough that we couldn't stop her. But I couldn't think about that now. All I could think about right now was getting Allie back.

I'd get her back, or I'd die trying.

And if I could take Lilith down with me, so much the better.

Not that I could see any way of that happening. The bitch was powerful. Too powerful. The most I could hope for was to get my daughter back and to escape. And to hope that once Lilith had her lover, that she would go off on some sort of demonic honeymoon and leave the rest of my family alone.

I'd lose Eric—dear God, I could hardly bear to think of it—but if my kids were safe . . .

I knew, of course, why they wanted Allie. I'd realized the moment Lilith had taken her. Eric had told me, though I don't think he'd ever realized that his daughter was in danger. *They needed his blood for the ceremony to bind him and*

Odayne. But Eric's blood was no more, because Eric's body was dead and buried. David's blood would never suffice, not for that kind of magic.

And the only remaining blood of Eric Crowe flowed in the veins of his daughter.

I prayed that they needed only a drop. If they needed a sacrifice . . . Well, I couldn't even bear to think of it.

"Have we got any chance at all?" Stuart asked. "Any chance of stopping her?"

"Car's stocked," Eddie said. "Made sure it was before we left for the party. Trunk's full of holy water super shooters and a few more Tasers. Got a selection of knives and crossbows. And I got a few handguns, too. Won't stop the bitch, but she'll look a damn sight less pretty with a chunk of her face missing. And we got one other thing, too. If you kill Odayne, you're gonna hurt her. Gonna hurt her bad."

"Except to do that," Stuart said, as he sped along the Coast Highway toward the cutoff to the canyon, "we need that dagger. And we've never found it."

"Don't even really know it existed," Eddie said, his eyes on the tracking device. "If it did, you'd think Odayne woulda found it. Found it and hidden it away just in case Eric was tempted to pass it on in one of his lucid moments."

"Eric looked," I said, twisting around to speak to Eddie, who was in the backseat. "He would have told me if he—"

"What?" Eddie said, his eyes narrowed as he peered at my face.

"Here!" I shouted, grabbing Stuart's arm. "Turn here."

"You can't get to the national forest through here," Stuart said.

"Do it!" I shouted, with such force that he complied, apparently without thinking. "I know where the dagger is."

"You sure?" Eddie asked. "'Cause our girl's in trouble, and if we take too long . . ."

"I'm sure," I said, hoping, praying that I was right. Hoping that Eric's cryptic words about the hidden and the secret had been a message and not mere ramblings.

I pointed the turns out to Stuart, and when he slammed on the brakes in front of the house I'd once shared with Eric, I had the door open before the car had completely halted. I raced toward the house, burst through the broken doorway, and threw myself down in front of the window seat. I pried it open and found nothing, then broke my fingernails as I clawed open the loose board.

And there it was. The dagger. Odayne must have forced Eric not to tell me. But Eric had fought. And though he couldn't speak it directly, he'd managed to hide it for me. And he'd managed to give me a clue.

It was a magnificent weapon. An ornate hilt in the middle from which a curved blade extended on either side. As a whole, it formed a deadly crescent, but I also realized that the blades could slide apart at the hilt and it could be used as two daggers.

They're bound, I thought as I raced with my prize back to the car. Eric had explained how Lilith and Odayne were essentially one and the same.

So that should mean that if this dagger was capable of killing Odayne, then it should also be capable of killing Lilith as well.

The trick, of course, would be getting close enough to her to do it.

That, however, I'd worry about when we got there.

"We still have a chance," I said, climbing back into the car. "We still have a chance to rescue Allie and destroy Lilith, too. Hurry," I said, but it wasn't necessary.

Stuart had already pulled away from the curb, and we were speeding back the way we came, heading toward the forest.

Heading for my daughter and the battle still to come.

* * *

As we hit the main entrance to the national forest, I realized that we didn't need the GPS tracker anymore. I knew where we were going. "The Stone Table," I said. Discovered by botanists who had been investigating plant life, the table was in a near-inaccessible part of the forest, well off the beaten path, and experts assumed it had been used in ancient times by native tribes performing various rituals.

"You can't be sure—" Stuart said.

I gave him a wry look. "I can. Nadia's used it before. She's the one who broke it," I added, referring to the way the table had broken clean down the center in the midst of a demonic ritual not too long ago. The result—though not the cause—had made the local papers, with historical experts speculating all sorts of reasons for the table's destruction, most arguing that a small earthquake had rendered the table unstable.

"Right," he said, making a hard left onto a walking trail as I gasped. He pushed the Infiniti as hard as he could for as long as he could, but soon it became clear that the car would go no farther. "Out," he said. "We run the rest of the way."

"Eddie?" I glanced quickly down at the tracking device. "I'm right, aren't I?"

"Looks like," he confirmed, already half out of the car.

We grabbed gear from the trunk and started hauling ass toward the table, using our blades to cut through the growth where necessary. In fact, though, the path was clear. Lilith had come before us, and as she'd blown a path through the mansion, she'd cut a path through the forest.

Apparently, she wasn't terribly worried about being followed. Considering what I'd seen her do, I couldn't say I blamed her.

I held up a finger to my lips, signaling the others to be quiet as we approached. A group of trees stood off the path at the edge of the clearing where the Stone Table stood. We eased that way, using the cover of the trees to remain hidden as we assessed the situation. And the situation really wasn't good.

Lilith moved in front of the remains of the Stone Table, her palm split open, and she marked the table with her blood, readying it for the ritual.

Odayne leaned against one broken half, his expression as he looked at her one of utter adoration. My baby lay on the other slab, bound there, her shirt ripped to form a V over her chest. The necklace had been ripped away, probably tossed to the ground somewhere, and I said a silent thank-you that they'd kept it on her neck long enough for us to find her.

Tears streamed down her face, but she was quiet, her jaw set in a firm line, and her eyes hard. She was terrified, yet she was holding. Dear God, my baby was holding.

I only hoped I could do the same.

Beside me, Stuart silently squeezed my hand, and when he looked at me, a thousand words passed between us. Words of comfort and hope and love. But it wasn't until he whispered, "We will get her, and that bitch will die," that the sob broke free. I pressed my hand over my mouth, determined to be silent. Determined to be strong. Because I couldn't save Allie if I broke down.

Right then, she needed a Hunter, not her mother, and that's just what I intended to be.

Eddie pressed a hand to my forehead, his voice barely audible. "You steady?"

I nodded, then straightened my shoulders. Yeah. I was steady.

"I figure your boy and I will go in full blast with the holy water," he said, his voice little more than a whisper. "You go in straight and fast with the dagger. She knows we know how strong she is. She won't be expecting a straight-on attack. And because she is one hell of a strong she-bitch, we gotta take her down first. We don't manage that, and I think it's safe to say we're all dead."

He was right, and I knew it. And although the plan had risks—huge, horrible risks—I didn't have a better one. More than that, we were running out of time. Lilith had finished marking the table. Now she was positioning herself in front of it, Odayne and Allie behind her, an athame held high in her hand. I swallowed, imagining that ceremonial knife being thrust down into my daughter, and I knew with a desperate certainty that this was not a ceremony Allie would survive.

Even if they only needed a drop of her blood, Lilith would kill my daughter. Not because she was mine, but because she was Eric's. She would do it because it would prove, once and for all, that Odayne and Eric had fully merged. Eric wouldn't stop her. Instead, his grief and guilt would force him inside, even as her demonic lover took control of the body.

I held the double-bladed dagger at the hilt in the middle, ready to thrust it hard into Lilith's eye, relishing the moment when I could do that. "On three," I said, then counted down, the men beside me with super-squirter water guns at the ready.

On three, we burst out, rushing forward even as Allie's screams of "Mom!" and "Stuart!" and "Gramps!" filled my ears. I kept my focus on Lilith who, I was rather distressed to see, didn't look the least bit surprised. The blasts of holy water from Stuart and Eddie were sizzling on her skin, rising as steam, but not leaving the familiar welts. Not a good sign—definitely not a good sign—and I could only hope that her false sense of security came from the fact that she didn't know we had the dagger.

"Now, Kate!" Stuart screamed, even as Odayne leaped from the table to knock the squirt gun from Stuart's hands. I couldn't worry about that—had to trust that Stuart could take care of himself—and I launched myself forward, landing on Lilith with enough force that she was knocked backward. I didn't hesitate, simply shoved the blade down, hard, into her eye, then pulled it free again, my breath hitching as I waited for the familiar moment when the demon would leave. I waited for her to drop down, destroyed, as foretold in the dagger's legend.

That didn't happen.

She was fine. The bitch was fine. And I was straddling the strongest demon I'd ever encountered walking the earth. A demon that could toss me across the park with only the force of her mind.

"Little fool," she hissed. "Do you think I'm so easy to kill?"

I said nothing—my thoughts racing—and I realized she was right. I was a fool. I'd believed that the connection between her and Odayne would have allowed the weapon against him to kill her, too, and I'd risked all our lives by following that hunch. A foolish hunch.

A wrong hunch, that was now going to get us all killed.

I met her eyes, saw the pure hatred there, and knew then that I wasn't going down. Not without a fight.

"Let. My. Daughter. Go."

Her lips curved into a sneer. "No."

"Bitch!" I screamed, undone by both fury and fear, and without thinking, I brought the blade down, hacking at Nadia's face with the razor-sharp blade.

"Beloved!" Beside us, Odayne kicked Stuart to the ground. His face and arms were covered with burns from Stuart's holy water, but he appeared not to notice. He rushed toward Lilith, plucked me off of her, and thrust his fist hard into my gut.

All the air left my body and I gasped, the dagger still tight in my hand. My eyes locked on his face as I tried to process the fact that Eric was attacking me. I knew I had to lash out—to get him with the dagger—but this was Eric. I couldn't help believing that Eric would fight his way back to the surface. That he would break free.

It was Eric, or so I thought.

And I hesitated.

I hesitated, and it cost me, because as his fingers tightened around my neck—as his thumbs pressed down against my windpipe, I kicked uselessly, the world turning gray and the dagger slipping from my fingers. Slipping away now that I'd finally realized that the dagger really was my only chance.

I'd lost that chance, I knew. And as the world began to fade around me, I saw both Eric and the demon in those silver-gray eyes. And knew for certain that I'd lost him at last.

Around me, I could hear Allie's cries, but there was nothing—*nothing*—I could do.

And then a sharp scream rent the sky, and pure, sweet air flowed into my lungs. I was on the ground, he'd dropped me, and as I looked up, I realized that it was Eric who had screamed. Eric, with one blade of the dagger still thrust into his eye.

And Stuart standing there, the one who had wielded it. For the first time in his hunting career, he'd wielded a knife and thrust it straight into a demon's eye.

Into Eric's eye.

"You did it," Eddie whispered, as Stuart clutched my hand. "Killed the demon, in its true form."

I didn't say the other—that Eric was dead, too. I couldn't think about that. Couldn't think about the fact that Eric had died for me already, dead and gone when Odayne had tried to kill me.

"Or maybe not," Stuart said, and as we watched Eric's body writhe on the ground. I saw the familiar shimmer emerge from the wound in his eye, but instead of disappearing, it took form. And as I lay on the ground, still gasping for breath, the shimmer became a beast, and the beast became solid, and the beast became Odayne.

He was alive. His flesh gray and scaled. His fingers clawed. His eyes bulbous and red.

He was alive, and he was free of Eric.

And he was right there. Right there to kill or be killed.

I lunged for Eric's body and the knife still lodged in his eye, and was shocked to see him stuttering for breath. I had no time to do anything about that, not with a demon about to swallow me whole. Gently, I disconnected the knives, leaving one blade in Eric. I closed my hand over the other half, but didn't move. I didn't want them to realize. I couldn't let them know. And so I stayed near Eric, listening to his slow, gasping breaths, and turned my head to see what horrors lay behind me.

Lilith had moved beside the monster Odayne, her eyes full of mirth. There was no concern at all on her face, and once again, I feared that I was wrong. That I didn't understand how this worked.

But I had to be right. I had to. Because if I wasn't, then we all were truly dead.

Beside her, Odayne roared, and Lilith screamed, "Kill her! Kill the one who stole your humanity. Kill her, my beloved. Kill her in my name!"

And with that, I whipped around. And as the snarling beast lunged for me, I thrust the dagger home, sliding it deep into the true demon's chest and spilling a black mass of demon blood.

There was a flash of light and then the world seemed to turn red all around us. I heard Allie scream, and I felt the hair on my body stand up, as if lightning had struck only inches away.

Then the red passed and the world shifted back to normal, and when I looked around, Odayne was gone, and Lilith with him.

Eric had been right. They *were* bound.

And the death of Odayne in his true form had destroyed Lilith as well.

She hadn't known, hadn't even suspected that her love for Odayne would ultimately provide the means to kill her.

It was over.

We were alone, and Allie was safe, and Eric was alive.

I crouched again at his side, not certain if I'd find Eric in the body or a new demon or even the original David, back to claim what was his.

But as I leaned over him, all questions faded.

It was Eric.

He was back. And, miraculously, he was alive.

Eighteen

"Not too long now," the nurse said, her eyes kind despite her stern expression. "You two relatives?"

"I—" I began, but Allie cut me off.

"No," she said, turning flat eyes on me. "Not relatives."

My heart twisted in my chest, and I took a deep breath as the nurse nodded briskly. "Nonfamily visiting hours ends in ten minutes. But you go on in and visit. Maybe you can cheer him up. I would've thought a man who survived what he went through would have a smile on his face, but not our Mr. Long," she said. A quick smile flitted across her face, and she fluttered her hands as if maybe, just maybe, she thought she'd spoken out of turn.

"These things take time," I said, taking Allie's hand and giving it a quick squeeze as I led her toward the door to Eric's room. He'd been moved down from ICU that morning, and this was the first time we'd been allowed to see him, the ICU visits having been restricted only to relatives.

As Allie had pointed out, we were only a friend and a student.

"Are you okay?" I asked, pausing outside the heavy wooden door. "That wasn't your father who did that to you. It was the demon. Odayne had taken over."

I kept my voice firm and hard, as if by force alone I could will myself to believe what I was telling Allie. But the truth, I knew, was so very different. Odayne may have come out fighting, but Eric had still been in there, too. He'd been inside when it was happening, and he hadn't saved Allie, and he hadn't saved me.

I wanted to be the bigger person, to see Eric as the victim. But I was having one hell of a hard time with that.

Harder still was my certain knowledge that we might never have gotten here if he'd shared his secrets with me all those years ago. We'd been good together, or so I'd thought. And yet that essential trust had never been there.

I'd thought it had, but I'd been wrong.

No way, though, was I going to let what happened destroy Allie's love for her father, no matter how intense my own doubts might be.

"It really is okay, Mom." She squeezed my hand. "Honest. My head totally gets it. I've just gotta get my heart with the program."

"He loves you, Al. Nothing will ever change that."

She looked at me, her eyes older than her fifteen years. "I'm not the only one who got hurt. Do you want me to say the same thing right back at you?"

A whisper of a smile touched my lips, and I pressed a soft kiss to her forehead. "I love you," I said, then grabbed hold of the handle and pushed the door open.

I saw his face first. His one eye closed, the area around it the deep purple of a stormy twilight. I could see nothing of the other, now-useless, eye, completely covered as it was with white gauze and surgical tape. The blade had sliced through the optic nerve before burying itself ten centimeters into his brain and missing his carotid artery by less than a millimeter. He'd lost the sight in his right eye, but that seemed a small price to pay for life. For his soul.

For himself.

A miracle, the doctors had said, and I had to admit I agreed. I believed in miracles, after all. But I knew better than to rely on them.

His bland, gray face shifted as his mouth curved up into a small smile. "Company," he rasped, and when he opened his one eye, his smile grew bigger before fading as his eye clouded with worry. He held out his hand to Allie, and I could see the pain flicker across his face. Not from the surgery, but from the memories of what had happened. What he'd done.

"I'm sorry, baby," he said. "I'm so, so sorry."

The dam broke then, my daughter's stony face collapsing into a waterfall of tears. She rushed to him, taking his hand and perching on the hospital bed so close to him I winced for fear she'd accidentally rip out a tube or something.

"It's okay," Eric said, apparently reading my mind, and with that simple comment, my heart swelled a little.

"Pretty crowded in this tiny room," I said. "But at least you're not sharing."

"It's the lap of luxury," he said, and Allie giggled.

"You two haven't had much time alone recently," I said. "How about I go get a coffee for me and a soda for Allie. I'd smuggle contraband in for you, but I don't want to get my hand slapped by the nurses."

"That would be great," Eric said, the light blooming in his eyes telling me all I needed to know.

"Allie? Soda?" I asked, although I was really asking if it was okay for me to leave. She knew it, too, and answered with a quick nod. "Great. Anything. Thanks."

I shot Eric one last look, our eyes lingering together for

only a moment before I slid back through the door and parked myself on one of the uncomfortable plastic chairs in the hallway. And then, silently, I began to cry. Not huge gasping sobs, but silent tears that streamed down my cheeks as if cleansing me of fear and stress. This chapter was finally over. Eric's body was clean, his soul free.

The past still loomed between us, though. A wall of secrets and harsh memories that I knew we'd have to work through, brick by brick. It had, I realized now, always been there. Those secrets stacked up between us. Only recently had I been able to see it.

He'd shared his secrets too late, and it had almost cost him his soul. Almost cost him his daughter. *My daughter.*

That wasn't something I knew how to forgive.

"You okay, honey?" A squat nurse in Scooby-Doo scrubs handed me a tissue, and I realized that my cheeks were still wet. "He's doing real good. Don't you worry."

"Thanks. I'm fine."

"Only five minutes left. You hold on and let's make sure you get your turn." She pushed open the door and I heard her relay the five-minute warning to Allie and Eric. A moment later, she came out, with Allie trailing behind.

"He said he wanted to talk to you alone."

"I never did get that soda for you," I said.

"I'll go. Meet you back here in five." She hurried off down the hall without waiting for my answer.

I took a deep breath and went back into the room, was greeted by Eric's wide smile.

"She's remarkable," he said.

"Yeah. She is. Resilient, too."

"So were we," he reminded me.

I sat in the chair Allie had abandoned, but I said nothing.

"Katie." He reached for my hand, but I pulled it back, held my hands together in my lap.

"I see," he said, then drew in a long breath. "Well, at least that makes this easier. I'm leaving San Diablo. I need to work this out."

I tilted my head, suddenly realizing what he meant. "The demon's gone," I said slowly, working to keep the fear out of my voice. "We beat it."

"It's gone," he agreed. "But I have to figure this out. What I am. What I did." He looked at me hard. "Kate, I'm leaving."

His words hit me with the force of a slap. And though I opened my mouth to speak, he held up a hand to cut me off. "*I* did this. Me. Do you think I can look at you, knowing what I did to you? What I did to Allie? Do you think I can live every day knowing that I almost killed both of you?" His voice, soft but harsh, slid over the room on an undercurrent of rage. "Or that Stuart saved you. And not from a distant threat, but from me. Do you think I can live with that?"

"Do you think I can?" I spat back. "But you're her father, and you can't just run away from this."

"I'm not running. Don't you see? Don't you see what I'd become? If it was only the demon, I'd have handed over the dagger to Nadia. Let her destroy it. But it was me in there, too, Kate, with enough control to keep my own secrets, even from a bastard who was living inside my head."

"And in the end, you used that control to save us. You told me where you'd hidden the dagger."

"That's not enough," he said. "It doesn't make up for anything."

No, I thought, it didn't. But I didn't say that. Instead, I forced myself to meet his eyes. "I can live with it," I said. "I can deal. For Allie's sake, we both have to."

"Maybe you can," he said. "But I can't."

"She loves you," I whispered. And so did I, I thought. Despite everything that had happened, I loved him still. And I mourned the loss of what had once been between us.

He closed his eyes, and I felt a twinge of guilt, as if I'd been playing dirty. "I'm sorry, Katie," he said, and I knew then that it was over.

I'd lost him.

And Allie was the one who'd pay the dearest price.

I dropped Allie at home, expecting to find Stuart there, holding tight to Timmy as had been his habit in these days since the battle. He was gone, though, and so I left my daughter with Eddie and her brother, then hurried to the mansion.

I had no way of knowing that he'd be there—he hadn't told Eddie where he was going—yet I was certain I was right. And when I walked in, I found him sitting on the bottom step of the battered staircase, surveying the destruction.

There was a lot to survey. Deep gouges marred the beautiful wood flooring. Wallpaper hung in strips from the walls. Scorch marks marred the ceiling. And spiderweb cracks danced across what little glass was left in the doors to the balcony.

The entire wall between the entrance and the front parlor had crumbled to the ground, and now lay in a pile of wooden splinters and plaster rubble.

"Stuart," I said, and then stopped. There really weren't words.

"I'd been staying away," he said, his attention on the floor, the ceiling, anywhere but me. "Staying home with you. With Allie. With Timmy. Watching television. Drinking beer. Pretending there was one thing—just one thing—in our life that didn't kill or maim or hurt."

"Stuart, please." I tried, but I'm not sure the words came out. My throat was too thick, too clogged with unshed tears.

He stood and moved toward me, kicking debris out of his way as he did. "I was going to buy this place for us," he said.

"I'd worked it out with Bernie and everything. It seemed like the perfect house for our crazy family, especially once I learned about the safe room."

I swallowed, unreasonably touched by the gesture. And feeling horribly guilty for all the years I'd kept my own secrets—building between Stuart and me a wall as impenetrable as the one Eric had built, and which I despised.

I realized now my mistake. I'd clung to a past I didn't even fully understand so hard that I'd risked my future with Stuart. A good man, who loved me.

The second man in my life who I loved with all my heart.

"I could picture Timmy in here with his trains," he continued, "getting underfoot even though we'd tell him to keep them upstairs. And Allie would turn the attic into a workout room. I figured that much was inevitable. And you'd be that much closer to the beach and Old Town and the cemetery for patrols. Not that demons roam cemeteries very often," he said, holding up a hand as though I were about to interrupt him. "But there was something so very Demon Hunterish about having a house that overlooked a graveyard." He turned once, taking in the room with a sigh. "We worked so hard to make this place special. And all of it was destroyed in less than ten minutes."

I realized then that I was crying. "It still is special," I said, hearing the desperation in my voice. "And all of this is fixable."

"The house, maybe," he said, and the first jolt of fear shot through me, that wall I'd built taking on form and substance. My mistakes and secrets crying out to me. Mocking me.

I shoved the fears away, forcing myself not to cry. "What are you saying, Stuart?" I asked, even though I didn't want to ask. Didn't want to know.

"I'm sorry, Kate," he said, as I felt the world fall out from underneath my feet. "I thought being together was enough. I thought I could stomach it. Out there, in the world, and us standing together to keep it at bay. But it came in, Kate. It touched our family. It touched our lives, and that's not something I can live with. It's not something I want Timmy to live with."

"I'm his mother no matter what," I said, forcing my voice to stay calm as fear sparked through me. "Nothing can change that. Not ever."

"No," Stuart agreed. "Nothing can." He met my eyes. "I'm sorry, Kate."

I shook my head, as if the force of my will could change his direction. "You told me once you were going to fight for me. For *us*. But you're not fighting, Stuart. You're running away. And you're punishing me for being the woman I am." I wanted to fight him. Wanted to get a rise out of him, have this out, and have our life get back to normal.

Stuart, however, was having none of that. Instead he simply looked at me with that calm, media-ready face. "I love you, Kate. Nothing will ever change that."

My legs gave out, and I slid to the floor, hugging my knees to my chest and rocking. "Then stay," I said, resorting to begging. "Please, please stay."

"I can't," he said simply. "I'm sorry, but I can't."

I sat on the mansion's broken and battered flagstone balcony, looking out over the cemetery toward the ocean and the setting sun.

Days had passed since Stuart had moved out of our house, since Eric had packed his car and driven south toward Los Angeles.

In my whole life, I'd loved only two men, and now they were gone.

Stuart wasn't ass enough to deny me access to Timmy, so

I was still seeing my little boy every day, thanks to Laura's willingness to play intermediary. I hated putting her in that position, but she swore she didn't mind. It was, she said, only temporary, and I desperately hoped she was right. The thought of divorce and custody arrangements and shuttling my baby back and forth for years and years overwhelmed me. And every time I let my mind go there, I began to cry all over again.

"Mom?"

I closed my eyes, willing the tears to stop flowing, needing to be strong for my daughter. But I couldn't manage it. I'd been fighting for too damn long, and the strength I tried to compel eluded me.

I pressed my forehead to my knees, then felt Allie's soft hand press against my back.

"It'll be okay," she said, and her voice was so calm, so full of strength, that it compelled me to turn my head and look at my daughter through the haze of tears.

"You grew up," I said. "Sometime when I wasn't looking, you managed to grow up."

"Maybe a little," she said modestly, but I could see the pleasure in her eyes. "And I had really excellent help."

She sank down on the balcony beside me, mimicking my pose, arms around her knees, toes pointed out toward the ocean. "He's not gone forever, you know," she said. And before I could ask which of our men she was referring to, she amended the statement. "They'll be back. Both of them. I know a little bit about how they feel," she said. "And I'm certain they're not gone for good."

She took her gaze off the Pacific long enough to meet my eyes, her steady gaze unblinking and sure, filled with far more maturity than I gave her credit for. My heart stuttered in my chest, and I put my arm around her, sighing as she leaned her head against me.

I sighed, too, overcome suddenly by a need to be parented. To have firm, sure arms hold me tight and rock me and tell me that everything was going to be all right. An image of Father Corletti filled my head, and the tears threatened again. My breath hitched as I fought them back, but not soon enough to escape Allie's notice.

"Mom?"

"Rome," I said. "It's not a lazy beach vacation, but we can go for a couple of weeks. Let you meet Father. Try out some formal training. See the sights." I managed a smile. "Will that do?"

Her eyes widened as she nodded, and I watched the melancholy vanish from her face, her sad memories undoubtedly shoved aside by fantasies of swordplay on the *Forza* training floor.

As for me, I settled comfortably into the idea of going home. I needed the visit. I needed to get centered again. To go back to my roots. And I needed to get past what had become my new habit—jumping when the phone rang or the doorbell chimed, expecting it to be Eric or Stuart.

The real truth was that I didn't really know what I'd do if the two men I loved walked back into my life. Things had changed, and there was no going back. But hopefully, with time, we'd move slowly forward.

And as the horizon burst into a cacophony of orange and red, one emotion fought its way upstream through the pain to settle quietly around my heart.

Hope.

Right then, that was enough.

"Mom! Have you seen my passport?"

I took a deep breath, carefully slid our plane tickets back into my purse, and aimed the evil eye at my daughter, who'd come careening into the kitchen, ponytail bouncing, her mouth pursed in frustration.

"Alison Elizabeth Crowe, the shuttle is supposed to be here in less than fifteen minutes, and *now* you tell me you can't find your passport?"

"Did you check your desk drawer?" Laura asked, stifling a yawn. Despite the fact that we were heading out even before the sun, Laura and Mindy had come over to see us off.

"Want me to help you look?" Mindy asked. "Under the bed, maybe? God! I'm so jealous. *I* want to go to Rome."

I shot Laura a quick look, but she gave me the slightest shake of her head. We'd talked about her and Mindy joining us for a few days, but as we hadn't yet made specific plans, Laura didn't want to say anything and get Mindy's hopes up.

Eddie rattled the newspaper and snorted. "You check the purse, girlie?"

Allie rolled her eyes, then held up her leather backpack. "I'm not taking a purse, Gramps."

He tapped his chest, and I watched Allie's cheeks go pink. "Oh. Right." She reached beneath her shirt and tugged out a black traveler's wallet. She unzipped it, rifled through it, and smiled sheepishly at everyone in the room. "Got it."

"I'm very glad to hear it," I said, as Laura hid her smile behind the rim of her coffee cup.

I drew in a breath and looked around the kitchen, wondering what I was forgetting. "I'll call you when we get settled. You don't mind playing Internet liaison?"

"I told you I didn't," Laura said. Stuart had temporarily settled himself and Timmy in Bernie's beach cottage, and the lure of tidal pools and the nearby Playscape was keeping my little boy occupied. I'd gone over there last night to say good-bye, and Stuart had conveniently remembered urgent business at the office. But since I had no intention of not seeing Timmy during our Roman holiday, Laura had set up my laptop with video chatting. That alone would have qualified her for sainthood, but the fact that she had offered to watch

Timmy during Stuart's working hours meant that I could see my little boy across the miles each and every day.

The arrangement eased some of my guilt about leaving. Guilt or no, I knew I had to go. Timmy would survive Mommy's long vacation, and Allie needed this. For that matter, so did I.

"You taking that knife?" Eddie said. "The one demon boy gave you?" That earned him a scowl from everyone in the room, and he tossed his hands up and harumphed. "What? It's true, ain't it?"

"Yes," I said, thinking of the double-action blade that Eric had once given me. "Of course. It's in my suitcase."

"Won't be there when you get to Italy," he said, crossing his arms over his chest and leaning back.

"Excuse me?"

His caterpillar-like eyebrows twitched. "They search. They search, then they take what they want. It's a whole big conspiracy."

I stared him down. "No it's not."

"Eh, do what you want then, but mark my words," he added, pointing a bony finger at me. "You're gonna get to your hotel, unpack, and that knife's gonna be gone."

"We're staying at a hotel?" Allie asked, her voice suddenly frantic. "I thought were were gonna stay in the *Forza* dorms. Mom!"

"We are," I told her. To Eddie, I added, "You've been watching too many movies."

"Your loss," he said, which had me rolling my eyes again.

"I'm going to go make sure we've got luggage tags on everything," I said, then moved to the hallway. Which is where I was when Laura found me, rummaging in my suitcase for the knife I'd decided to leave behind.

"Sucker," she said.

"He might be right. Besides, I can get another knife in Rome."

Her brows rose slightly. "Are you going to need one? You're going to see Father Corletti and let Allie get a taste of real training, right? Maybe do some sightseeing? It's not like you're going to be sliding into the catacombs hunting demons."

She had a point, but I only shrugged, noncommittal. If I'd learned one thing for certain, it was to never take a demon for granted.

The sharp toot of a horn sounded outside, and my eyes darted to Laura's, even as a surge of excitement mixed with grief swept through me, making me more than a little unsteady. "We're really going. I can't believe we're really going." Part of me wished we were already gone, both so that I could see the place I'd once known as home, and also so that I could escape the sadness that clung to me as I walked the halls of this house. Another part of me didn't ever want to leave, wanted instead to cling to that sadness. Because the longer I held on to it, the longer it was real. And if it was real, there was a possibility I'd have that life again. A happy, suburban life with my husband, my kids, and my cat.

Those days, I knew, were behind me.

I just didn't want to accept reality.

"You okay?" Laura asked, looking so hard at me I was certain she could read my mind.

"I will be. Ten hours in coach will set me right." I gave her a hug, then hauled my carry-on bag to my shoulder as Allie and Mindy bounded into the room.

"The shuttle's here! Come on, Mom! Let's go!" She jumped in front of me, yanked open the door, then froze, emitting a tiny puff of air that formed into a single word: "Oh."

Alarmed, I rushed to her side, expecting a demonic horde. Instead, I saw Stuart.

The Infiniti was parked in the drive, and my husband stood beside it, my sleepy son curled in his arms. At his feet were a suitcase, a briefcase, and a Thomas the Tank backpack.

I opened my mouth, but no sound came out.

"Oh my God!" Allie hooted, then ran to give him a hug. She stared down at the suitcases. "You're coming? You're coming, too?"

Stuart put a hand on her head, then looked at me. He said nothing, but reached into his briefcase and held up two plane tickets and two passports. "It was easier to run than to fight," he said. "But I've been doing a lot of thinking, and I've come to the rather astounding conclusion that life isn't always easy."

"No," I said, managing to talk through the tears that had begun to silently stream down my face. "No, it really isn't."

A pair of headlights cut through the night, and the airport shuttle slid to a halt in front of the house. Stuart looked over his shoulder at it, then looked at me. "What do you say? You ready for the next adventure?"

The band that had been constricting my heart for so many days loosened, and I nodded. "Yeah," I said, taking a step toward him. Toward my family. "Yeah, I really am."

San Diablo, California.

The perfect place to raise a couple of kids.

And a lot of hell.

Carpe Demon
California Demon
Demons Are Forever
Deja Demon
Demon Ex Machina

Praise for Julie Kenner's Demon novels:

"A HOOT!"
—Charlaine Harris

"FABULOUS."
—*The Best Reviews*

"SASSY."
—Richmond.com

penguin.com

M254AS0609

DON'T MISS THE FIRST BOOK IN THE
BLOOD LILY CHRONICLES
BY JULIE KENNER

TAINTED

*Lily Carlyle has lied, cheated, and stolen
her way through life. But in death,
she'll really get to be bad…*

When her little sister is brutalized, a vengeful Lily decides
to exact her own justice. She succeeds—at the cost of her
own life. But as she lies dying, she is given a second chance.
Lily can earn her way into paradise by becoming an
assassin for the forces of good.

It's a job Lily believes she can really get into—but she
doesn't realize that she may not be able to get out.

M529T0709

Explore the outer reaches
of imagination—don't miss these authors
of dark fantasy and urban noir who take you
to the edge and beyond . . .

Patricia Briggs	Anne Bishop
Simon R. Green	Marjorie M. Liu
Jim Butcher	Jeanne C. Stein
Kat Richardson	Christopher Golden
Karen Chance	Ilona Andrews
Rachel Caine	Anton Strout

M15G0610